Ovington's Bank

STANLEY WEYMAN

With an essay by Jim Lawley

MERLIN UNWIN BOOKS

First published by John Murray Ltd, 1922
This edition published by Merlin Unwin Books, 2018

Merlin Unwin Books Ltd
Palmers House
7 Corve Street
Ludlow
Shropshire SY8 1DB
U.K.

www.merlinunwin.co.uk

ISBN 978-1-910723-82-1

Typeset in 12 point Adobe Caslon Pro by Merlin Unwin Books

Printed by TJ International Ltd, Padstow, Cornwall

Contents

Chapter One

It was market day at Aldersbury, the old county town of Aldshire, and the busiest hour of the day. The clock of St. Juliana's was on the point of striking three, and the streets below it were thronged. The gentry, indeed, were beginning to take themselves homeward; a carriage and four, with postilions in yellow jackets, awaited its letters before the Post Office, and near at hand a red-wheeled tandem-cart, the horses tossing their small, keen heads, hung on the movements of its master, who was gossiping on the steps of Ovington's Bank, on Bride Hill. But only the vans bound to the more distant valleys had yet started on their lagging journey; the farmers' gigs, the hucksters' carts, the pack-asses still lingered, filling the streets with a chattering, moving multitude. White-coated yeomen and their wives jostled their betters – but with humble apologies – in the low-browed shops, or hardily pushed smocked-frocks from the narrow pavements, or clung together in obstinate groups in the roadway. Loud was the babel about the yards of the inns, loudest where the tap-rooms poured forth those who, having dined well, had also drunk deep, after the fashion of our great-grandsires.

Through all this medley and hubbub a young man threaded his way. He wore a blue coat with gilt buttons, a waistcoat to match, and drab trousers, and as he hurried along, his hat tilted back, he greeted gentle and simple with the same laughing nod. He had the carriage of one who had a fixed position in the world and knew his worth; and so attractive was his smile, so gallant his confidence, that liking ran before him, and two out of three of the faces that he encountered mirrored his good humour. As he passed along the High Street, and skirted the Market Place, where the quaint stone figure of an ancient Prince, great in his day, looked down on the turmoil from the front of the Market House, he glanced up at the clock, noted the imminence of the hour, and quickened his pace.

A man touched him on the sleeve. 'Mr Bourdillon, sir,' he said, trying to stop him, 'by your leave! I want to—'

'Not now. Not now, Broadway,' the young man answered quickly. 'I'm meeting the mail.' And before the other had fairly taken in his words he was a dozen paces away, now slipping deftly between two lurching farmers, now coasting about the more obstinate groups.

A moment later St Juliana's clock, hard put to it to raise its wheezy voice above the noise, struck the hour. The young man slackened his pace. He was in time, but only barely in time, for as he paused, the distant notes of the guard's bugle sprang like fairy music above the turbid current of sound and gave notice that the coach was at hand. Hurriedly gigs and carts drew aside, the crowd sought the pavements, the more sober drew the heedless out of danger, half a dozen voices cried 'Look out! Have a care!' and with a last shrill Tantivy! Tantivy! Tantivy! the four sweating bays, the leaders cantering, the wheelers trotting, the bars all taut, emerged from the crest of the steep Cop, and the Holyhead Mail, within a minute of its time, drew up before the door of the Lion, the Royal Arms shining bravely from its red panels.

Shopkeepers ran to their doors, the crowd closed up about it, the yokels gaped – for who in those days felt no interest in its advent! By that coach had come, eleven years before, the news of the abdication of the Corsican and the close of the Great War. Laurelled and flagged, it had thrilled the town a year afterwards with the tidings of Waterloo. Later it had signalled the death of the old blind king, and later still, the acquittal – as all the world regarded it – of Queen Caroline. Ah, how the crowd had cheered then! And how lustily old Squire Griffin of Garth, the great-uncle of this young man, now come to meet the mail, had longed to lay his cane about their disloyal shoulders!

The coachman, who had driven the eleven-mile stage from Haygate in fifty-eight minutes, unbuckled and flung down the reins. The guard thrust his bugle into its case, tossed a bundle of journals to the waiting boys, and stepped nimbly to the ground. The passengers followed more slowly, stamping their chilled feet, and stretching their cramped limbs. Some, who were strangers, looked about them with a travelled air, or hastened to the blazing fires that shone from the Lion windows, while two or three who were at their journey's end bustled about, rescuing shawls and portmanteaux, or dived into inner pockets for the coachman's fee.

The last to appear, a man, rather below the middle height, in a handsome caped travelling-coat, was in no hurry. He stepped out at his ease and found the young man who has been described at his side. 'That you, Arthur?' he said, his face lighting up. 'All well?'

'All well, sir. Let me take that!'

'Isn't Rodd here? Ah!' to a second young man, plainer, darker, and more soberly garbed, who had silently appeared at his forerunner's elbow. 'Take this, Rodd, will you?' handing him a small leather case. 'Don't let it go, until it is on my table. All well?'

'All well, sir, thank you.'

'Then go on at once, will you? I will follow with Mr Bourdillon. Give me your arm, Arthur.' He looked about him as he spoke. One or two hats were lifted, he acknowledged the courtesy with a smile. 'Betty well?'

'You'll find her at the window looking out. All gone swimmingly, I hope, sir?'

'Swimmingly?' The traveller paused on the word, perhaps questioning its propriety; and he did not continue until they had disengaged themselves from the group round the coach. He and the young man came, though there was nothing to show this, from different grades of society, and the one was thirty years older than the other and some inches shorter. Yet there was a likeness. The lower part of the face in each was strong, and a certain brightness in the eyes, that was alertness in the younger man and keenness in the elder, told of a sanguine temperament; and they were both good-looking. 'Swimmingly?' the traveller repeated when they had freed themselves from their immediate neighbours. 'Well, if you choose to put it that way, yes. But, it's wonderful, wonderful,' in a lower tone, as he paused an instant to acknowledge an acquaintance, 'the state of things up there, my boy.'

'Still rising?'

'Rising as if things would never fall. And upon my word I don't know why, with the marvellous progress everything is making – but I'll tell you all that later. It's a full market. Is Acherley at the bank?'

'Yes, and Sir Charles. They came a little before time.'

'Clement is with them, I suppose?'

'Well, no, sir.'

'Don't say he's away today!' in a tone of vexation.

'I'm afraid he is,' Arthur admitted. 'But they are all right. I offered Sir Charles the paper, but they preferred to wait outside.'

'D—n!' muttered the other, nodding right and left. 'Too bad of the boy! Too bad! No,' to the person who had lain in wait for Bourdillon and now put himself in their way, 'I can't stop now, Mr Broadway.'

'But, Mr Ovington! Just a—'

'Not now!' Ovington answered curtly. 'Call tomorrow.' And when they had left the man behind, 'What does he want?'

'What they all want,' Arthur answered, smiling. 'A good thing, sir.'

'But he isn't a customer.'

'No, but he will be tomorrow,' the young man rejoined. 'They are all agog. They've got it that you can make a man's fortune by a word, and of course they want their fortunes made.'

'Ah!' the other ejaculated drily. 'But seriously, look about you, Arthur. Did you ever see a greater change in men's faces – from what they were this time two years? Even the farmers!'

'Well, they are doing well.'

'Better, at any rate. Better, even they. Yes, Mr Wolley,' to a stout man, much wrapped up, who put himself in the way, 'follow us, please. Sir Charles is waiting. Better,' Ovington continued to his companion, as the man fell behind, 'and prices rising, and demand – demand spreading in everything.'

'Including Stocks?'

'Including Stocks. I've some news for Sir Charles, that, if he has any doubts about joining us, will fix him. Well, here we are, and I'm glad to be at home. We'll go in by the house door, Arthur, or Betty will be disappointed.'

The bank stood on Bride Hill, looking along the High Street. The position was excellent and the house good. Still, it was no more than a house, for in 1825 banks were not the institutions that they have since become; they had still for rivals the old stocking and the cracked teapot, and among banks, Ovington's at Aldersbury was neither of long standing nor of more than local repute.

Mr Ovington led the way into the house, and had barely removed his hat when a girl flew down the wide oak staircase and flung herself upon him. 'Oh, father!' she cried. 'Here at last! Aren't you cold? Aren't you starving?'

'Pretty well for that,' he replied, stroking her hair in a way that proved that, whatever he was to others, he had a soft spot for his daughter. 'Pretty well for that, Betty.'

'Well, there's a good fire! Come and warm yourself!'

'That's what I can't do, my dear,' he said, taking off his great coat. 'Business first.'

'But I thought you had done all that in London?' pouting.

'Not all, but some. I shall be an hour, perhaps more.'

She shot a mutinous glance at Arthur. 'Why can't he do it ? And Mr Rodd?'

'You think we are old enough, Betty?'

'Apprentices should be seen, and not heard!' she snapped.

Arthur's position at the bank had been hardly understood at first, and in some fit of mischief, Betty, determined not to bow down to his pretensions, had christened him the 'Apprentice.'

'I thought that that proverb applied to children,' he retorted.

The girl was a beauty, dark and vivid, but small, and young enough to feel the gibe. Before she could retaliate, however, her father intervened. 'Where's Clement?' he asked. 'I know that he is not here.'

'Tell-tale!' she flung at Arthur. 'If you must know, father,' mildly, 'I think that he's—'

'Mooning somewhere, I suppose, instead of being in the bank, as he should be. And market day of all days! There, come, Bourdillon, I mustn't keep Sir Charles and Acherley waiting.' He led the way to the rear of the hall, where a door on the left led into the bank parlour. Betty made a face after them.

In the parlour which lay behind the public office were two men. One, seated in an armchair by the fire, was reading the *Morning Post*. The other stood at the window, his very shoulders expressing his impatience. But it was to the former, a tall, middle-aged man, stiff and pompous, with thin sandy hair but kindly eyes, that Ovington made the first advance. 'I am sorry to have kept you waiting, Sir Charles,' he said. 'Very sorry. But I assure you I have not wasted a minute. Mr Acherley,' to the other, 'pardon me, will you? Just a word with Sir Charles before we begin.'

And leaving Bourdillon to make himself agreeable to the impatient Acherley, Ovington drew Sir Charles Woosenham aside. 'I have gone a little beyond my instructions,' he said in a low tone, 'and sold your Monte Reales.'

The Baronet's face fell. 'Sold!' he ejaculated. 'Parted with them? But I never – my dear sir, I never—'

'Authorised a sale?' the banker agreed suavely. 'No, perfectly right, Sir Charles. But I was on the spot and I felt myself responsible. There was a favourable turn and' – forestalling the other as he would have interrupted – 'my rule is little and sure – little and sure, and sell on a fair rise. I don't think you will be dissatisfied with the transaction.'

But Sir Charles' displeasure showed itself in his face. He was a man of family and influence, honourable and straightforward, but his abilities were hardly on a par with his position, and though he had at times an inkling of the fact it only made him the more jealous of interference. 'But I never contemplated,' he said, the blood rising to his face, 'never for a moment, that you would part with the stocks without reference to me, Mr Ovington.'

'Precisely, precisely – without your authority, Sir Charles – except at a really good profit. I think that four or five hundred was mentioned? Just so. Well, if you will look at this draft, which of course includes the price of the stocks – they cost, if I remember, fourteen hundred or thereabouts – you will, I hope, – I really hope – approve of what I did.'

Sir Charles adjusted his glasses, and frowned at the paper. He was prepared to be displeased and to show it. 'Two thousand six hundred,' he muttered, 'two thousand six hundred and twenty-seven!' his jaw dropping in his surprise. 'Two thousand six – really! Ah, well, I certainly think' – with a quick change to cordiality that would have amused an onlooker – 'that you acted for the best. I am obliged to you, much obliged, Mr Ovington. A handsome profit.'

'I felt sure that you would approve,' the banker assented gravely. 'Shall Bourdillon put the draft – Arthur, be good enough to place this draft to Sir Charles Woosenham's account. And tell Mr Wolley and Mr Grounds – I think they are waiting – to come in. I ask your pardon, Mr Acherley,' approaching him in turn.

'No plum for me, I suppose?' growled that gentleman, whom the gist of the interview with Sir Charles had not escaped. He was a tall, hatchet-faced, dissipated-looking man, of an old family, Acherley of Acherley. He had been a dandy with Brummell, had shaken his elbow at Watier's when Crockford managed it, had dined at the Pavilion; now he vegetated in the country on a mortgaged estate, and on Sundays attended cock-fights behind the village public-house.

'Well, not today,' Ovington answered pleasantly. 'But when we have shaken the tree a little—'

'One may fall, you think?'

'I hope so. You will be unlucky if one does not.'

The two men who had been summoned came in, each after his fashion. Wolley entered first, endeavouring to mask under a swaggering manner his consciousness that he stood in the presence of his betters. A clothier from the Valleys and one of Ovington's earliest customers, he had raised himself, as the banker had, and from the same stratum; but by enlarging instead of selling his mill. During the war he had made much money and had come to attribute his success a little more to his abilities and a little less to circumstances than was the fact. Of late there were whispers that in the financial storm of '16, which had followed the close of the war, he had come near the rocks, but if so he had put a bold face on the crisis, and by steadily putting himself forward he had impressed most men with a belief in his wealth. 'Afternoon, Sir Charles,' he grunted with as much ease as he could compass. 'Afternoon,' to Acherley. He took a seat at the table and slapped down his hat. He was here on business and he meant to show that he knew what business was.

Grounds, who followed, was a man of a different type. He was a maltster and had been a dairyman; a leading tradesman in the town, cautious, penurious, timid, putting pound to pound without saying much about it, and owning that respect for his superiors which became one in his position. Until lately he had hoarded his savings, or put them into the five per cents; he had distrusted even the oldest bank. But progress was in the air, new enterprises, new discoveries were the talk of the town, the interest on the five per cents had been reduced to four, and in a rare moment of rashness, he had taken a hint dropped by Ovington, had ventured, and won. He still trembled at his temerity, he still vowed in wakeful moments that he would return to the old safe road, but in the meantime easy gains tempted him and he was now fairly embarked on modern courses. He was a byword in Aldersbury for caution and shrewdness, and his adhesion to any scheme would, as Ovington well knew, commend it to the town.

He hung back, but, 'Come, Mr Grounds, take a seat,' said the banker. 'You know Sir Charles and Mr Acherley? Sir Charles, will you sit on my right, and Mr Acherley here, if you please? Bourdillon, will you take a note? We are met, as you know, gentlemen, to consider the formation of a Joint

Stock Company, to be called' – he consulted a paper – 'the Valleys Steam Railroad Company, for the purpose of connecting the woollen business of the Valleys with the town, and of providing the public with a superior mode of transport. The Bill for the Manchester and Liverpool Railroad is on the point of passing, and that great enterprise is as good as carried through. The Bill for the London and Birmingham Railroad is before the House; a Bill for a line from Birmingham to Aldersbury is preparing. Those projects are, gentlemen, in stronger hands than ours, and it might seem to some to be too early to anticipate their success and to provide the continuation we propose. But nothing is more certain than that the spoils are to those who are first in the field. The Stockton and Darlington Railway is proving what can be done by steam in the transport of the heaviest goods. There a single engine draws a load of fifty tons at the rate of six miles an hour, and has been known to convey a load of passengers at fifteen miles. Higher speeds are thought to be possible—'

'I'll never believe it!' Wolley growled, anxious to assert himself.

'But not desirable,' Ovington continued blandly. 'At any rate, if we wait too long—'

'There's no talk of waiting!' Acherley exclaimed. Neither he nor Sir Charles was in the habit of meeting on an equal footing the men with whom they were sitting today; he found the position galling, and what was to be done he was anxious should be done quickly. He had heard the banker's exordium before.

'No, we are here to act,' Ovington assented, with an eye on Grounds, for whose benefit he had been talking. 'But on sober and well-considered lines. We are all agreed, I think, that such a railroad will be a benefit to the trade and district?'

Now, to this proposition not one of those present would have assented a year before. 'Steam railroads!' they would have cried. 'Fantastic and impossible!' But the years 1823 and 1824 had been years not only of great prosperity but of abnormal progress. The seven lean years, the years of depression and repression, which had followed Waterloo had come to an end. The losses of war had been made good, and simultaneously a more liberal spirit had been infused into the Government. Men had breathed freely, had looked about them, had begun to hope and to venture, to talk of a new world. Demand had overtaken and outrun supply, large profits had been made, money had become cheap, and, fostered by credit, the growth of enterprise throughout the country had been marvellous. It was as if, after the frosts of winter, the south wind had blown and sleeping life had everywhere awakened. Men doubled their operations and still had money to spare. They put the money in the funds – the funds rose until they paid no more than three per cent. Dissatisfied, men sought other channels for their savings, nor sought in vain. Joint Stock Companies arose on every side. Projects, good and bad, sprang up like mushrooms in a night. Old lodes and new harbours, old canals and new fisheries, were taken in hand, and for all these there seemed to be capital. Shares rose to a premium before the companies were floated, and soon the bounds of our shores were found to be too narrow for British enterprise. At that moment the separation of the South American countries from Spain fell out, and these were at once seen to offer new outlets. The romantic were dazzled with legends of mines of gold and pockets of diamonds, while the gravest saw gain in pampas waving with wheat and prairies grazed by countless herds. It was felt, even by the most cautious, that a new era had set in. Trade, soaring on a continual rise in prices, was to know no bounds. If the golden age of commerce had not begun, something very like it had come to bless the British merchant.

Under such circumstances the Valleys Railroad seemed a practical thing even to Grounds, and Ovington's question was answered by a general assent.

'Very good, gentlemen,' he resumed. 'Then I may take that as agreed.' He proceeded to enter upon the details of the scheme. The length of the line would be fourteen miles. The capital was to be £45,000, divided into 4,500 shares of £10 each, £1 a share to be paid at once, the sum so raised to be used for the preliminary expenses; £1 10s per share to be paid three months later, and the rest to be called up as required. The directors' qualification would be fifty shares. The number of directors would be seven – the five gentlemen now present and two to be named, as to whom he would have a word to say by-and-by. Mr Bourdillon, of whose abilities he thought highly – here several at the table looked kindly at the young man – and who for other reasons was eminently fitted for the position, would be secretary.

'But will the forty-five thousand be enough, sir?' Grounds ventured timidly. He alone was not directly interested in the venture. Wolley was the tenant of a large mill. Sir Charles was the owner of two mills and the hamlets about them, Acherley of a third. Ovington had various interests.

'To complete the line, Mr Grounds? We believe so. To provide the engine and coaches another fifteen thousand will be needed, but this may be more cheaply raised by a mortgage.'

Sir Charles shied at the word. 'I don't like a mortgage, Mr Ovington,' he said.

'No, d—n a mortgage!' Acherley chimed in. He had had much experience of them.

'The point is this,' the banker explained. 'The road once completed, we shall be able to raise the fifteen thousand at five per cent. If we issue shares they must partake, equally with ourselves, in the profits, which may be fifteen, twenty, perhaps twenty-five per cent.'

A twinkle of greed passed from eye to eye. Fifteen, twenty, twenty-five per cent! Ho, ho!

'The next question,' Ovington continued, 'is important. We cannot use the highway, the gradients and angles render that impossible. We must acquire a right of way. But, fortunately, the estates we run over are few, no more than thirteen in all, and for a full third of the distance they are represented at this table.' He bowed gracefully to the two landowners. 'Sir Charles will, of course, be President of the Road and Chairman of the Directors. We are fortunate in having at our head a country gentleman who has' – he bowed again – 'the enlightenment to see that the landed interest is best served by making commerce contributory to its well-being.'

'But what about the game?' Sir Charles asked anxiously. 'You don't think—'

'On that point the greatest care will be taken. We shall see that no covert is closely approached.'

'And the – you won't bring the line within sight of—'

'Of the Park? God forbid! The amenities of every estate must be carefully guarded. And, of course, a fair price for the right of way will be agreed. Seven of the smaller landowners I have sounded, and we shall have no trouble with them. The largest estate outstanding—'

'Is my landlord's, I'll bet!' Wolley exclaimed.

'Yes – is Garth. Mr Griffin's.'

Wolley laughed rudely. 'Garth? Ay, you'll have your work cut out there!'

'Oh, I don't know!'

'I do. And you'll find I'm right.'

'Well, I hope—'

'You may hope what you like!' Wolley rejoined, and Sir Charles shuddered at the man's brusqueness. 'The Squire's a hard nut to crack, and so you'll find, banker. If you can get him to do a thing he don't wish to do, you'll be the first that ever has. He hates the name of trade as he hates the devil!'

'The baronet sat up. 'Trade?' he exclaimed. 'Oh! but I am not aware, sir, that this is— Surely a railroad is on another footing?' Alarm was written on his face.

'Quite!' Ovington struck in. 'Entirely different! Another thing altogether, Sir Charles. There can be only one opinion on that.'

'Of course, if I thought I was entering on anything like—'

'A railroad is on an entirely different footing,' the banker repeated, with an angry glance at Wolley, who, unrepentant, continued to stare before him, a sneer on his face. 'On an entirely different footing. Even Mr Griffin, prejudiced as I venture with all respect to think he is – even he would agree to that. But I have considered the difficulty, gentlemen, and I have no doubt we can surmount it. I propose to see him on Monday, accompanied by Mr Bourdillon, his great-nephew, and between us I have no doubt that we shall be able to persuade him.'

Acherley looked over his shoulder at the secretary, who sat at a small table at Ovington's elbow. 'Like the job, Arthur?' he asked.

'I think Sir Charles' example will go a long way with him,' Bourdillon answered. He was a tactful young man.

The banker put the interruption aside. 'I shall see Mr Griffin on Monday, and with your consent, gentlemen, I propose to offer him the sixth seat at the Board.'

'Quite right, quite right,' Sir Charles murmured, much relieved.

'He'll not take it!' Wolley persisted.

'My dear sir!'

'You will see I am right.'

'Well, there are more ways than one. At any rate I will see him and report to the next meeting, when, with the chairman's approbation, we shall draw up the prospectus. In that connection' – he consulted his paper – 'I have already received overtures from customers of the bank for four hundred shares.' There was a murmur of applause and Grounds' face betrayed relief. 'Then Sir Charles has put himself down for three hundred.' He bowed deferentially to Woosenham. 'Mr Acherley for one hundred and fifty, Mr Wolley has taken up one hundred and twenty-five, and Mr Grounds – I have not heard from Mr Grounds, and there is no hurry. No hurry at all!'

But Grounds, feeling that all eyes were on him, and feeling also uncomfortable in his company, took the fence up to which he had been brought. He murmured that he would take one hundred and twenty-five.

'Excellent!' said Ovington. 'And I, on behalf of the bank, propose to take four hundred.' Again there was a murmur of applause. 'So that before we go to the public we have already one-third of the shares taken up. That being so, I feel no doubt that we shall start at a premium before we cut the first sod.'

There followed a movement of feet, an outburst of hilarity. For this was what they all wished to hear; this was the point. Chairs were pushed back, and Sir Charles, who was as fearful for his prestige as Grounds for his money, recovered his cheerfulness. Even Acherley became good-humoured. 'Well, here's to the Valleys Railroad!' he cried. 'Damme, we ought to have something to drink it in!'

The banker ignored this, and Sir Charles spoke. 'But as to the seventh seat at the Board? We have not arranged that, I think?' He liked to show that nothing escaped him, and that if he was above business he could still, when he condescended, be a business man.

'No,' Ovington agreed. 'But I suggest that, with your permission, we hold that over. There may be a big subscriber taking three or four hundred shares?'

'Quite so, quite so.'

'Somebody may come forward, and the larger the applications the higher the premium, gentlemen.'

Again eyes glistened, and there was a new movement. Woosenham took his leave, bowing to Wolley and Grounds, and shaking hands with the others. Acherley went with him and Ovington accompanied them, bareheaded, to Sir Charles' carriage, which was waiting before the bank. As he returned Wolley waylaid him and drew him into a corner. A conference took place, the banker turning the money in his fob as he listened, his face grave. Presently the clothier entered on a second explanation. In the end Ovington nodded. He called Rodd from the counter and gave an order. He left his customer in the bank.

When he re-entered the parlour Grounds had disappeared, and Arthur, who was bending over his papers, looked up. 'Wolley wanted his notes renewed, I suppose?' he said. The bank had few secrets for this shrewd young man, who had learnt as much of business in eighteen months as Rodd the cashier had learned in ten years, or as Clement Ovington would learn in twenty.

The banker nodded. 'And three hundred more on his standing loan.'

Arthur whistled. 'I wonder you go on carrying him, sir.'

'If I cut him loose now—'

'There would be a loss, of course.'

'Yes, but that is not all, lad. Where would the Railroad scheme be? Gone. And that's not all, either. His fall would deal a blow to credit. The money that we are drawing out of the old stockings and the cracked tea-pots would go back to them. Half the clothiers in the Valley would shiver, and neither I nor you would be able to say where the trouble would stop, or who would be in the *Gazette* next week. No, we must carry him for the present, and pay for his railway shares too. But we shall hold them, and the profits will eventually come to us. And if the railway is made it will raise the value of mills and increase our security; so that whether he goes on or we have to take the mills over – which Heaven forbid! – the ground will be firmer. It went well?'

'Splendidly! The way you managed them!' The lad laughed.

'What is it?'

'Grounds asked me if I did not think that you were like the pictures of old Boney. I said I did. The Napoleon of Finance, I told him. Only, I added, you knew a deal better where to stop.'

Ovington shook his head at the flatterer, but was pleased with the flattery. More than once, people had stopped him in the street and told him that he was like Napoleon. It was not only that he was stout and of middle height, with his head sunk between his shoulders; but he had the classic profile, the waxen complexion, the dominating brow and keen bright eyes, nay, something of the air of power of the great Exile who had died three years before. And he had something, too, of his ambition. Sprung from nothing, a self-made man, he seemed in his neighbours' eyes to have already reached a wonderful eminence. But in his own eyes he was still low on the hill of fortune. He was still a country banker, and new at that.

But if the wave of prosperity which was sweeping over the country and which had already wrought so many changes, if this could be taken at the flood, nothing, he believed, was beyond him. He dreamed of a union with Dean's, the old conservative steady-going bank of the town; of branches here and branches there; finally of an amalgamation with a London bank, of Threadneedle Street, and a directorship – but Arthur was speaking.

'You managed Grounds splendidly,' he said. 'I'll wager he's sweating over what he's done! But do you think' – he looked keenly at the banker as he put the question, for he was eager to know what was in his mind – 'the thing will succeed, sir?'

'The railroad?'

'Yes.'

'I think that the shares will go to a premium. And I see no reason why the railroad should not do. If I did not think so, I should not be fostering it. It may take time and, of course, more money than we think. But if nothing occurs to dash the public – no, I don't see why it should not succeed. And if it does it will give such an impetus to the trade of the Valleys, three-fourths of which passes through our hands, as will repay us many times over.'

'I am glad you think so. I was not sure.'

'Because I led Grounds a little? Oh, that was fair enough. It does not follow from that, that honesty is not the banker's only policy. Make no mistake about that. But I am going into the house now. Just bring me the note-issue book, will you? I must see how we stand. I shall be in the dining-room.'

But when Arthur went into the house a few minutes later he met Betty, who was crossing the hall. 'Your father wanted this book,' he said. 'Will you take it to him?'

But Betty put her hands behind her back. 'Why? Where are you going?'

'You have forgotten that it is Saturday. I am going home.'

'Horrid Saturday! I thought that tonight, with father just back—'

'I wouldn't go? If I don't my mother will think that the skies have fallen. Besides, I am riding Clement's mare, and if I don't go, how is he to come back?'

'As you go at other times. On his feet.'

'Ah, well, very soon I shall have a horse of my own. You'll see, Betty.

We are all going to make our fortunes now.'

'Fortunes?' – with disdain. 'Whose?'

'Your father's for one.'

'Silly! He's made his.'

'Then yours – and mine, Betty. Yours and mine – and Clement's.'

'I don't think he'll thank you.'

'Then Rodd's. But, no, we'll not make Rodd's. We'll not make Rodd's, Betty.'

'And why not Mr Rodd's?'

'Never mind. We'll not make it,' mischievously. 'I wonder why you've got such a colour, Betty?' And as she snatched the book from him and threatened him with it, 'Goodbye till Monday. I'm late now, and it will be dark before I am out of the town.'

With a gay nod he vanished through the door that led into the bank. She looked after him, the book in her hand. Her lip curled. 'Rodd indeed!' she murmured. 'Rodd? As if I should ever – oh, isn't he provoking!'

Chapter Two

The village of Garthmyle, where Arthur had his home, lay in the lap of the border hills more than seven miles from Aldersbury, and night had veiled the landscape when he rode over the bridge and up the village street. The squat church-tower, firm and enduring as the hopes it embodied, rose four-square above the thatched dwellings, and some half-mile away the rider could discern or imagine the blur of trees that masked Garth, on its sister eminence. But the bounds of the valley, in the mouth of which the village stood, were obscured by darkness; the steep limestone wall which fenced it on one side and the more distant wooded hills that sloped gently to it on the other were alike hidden. It was only when Arthur had passed through the hamlet, where all doors were closed against the chill of a January night, and he had ridden a few paces down the hillock, that the lights of the Cottage broke upon his view. Many a time had they, friendly beacons of home and rest, greeted him at that point.

Not that Arthur saw them as beacons, for at no time was he much given to sentiment. His outlook on life was too direct and vivid for that, and today in particular his mind was teeming with more practical thoughts, with hopes and plans and calculations. But the lights meant that a dull ride over a rough road was at an end, and so far they gave him pleasure. He opened the gate and rode round to the stable, gave up the horse to Pugh, the man-of-all-work, and made his way into the house.

He entered upon a scene as cheerful as any lights shining on weary traveller could promise. In a fair-sized room a clear grate held a coal fire the flames of which danced on the red-papered walls. A kettle bubbled on the hob, a tea tray gleamed on the table, and between the two a lady and gentleman sat, eating crumpets; the lady with much elegance and a napkin spread over her lavender silk dress, the gentleman in a green cutaway coat with basket buttons – a coat that ill concealed the splashed gaiters for which he had more than once asked pardon.

But fair as things looked on the surface, all was not perfect even in this pleasant interior. The lady held herself stiffly, and her eyes rested rather more often than was courteous on the spatter-dashes. Secretly she thought her company not good enough for her, while the gentleman was frankly bored. Neither was finding the other as congenial as a first glance suggested, and it would have been hard to say which found Arthur's entrance the more welcome interruption.

'Hallo, Mother!' he said, stooping carelessly to kiss her. 'Hallo, Clement.'

'My dear Arthur!' the lady cried, the lappets of her cap shaking as she embraced him. 'How late you are! That horrid bank! I am sure that some day you will be robbed and murdered on your way home!'

'I! No, Mother. I don't bring the money, more's the pity! I am late, am I? The worse for Clement, who has to ride home. But I have been doing your work, my lad, so you mustn't grumble. What did you get?'

'A brace and a wood-pigeon. Has my father come?'

'Yes he has come, and I am afraid has a wigging in store for you. But – a brace and a wood-pigeon? Lord man,' with a little contempt in his tone, 'what do you do with your gun all day? Why, Acherley told me that in that rough between the two fallows above the brook—'

'Oh, Arthur,' Mrs Bourdillon interposed, 'never mind that!' She had condescended sufficiently, and she wished to hear no more of Clement Ovington's doings. 'I've something more important to tell you, much more important. I've had a shock, a dreadful shock today.'

She was a faded lady, rather foolish than wise, and very elegant: one who made the most of such troubles as she had, and the opening her son now heard was one which he had heard before.

'What's the matter now, Mother?' he asked, stooping to warm his hands.

'Your uncle has been here.'

'Well, that's no new thing.'

'But he has behaved dreadfully, perfectly dreadfully to me.'

'I don't know that that is new, either.'

'He began again about your refusal to take Orders, and your going into that dreadful bank instead.'

Arthur shrugged his shoulders. 'That's one for you, Clement.'

'Oh, that wasn't the half,' the lady continued, unbending. 'He said, there was the living, three hundred and fifty a year, and old Mr Trubshaw seventy-eight. And he'd have to sell it and put in a stranger and have quarrels about tithes. He stood there with his great stick in his hand and his eyes glaring at me like an angry cat's, and scolded me till I didn't know whether I stood on my head or my heels. He wanted to know where you got your low tastes from.'

'There you are again, Clement!'

'And your wish to go into trade, and I answered him quite sharp that you didn't get them from me; as for Mr Bourdillon's grandfather, who had the plantations in Jamaica, it wasn't the same at all, as everybody knows and agrees that nothing is genteeler than the West Indies with black men to do the work!'

'You confounded him there, Mother, I'm sure. But as we have heard this before, and Clement is not much interested, if that is all—'

'Oh, but it is not all! Very far from it!' Mrs Bourdillon's head shook till the lappets swung again. 'The worst is to come. He said that we had had the Cottage rent-free for four years – and I'm sure I don't know who has a better right to it – but that that was while he still hoped that you were going to live like a gentleman, like the Griffins before you – and I am sure the Bourdillons were gentry, or I should have been the last to marry your father! But as you seemed to be set on going your own way and into the bank for good – and I must say I told him it wasn't any wish of mine and I'd said all I could against it, as you know, and Mr Clement knows the same – why, it was but right that we should pay rent like other people! And it would be thirty pounds a year from Lady Day!'

'The d—d old hunks!' Arthur cried. He had listened unmoved to his mother's tirade, but this touched him. 'Well, he is a curmudgeon! Thirty pounds a year? Well, I'm d—d! And all because I won't starve as a parson!'

But his mother rose in arms at that. 'Starve as a parson!' she cried. 'Why, I think you are as bad, one as the other. I'm sure your father never starved!'

'No, I know, Mother. He was passing rich on four hundred pounds a year. But that is not going to do for me.'

'Well, I don't know what you want!'

'My dear Mother, I've told you before what I want.' Arthur was fast regaining the good temper that he seldom lost. 'If I were a bishop's son and could look to be a bishop, or if I were an archdeacon's son with the prospect of a fat prebend and a rectory or two with it, I'd take Orders. But with no prospect except the Garthmyle living, and with tithes falling—'

'But haven't I told you over and over again that you have only to make up to – but there, I haven't told you that Jos was with him, and I will say this for her, that she looked as ashamed for him as I am sure I was! I declare I was sorry for the girl and she not daring to put in a word – such an old bear as he is to her!'

'Poor Jos!' Arthur said. 'She has not a very bright life of it. But this does not interest Clement, and we're keeping him.'

The young man had indeed made more than one attempt to take leave, but every time he had moved Mrs Bourdillon had either ignored him, or by a stately gesture had claimed his silence. He rose now.

'I dare say you know my cousin?' Arthur said.

'I've seen her,' Clement answered. And his mind went back to the only occasion on which he had remarked Miss Griffin. It had been at the last Race Ball at Aldersbury that he had noticed her – a gentle, sweet-faced girl, plainly and even dowdily dressed, and so closely guarded by her proud old dragon of a father that, warned by the fate of others and aware that his name was not likely to find favour with the Squire, he had shrunk from seeking an introduction. But he had noticed that she sat out more than she danced; sat, indeed, in a kind of isolation, fenced in by the old man, and regarded with glances of half-scornful pity by girls more smartly dressed. He had had time to watch her, for he also, though for different reasons, had been a little without the pale, and he had found her face attractive. He had imagined how differently she would look were she suitably dressed. 'Yes,' he continued, recalling it, 'she was at the last Race Ball, I think.'

'And a mighty poor time she had of it,' Arthur answered, half carelessly, half contemptuously. 'Poor Jos! She hasn't at any time much of a life with my beauty of an uncle. Two-pence to get and a penny to spend!'

Mrs Bourdillon protested. 'I do wish you would not talk of your cousin like that,' she said. 'You know that she's your uncle's heiress, and if you only—'

Arthur cut her short. 'There! There! You don't remember, Mother, that Clement has seven miles to ride before his supper. Let him go now! He'll be late enough.'

That was the end, and the two young men went out together. When Arthur returned, the tea had been removed and his mother was seated at her tambour work. He took his stand before the fire. 'Confounded old screw!' he fumed. 'Thirty pounds a year? And he's three thousand, if he's a penny! And more likely four!'

'Well, it may be yours some day,' with a sniff. 'I'm sure Jos is ready enough.'

'She'll have to do as he tells her.'

'But Garth must be hers.'

'And still she'll have to do as he tells her. Don't you know yet, Mother, that Jos has no more will than a mouse? But never mind, we can afford his thirty pounds. Ovington is giving me a hundred and fifty, and I'm to have another hundred as Secretary to this new Company – that's news for you. With your three hundred we shall be able to pay his rent and still be better off than before. I shall buy a nag – Packham has one to sell – and move to better rooms in town – on the Walls, I think.'

'But you'll still be in that dreadful bank,' Mrs Bourdillon sighed. 'Really, Arthur, with so much money it seems a pity you should lower yourself to it.'

He had some admirable qualities besides the gaiety, the alertness, the good looks that charmed all comers; ay, and besides the rather uncommon head for figures and for business which came, perhaps, of his Huguenot ancestry, and had commended him to the banker. Of these qualities patience with his mother was one. So, instead of snubbing her, 'Why dreadful?' he asked good-humouredly. 'Because all our county fogies look down on it? Because having nothing but land, and drawing all their importance from land, they're jealous of the money that is shouldering them out and threatening their pride of place? Listen to me, Mother. There is a change coming! Whether they see it or not, and I think they do see it, there is a change coming, and stiff as they hold themselves, they will have to give way to it. Three thousand a year? Four thousand? Why, if Ovington lives another ten years what do you think that he will be worth? Not three thousand a year, but ten, fifteen, twenty thousand!'

'Arthur!'

'It is true, Mother. Ay, twenty, it is possible! And do you think that when he can buy up half a dozen of these thick-headed Squires who can just add two to two and make four – that he'll not count? Do you think that they'll be able to put him on one side? No! And they know it. They see that the big manufacturers and the big ironmasters and the big bankers who are putting together hundreds of thousands are going to push in among them and can't be kept out! And therefore trade, as they call it, stinks in their nostrils!'

'Oh, Arthur, how horrid!' Mrs Bourdillon protested, 'you are growing as coarse as your uncle. And I'm sure we don't want a lot of vulgar purse-proud—'

'Purse-proud? And what is the Squire? Land-proud! But,' growing more calm, 'never mind that. You will take a different view when I tell you something that I heard today. Ovington let drop a word about a – partnership.'

'La, Arthur! But—'

'A partnership! Nothing definite, and not yet, but in the future. It was but a hint. But think of it, Mother! It is what I have been aiming at, but I didn't expect to hear of it yet. Not one or two hundred a year, but say, five hundred to begin with, and three, four, five thousand by and by! Five thousand!' His eyes sparkled and he threw back the hair from his forehead with a characteristic gesture. 'Five thousand a year! Think of that and don't talk to me of Orders. Take Orders! Be a beggarly parson while I have that in my power, and in my power while I am still young! For trust me, with Ovington at the helm and the tide at flood we shall move. We shall move, Mother! The money is there, lying there, lying everywhere to be picked up. And we shall pick it up.'

'You take my breath away!' his mother protested, her faded, delicate face unusually flushed. 'Five thousand a year! Gracious me! Why, it is more than your uncle has!' She raised her mittened hands in protest. 'Oh, it is impossible!' The vision overcame her.

But 'It is perfectly possible,' he repeated. 'Clement is of no use. He is for ever wanting to be out of doors – a farmer spoiled. Rodd's a mere mechanic. Ovington cannot do it all, and he sees it. He must have someone he can trust. And then it is not only that I suit him. I am what he is not – a gentleman.'

'If you could have it without going to the bank!' Mrs Bourdillon said. And she sighed, golden as was the vision. But before they parted his eloquence had almost persuaded her. She had heard such things, had listened to such hopes, had been dazzled by such sums that she was well-nigh reconciled even to that which the old Squire dubbed 'the trade of usury.'

Chapter Three

Meanwhile Clement Ovington jogged homeward through the darkness, his thoughts divided between the discussion at which he had made an unwilling third, and the objects about him which were never without interest for this young man. He had an ear, and a very sharp one, for the piping of the pee-wits in the low land by the river, and the owl's cadenced cry in the trees about Garth. He marked the stars shining in a depth of heaven opened amid the flying wrack of clouds; he picked out Jupiter sailing with supreme dominion, and the Dog-star travelling across the southern tract. His eye caught the gleam of water on a meadow, and he reflected that old Gregory would never do any good with that ground until he made some stone drains in it. Not a sound in the sleeping woods, not the barking of a dog at a lonely homestead – and he knew every farm by name and sight and quality – escaped him; nor the shape of a covert, blurred though it was and leafless. But amid all these interests, and more than once, his thoughts as he rode turned inwards, and he pictured the face of the girl at the ball. Long forgotten, it recurred to him with strange persistence.

He was an out-of-door man, and that, in his position, was the pity of it. Aldersbury School – and Aldersbury was a very famous school in those days – and Cambridge had done little to alter the tendency: possibly the latter, seated in the midst of wide open spaces, under a wide sky, the fens its neighbours, had done something to strengthen his bent. Bourdillon thought of him with contempt, as a clodhopper, a rustic, hinting that he was a throw-back to an ancestor, not too remote, who had followed the plough and whistled for want of thought. But he did Clement an injustice. It was possible that in his love of the soil he was a throw-back; he would have made, and indeed he was, a good ploughman. He had learnt the trick with avidity, giving good money, solid silver shillings, that Hodge might rest while he worked. But, a ploughman, he would not have turned a clod without noticing its quality, nor sown a seed without considering its fitness, nor observed a rare plant without wondering why it grew in that position, nor looked up without drawing from the sky some sign of the weather or the hour. Much less would he have gazed down a woodland glade, flecked with sunlight, without perceiving its beauty.

He was, indeed, both in practice and theory a lover of Nature; breathing freely its open air, understanding its moods, asking nothing better than to be allowed to turn them to his purpose. Though he was no great reader, he read Wordsworth, and many a line was fixed in his memory and, on occasions when he was alone, rose to his lips.

But he hated the desk and he hated figures. His thoughts as he stood behind the bank counter, or drummed his restless heels against the legs of his high stool, were far away in fallow and stubble, or where the trout, that he could tickle as to the manner born, lay under the caving bank. And to his father and to those who judged him by the bank standard, and felt for him a half scornful liking, he seemed to be an inefficient, a trifler. They said in Aldersbury that it was lucky for him that he had a father.

Perhaps of all about him it was from that father that he could expect the least sympathy. Ovington was not only a banker, he was a banker to whom his business was everything. He had created it. It had made him. It was not in his eyes a mere adjunct, as in the eyes of one born in the purple and to the leisure which invites to the higher uses of wealth. Able he was, and according to his lights honourable; but a narrow education had confined his views, and he saw in his money merely the means to rise in the world and eventually to become one of the landed class which at that time monopolised all power and all influence, political as well as social. Such a man could only see in Clement a failure, a reversion to the yeoman type, and own with sorrow the irony of fortune that so often delights to hand on the sceptre of an Oliver to a Tumble-down-Dick.

Only from Betty, young and romantic, yet possessed of a woman's intuitive power of understanding others, could Clement look for any sympathy. And even Betty doubted while she loved – for she had also that other attribute of woman, a basis of common-sense. She admired her father. She saw more clearly than Clement what he had done for them and to what he was raising them. And she could not but grieve that Clement was not more like him, that Clement could not fall in with his wishes and devote himself to the attainment of the end for which the elder man had worked. She could enter into the father's disappointment as well as into the son's distaste.

Meanwhile Clement, dreaming now of a girl's face, now of a new drill which he had seen that morning, now of the passing sights and sounds which would have escaped nine men out of ten but had a meaning for him, drew near to the town. He topped the last eminence, he rode under the ancient oak, whence, tradition had it, a famous Welshman had watched the wreck of his fortunes on a pitched field. Finally he saw, rising from the river before him, the amphitheatre of dim lights that was the town. Descending he crossed the bridge.

He sighed as he did so. For to him to pass from the silent lands and to enter the brawling streets where apprentices were putting up the shutters and beggars were raking among heaps of market garbage was to fall half way from the clouds. To right and left the inns were roaring drunken choruses, drabs stood in the mouths of the alleys – dubbed in Aldersbury 'shuts' – tradesmen were hastening to wet their profits at the Crown or the Gullet. When at last he heard the house door clang behind him, and breathed the confined air of the bank, redolent for him of ledgers and day-books, the fall was complete. He reached the earth.

If he had not done so, his sister's face when he entered the dining-room would have brought him to his level.

'My eye and Betty Martin!' she said. 'But you've done it now, my lad!'

'What's the matter?'

'Father will tell you that. He's in his room and as black as thunder. He came home by the mail at three – Sir Charles waiting, Mr Acherley waiting, the bank full, no Clement! You are in for it. You are to go to him the moment you come in.'

He looked longingly at the table where supper awaited him. 'What did he say?' he asked.

'He said all I have said and d—n besides. It's no good looking at the table, my lad. You must see him first and then I'll give you your supper.'

'All right!' he replied, and he turned to the door with something of a swagger.

But Betty, whose moods were as changeable as the winds, and whose thoughts were much graver than her words, was at the door before him. She took him by the lapel of his coat and looked up in his face. 'You won't forget that you're in fault, Clem, will you?' she said in a small voice. 'Remember that if he had not worked there would be no walking about with a gun or a rod for you. And no looking at new drills, whatever they are, for I know that that is what you had in your mind this morning. He's a good dad, Clem – better than most. You won't forget that, will you?'

'But after all a man must—'

'Suppose you forget that "*after all*" she said sagely. 'The truth is you have played truant, haven't you? And you must take your medicine. Go and take it like a good boy. There are but three of us, Clem.'

She knew how to appeal to him, and how to move him; she knew that at bottom he was fond of his father. He nodded and went, knocked at his father's door and, tamed by his sister's words, took his scolding – and it was a sharp scolding – with patience. Things were going well with the banker, he had had his usual four glasses of port, and he might not have spoken so sharply if the contrast between the idle and the industrious apprentice had not been thrust upon him that day with a force which had startled him. That little hint of a partnership had not been dropped without a pang. He was jealous for his son, and he spoke out.

'If you think,' he said, tapping the ledger before him, to give point to his words, 'that because you've been to Cambridge this job is below you, you're mistaken, Clement. And if you think that you can do it in your spare time, you're still more mistaken. It's no easy task, I can tell you, to make a bank and keep a bank, and manage your neighbour's money as well as your own, and if you think it is, you're wrong. To make a hundred thousand pounds is a deal harder than to make Latin verses – or to go tramping the country on a market day with your gun! That's not business! That's not business, and once for all, if you are not going to help me, I warn you that I must find someone who will! And I shall not have far to look!'

'I'm afraid, sir, that I have not got a turn for it,' Clement pleaded.

'But what have you a turn for? You shoot, but I'm hanged if you bring home much game. And you fish, but I suppose you give the fish away. And you're out of town idling and doing God knows what, three days in the week! No turn for it? No will to do it, you mean. Do you ever think,' the banker continued, joining the fingers of his two hands as he sat back in his chair, and looking over them at the culprit, 'where you would be and what you would be doing if I had not toiled for you? If I had not made the business at which you do not condescend to work? I had to make my own way. My grandfather was little better than a labourer, and but for what I've done you might be a clerk at a pound a week, and a bad clerk, too! Or behind a shop-counter, if you liked it better. And if things go wrong with me – for I'd have you remember that nothing in this world is quite safe – that is where you may still be! Still, my lad!'

For the first time Clement looked his father fairly in the face – and pleased him. 'Well, sir,' he said, 'if things go wrong I hope you won't find me wanting. Nor ungrateful for what you have done for us. I know how much it is. But I'm not Bourdillon, and I've not got his head for figures.'

'You've not got his application. That's the mischief! Your heart's not in it.'

'Well, I don't know that it is,' Clement admitted. 'I suppose you couldn't—' he hesitated, a new hope kindled within him. He looked at his father doubtfully.

'Couldn't what?'

'Release me from the bank, sir! And give me a – a very small capital to—'

'To go and idle upon?' the banker exclaimed, and thumped the ledger in his indignation at an idea so preposterous. 'No, by G–d, I couldn't! Pay you to go idling about the country, more like a dying duck in a thunderstorm, as I am told you do, than a man! Find you capital and see you loiter your life away with your hands in your pockets? No, I couldn't, my boy, and I would not if I could! Capital, indeed? Give you capital? For what?'

'I could take a farm,' sullenly, 'and I shouldn't idle. I can work hard enough when I like my work. And I know something about farming, and I believe I could make it pay.'

The other gasped. To the banker, with his mind on thousands, with his plans and hopes for the future, with his golden visions of Lombard Street and financial sway, to talk of a farm and of making it pay! It seemed – it seemed worse than lunacy. His son must be out of his mind. He stared at him, honestly wondering. 'A farm!' he ejaculated at last. 'And make it pay? Go back to the clodhopping life your grandfather lived before you and from which I lifted you? Peddle with pennies and sell ducks and chickens in the market? Why – why, I don't know what to say to you?'

'I like an outdoor life,' Clement pleaded, his face scarlet.

'Like a – like a –' Ovington could find no word to express his feelings and with an effort he swallowed them down. 'Look here, Clement,' he said more mildly; 'what's come to you? What is it that is amiss with you? Whatever it is you must straighten it out, boy; there must be an end of this folly, for folly it is. Understand me, the day that you go out of the bank you go to stand on your own legs, without help from me. If you are prepared to do that?'

'I don't say that I could – at first.'

'Then while I keep you I shall certainly do it on my own terms. So, if you please, I will hear no more of this. Go back to your desk, go back to your desk, sir, and do your duty. I sent you to Cambridge at Butler's suggestion, but I begin to fear that it was the biggest mistake of my life. I declare I never heard such nonsense except from a man in love. I suppose you are not in love, eh?'

'No!' Clement cried angrily, and he went out.

For he could not own to his father that he was in love; in love with the brown earth, the woods, and the wide straggling hedgerows, with the whispering wind and the music of the river on the shallows, with the silence and immensity of night. Had he done so, he would have spoken a language which his father did not and could not understand. And if he had gone a step farther and told him that he felt drawn to those who plodded up and down the wide stubbles, who cut and bound the thick hedgerows, who wrought hand in hand with Nature day in and day out, whose lives were spent in an unending struggle with the soil until at last they sank and mingled with it – if he had told him that he felt his kinship with those humble folk who had gone before him, he would only have mystified him, only have angered him the more.

Yet so it was. And he could not change himself.

He went slowly to his supper and to Betty, owning defeat; acknowledging his father's strength of purpose, acknowledging his father's right, yet vexed at his own impotence. Life pulsed strongly within him. He longed to do something. He longed to battle, the wind in his teeth and the rain in his face, with some toil, some labour that would try his strength and task his muscles, and send him home at sunset weary and satisfied. Instead he saw before him an endless succession of days spent with his head in a ledger and his heels on the bar of his stool, while the sun shone in at the windows of the bank and the flies buzzed sleepily about him; days arid and tedious, shared with no companion more interesting than Rodd, who, excellent fellow, was not amusing, or more congenial than Bourdillon, who patronised him when he was not using him. And in future he would have to be more punctual, more regular, more assiduous! It was a dreary prospect.

He ate his supper in morose silence until Betty, who had been quick to read the upshot of the interview in his face, came behind him and ruffled his hair. 'Good boy!' she whispered, leaning over him. 'His days shall be long in the land!'

'I wish to heaven,' he answered, 'they were in the land! I am sure they will be long enough in the bank!'

But after that he recovered his temper.

Chapter Four

In remote hamlets a few churches still recall the fashion of Garthmyle.
It was a wide church of two aisles having clear windows, through which
a flood of cold light fell on the whitewashed walls, and on the maze of
square pews, some coloured drab, some a pale blue, through which narrow
alleys, ending in culs-de-sac, wound at random. The Griffin memorials,
though the earliest were of Tudor date, were small and mean, and the one
warm scrap of colour in the church was furnished by the faded red curtain
which ran on iron rods round the Squire's pew and protected his head from
draughts. That curtain was watched with alarm by many, for at a certain
point in the service it was the Squire's wont to draw it aside, and to stand
for a time with his back to the east while his hard eyes roved over the
congregation. Woe to the absentees! His scrutiny completed, with a grunt
which carried terror to the hearts of their families, he would draw the
curtain, turn about again, and compose himself to sleep.

In its severity and bleakness the church fairly matched the man,
who, old and gaunt and grey, was its central figure; who, like it, embodied,
meagrely and plainly as he dressed, the greatness of old associations, and
like it, if in a hard and forbidding way, owned and exacted an unchanging
standard of duty.

For he was the Squire. Whatever might be done elsewhere, nothing
was done in that parish without him. The parson, aged and apathetic,
knew better than to cross his will – had he not to get in his tithes? The
farmers were his tenants, the overseers rested in the hollow of his hand.
Hardly a man was hired, and no man was relieved, no old wife sent back
to her distant settlement, no lad apprenticed, but as he pleased. He was the
Squire. On Sundays the tenants waited in the churchyard until he arrived,
and it was this which deceived Arthur when, Mrs Bourdillon feeling

unequal to the service, he reached the church next morning. He found the porch empty, and concluding that his uncle had entered, he made his way to the Cottage pew, which was abreast of the great man's. But in the act of sitting down he saw, glancing round the red curtain; that Josina was alone. It struck him then that it would be pleasant to sit beside her and entertain himself with her conscious face, and he crossed over and let himself into the Squire's pew. He had the satisfaction of seeing the blood mount swiftly to her cheeks, but the next moment he found the old man – who had that morning sent word that he would be late – at his elbow, in the act of entering behind him.

It was too late to retreat, and with a face as hot as Josina's he stumbled over the straw-covered footstool and sat down on her other hand. He knew that the Squire would resent his presence after what had happened, and when he stood up his ears were tingling. But he soon recovered himself. He saw the comic side of the situation, and long before the sermon was over, he found himself sufficiently at ease to enjoy some of the *agréments* which he had foreseen.

Carved roughly with a penknife on the front of the pew was a heart surmounting two clasped hands. Below each hand were initials – his own and Josina's; and he never let the girl forget the August afternoon, three years before, when he had induced her to do her share. She had refused many times; then, like Eve in the garden, she had succumbed on a drowsy afternoon when they had had the pew to themselves and the drone of the preacher's voice had barely risen above the hum of the bees. She had been little more than a child at the time, and ever since that day the apple had been to her both sweet and bitter. For she was not a child now, and, a woman, she rebelled against Arthur's power to bring the blood to her cheeks and to play – with looks rather than words, for of these he was chary – upon feelings which she could not mask.

Of late resentment had been more and more gaining the upper hand. But today she forgave. She feared that which might pass between him and his uncle at the close of the service, and she had not the heart to be angry. However, when the dreaded moment came she was pleasantly disappointed. When they reached the porch, 'Take my seat, take my meat,' the Squire said grimly. 'Are you coming up?'

'If I may, sir?'

'I want a word with you.'

This was not promising, but it might have been worse, and little more was said as the three passed, the congregation standing uncovered, down the Churchyard Walk and along the road to Garth.

The Squire, always taciturn, strode on in silence, his eyes on his fields. The other two said little, feeling trouble in the air. Fortunately at the early dinner there was a fourth to mend matters in the shape of Miss Peacock, the Squire's housekeeper. She was a distant relation who had spent most of her life at Garth; who considered the Squire the first of men, his will as law, and who from Josina's earliest days had set her an example of servile obedience. To ask what Mr Griffin did not offer, to doubt where he had laid down the law, was to Miss Peacock flat treason, and where a stronger mind might have moulded the girl to a firmer shape, the old maid's influence had wrought in the other direction. A tall meagre spinster, a weak replica of the Squire, she came of generations of women who had been ruled by their men and trained to take the second place. The Squire's two wives, his first, whose only child had fallen, a boy-ensign, at Alexandria, his second, Josina's mother, had held the same tradition, and Josina promised to abide by it.

When the Peacock rose Jos hesitated. The Squire saw it. 'Do you go, girl,' he said. 'Be off!'

For once she wavered – she feared what might happen between the two. But 'Do you hear?' the Squire growled. 'Go when you are told.'

She went then, but Arthur could not restrain his indignation. 'Poor Jos!' he muttered.

Unluckily the Squire heard the words, and 'Poor Jos!' he repeated, scowling at the offender. 'What the devil do you mean, sir? Poor Jos, indeed? Confound your impudence! What do you mean?'

Arthur quailed, but he was not lacking in wit. 'Only that women like a secret, sir,' he said. 'And a woman, shut out, fancies that there is a secret.'

'Umph! A devilish lot you know about women!' the old man snarled. 'But never mind that. I saw your mother yesterday.'

'So she told me, sir.'

'Ay! And I dare say you didn't like what she told you! But I want you to understand, young man, once for all, that you've got to choose between Aldersbury and Garth. Do you hear? I've done my duty. I kept the living for you, as I promised your father, and whether you take it or not, I expect you to do yours, and to live as the Griffins have lived before you. Who the devil is this man, Ovington? Why do you want to mix yourself up with him? Eh? A man whose father touched his hat to me and would no more have thought of sitting at my table than my butler would! There, pass the bottle.'

'Would you have no man rise, sir?' Arthur ventured.

'Rise?' The Squire glared at him from under his great bushy eyebrows. 'It's not to his rise, it's to your fall I object, sir. A d—d silly scheme this, and one I won't have. D'you hear, I won't have it.'

Arthur kept his temper, oppressed by the other's violence. 'Still, you must own, sir, that times are changed,' he said.

'Changed? Damnably changed when a Griffin wants to go into trade in Aldersbury.'

'But banking is hardly a trade.'

'Not a trade? Of course it's a trade – if usury is a trade! If pawn-broking is a trade! If loan-jobbing is a trade! Of course it's a trade.'

The gibe stung Arthur and he plucked up spirit. 'At any rate, it is a lucrative one,' he rejoined. 'And I've never heard, sir, that you were indifferent to money.'

'Oh! Because I'm going to charge your mother rent? Well, isn't the Cottage mine? Or because fifty years ago I came into a cumbered estate and have pinched and saved and starved to clear it? Saved? I have saved. But I've saved out of the land like a gentleman, and like my fathers before me, and not by usury. Not by money-jobbing. And if you expect to benefit – but there, fill your glass, and let's hear your tongue. What do you say to it?'

'As to the living,' Arthur said mildly, 'I don't think you consider, sir, that what was a decent livelihood no longer keeps a gentleman as a gentleman. Times are changed, incomes are changed, men are richer. I see men everywhere making fortunes by what you call trade, sir; making fortunes and buying estates and founding houses.'

'And shouldering out the old gentry? Ay, damme, and I see it too,' the Squire retorted, taking the word out of his mouth. 'I see plenty of it. And you think to be one of them, do you? To join them and be another Peel, or one of Pitt's money-bag peers? That's in your mind, is it? A Mr Coutts? And to buy out my lord and drive your coach and four into Aldersbury, and splash dirt over better men than yourself?'

'I should be not the less a Griffin.'

'A Griffin with dirty hands!' with contempt. 'That's what you'd be. And vote Radical and prate of Reform and scorn the land that bred you. And talk of the Rights of Men and moneybags, eh? That's your notion, is it, by G–d?'

'Of course, sir, if you look at it in that way—'

'That's the way I do look at it!' The Squire brought down his hand on the table with a force that shook the glasses and spilled some of his wine. 'And it's the way you've got to look at it, or there won't be much between you and me – or you and mine. Or mine, do you hear! I'll have no tradesman at Garth and none of that way of thinking. So you'd best give heed before it's too late. You'd best look at it all ways.'

'Very well, sir.'

'Any more wine?'

'No, thank you.' Arthur's head was high. He did not lack spirit.

'Then hear my last word. I won't have it! That's plain. That's plain, and now you know. And, hark ye, as you go out, send Peacock to me.'

But before Arthur had made his way out, the Squire's voice was heard, roaring for Josina. When Miss Peacock presented herself, 'Not you! Who the devil wants you?' he stormed. 'Send the girl! D'you hear? Send the girl!'

And when Josina, scared and trembling, came in her turn, 'Shut the door!' he commanded. 'And listen! I've had a talk with that puppy, who thinks that he knows more than his betters. D—n his impertinence, coming into my pew when he thought I was elsewhere! But I know very well why he came, sneaking in to sit beside you and make sheep's eyes when my back was turned. Now, do you listen to me. You'll keep him at arm's length. Do you hear, miss? You'll have nothing to say to him unless I give you leave. He's got to do with me now, and it depends on me whether there's any more of it. I know what he wants, but by G–d, I'm your father, and if he does not mend his manners, he goes to the right-about. So let me hear of no more billing and cooing and meeting in pews, unless I give the word! D'you understand, girl?'

'But I think you're mistaken, sir,' poor Jos ventured. 'I don't think that he means—'

'I know what he means. And so do you. But never you mind! Till I say the word there's an end of it. The puppy, with his Peels and his peers! Men my father wouldn't have – but there, you understand now, and you'll obey, or I'll know the reason why!'

'Then he's not to come to Garth, sir?'

But the Squire checked at that. Family feeling and the pride of hospitality were strong in him, and to forbid his only nephew the family house went beyond his mind at present.

'To Garth?' angrily. 'Who said anything about Garth? No, Miss, but when he comes, you'll stand him off. You know very well how to do it, though you look as if butter wouldn't melt in your mouth! You'll see that he keeps his distance. And let me have no tears, or – d—n the fellow, he's spoiled my nap. There, go! Go! I might as well have a swarm of wasps about me as such folks! Pack o' fools and idiots! Go into a bank, indeed!'

Jos did go, and shutting herself up in her room would not open to Miss Peacock, who came fluttering to the door to learn what was amiss. And she cried a little, but it was as much in humiliation as grief. Her father was holding her on offer, to be given or withheld, as he pleased, while all the time she doubted, and more than doubted, if he to whom she was on offer, he from whom she was withheld, wanted her. There was the rub.

For Arthur, ever since he had begun to attend at the bank, had been strangely silent. He had looked and smiled and teased her, had pressed her hand or touched her hair, but in sport rather than in earnest, meaning little. And she had been quick to see this, and with the womanly pride, of which, gentle and timid as she was, she had her share, she had schooled herself to accept the new situation. Now, her father had taken Arthur's suit for granted and humbled her. So Jos cried a little. But they were not very bitter tears.

Chapter Five

Arthur was taken aback by his uncle's harshness, and he made haste to be at the bank early enough on the Monday to anticipate the banker's departure for Garth. He was certain that to approach the Squire at the moment in the matter of the railroad was to invite disaster, and he gave Ovington such an account of the quarrel as he thought would deter him from going over.

But the banker had a belief in himself which success and experience in the management of men had increased. He was convinced that self-interest was the spring which moved nine men out of ten, and though he admitted that the family quarrel was untimely, he did not agree that as between the Squire and a good bargain it would have weight.

'But I assure you, sir, he's like a bear with a sore head,' Arthur urged.

'A bear will come to the honey if its head be sore,' the banker answered, smiling.

'And perhaps upset the hive?'

Ovington laughed. 'Not in this case, I think. And we must risk something. Time presses and he blocks the way. However, I'll let it stand over for a week and then I'll go alone. We must have your uncle.'

Accordingly a week later, discarding the tilbury and smart man-servant that he had lately set up, he rode over to Garth, considering as he journeyed the man whom he was going to meet and of whom, in spite of his self-assurance, he stood in some awe.

Round Aldersbury were larger landowners and richer men than the Squire. But his family and his name were old, and by virtue of long possession he stood high among the gentry of the county. He had succeeded at twenty-two to a property neglected and loaded with debt, and his father's friends – this was far back in the old King's reign – had advised him to sell; let him keep the house and the home-farm and pay his debts with the rest. But pride of race was strong in him, he had seen that to sell was to lose the position which his forebears had held, and he had refused. Instead he had set himself to free the estate, and he had pared, he had pinched, he had almost starved himself and others. He had become a byword for parsimony. In the end, having benefited much by enclosures in the 'nineties, he had succeeded. But no sooner had he deposited in the bank the money to pay off the last charge than the loss of his only son had darkened his success. He had married again – he was by this time past middle age – but only a daughter had come of the marriage, and by that time to put shilling to shilling and acre to acre had become a habit of which he could not break himself, though he knew that only a woman would follow him at Garth.

Withal he was a great aristocrat, a Tory of the Tories, stern and unbending. Fear of France and of French doctrines and pride in his caste were in his blood. The *Quarterly Review* ranked with him after his Bible, and very little after it. Reform under the most moderate aspect was to him a shorter name for Revolution. He believed implicitly in his class, and did not believe in any other class. Manufacturers and traders he hated and distrusted, and of late jealousy had been added to hatred and distrust. The inclusion of such men in the magistracy, the elevation of Peel to the Ministry had made him fancy that there was something in the Queen's case after all; when Canning and Huskisson had also risen to power he had said that Lord Liverpool was ageing and the Duke was no longer the man he had been.

He was narrow, choleric, proud, miserly; he had been known to carry an old log a hundred yards to add it to his wood-pile, and to travel a league to look for a lost sixpence. He dressed shabbily, which was not so much remarked now that dandies aped coachmen, as it had been in his younger days; and he rode about his fields on an old white mare which he was believed to hold in affection next after his estate and much before his daughter. He ruled his parish with a high hand. He had no mercy for poachers. But he was honest and he was just. The farmers must pay the wage he laid down – it was a shilling above the allowed rate. But the men must work it out, and woe betide the idle; they had best seek work abroad, and heaven help them if a foreign parish sent them home. In one thing he was before his time: he was resolved that no able-bodied man should share in the rates. The farmers growled, the labourers grumbled, there were hard cases. But he was obdurate – work your worth, or starve! And presently it began to be noticed that the parish was better off than its neighbours. He was a tyrant, but a just tyrant.

Such was the man whom Ovington was going to meet, and from whose avarice he hoped much. He had made his market of it once, for it was by playing on it that he had lured the Squire from Dean's, and so had gained one of his dearest triumphs over the old Aldersbury Bank.

His hopes would not have been lessened had he heard a dialogue which was at that moment proceeding in the stable-yard at Garth to an accompaniment of clattering pails and swishing besoms. 'He've no bowels!' Thomas the groom declared with bitterness. 'He be that hard and grasping he've no bowels for nobody!'

Old Fewtrell, the Squire's ancient bailiff, sniggered. 'He'd none for you, Thomas,' he said, 'when you come back gallus drunk from Baschurch Fair. None of your Manchester tricks with me, says Squire, and, lord, how he did leather 'ee.'

Thomas did not like the reminiscence. 'What other be I saying!' he snarled. 'He've no bowels even for his own flesh and blood! Did'ee ever watch him in church? Well, where be he a-looking? At his son's moniment as is at his elbow? Never see him, never see him, not once!'

'Well, I dunno as I 'ave, either,' Fewtrell admitted.

'No, his eyes is allus on t'other side, a-counting up the Griffins before him, and filling himself up wi' pride.'

'Dunno as I couldn't see it another way,' said the bailiff thoughtfully.

'What other way? Never to look at his own son's moniment?'

'Well, mebbe—'

'Mebbe?' Thomas cried with scorn. 'Look at his darter! He an't but one, and he be swilling o' money! Do he make much of her, James Fewtrell? And titivate her, and pull her ears bytimes same as you with your grand-darters? And get her a horse as you might call a horse? You know he don't. If she's not quick, it's a nod and be damned, same as to you and me!'

Old Fewtrell considered. 'Not right out the same,' he decided.

'Right out, I say. You've been with him all your life. You've never knowed no other and you're getting old, and Calamity, he be old too, and may put up with it. But I don't starve for no Squire, and I'm for more wage. I was in Aldersbury Saturday and wages is up and more work than men!

While here I'm a-toiling for what you got twenty year ago. But not me! I
bin to Manchester. And so I'm going to tell Squire.'

The bailiff grinned. 'Mebbe he'll take a stick same as before.'

'He'd best not!' Thomas said; with an ugly look. 'He'd best take care,
or—'

'Whist! Whist! lad. You be playing for trouble. Here be Squire.'

The Squire glared at them, but he did not stop. He stalked into the
house and, passing through it, went out by the front door. He intended
to turn righthanded, and enter the high-terraced garden facing south, in
which he was wont to take, even in winter, a few turns of a morning. But
something caught his eye, and he paused. 'Who's this!' he muttered, and
shading his eyes made out a moment later that the stranger was Ovington.
A visit from him was rare enough to be a portent, and the figure of his bank
balance passed through the Squire's mind. Had he been rash? Ovington's
was a new concern; was anything wrong? Then another idea, hardly more
welcome, occurred to him: had the banker come on his nephew's account?

If so – however, he would soon know, for the visitor was by this time
half-way up the winding drive. Sunk between high banks, it left the road
a third of a mile from the house, and presently forked, the left branch
swerving through a grove of beech trees to the front entrance, the right
making straight for the stables.

The Squire met his visitor at the gate and, raising his voice, shouted
for Thomas. 'I am sorry to trespass on you so early,' Ovington said as he
dismounted. 'A little matter of business, Mr Griffin, if I may trouble you.'

The old man did not say that it was no trespass, but he stood aside
punctiliously for the other to precede him through the gate. Then, 'You'll
stay to eat something after your ride?' he said.

'No, I thank you. I must be in town by noon.'

'A glass of Madeira?'

'Nothing, Squire, I thank you. My business will not take long.'

By this time they stood in the room in which the Squire lived and
did his business. He pointed courteously to a chair. He was shabby, in
well-worn homespun and gaiters, and the room was shabby, walled with
bound Quarterlies and old farm books, and littered with spurs and dog
leashes – its main window looked into the stable yard. But there was about
the man a dignity implied rather than expressed, which the spruce banker
in his shining Hessians owned and envied. The Squire could look at men

so that they grew uneasy under his eye, and for a moment, owning his domination, the visitor doubted of success. But then again the room was so shabby. He took heart of grace.

'I shouldn't trouble you, Mr Griffin,' he said, sitting back with an assumption of ease, while the Squire from his old leather chair observed him warily, 'except on a matter of importance. You will have heard that there is a scheme on foot to increase the value of the woollen industry by introducing a steam railroad. It is a new invention which, I admit, has not yet been proved, but I have examined it as a business man, and I think that much is to be expected from it. A limited company is being formed to carry out the plan, if it prove to be feasible. Sir Charles Woosenham has agreed to be Chairman, Mr Acherley and other gentlemen of the county are taking part, and I am commissioned by them to approach you. I have the plans here—'

'What do you want?' The Squire's tone was uncompromising, and he made no movement towards taking the plans.

'If you will allow me to explain?'

The old man sat back in his chair.

'The railroad will be a continuation of the Birmingham and Aldersbury railroad, which is in strong hands at Birmingham. Such a scheme would be too large for us. That, again, is a continuation of the London and Birmingham railroad.'

'Built?'

'No. Not yet, of course.'

'Begun, then?'

'No but—'

'Projected?'

'Precisely, projected, the plans approved, the Bill in preparation.'

'But nothing done?'

'Nothing actually done as yet,' the banker admitted, somewhat dashed. 'But if we wait until these works are finished we shall find ourselves anticipated.'

'Ah!'

'We wish, therefore, to be early in the field. Much has appeared in the papers about this mode of transport, and you are doubtless familiar with it. I have myself inquired into it, and the opinion of financial men in London is that these railroads will be very lucrative, paying dividends of from ten to twenty-five per cent.'

The Squire raised his eyebrows.

'I have the plans here,' the banker continued, once more producing them. 'Our road runs over the land of six small owners, who have all agreed to the terms offered. It then enters on the Woosenham outlying property, and thence, before reaching Mr Acherley's, proceeds over the Garth estate, serving your mills, the tenant of one of which joins our board. If you will look at the plans?' Again Ovington held them out.

But the old man put them aside. 'I don't want to see them,' he said.

'But, Squire, if you would kindly glance—'

'I don't want to see them. What do you want?'

Ovington paused to consider the most favourable light in which he could place the matter. 'First, Mr Griffin, your presence on the Board. We attach the highest importance to that. Secondly, a wayleave over your land for which the Company will pay – pay most handsomely, although the value added to your mills will far exceed the immediate profit.'

'You want to carry your railroad over Garth?'

'Yes.'

'Not a yard!' The old man tapped the table before him. 'Not a foot!'

'But our terms – if you would allow me to explain them?'

'I don't want to hear them. I am not going to sell my birthright, whatever they are. You don't understand me? Well, you can understand this.' And abruptly the Squire sat up. 'I'll have none of your d—d smoking, stinking steam-wagons on my land in my time! Oh, I've read about them in more places than the papers, sir, and I'll not sell my birthright and my people's birthright – of clean air and clean water and clean soil for any mess of pottage you can offer! That's my answer, Mr Ovington.'

'But the railroad will not come within a mile of Garth.'

'It will not come on to my land! I am not blind, sir. Suppose you succeed. Suppose you drive the mails and coaches and the stage-wagons off the road. Where shall I sell my coach-horses and hackneys and my tenants their heavy nags? And their corn and their beans? No, by G—d,' stopping Ovington, who wished to interrupt him. 'You may delude some of my neighbours, sir, and you may know more about money-making, where it is no question how the money is made, than I do! But I'll see that you don't delude me! A pack of navigators upsetting the country, killing game and robbing hen-roosts, raising wages and teaching honest folks tricks? Not here! If Woosenham knew his own business, and Acherley were not up to his neck in debt, they'd not let themselves be led by the nose by—'

'By whom, sir?' Ovington was on his feet by this time, his eyes smouldering, his face paler than usual. They confronted each other. It was the meeting, the collision of two powers, of two worlds, the old and the new.

'By whom, sir?' the Squire replied sternly – he too had risen. 'By one whose interests and breeding are wholly different from theirs and who looks at things from another standpoint! That's by whom, sir. And one word more, Mr Ovington. You have the name of being a clever man and I never doubted it until today; but have a care that you are not over clever, sir. Have a care that you do not lead your friends and yourself into more trouble than you think for I read the papers and I see that everybody is to grow rich between Saturday and Monday. Well, I don't know as much about money business as you do, but I am an old man, and I have never seen a time when everybody grew rich and nobody was the loser.'

Ovington had controlled himself well, and he still controlled himself, but there was a dangerous light in his eyes. 'I am sorry,' he said, 'that you can give me no better answer, Mr Griffin. We hoped to have, and we set some value on your support. But there are, of course – other ways.'

'You may take your railroad any way you like, so long as you don't bring it over Garth.'

'I don't mean that. If the railroad is made at all it must pass over Garth – the property stretches across the valley. But the Bill, when presented, will contain the same powers which are given in the later Canal Acts – a single proprietor cannot be allowed to stand in the way of the public interests, Mr Griffin.'

'You mean – by G–d, sir,' the Squire broke out, 'you mean that you will take my land whether I will or no?'

'I am not using any threat.'

'But you do use a threat!' roared the Squire, towering tall and gaunt above his opponent. 'You do use a threat! You come here—'

'I came here' – the other answered – he was quietly drawing on his gloves – 'to put an excellent business investment before you, Mr Griffin. As you do not think it worth while to entertain it, I can only regret that I have wasted your time and my own.'

'Pish!' said the Squire.

'Very good. Then with your permission I will seek my horse.'

The old man turned to the window and opened it. 'Thomas,' he shouted violently. 'Mr Ovington's horse.'

When he turned again, 'Perhaps you may still think better of it,' Ovington said. He had regained command of himself. 'I ought to have mentioned that your nephew has consented to act as Secretary to the Company.'

'The more fool he!' the Squire snarled. 'My nephew! What the devil is he doing in your Company? Or for the matter of that in your bank either?'

'I think he sees more clearly than you that times are changed.'

'Ay,' the old man retorted, feeling the hit, and well aware that the other had found a joint in his armour. 'And he had best have a care that these fine times don't lead him into trouble!'

'I hope not, I hope not. Good-day, Mr Griffin. I can find my way out. Don't let me trouble you.'

'I will see you out, if you please. After you, sir.' Then, with an effort which cost him much, but which he thought was due to his position, 'You are sure that you will take nothing?'

'Nothing, I thank you.'

The Squire saw his visitor to the door; but he did not stay to see him ride away. He went back to his room and to a side window at which it was his custom to spend much time. It looked over the narrow vale, little more than a glen, which the eminence, on which the house stood, cut off from the main valley. It looked on its green slopes, on the fern-fringed brook that babbled and tossed in its bottom, on the black and white mill that spanned the stream, and on the Thirty Acre covert that clothed the farther side and climbed to the foot of the great limestone wall that towered alike above house and glen and rose itself to the knees of the boundary hills. And looking on all this, the Squire in fancy saw the railroad scoring and smirching and spoiling his beloved acres. It was nothing to him, that in fact the railroad would pass up the middle of the broad vale behind him – he ignored that. He saw the hated thing sweep by below him, a long black ugly snake, spewing smoke and steam over the green meadows, fouling the waters, darkening the air.

'Not in my time, by G–d!' he muttered, his knees quivering a little under him – for he was an ageing man and the scene had tried him. 'Not in my time!' And at the thought that he, the owner of all, hill and vale, within his sight, and the descendant of generations of owners – that he had been threatened by this upstart, this loan-monger, this town-bred creature of a day, he swore with fresh vigour.

He had at any rate the fires of indignation to warm him, and the satisfaction of knowing that he had spoken his mind and had not had the worst of the bout. But the banker's feelings as he jogged homewards on his hackney were not so happy. In spite of Bourdillon's warning he had been confident that he would gain his end. He had fancied that he knew his man and could manage him. He had believed that the golden lure would not fail. But it had failed, and the old man's gibes accompanied him, and like barbed arrows clung to his memory and poisoned his content.

It was not the worst that he must return and own that Arthur had been wiser than he; that he must inform his colleagues that his embassy had failed. Worse than either was the hurt to his pride. Certain things that the Squire had said about money-making, his sneer about the difference in breeding, his warning that the banker might yet find that he had been too clever – these had pricked him to the quick, and the last had even caused him a pang of uneasiness. And then the Squire had shown so clearly the gulf that in his eyes lay between them!

Ay, it was that which rankled: the knowledge, sharply brought home to him, that no matter what his success, no matter what his wealth, nor how the common herd bowed down to him, this man and his like would ever hold themselves above him, would always look down on him. The fence about them he could not cross. Add thousands to thousands as he might, and though he conquered Lombard Street, these men would not admit him of their number. They would ever hold him at arm's length, would deal out to him a cold politeness. He could never be of them.

As a rule Ovington was too big a man to harbour spite, but as he rode and fumed, a plan which he had already considered put on a new aspect, and by and by his brow relaxed and he smote his thigh. Something tickled him and he laughed. He thought that he saw a way to avenge himself and to annoy his enemy, and by the time he reached the bank he was himself again. Indeed, he had not been human if he had not by that time owned that whatever Garth thought of him he was something in Aldersbury.

Three times men stopped him, one crossing the street to intercept him, one running bare-headed from a shop, a third seizing his rein. And all three sought favours, or craved advice, all, as they retreated, did so, eyed askance by those who lacked their courage or their impudence. For the tide of speculation was still rising in the country, and even in Aldersbury had reached many a back-parlour where the old stocking or the money-box was scarcely out of date. Thousands sold their Three per cents, and the proceeds had to go somewhere, and other proceeds, for behind all there was real prosperity. Men's money poured first into a higher and then into a lower grade of security and raised each in turn, so that fortunes were made with astonishing speed. The banks gave extended credit; everything rose. Many who had bought in fear found that they had cleared a profit before they had had time to tremble. They sold, and still there were others to take their place. It seemed as if all had only to buy and to sell and to grow rich. Only the very cautious stood aside, and one by one even these slid tempted into the stream.

The more venturesome hazarded their money afar, buying shares in steamship companies in the West Indies, in diamond mines in Brazil, or in cattle companies in Mexico. The more prudent preferred undertakings which they could see and which their limited horizon could compass, and to these such a local scheme as the Valleys Railroad held out a tempting bait. They knew nothing about a railroad, but they knew that steam had been applied to ocean travel, and they knew Aldersbury and the woollen district. Here was something the growth and progress of which they could watch, and which once begun could not vanish in a night.

Then the silence of those within and the rumours spread without added to its attractions. Each man felt that his neighbour was stealing a march upon him, and that if he were not quick he would not get in on equal terms.

One of Ovington's waylayers wished to know if the limit at which he had been advised to sell his stock was likely to he reached. 'I sold on Saturday,' the banker answered, 'two pounds above your limit, Davies. The money will be in the bank in a week.' He spoke with Napoleonic curtness, and rode on, leaving the man, amazed and jubilant, to calculate his gains.

The next wanted advice. He had a hundred in hand if Mr Ovington would not think it too small. 'Call tomorrow – no, Thursday,' Ovington said, hardly looking at him. 'I'll see you then.'

The third ran bare-headed out of a shop. He was a man of more weight, Purslow the big draper on Bride Hill, who had been twice Mayor of Aldersbury; a tradesman, bald and sleek, whom fortune had raised so rapidly that old subservience was continually at odds with new importance. 'Just a word, Mr Ovington,' he stuttered, 'a word, sir, by your leave? I'm a good customer.' He had not laid aside his black apron but merely twisted it round his waist, a sure sign, in these days of his greatness, that he was flustered.

The banker nodded. 'None better, Purslow,' he answered. 'What is it?'

'What I says, then – excuse me – is, if Grounds, why not me? Why not me, sir ?'

'I don't quite—'

'If he's to be on the Board, he and his mashtubs—'

'Oh!' The banker looked grave. 'You are thinking of the Railroad, Purslow?'

'To be sure! What else? – excuse me, sir! And what I say is, if Grounds, why not me? I've been mayor twice and him not even on the Council? And I'm not a pauper, as none knows better than you, Mr Ovington. If it's only that I'm a tradesman, why, there ought to be a tradesman on it, and I'll be bound as many will follow my lead as Grounds'.'

The banker seemed to consider. 'Look here, Purslow,' he said, 'you are doing very well, not a man in Aldersbury better. Take my advice and stick to the shop.'

'And slave for every penny I make!'

'Slow and sure is a good rule.'

'Oh, damn slow and sure!' cried the draper, forgetting his manners. 'No offence, sir, I'm sure. Excuse me. But slow and sure, while Grounds is paid for every time he crosses the street, and doubles his money while he wears out his breeches!'

'Well,' said Ovington, with apparent reluctance, 'I'll think it over. But to sit on the Board means putting in money, Purslow. You know that, of course.'

'And haven't I the money?' the man cried, inflamed by opposition. 'Can't I put down penny for penny with Grounds? Ay, though I've served the town twice, and him not even on the Council!'

'Well, I'll bear it in mind. I can say no more than that,' Ovington rejoined. 'I must consult Sir Charles. It's a responsible position, Purslow. And, of course, where there are large profits, as we hope there may be, there must be risk. There must be some risk. Don't forget that. Still,' touching up his horse with his heel, 'I'll see what I can do.'

He gained the bank without further stay, and there the stir and bustle which his practised eye was quick to mark sustained the note already struck. There were customers coming and going: some paying in, others seeking to have bills renewed, or a loan that they might pay calls, or accommodation of one kind or another. But with easy money these demands could be granted, and many a parcel of Ovington's notes passed out amid smiling and general content. The January sun was shining as if March winds would never blow, and credit seemed to be a thing to be had for the asking.

It was only within the last seven years that Ovington's had ventured on an issue of notes. Then, a little before the resumption of cash payments, they had put them forth with a tentative, 'If you had rather have bank paper it's here.' Some had had the bad taste to prefer the Abraham Newlands, a few had even asked for Dean's notes. But borrowers cannot be choosers, the notes had gradually got abroad, and though at first they had returned with the rapidity of a homing pigeon, the readiness with which they were cashed wrought its effect, and by this time the public were accustomed to them.

Dean's notes bore a big D, and Ovington's, for the benefit of those who could not read, were stamped with a large C.O., for Charles Ovington.

Alone with his daughter that evening the banker referred to this. 'Betty,' he said, after a long silence, 'I am going to make a change. I am going to turn C.O. into Company.'

She understood him at once, and 'Oh, Father!' she cried, laying down her work. 'Who is it? Is it Arthur?'

'Would you like that?'

She replied by another question. 'Is he really so clever?'

'He's a gentleman – that's much. And a Griffin, and that's more, in a place like this. And he's – yes, he's certainly clever.'

'Cleverer than Mr Rodd?'

'Rodd! Pooh! Arthur's worth two of him.'

'Quite the industrious apprentice!' she murmured, her hands in her lap.

'Well, you know,' lightly, 'what happened to the industrious apprentice, Betty?'

She coloured. 'He married his master's daughter, didn't he? But there are two words to that, Father. Quite two words.'

'Well, I am going to offer him a small share. Anything more will depend upon himself – and Clement.'

She sighed. 'Poor Clement!'

'Poor Clement!' The banker repeated her words pettishly. 'Not poor Clement, but idle Clement! Can you do nothing with that boy? Put no sense into him? He's good for nothing in the world except to moon about with a gun. The other day he began to talk to me about Cobbett and some new wheat. New wheat, indeed! Rubbish!'

'But I think,' timidly, 'that he does understand about those things, Father.'

'And what good will they do him? I wish he understood a little more about banking! Why, even Rodd is worth two of him. He's not in the bank four days in the week. Where is he today?'

'I am afraid that he took his gun – but it was the last day of the season. He said that he would not be out again. He has been really better lately.'

'Though I was away!' the banker exclaimed. And he said some strong things upon the subject, to which Betty had to listen.

However, he had recovered his temper when he sent for Arthur next day. He bade him close the door. 'I want to speak to you,' he said; then he paused a moment while Arthur waited, his colour rising. 'It's about yourself. When you came to me I did not expect much from the experiment. I thought that you would soon tire of it, being what you are. But you have stood to it, and you have shown a considerable aptitude for the business. And I have made up my mind to take you in – on conditions, of course.'

Arthur's eyes sparkled. He had not hoped that the offer would be made so soon, and, much moved, he tried to express his thanks. 'You may be sure that I shall do my best, sir,' he said.

'I believe you will, lad. I believe you will. Indeed, I am thinking of myself as well as of you. I had not intended to make the offer so soon – you are young and could wait. But you will have to bring in a certain sum, and capital can be used at present to great advantage.'

Arthur looked grave. 'I am afraid, sir—'

'Oh, I'll make it easy,' Ovington said. 'This is my offer. You will put in five thousand pounds, and will receive for three years twelve per cent upon this in lieu of your present salary of one hundred and fifty – the hundred you are to be paid as Secretary to the Company is beside the matter. At the end of three years, if we are both satisfied, you will take an eighth share – otherwise you will draw out your money. On my death, if you remain in the bank, your share will be increased to a third on your bringing in another five thousand. You know enough about the accounts to know—'

'That it's a most generous offer,' Arthur exclaimed, his face aglow. And with the frankness and enthusiasm, the sparkling eye and ready word that won him so many friends, he expressed his thanks.

'Well, lad,' the other answered pleasantly, 'I like you. Still, you had better take a short time to consider the matter.'

'I want no time,' Arthur declared. 'My only difficulty is about the money. My mother's six thousand is charged on Garth, you see.'

This was a fact well known to Ovington, and one which he had taken into his reckoning. Perhaps, but for it, he had not been making the offer at this moment. But he concealed his satisfaction and a smile, and 'Isn't there a provision for calling it up?' he said.

'Yes, there is – at three months. But I am afraid that my mother—'

'Surely she will not object under the circumstances. The increased income might be divided between you so that it would be to her profit as well as to your advantage to make the change. Three months, eh? Well, suppose we say the money to be paid and the articles of partnership to lie signed four months from now?'

Difficulties never loomed very large in this young man's eyes. 'Very good, sir,' he said. 'Upon my honour, I don't know how to thank you.'

'It won't be all on your side,' the banker answered good-humouredly. 'Your name's worth something, and you are keen. I wish to heaven you could infect Clement with a tithe of your keenness.'

'I'll try, sir,' Arthur replied. At that moment he felt that he could move mountains.

'Well, that's settled, then. Send Rodd to me, will you, and do you see if I have left my pocket-book in the house. Betty may know where it is.'

Arthur went through the bank, stepping on air. He gave Rodd his message, and in a twinkling he was in the house. As he crossed the hall his heart beat high. Lord, how he would work! What feats of banking he would perform! How great would he make Ovington's, so that not only Aldshire but Lombard Street should ring with its fame! What wealth would he not pile up, what power would he not build upon it, and how he would crow, in the days to come, over the dull-witted clod-hopping Squires from whom he sprang, and who had not the brains to see that the world was changing about them and their reign approaching its end!

For at this moment he felt that he had it in him to work miracles. The greatest things seemed easy. The fortunes of Ovington's lay in the future, the cycle half turned – to what a point might they not carry them! During the last twelve months he had seen money earned with an ease which made all things appear possible; and alert, eager, sanguine, with an inborn talent for business, he felt that he had but to rise with the flowing tide to reach any position which wealth could offer in the coming age – that age which enterprise and industry, the loan, the mill, the furnace were to make their own. The age of gold!

He burst into song. He stopped. 'Betty!' he cried.

'Who is that rude boy?' the girl retorted, appearing on the stairs above him.

He bowed with ceremony, his hand on his heart, his eyes dancing. 'You see before you the Industrious Apprentice!' he said. 'He has received the commendation of his master. It remains only that he should lay his success at the feet of – his master's daughter!'

She blushed, despite herself. 'How silly you are!' she cried. But when he set his foot on the lowest stair as if to join her, she fled nimbly up and escaped. On the landing above she stood. 'Congratulations, sir,' she said, looking over the balusters. But a little less forwardness and a little more modesty, if you please! It was not in your articles that you should call me Betty.'

'They are cancelled! They are gone!' he retorted. 'Come down, Betty! Come down and I will tell you such things!'

But she only made a mocking face at him and vanished. A moment later her voice broke forth somewhere in the upper part of the house. She, too, was singing.

Chapter Six

Between the village and Garth the fields sank gently, to rise again to the clump of beeches which masked the house. On the farther side the ground fell more sharply into the narrow valley over which the Squire's window looked, and which separated the knoll whereon Garth stood from the cliffs. Beyond the brook that babbled down this valley and turned the mill rose, first, a meadow or two, and then the Thirty Acre covert, a tangle of birches and mountain-ashes which climbed to the foot of the rock-wall. Over this green trough, which up-stream and down merged in the broad vale, an air of peace, of remoteness and seclusion brooded, making it the delight of those who, morning and evening, looked down on it from the house.

Viewed from the other side, from the cliffs, the scene made a different impression. Not the intervening valley but the house held the eye. It was not large, but the knoll on which it stood was scarped on that side, and the walls of weathered brick rose straight from the rock, fortress-like and imposing, displaying all their mass. The gables and the stacks of fluted chimneys dated only from Dutch William, but tradition had it that a strong place, Castell Coch, had once stood on the same site; and fragments of pointed windows and Gothic work, built into the walls, bore out the story.

The road leaving the village made a right-angled turn round Garth and then, ascending, ran through the upper part of the Thirty Acres, skirting the foot of the rocks. Along the lower edge of the covert, between wood and water, there ran also a field-path, a right-of-way much execrated by the Squire. It led by a sinuous course to the Acherley property, and, alas, for good resolutions, along it on the afternoon of the very day which saw the elder Ovington at Garth came Clement Ovington, sauntering as usual.

He carried a gun, but he carried it as he might have carried a stick, for he had long passed the bounds within which he had a right to shoot; and at all times, his shooting was as much an excuse for a walk among the objects he loved as anything else. He had left his horse at the Griffin Arms in the village, and he might have made his way thither more quickly by the road. But at the cost of an extra mile he had preferred to walk back by the brook, observing as he went things new and old; the dipper curtseying on its stone, the water-vole perched to perform its toilet on the leaf of a brook-plant, the first green shoots of the wheat piercing through the soil, an old labourer who was not sorry to unbend his back, and whose memory held the facts and figures of fifty-year-old harvests. The day was mild, the sun shone, Clement was happy. Why, oh, why were there such things as banks in the world?

At a stile which crossed the path he came to a stand. Something had caught his eye. It was a trifle, to which nine men out of ten would not have given a thought, for it was no more than a clump of snowdrops in the wood on his right. But a shaft of wintry sunshine, striking athwart the tiny globes, lifted them, star-like, above the brown leaves about them, and he paused, admiring them – thinking no evil, and far from foreseeing what was to happen. He wondered if they were wild, or – and he looked about for any trace of human hands – a keeper's cottage might have stood here. He saw no trace, but still he stood, entranced by the white blossoms that, virgin-like, bowed meek heads to the sunlight that visited them.

He might have paused longer, if a sound had not brought him abruptly to earth. He turned. To his dismay he saw a girl, three or four paces from him, waiting to cross the stile. How long she had waited, how long watched him, he did not know, and in confusion – for he had not dreamed that there was a human being within a mile of him – and with a hurried snatch at his hat, he moved out of the way.

The girl stepped forward, colouring a little, for she foresaw that she must climb the stile under the young man's eye. Instinctively, he held out a hand to assist her, and in the act – he never knew how, nor did she – the gun slipped from his grasp, or the trigger caught in a bramble. A sheet of flame tore between them, the blast of the powder rent the air.

'O my God!' Clement cried, and he reeled back, shielding his eyes with his hands.

The smoke hid the girl, and for a long moment, a moment of such agony as he had never known, Clement's heart stood still. What had he done? Oh, what had he done at last, with his cursed carelessness! Had he killed her?

Slowly, the smoke cleared away, and he saw the girl. She was on her feet – thank God, she was on her feet! She was clinging with both hands to the stile. But was she – 'Are you— are you—' He tried to frame words, his voice a mere whistle.

She clung in silence to the rail, her face whiter than the quilted bonnet she wore. But he saw – thank God, he saw no wound, no blood, no hurt, and his own blood moved again, his lungs filled again with a mighty inspiration. 'For pity's sake, say you are not hurt!' he prayed. 'For God's sake, speak!'

But the shock had robbed her of speech, and he feared that she was going to swoon. He looked helplessly at the brook. If she did, what ought he to do? 'Oh, a curse on my carelessness!' he cried. 'I shall never, never forgive myself.'

It had in truth been a narrow, a most narrow escape, and at last she found words to say so. 'I heard the shot – pass,' she whispered, and shuddering closed her eyes again, overcome by the remembrance.

'But you are not hurt? They did pass!' The horror of that which might have been, of that which had so nearly been, overcame him anew, gave a fresh poignancy to his tone. 'You are sure – sure that you are not hurt?'

'No, I am not hurt,' she whispered. 'But I am very – very frightened. Don't speak to me. I shall be right – in a minute.'

'Can I do anything? Get you some water?'

She shook her head and he stood, looking solicitously at her, still fearing that she might swoon, and wondering afresh what he ought to do if she did. But after a minute or so she sighed, and a little colour came back to her face. 'It was near, oh, so near!' she whispered, and she covered her face with her hands. Presently, and more certainly, 'Why did you have it – at full cock?' she asked.

'God knows!' he owned. 'It was unpardonable. But that is what I am! I am a fool, and forget things. I was thinking of something else, I did not hear you come up, and when I found you there I was startled.'

'I saw.' She smiled faintly. 'But it was – careless.'

'Horribly! Horribly careless! It was wicked!' He could not humble himself enough.

She was herself now, and she looked at him, took him in, and was sorry for him. She removed her hands from the rail, and though her fingers trembled she straightened her bonnet. 'You are Mr Ovington?'

'Yes. And you are Miss Griffin, are you not?'

'Yes.'

'May I help you over the stile? Oh, your basket!'

She saw that it lay some yards away, blackened by powder, one corner shot away; so narrow had been the escape! He had a feeling of sickness as he took it up. 'You must not go on alone,' he said. 'You might faint.'

'Not now. But I shall not go on. What—' Her eyes strayed to the wood, and curiosity stirred in her. 'What were you looking at so intently, Mr Ovington, that you did not hear me?'

He coloured. 'Oh, nothing!'

'But it must have been something!' Her curiosity was strengthened.

'Well, if you wish to know,' he confessed, shamefacedly, 'I was looking at those snowdrops.'

'Those snowdrops?'

'Don't you see how the sunlight touches them? What a little island of light they make among the brown leaves?'

'How odd!' She stared at the snowdrops and then at him. 'I thought that only painters and poets, Mr Wordsworth and people like that, noticed those things. But perhaps you are a poet?'

'Goodness, no!' he cried. 'A poet? But I am fond of looking at things – out of doors, you know. A little way back' – he pointed up-stream, the way he had come – 'I saw a rat sitting on a lily leaf, cleaning its whiskers in the sun – the prettiest thing you ever saw. And an old man working at Bache's told me that he – but Lord, I beg your pardon! How can I talk of such things when I remember—?'

He stopped, overcome by the recollection of that through which they had passed. She, for her part, was inclined to ask him to go on, but remembered that this, all this was very irregular. What would her father say? And Miss Peacock? Yet, if this was irregular, so was the adventure itself. She would never forget his face of horror, the appeal in his eyes, his poignant anxiety. No, it was impossible to act as if nothing had happened between them, impossible to be stiff and to talk at arm's length about prunes and prisms with a person who had all but taken her life – and who was so very penitent. And then it was all so interesting, so out of the common, so like the things that happened in books, like that dreadful fall from the Cobb at Lyme in *Persuasion*. And he was not ordinary, not like other people. He looked at snowdrops!

But she must not linger now. Later, when she was alone in her room, she could piece it together and make a whole of it, and think of it, and compass the full wonder of the adventure. But she must go now. She told him so, the primness in her tone reflecting her thoughts. 'Will you kindly give me the basket?'

'I am going to carry it,' he said. 'You must not go alone. Indeed you must not, Miss Griffin. You may feel it more by and by. You may – go off suddenly.'

'Oh,' she replied, smiling, 'I shall not go off, as you call it, now.'

'I will only come as far as the mill,' humbly. 'Please let me do that.'

She could not say no, it could hardly be expected of her; and she turned with him. 'I shall never forgive myself,' he repeated. 'Never! Never! I shall dream of the moment when I lost sight of you in the smoke and thought that I had killed you. It was horrible! Horrible! It will come back to me often.'

He thought so much of it that he was moving away without his gun, leaving it lying on the ground. It was she who reminded him. 'Are you not going to take your gun?' she asked.

He went back for it, covered afresh with confusion. What a stupid fellow she must think him! She waited while he fetched it, and as she waited she had a new and not unpleasant sensation. Never before had she been on these terms with a man. The men whom she had known had always taken the upper hand with her. Her father, Arthur even, had either played with her or condescended to her. In her experience it was the woman's part to be ordered and directed, to give way and to be silent. But here the parts were reversed. This man – she had seen how he looked at her, how he humbled himself before her! And he was – interesting. As he came back to her carrying the gun, she eyed him with attention. She took note of him.

He was not handsome, as Arthur was. He had not Arthur's sparkle, his brilliance, his gay appeal, the carriage of the head that challenged men and won women. But he was not ugly, he was brown and clean and straight, and he looked strong. He bent to her as if he had been a knight and she his lady, and his eyes, grey and thoughtful – she had seen how they looked at her.

Now, she had never given much thought to any man's eyes before, and that she did so now, and criticised and formed an opinion of them, implied a change of attitude, a change in her relations and the man's; and instinctively she acknowledged this by the lead she took. 'It seems so strange,' she said half-playfully – when had she ever rallied a man before? – 'that you should think of such things as you do. Snowdrops, I mean. I thought you were a banker, Mr Ovington.'

'A very bad banker,' he replied ruefully. 'To tell the truth, Miss Griffin, I hate banking. Pounds, shillings, and pence – and this!' He pointed to the country about them, the stream, the sylvan path they were treading, the wood beside them, with its depth gilded here and there by a ray of the sun. 'A desk and a ledger – and this! Oh, I hate them! I would like to live out of doors. I want' – in a burst of candour – 'to live my own life! To be able to follow my own bent and make the most of myself.'

'Perhaps,' she said with naïveté, 'you would like to be a country gentleman?' And indeed the lot of a country gentleman in that day was an enviable one.

'Oh no,' he said, his tone deprecating the idea. He did not aspire to that.

'But what, then?' She did not understand. 'Have you no ambition?'

'I'd like to be – a farmer, if I had my way.'

That surprised as well as dashed her. She thought of her father's tenants and her face fell. 'Oh, but,' she said, 'a farmer? Why?' He was not like any farmer she had ever seen.

But he would not be dashed. 'To make two blades of grass grow where one grew before,' he answered stoutly, though he knew that he had sunk in her eyes. 'Just that; but after all isn't that worth doing? Isn't that better than burying your head in a ledger and counting other folk's money while the sun shines out of doors, and the rain falls sweetly, and the earth smells fresh and pure? Besides, it is all I am good for, Miss Griffin. I do think I understand a bit about that. I've read books about it and I've kept my eyes open, and – and what one likes one does well, you know.'

'But farmers—'

'Oh, I know,' sorrowfully, 'it must seem a very low thing to you.'

'Farmers don't look at snowdrops, Mr Ovington,' with a gleam of fun in her eyes.

'Don't they? Then they ought to, and they'd learn a lot that they don't know now. I've met men, labouring men who can't read or write, and it's wonderful the things they know about the land and the way plants grow on it, and the live things that are only seen at night, or stealing to their homes at daybreak. And there's a new wheat, a wheat I was reading about yesterday, Cobbett's corn, it is called, that I am sure would do about here if anyone would try it. But there,' remembering himself and to whom he was talking, 'this can have no interest for you. Only wouldn't you rather plod home weary at night, feeling that you had done something, and with all this' – he waved his hand – 'sinking to rest about you, and the horses going down to water, and the cattle lowing to be let into the byres, and – and all that,' growing confused, as he felt her eyes upon him, 'than get up from a set of ledgers with your head aching and your eyes muddled with figures?'

'I'm afraid I have not tried either,' she said. But she smiled. She found him new, his notions unlike those of the people about her, and certainly unlike those of a common farmer. She did not comprehend all his half-expressed thoughts, but not for that was she the less resolved to remember them, and to think of them at her leisure. For the present here was the mill, and they must part. At the mill the field-path which they were following fell into a lane, which on the right rose steeply to the road, on the left crossed a cart-bridge, shaken perpetually by the roar and wet with the spray of the great mill-wheel. Thence it wound upwards, rough and stony, to the back premises of Garth.

He, too, knew that this division of the ways meant parting, and humility clothed him. 'Heavens, what a fool I've been,' he said, blushing, as he met her eyes. 'What must you think of me, prating about myself when I ought to have been thinking only of you and asking your pardon.'

'For nearly shooting me?'

'Yes – and thank God, thank God,' with emotion, 'that it was not worse. I ought never to carry a gun again!'

'I won't exact that penalty.' She looked at him very kindly.

'And you will forgive me! You will do your best to forgive me?'

'I will do my best, if you will not carry off my basket,' she replied, for he was turning away with the basket on his arm. 'Thank you,' as he restored it, and in his embarrassment nearly dropped his gun. 'Goodbye.'

'You are sure that you will be safe now?'

'If you have no fresh accident with your firearms,' she laughed. 'Please be careful.'

She nodded, and turned and tripped away. But she had hardly left him, she had not passed ten paces beyond the bridge, before her mood changed. The cloak of playfulness fell from her, reaction did its work. The colour left her cheeks, her knees shook as she remembered. She felt again the hot blast on her cheek, lived through the flash, the shock, the onset of faintness. Again she clung to the stile, giddy, breathless, the landscape dancing about her. And through the haze she saw his face, white, drawn, terror-stricken – saw it and strove vainly to reassure him.

And now – now he was soothing her. He was pouring out his penitence, he was upbraiding himself. Presently she was herself again; her spirits rising, she was playing with him, chiding him, exercising a new sense of power, becoming the recipient of a man's thoughts, a man's hopes and ambitions. The colour was back in her cheeks now, her knees were steady, she could walk. She went on, but slowly and more slowly, full of thought, reviewing what had happened.

Until, near the garden door, she was roughly brought to earth. Miss Peacock, visiting the yard on some domestic errand, had discerned her. 'Josina!' she cried. 'My certy, girl, but you have been quick! I wish the maids were half as quick when they go! A whole afternoon is not enough for them to walk a mile. But you've not brought the eggs?'

'I didn't go,' said Josina. 'I was frightened by a gun.'

'A gun?'

'And I felt a little faint.'

'Faint? Why, you've got the colour of a rose, girl. Faint? Well, when I want galeny eggs again I shan't send you. Where was it?'

'Under the Thirty Acres – by the stile. A gun went off, and—'

'Sho!' Miss Peacock cried contemptuously. 'A gun went off, indeed! At your age, Josina! I don't know what girls are coming to! If you don't take care you'll be all nerves and vapours like your aunt at the Cottage! Go and take a dose of gilly-flower-water this minute, and the less said to your father the better. Why, you'd never hear the end of it! Afraid because a gun went off!'

Josina agreed that it was very silly, and went quickly to her room. Yes, the less said about it the better!

Chapter Seven

The terraced garden at Garth rested to the south and east on a sustaining wall so high that to build it today would tax the resources of three Squires. Unfortunately, either for defence or protection from the weather, the wall rose high on the inner side also, so that he who walked in the garden might enjoy the mellow tints of the old brickwork, but had no view of the country except through certain loop-holes, gable-shaped, which pierced the wall at intervals, like the port-holes of a battleship. If the lover of landscape wanted more, he must climb half a dozen steps to a raised walk which ran along the south side. Thence he could look, as from an eyrie, on the green meadows below him, or away to the line of hills to westward, or turning about he could overlook the operations of the gardener at his feet.

More, if it rained or blew there was at the southwest corner, and entered from the raised walk, an ancient Dutch summer-house of brick, with a pyramidal roof. It had large windows and, with much at Garth that served for ornament rather than utility, it was decayed, time and damp having almost effaced its dim frescoes. But tradition hallowed it, for it was said that William of Orange, after dining in the hall at the oaken table which still bore the date 1691, had smoked his pipe and drunk his Schnapps in this summer-house; and thence had watched the roll of the bowls and the play of the bias on the turf below. For in those days the garden had been a bowling green.

There on summer evenings the Squire would still drink his port, but in winter the place was little used, tools desecrated it, and tubers took refuge in it. So when Josina began about this time to frequent it, and, as winter yielded to the first breath of spring, began to carry her work thither of an afternoon, Miss Peacock should have had her suspicions. But the good lady saw nothing, being a busy woman. Thomas the groom did

remark the fact, for idle hands make watchful eyes, but for a time he was
none the wiser.

'What's young Miss doing up there?' he asked himself. 'Must be
tarnation cold! And her look's fine, too! Ay, 'tis well to be them as has
nought to do but traipse up and down and sniff the air!'

'Naturally it did not at once occur to him that the summer-house
commanded a view of the path which ran along the brook side; nor did
he suppose that Miss had any purpose, when, as might happen, perhaps
once a week, she would leave her station at the window and in an aimless
fashion wander down to the mill – and beyond it. She might be following
a duck inclined to sit, or later – for turkeys will stray – be searching for a
turkey's nest. She might be doing fifty things, indeed – she was sometimes
so long away. But the time did come when, being by chance at the mill,
Thomas saw a second figure on the path beside the water, and he laid by
the knowledge for future use. He was a sly fellow, not much in favour with
the other servants.

Presently there came a cold Saturday in March, a wet, windy day,
when to saunter by the brook would have too odd an air. But would it have
an odd look, Josina wondered, standing before the glass in her room, if she
ran across to the Cottage for ten minutes about sunset? The bank closed
early on Saturdays, and men were not subject to the weather as women
were. Twice she put on her bonnet, and twice she took it off and put it
back in its box – she could not make up her mind. He might think that she
followed him. He might think her bold. Or suppose that when they met
before others, she blushed; or that they thought the meeting strange? And,
after all, he might not be there – he was no favourite with Mrs Bourdillon,
and his heart might fail him. In the end the bonnet was put away, but it is
to be feared that that evening Jos was a little snappish with Miss Peacock
when arraigned for some act of forgetfulness.

Had she gone she might have come off no better than Clement, who,
braving all things, did go. Mrs Bourdillon did not, indeed, say when he
entered, 'What, here again?' but her manner spoke for her, and Arthur,
who had arrived before his time, received the visitor with less than his usual
good humour. Clement's explanation, that he had left his gun, fell flat, and
so chilly were the two that he stayed but twenty minutes, then faltered an
excuse, and went off with his tail between his legs. He did not guess that
he had intruded on a family difference, a trouble of some standing, which

the passage of weeks had but aggravated. It turned on Ovington's offer, which Arthur, pluming himself on his success and proud of his prospects, had lost no time in conveying to his mother. He had supposed that she would see the thing with his eyes, and be as highly delighted. To become a partner so early, to share at his age in the rising fortunes of the house! Surely she would believe in him now, if she had never believed in him before.

But Mrs Bourdillon had been imbued by her husband with one fixed idea – that whatever happened she must never touch her capital; that under no circumstances must she spend it, or transfer it or alienate it. That way lay ruin. No sooner, therefore, had Arthur come to that part of his story than she had taken fright; and nothing that he had been able to say, no assurance that he had been able to give, no gilded future that he had been able to paint, had sufficed to move the good woman from her position.

'Of course,' she said, looking at him piteously, for she hated to oppose him, 'I'm not saying that it does not sound nice, dear.'

'It is nice! Very nice!'

'But I'm older than you, and oh, dear, dear, I've known what disappointment is! I remember when your father thought that he had the promise of the Benthall living and we bought the drawing-room carpet, though it was blue and buff and your father did not like the colour – something to do with a fox, I remember, though to be sure a fox is red! Well, my dear,' drumming with her fingers on her lap in a placid way that maddened her listener, 'he was just as confident as you are, and after all the Bishop gave the living to his own cousin, and the money thrown clean away, and the carpet too large for any room we had, and woven of one piece so that we couldn't cut it! I'm sure that was a lesson to me that there's many a slip between the cup and the lip. Believe me, a bird in the hand—'

'But this is in the hand!' Arthur cried, restraining himself with difficulty. 'This is in the hand!'

'Well, I don't know how that may be. I never was a business woman, whatever your uncle may say when he is in his tantrums. But I do know that your father told me, nine or ten times—'

'And you've told me a hundred times!'

'Well, and I'm sure your uncle would say the same! But, indeed, I don't know what he wouldn't say if he knew what we were thinking of!'

'The truth is, Mother, you are afraid of the Squire.'

'And if I am,' plaintively, 'it is all very well for you, Arthur, who are away six days out of seven. But I'm here and he's here. And I have to listen to him. And if this money is lost—'

'But it cannot be lost, I tell you!'

'Well, if it is lost, we shall both be beggars! Oh, dear, dear, I'm sure if your father told me once he told me a hundred times—'

'Damn!' Arthur cried, fairly losing his temper at last. 'The truth is, Mother, that my father knew nothing about money.'

At that, however, Mrs Bourdillon began to cry and Arthur found himself obliged to drop the matter for the time. He saw, too, that he was on the wrong tack, and a few days later, under pressure of necessity, he tried another. He humbled himself, he wheedled, he cajoled, and when he had by this means got on the right side of his Mother he spoke of Ovington's success.

'In a few years he will be worth a quarter of a million,' he said.

The figure flustered her. 'Why, that's—'

'A quarter of a million,' he repeated impressively. 'And that's why I consider this the chance of my life, mother. It is such an opportunity as I shall never have again. It is within my reach now, and surely, surely,' his voice shook with the fervour of his pleading, 'you will not be the one to dash it from my lips?' He laid his hand upon her wrist. 'And ruin your son's life, Mother?'

She was shaken. 'You know, if I thought it was for your good!'

'It is! It is, Mother!'

'I'd do anything to make you happy, Arthur! But I don't believe,' with a sigh, 'that whatever I did your uncle would pay the money.'

'Is it his money or yours?'

'Why, of course, Arthur, I thought that you knew that it was your father's.' She was very simple, and her pride was touched.

'And now it is yours. And I suppose that some day – I hope it will be a long day, Mother – it will be mine. Believe me, you've only to write to my uncle and tell him that you have decided to call it up, and he will pay it as a matter of course. Shall I write the letter for you to sign?'

Mrs Bourdillon looked piteously at him. She was very, very unwilling to comply, but what was she to do? Between love of him and fear of the Squire, what was she to do? Poor woman, she did not know. But he was with her, the Squire was absent, and she was about to acquiesce when a last argument occurred to her. 'But you are forgetting,' she said, 'if your uncle takes offence, and I'm sure he will, he'll come between you and Josina.'

'Well, that is his look-out.'

'Arthur! You don't mean that you've changed your mind, and you so fond of her? And the girl heir to Garth and all her father's money!'

'I say nothing about it,' Arthur declared. 'If he chooses to come between us that will be his doing, not mine.'

'But Garth!' Mrs Bourdillon was altogether at sea. 'My dear boy, you are not thinking! Why, Lord ha' mercy on us, where would you find such another, young and pretty and all, and Garth in her pocket? Why, if it were only on Jos' account you'd be mad to quarrel with him.'

'I'm not going to quarrel with him,' Arthur replied sullenly. 'If he chooses to quarrel with me, well, she's not the only heiress in the world.'

His mother held up her hands. 'Oh dear me,' she said wearily. 'I give it up, I don't understand you. But I'm only a woman and I suppose I don't understand anything.'

He was accustomed to command and she to be guided. He saw that she was wavering, and he plied her afresh, and in the end, though not without another outburst of tears, he succeeded. He fetched the pen, he smoothed the paper, and before he handed his mother her bed-candle he had got the fateful letter written, and had even by lavishing on her unusual signs of affection brought a smile to her face. 'It will be all right, Mother, you'll see,' he urged as he watched her mount the stairs. 'It will be all right! You'll see me a millionaire yet.'

And then he made a mistake which was to cost him dearly. He left the letter on the mantel-shelf. An hour later, when he had been some time in bed, he heard a door open and he sat up and listened. Even then, had he acted on the instant, it might have availed. But he hesitated, arguing down his misgivings, and it was only when he caught the sound of footsteps stealthily re-ascending that he jumped out of bed and lit a candle. He slipped downstairs, but he was too late. The letter was gone.

He went up to bed again, and though he wondered at the queer ways of women he did not as yet doubt the issue. He would recover the letter in the morning and send it. The end would be the same.

There, however, he was wrong. Mrs Bourdillon was a weak woman, but weakness has its own obstinacy, and by the morning she had reflected. The sum charged on Garth was her whole fortune, her sole support, and

were it lost she would be penniless, with no one to look to except the Squire,
whom she would have offended beyond forgiveness. True, Arthur laughed
at the idea of loss, and he was clever. But he was young and sanguine, and
before now she had heard of mothers beggared through the ill-fortune or
the errors of their children. What if that should be her lot!

Nor was this the only thought which pressed upon her mind. That
Arthur should marry Josina and succeed to Garth had been for years her
darling scheme, and she could not, in spite of the hopes with which he
had for the moment dazzled her, imagine any future for him comparable
to that. But if he would marry Josina and succeed to Garth he must not
offend his uncle.

So, when Arthur came down in the morning, and with assumed
carelessness asked for the letter she put him off. It was Sunday. She would
not discuss business on Sunday, it would not be lucky. On Monday, when,
determined to stand no more nonsense, he returned to the subject, she
took refuge in tears. It was cruel of him to press her so, when – when she
was not well! She had not made up her mind. She did not know what she
should do. To tears there is no answer, and, angry as he was, he had to
start for Aldersbury, leaving the matter unsettled, much to his disgust and
alarm, for the time was running on.

And that was the beginning of a tragedy in the little house under
Garthmyle. It was a struggle between strength and weakness, and
weakness, as usual, sought shelter in subterfuge. When Arthur came home
at the end of the week his mother took care to have company, and he could
not get a word with her. She had no time for business – it must wait. On
the next Saturday she was not well, and kept her bed, and on the Sunday
met him with the same fretful plea – she would do no business on Sunday!
Then, convinced at last that she had made up her mind to thwart him,
he hardened his heart. He loved his mother, and to go beyond a certain
point did not consort with his easy nature, but he had no option; the thing
must be done if his prospects were not to be wrecked. He became hard,
cruel, almost brutal; threatening to leave her, threatening to take himself
off altogether, harassing her week after week, in what should have been her
happiest hours, with pictures of the poverty, the obscurity, the hopelessness
to which she was condemning him! And, worst of all, torturing her with
doubts that after all he might be right.

And still she resisted, and weak, foolish woman as she was, resisted with an obstinacy that was infinitely provoking. Meanwhile only two things supported her: her love for him, and the belief that she was defending his best interests and that some day he would thank her. She was saving him from himself. The odds were great, she was unaccustomed to oppose him, and still she withstood him. She would not sign the letter. But she suffered, and suffered terribly.

She took to bringing in guests as buffers between them, and once or twice she brought in Josina. The girl, who knew them so well, could not fail to see that there was something wrong, that something marred the relations between mother and son. Arthur's moody brow, his silence, or his snappish answers, no less than Mrs Bourdillon's scared manner, left her in no doubt of that. But she fancied that this was only another instance of the law of man's temper and woman's endurance – that law to which she knew but one exception. And if the girl hugged that exception, trembling and hoping, to her breast, if Arthur's coldness was a relief to her, if she cared little for any secret but her own, she was no more of a mystery to them than they were to her. When the door closed behind her, and, accompanied by a maid, she crossed the dark fields, she thought no more about them. The two ceased – such is the selfishness of love – to exist for her. Her thoughts were engrossed by another, by one who until lately had been a stranger, but whose figure now excluded the world from her view. Her secret monopolised her, closed her heart, blinded her eyes. Such is the law of love – at a certain stage in its growth.

Meanwhile life at the Cottage went on in this miserable fashion until April had come in and the daffodils were in full bloom in the meadows beside the river. And still Arthur could not succeed in his object, and wondering what the banker thought of the delay and his silence, was almost beside himself with chagrin. Then there came a welcome breathing space. Ovington despatched him to London on a confidential mission. He was to be away rather more than a fortnight, and the relief was much even to him. To his mother it had been more, if he had not, with politic cruelty, kept from her the cause of his absence. She feared that he was about to carry out his threat and to make a home elsewhere – that this was the end, that he was going to leave her. And perhaps, she thought, she had been wrong. Perhaps, after all, she had sacrificed his love and lost his dear presence for nothing! It was a sad Easter that she passed, lonely and anxious, in the little house.

Chapter Eight

It was in the third week of April that Arthur returned to Aldersbury. Ovington had not failed to let his correspondents know that the lad was no common mercantile person, but came of a county family; and Arthur had been fêted by the bank's agents and made much of by their friends. The negotiation which Ovington had entrusted to him had gone well, as all things went well at this time. His abilities had been recognised in more than one counting-house, and in the general elation and success, civilities and hospitality had been showered upon him. Mothers and daughters had exerted themselves to please the nephew – it was whispered the heir – of the Aldshire magnate; and what Arthur's letters of credit had not gained for him, his handsome face and good breeding had won. He came back, therefore, on the best of terms with himself and more in love than ever with the career which he had laid out. And, but for the money difficulty, and his mother's obstinacy, he would have seen all things in rose colour.

He returned at the moment when speculation in Aldersbury – and Aldersbury was in this but a gauge of the whole country – was approaching its fever point. The four per cent consols, which not long before had stood at 72, were 106. The three per cents, which had been 52, had risen to 93. India stock was booming at 280, and these prices, which would have seemed incredible to a former generation, were justified by the large profits accruing from trade and seeking investment. They were, indeed, nothing beside the heights to which more speculative stocks were being hurried. Shares in one mine, bought at ten pounds, changed hands at a hundred and fifty. Shares in another, on which seventy pounds had been paid, were sold at thirteen hundred. An instalment of £5 was paid on one purchase, and ten days later the stock was sold for one hundred and forty!

Under such circumstances new ventures were daily issued to meet the demand. Proposals for thirty companies came out in a week, and still there appeared to be money for all, for the banks, tempted by the prevailing prosperity, increased their issues of notes. It seemed an easy thing to borrow at seven per cent, and lay out the money at ten or fifteen, with certainty of a gain in capital. Men who had never speculated saw their neighbours grow rich, and themselves risked a hundred and doubled it, ventured two and saw themselves the possessors of six. It was like, said one, picking up money in a hat. It was like, said another, baling it up in a bucket. There seemed to be money everywhere – money for all. Peers and clergymen, shop-keepers and maiden ladies, servants even, speculated; while those who knew something of the market, or who could allot shares in new ventures, were courted and flattered, drawn into corners and consulted by troops of friends.

All this approached its height at the end of April, and Arthur, sanguine and eager, laden with the latest news from Lombard Street, returned to Aldersbury to revel in it. He trod the Cop and the High Street as if he walked on air. He moved amid the excitement like a young god. His nod was confidence, his smile a promise. A few months before he had doubted. He had viewed the rising current of speculation from without, and had had his misgivings. Now the stream had caught him, and if he ever reflected that there might be rocks ahead, he flattered himself that he would be among the first to take the alarm.

The confidence which he owed to youth, the banker drew from a past of unvarying success. But the elder man did have his moments of mistrust. There were hours when he saw hazards in front, and the days on which he did not call for the Note Issues were few. But even he found it easier to go with the current, and once or twice, so high was his opinion of Arthur's abilities, he let himself be persuaded by him. Then the mere bustle was exhilarating. The door of the bank that never rested, the crowded counter, the incense of the streets, the whispers where he passed, all had their intoxicating effect. The power to put a hundred pounds into a man's pocket – who can abstain from, who is not flattered by, the use of this, who can at all times close his mouth? And often one thing leads to another, and advice is the prelude to a loan.

It was above all when the railroad scheme was to the fore that the banker realised his importance. It was his, he had made it, and it was on its behalf that he was disposed to put his hand out farthest. The Board, upon Sir Charles' proposal – the fruit of a hint dropped by Ovington – had fixed the fourth market-day in April for the opening of the subscription list. Though the season was cold and late, the farmers would be more or less at liberty; and for a wonder the day turned out to be one of the few warm days of that spring. The sun shone, the public curiosity was tickled, the town was full, men in the streets quoted the tea-kettle and explained the powers of steam; and Arthur, as he forged his way through the good-tempered, white-coated throng, felt to the full his importance.

Near the door of the bank he met Purslow, and the draper seized his arm. 'One moment, sir, excuse me,' he whispered. 'I've a little more I can spare at a pinch. What do you advise, Mr Bourdillon?'

Arthur knew that it was not in his province to advise, and he shook his head. 'You must ask Mr Ovington,' he said.

'And he that busy that he'll snap my nose off! And you're just from London. Come, Mr Bourdillon, just for two or three hundred pounds. A good 'un! A real good 'un! I know you know one!'

Arthur gave way. The man's wheedling tone, the sense of power, the ability to confer a favour were too much for him. He named the Antwerp Navigation Company. 'But don't stop in too long,' he added. And he snatched himself away, and hurried on, and many were those who found his frank eager face irresistible.

As he ploughed his way through the crowd, his head on a level with the tallest, he seemed to be success itself. His careless greeting met everywhere a cheery answer, and more than one threw after him, 'There goes the old Squire's nevvy! See him? He's a clever 'un if ever there was one!' They gave him credit for knowing mysteries dark to them, yet withal they owned a link with him. He too belonged to the land. A link with him and some pride in him.

In the parlour where the Board met he had something of the same effect. Sir Charles and Acherley had taken their seats and were talking of county matters, their backs turned on their fellows. Wolley stood before the fire, glowering at them and resenting his exclusion. Grounds sat meekly on a chair within the door. But Arthur's appearance changed all. He had a word or a smile for each. He set Grounds at his ease, he had a joke for Sir Charles and Acherley, he joined Wolley before the fire. Ovington, who had left the room for a moment, noted the change, and his heart warmed to the Secretary. 'He will do,' he told himself, as he turned to the business of the meeting.

'Come, Mr Wolley, come, Mr Grounds,' he said, 'Pull up your chairs, if you please. It has struck twelve and the bank should be open to receive applications at half-past. I conveyed your invitation, gentlemen, to Mr Purslow two days ago, and I am happy to tell you that he takes two hundred shares, so that over one-third of the capital will be subscribed before we go to the public. I suppose, gentlemen, you would wish him to take his seat at once?'

Sir Charles and Acherley nodded, Wolley looked sullen but said nothing, Grounds submitted. Neither he nor Wolley was over-pleased at sharing with another the honour of sitting with the gentry. But it had to be done. 'Bring him in, Bourdillon,' Ovington said.

Purslow, who was in waiting, slid into the room and took his seat, between pride and humility. 'I have reason to believe, gentlemen,' Ovington went on, 'that the capital will be subscribed within twenty-four hours. It is for you to say how long the list shall remain open.'

'Not too long,' said Sir Charles, sapiently.

'Shall I say forty-eight hours? Agreed, gentlemen? Very good. Then a notice to that effect shall be posted outside the bank at once. Will you see to that, Bourdillon?'

'And what of Mr Griffin?' Wolley blurted out the question before Ovington could restrain him. The clothier was anxious to show Purslow that he was at home in his company.

'To be sure,' Ovington answered smoothly. 'That is the only point, gentlemen, in which my expectations have not been borne out. The interview between Mr Griffin and myself was disappointing, but I hoped to be able to tell you today that we were a little more forward. Mr Wolley, however, has handed me a letter which he has received from Garth, and it is certainly—'

'A d—d unpleasant letter,' said Wolley. 'The old Squire don't mince matters.' He had predicted that his landlord would not come in, and he was pleased to see his opinion confirmed. 'He says I'd better be careful, for if I and my fine railroad come to grief I need not look to him for time. By the Lord,' with unction, 'I know that, railroad or no railroad! He'd put me out as soon as look at me!'

Sir Charles shuffled his papers uncomfortably. To hear a man like

Wolley discuss his landlord shocked him – he felt it a kind of treason to listen to such talk. He feared – he feared more than ever – that the caustic old Squire was thinking him a fool for mixing himself up with this business. Good Heavens, if, after all, it ended in disaster!

Acherley took it differently. He cared nothing for Griffin's opinion. He was in money difficulties and had passed far beyond that. He laughed. 'Put you out? I'll swear he would! There's no fool like an old fool! But he won't have the chance.'

'No, I think not,' Ovington said blandly. 'But his attitude presents difficulties, and I am sure that our Chairman will agree with me that if we can meet his views, it will be worth some sacrifice.'

'Can't Arthur get round him?' Acherley suggested.

'No,' Arthur replied, smiling. 'Perhaps if you—'

'Will you see him, Mr Acherley?'

'Oh, I'll see him!' carelessly. 'I don't say I shall persuade him.'

'Still, we shall have done what we can to meet his views,' the banker replied. 'If we fail we must fall back – on my part most reluctantly – on the compulsory clauses. But that is looking ahead, and we need not consider it at present. I don't think that there is anything else? It is close on the half-hour. Will you see, Bourdillon, if all is ready in the bank?'

Arthur went out, leaving the door ajar. There came through the opening a murmur of voices and the noise of shuffling feet. Ovington turned over the papers before him. 'In the event of the subscriptions exceeding the sum required, what day will suit you to allot? Thursday, Sir Charles?'

'Friday would suit me better.'

'Friday be it then, if Mr Acherley – good. On Friday at noon, gentlemen. Yes, Bourdillon?'

Arthur did not sit down. He was smiling. 'It's something of a sight,' he said. 'By Jove it is! I think you ought to see it.'

Ovington nodded, and they rose, some merely curious, others eager to show themselves in their new role of dignity. Arthur opened the door and stood aside. Beyond the door the cashier's desk with its green curtains formed a screen which masked their presence. Ovington separated the curtains, and Sir Charles and Acherley peeped between them. The others looked round the desk.

The space devoted to the public was full. It hummed with low voices, but above the hum sharp sentences rang out. 'Here, don't push! It's struck,

Mr Rodd! Hand 'em out!' Then, louder than these, 'Here, get out o' my road! I want money for a cheque, man!'

The two clerks were at the counter, with piles of application forms before them and their eyes on the clock. Clement and Rodd stood in the background. The impassive attitude of the four contrasted strikingly with the scene beyond the counter, where eighteen or twenty persons elbowed and pushed one another, their flushed faces eloquent of the spirit of greed. For it had got about that there was easy money and much money to be made out of the Railroad shares – to be made in particular by those who were first in the field. Some looked to make the money by a sale at a premium, others foresaw a profit but hardly knew how it was to come, more had heard of men who had suddenly grown rich, and fancied that this was their chance. They had but to sign a form and pay an instalment, and profit would flow in, they did not care whence. They were certain, indeed, but of one thing, that there was gain in it; and with every moment their number grew, for with every moment a newcomer forced his way, smiling, into the bank. Meantime the crowd gave good-humoured vent to their impatience. 'Let's have 'em! Hand 'em out!' they murmured. What if there were not enough to go round?

The man with the cheque, hopelessly wedged in, protested. 'There, someone hand it on,' he cried at last. 'And pass me out the money, d—n you! And let me get out of this.'

The slip was passed from hand to hand, and 'How'll you have it, Mr Boumphry?' Rodd asked.

'In shares!' cried a wit.

'Notes and a pound in silver,' gasped Boumphry, who thought the world had gone mad. 'And dunno get on my back, man!' to one behind him. 'I'm not a bullock! Here, how'm I to count it when I canna get—'

'A form!' cried a second wit. 'Neither can we, farmer! Come, out with 'em, gentlemen. Hullo, Mr Purslow! That you? Ha' you turned banker?'

The draper, who had showed himself over-confidently, fell back purple with blushes. 'Certainly an odd sight,' said the banker quietly. 'It promises well, I think, Sir Charles.'

'Hanged well!' said Acherley. Sir Charles acquiesced. 'Er, I think so,' he said. 'I certainly think so.' But he felt himself a little out of place.

The minute hand touched the half-hour, and the clerks began to distribute the papers. After watching the scene for a moment the Board separated, its members passing out modestly through the house door. They parted on the pavement, even Sir Charles unbending a little, and the saturnine Acherley chuckling to himself as visions of fools and fat premiums floated before him. It was a vision which they all shared in their different ways.

Arthur was about to join the workers in the bank when Ovington beckoned him into the dining-room. 'You can be spared for a moment,' he said. 'Come in here. I want to speak to you.' He closed the door. 'I've been considering the matter I discussed with you some time ago, and I think, Bourdillon, that the time has come when it should be settled. But you've said nothing about it, and I've been wondering if anything was wrong. If so, you had better tell me.'

'Well sir—'

The banker was shrewd. 'Is it the money that is the trouble?'

The moment that Arthur had been dreading was come, and he braced himself to meet it. 'I'm afraid that there has been some difficulty,' he said, 'but I think now—'

'Have you given your uncle notice?'

Arthur hesitated. If he avowed that they had not given his uncle notice, how weak, how inept he would appear in the other's eyes! A wave of exasperation shook him, as he saw the strait into which his mother's obstinacy was forcing him. The opportunity which he valued so highly, the opening on which he had staked so much – was he to forfeit them through her folly? No, a hundred times, no! He would not let her ruin him; and, 'Yes, we have given it,' he said, 'but very late, I'm afraid. My mother had her doubts and I had to overcome them. I'm sorry, sir, that there has been this delay.'

'But the notice has been given now?'

'Yes.'

'Then in three months, as I understand—'

'The money will be ready, sir.' He spoke stoutly; the die was cast now, and he must go through with it. After all it was not his fault, but his mother's; and for the rest, if the notice was not already given it should be this very day. 'It will be ready in three months, but not earlier, I am afraid.'

Ovington reflected. 'Well,' he said, 'that must do. And we won't wait. We will sign the agreement now and it shall take effect from next Monday, the payment to be made within three months. Go through the articles' –

he opened his desk and took a paper from it and gave it to Arthur – 'and come in with one of the clerks at five o'clock and we will complete it.'

Arthur hardly knew what to say. 'It's uncommonly kind of you, sir!' he stammered. 'You may be sure I shall do my best to repay your kindness.'

'Well, I like you,' the banker rejoined. 'And, of course, I see my own advantage in it. So that is settled.'

Arthur went out taking the paper with him. But in the passage he paused, his face gloomy. After all it was not too late. He could go back and tell Ovington that his mother – but no, he could not risk the banker's good opinion. His mother must do it. She must do it. He was not going to see the chance of a lifetime wasted – for a silly scruple.

He moved at last, and as he went into the bank he jostled two persons who, sheltered by the cashier's desk, were watching, as the Board had watched a few minutes before, the scene of excitement which the bank presented. The one was Betty, the other was Rodd, the cashier. It had occurred to Rodd that the girl would like to view a thing so unusual, and he had slipped out and fetched her.

They faced about, startled by the contact. 'Oh, it's you!' said Betty.

'Yes,' drily. 'What are you doing here, Betty?'

'I came to see the Lottery drawn,' she retorted, making a face at him. 'Mr Rodd fetched me. No one else remembered me.'

'Well, I should have thought that he – ain't you wanted, Rodd?' There was a new tone in Arthur's voice. 'Mr Clement seems to have his hands full.'

Rodd's face reddened under the rebuke. For a moment he seemed about to answer, then he thought better of it. He left them and went to the counter.

'And what would you have thought?' Betty asked pertly, reverting to the sentence that he had not finished.

'Only that Rodd might be better employed – at his work. This is just the job he is fit for, giving out forms.'

'And Clement, too, I suppose? It is his job, too?'

'When he's here to do it,' with a faint sneer. 'That is not too often, Betty.'

'Well, more often of late, anyway. Do you know what Mr Rodd says?'

'No.'

'He says that he has seen just such a crowd as this in a bank before.

At Manchester seventeen years ago, when he was a boy. There was a run on the bank in which his father worked, and people fought for places as they are fighting today. He does not seem to think it – lucky.'

'What else does he think?' Arthur retorted with contempt. 'What other rubbish? He'd better mind his own business and do his work. He ought to know more than to say such things to you or to anyone.'

Betty stared. 'Dear me,' she replied, 'we are high and mighty today! Hoity toity!' And turning her shoulder on him, she became absorbed in the scene before her.

But that evening she was more than usually grave, and when her father, pouring out his fourth and last glass of port – for he was an abstemious man – told her that the partnership articles had been signed that afternoon, she nodded. 'Yes, I knew,' she said sagely.

'How, Betty? I didn't tell you. I have told no one. Did Arthur?'

'No, Father, not in so many words. But I guessed it.' And during the rest of the evening she was unusually pensive.

Chapter Nine

Spring was late that year. It was the third week in April before the last streak of snow faded from the hills, or the showers of sleet ceased to starve the land. Morning after morning the Squire tapped his glass and looked abroad for fine weather. The barley-sowing might wait, but the oats would not wait, and at a time when there should have been abundant grass he was still carrying hay to the racks. The lambs were doing ill.

Morning after morning, with an old caped driving-coat cast about his shoulders and a shabby hunting-cap on his grey head, he would walk down to the little bridge that carried the drive over the stream. There, a gaunt high-shouldered figure, he would stand, looking morosely out over the wet fields. The distant hills were clothed in mist, the nearer heights wore light caps, down the vale the clear rain-soaked air showed sombre woods and red soil, with here and there a lopsided elm, bursting into bud, and reddening to match the furrows. 'We shall lose one in ten of the lambs,' he thought, 'and not a sound foot in the flock!'

One morning as he stood there he saw a man turn off the road and come shambling towards him. It was Pugh, the man-of-all-work at the Cottage, and in his disgust at things in general, the Squire cursed him for a lazy rascal. 'I suppose they've nothing to do,' he growled, 'that they send the rogue traipsing the roads at this hour!' Aloud, 'What do you want, my man?' he asked.

Pugh quaked under the Squire's hard eyes. 'A letter from the mistress, your honour.'

'Any answer?'

Reluctantly Pugh gave up the hope of beer with Calamy the butler. 'I'd no orders to wait, sir.'

'Then off you go! I've all the idlers here I want, my lad.'

The Squire had not his glasses with him, and he turned the letter over to no purpose. Returning to his room he could not find them, and the delay aggravated a temper already oppressed by the weather. He shouted for his spectacles, and when Miss Peacock, hurrying nervously to his aid, suggested that they might be in the Prayer Book from which he had read the psalm that morning, he called her a fool. Eventually, it was there that they were found, on which he dismissed her with a flea in her ear. 'If you knew they were there, why did you leave them there!' he stormed. 'Silly fools women be!'

But when he had read the letter, he neither stormed nor swore. His anger was too deep. Here was folly, indeed, and worse than folly, ingratitude! After all these years, after forty years, during which he had paid them their five per cent to the day, five per cent secured as money could not be secured in these harum-scarum days – to demand their pound of flesh and to demand it in this fashion! Without warning, without consulting him, the head of the family! It was enough to make any man swear, and presently he did swear after the manner of the day.

'It's that young fool,' he thought. 'He's written it and she's signed it. And if they have their way in five years the money will be gone, every farthing, and the woman will come begging to me! But no, madam,' with rising passion, 'I'll see you farther before I'll pay down a penny to be frittered away by that young jackanapes! I'll go this moment and tell her what I think of her, and see if she's the impudence to face it out!'

He clapped on his hat and seized his cane. But when he had flung the door wide, pride spoke and he paused. No, he would not lower himself, he would not debate it with her. He would take no notice – that, by G–d, was what he would do. The letter should be as if it had not been written, and as to paying the money, why if they dared to go to law he would go all lengths to thwart them! He was like many in that day, violent, obstinate men who had lived all their lives among dependents and could not believe that the law, which they administered to others, applied to them. Occasionally they had a rude awakening.

But the old Squire did not lack a sense of justice; which, obscured in trifles, became apparent in greater matters. This quality came to his rescue now, and as he grew cooler his attitude changed. If the woman, silly and scatter-brained as she was, and led by the nose by that impudent son of hers – if she persisted, she should have the money, and take the consequences.

The six thousand was a charge; it must be met if she held to it. Little by little he accustomed himself to the thought. The money must be paid, and to pay it he must sell his cherished securities. He had no more than four hundred, odd – he knew the exact figure – in the bank. The rest must be raised by selling his India Stock, but he hated to think of it. And the demand, made without warning, hurt his pride.

He took his lunch, a hunch of bread and a glass of ale, standing at the sideboard in the dining-room. It was an airy room, panelled, like most of the rooms at Garth, and the pale-blue paint, which many a year earlier had been laid on the oak, was dingy and wearing off in places. His den lay behind it. On the farther side of the hall was the drawing-room, white-panelled and spacious, furnished sparsely and stiffly, with spindle-legged tables, and long-backed Stuart chairs set against the wall. It opened into a dull library never used, and containing hardly a book later than Junius' letters or Burke's speeches. Above, under the sloping roofs of the attics, were chests of discarded clothes, wig-boxes and queerly-shaped carriage-trunks, which nowadays would furnish forth a fancy-ball; an old-time collection almost as curious as that which Miss Berry once viewed under the attics of the Villa Pamphili, but dusty, moth-eaten, unregarded, unvalued. Cold and bare, the house owned everywhere the pinch of the Squire's parsimony; there was nothing in it new, and little that was beautiful. But it was large and shadowy, the bedrooms smelled of lavender, the drawing-room of pot-pourri, and in summer the wind blew through it from the hayfield, and garden scents filled the lower rooms.

An hour later, having determined how he would act, the old man walked across to the Cottage. As he approached the plank-bridge which crossed the river at the foot of the garden he caught a glimpse of a petticoat on the rough lawn. He had no sooner seen it than it vanished, and he was not surprised. His face was grim as he crossed the bridge, and walking up to the side door struck on it with his cane.

She was all of a tremble when she came to him, and for that he was prepared. That did not surprise him. It was due to him. But he expected that she would excuse herself and fib and protest and shift her ground, and pour forth a torrent of silly explanations, as in his experience women always did. But Mrs Bourdillon took him aback by doing none of these things. She was white-faced and frightened, but, strange thing in a woman, she was dumb, or nearly dumb. Almost all she had to say or would say, almost all that he could draw from her was that it was her letter – yes, it was her letter. She repeated that several times. And she meant it? She meant what she had written? Yes, oh yes she did. Certainly she did. It was her letter.

But beyond that she had nothing to say, and at length, harshly, but not as harshly as he had intended, 'What do you mean, then,' he asked, 'to do with the money, ma'am, eh? I suppose you know that much?'

'I am putting it into the bank,' she replied, her eyes averted. 'Arthur is going – to be taken in.'

'Into the bank?' The Squire glared at her. 'Into Ovington's?'

'Yes, into Ovington's,' she answered, with the courage of despair. 'Where he will get twelve per cent for it.' She spoke in the tone of one who repeated a lesson.

He struck the floor with his cane. 'And you think that it will be safe there? Safe, ma'am, safe?'

'I hope so,' she faltered.

'Hope so, by G–d? Hope so!' he rapped out, honestly amazed. 'And that's all! Hope so! Well, all I can say is that I hope you mayn't live to regret your folly. Twelve per cent indeed! Twelve—'

He was going to say more, but the silly woman burst into tears and wept with such self-abandonment that she fairly silenced him. After watching her a moment, 'Well, there, there, ma'am, it's no good crying like that,' he said irritably. 'But, damme, it beats me! It beats me. If that is the way you look at it, why do you do it? Why do you do it? Of course you'll have the money. But when it's gone, don't come to me for more. And don't say I didn't warn you! There, there, ma'am!' moved by her grief, 'for heaven's sake don't go on like that! Don't – God bless me, if I live to be a hundred, if I shall ever understand women!'

He went away, routed by her tears and almost as much perplexed as he was enraged. 'If the woman feels like that about it, why does she call up the money?' he asked himself. 'Hope that it won't be lost! Hope, indeed! No, I'll never understand the silly fools. Never! Hope, indeed! But I suppose that it's that son of hers has befooled her.'

He saw, of course, that it was Arthur who had pushed her to it, and his anger against him and against Ovington grew. He would take his balance from Ovington's on the very next market day. He would go back to Dean's, though it meant eating humble pie. He thought of other schemes of vengeance, yet knew that when the time came he would not act upon them.

He was in a savage mood as he crossed the stableyard at Garth, and unluckily his eye fell upon Thomas who was seated on a shaft in a corner of the cart-shed. The man espied him at the same moment and hurried away a paper – it looked like a newspaper – over which he had been poring. Now, the Squire hated idleness, but he hated still more to see a newspaper in one of his men's hands. A labourer who could read was, in his opinion, a labourer spoiled, and his wrath blazed up.

'You d—d idle rascal!' he roared, shaking his cane at the man. 'That's what you do in my time, is it! Read some blackguard twopenny trash when you should be cleaning harness! Confound you, if I catch you again with a paper, you go that minute! D'you hear? D'you think that that's what I pay you for?'

The worm will turn, and Thomas, who had been spelling out an inspiring speech by one Henry Hunt, did turn. 'Pay me? You pay me little enough!' he answered sullenly.

The Squire could hardly believe his ears. That one of his men should answer him!

'Ay, little enough!' the man repeated impudently. 'Beggarly pay, and 'tis time you knew it, Master.'

The Squire gasped. Thomas was a Garthmyle man, who ten years before had migrated to Lancashire. Later he had returned – some said that he had got into trouble up north. However that may be, the Squire had wanted a groom, and Thomas had offered himself at low wages and been taken. The village thought that the Squire had been wrong, for Thomas had learned more tricks in Manchester than just to read the newspaper, and, always an ill-conditioned fellow, was fond of airing his learning in the ale-house.

Perhaps the Squire now saw that he had made a mistake; or perhaps he was too angry to consider the matter. 'Time I knew it?' he cried, as soon as he could recover himself. 'Why, you idle, worthless vagabond, do you think that I do not know what you're worth? Ain't you getting what I've always given?'

'That's where it be!'

'Eh!'

'That's where it be! I'm getting what you gave thirty years agone! And you soaking in money, Master, and getting bigger rents and bigger profits. Ain't I to have my share of it?'

'Share of it!' the old man ejaculated, thunderstruck by an argument as new as the man's insolence. 'Share of it!'

'Why no?' Thomas knew his case desperate, and was bent on having something to repeat to the awe-struck circle at the Griffin Arms. 'Why not?'

'Why, begad?' the Squire exclaimed, staring at him. 'You're the most impudent fellow I ever set eyes on!'

'You'll see more like me before you die!' Thomas answered darkly. 'In hard times didn't we share 'em and fair clem? And now profits are up, the world's full of money, as I hear in Aldersbury, and be you to take all and us none?'

It was a revelation to the Squire. Share? Share with his men? Could there be a fool so foolish as to look at the matter thus? Labourers were labourers, and he'd always seen that they had enough in the worst times to keep soul and body together. The duty of seeing that they had as much as would do that was his; and he had always owned it and discharged it. If man, woman or child had starved in Garthmyle he would have blamed himself severely. But the notion that they should have more because times were good, the notion that aught besides the county rate of wages, softened by feudal charity, entered into the question, was a heresy as new to him as it was preposterous.

'You don't know what you are talking about,' he said, surprise diminishing his anger.

'Don't I?' the man answered, his little eyes sparkling with spite. 'Well, there's some things I know as you don't. You'd ought to go to the summer-house a bit more, master, and you'd learn. You'd ought to walk in the garden. There's goings-on and meetings and partings as you don't know, I'll go bail! But 'tain't my business and I say nought. I do my work.'

'I'll find another to do it this day month,' said the Squire. 'And you'll take that for notice, my man. You'll do your duty while you're here, and if I find one of the horses sick or sorry, you'll sleep in jail. That's enough. I want no more of your talk!'

He went into the house. Things had come to a pretty pass, when one of his men could face him out like that. The sooner he made a change and saw the rogue out of Garthmyle the better! He flung his stick into a corner and his hat on the table and damned the times. He would put the matter out of his mind.

But it would not go. The taunt the man had flung at him at the last haunted him. What did the rogue mean? And at whom was he hinting? Was Arthur working against him in his own house as well as opposing him out of doors? If so, by heaven, he would soon put an end to it! And by and by, unable to resist the temptation – but not until he had sent Thomas away on an errand – he went heavily out and into the terraced garden. He climbed to the raised walk and looked abroad, his brow gloomy.

The day had mended and the sun was trying to break through the clouds. The sheep were feeding along the brook-side, the lambs were running races under the hedgerows, or curling themselves up on sheltered banks. But the scene, which usually gratified him, failed to please today, for presently he espied a figure moving near the mill and made out that the figure was Josina's. From time to time the girl stooped. She appeared to be picking primroses.

It was the idle hour of the day, and there was no reason why she should not be taking her pleasure. But the Squire's brow grew darker as he marked her lingering steps and uncertain movements. More than once he fancied that she looked behind her, and by and by with an oath he turned, clumped down the steps, and left the garden.

He had not quite reached the mill when she saw him descending to meet her. He fancied that he read guilt in her face, and his old heart sank at the sight.

'What are you doing?' he asked, confronting her and striking the ground with his cane. 'Eh? What are you doing here, girl? Out with it! You've a tongue, I suppose?'

She looked as if she could sink into the ground, but she found her voice. 'I've been gathering – these, sir,' she faltered, holding out her basket.

'Ay, at the rate of one a minute! I've watched you. Now, listen to me. You listen to me, young woman. And take warning. If you're hanging about to meet that young fool, I'll not have it. Do you hear? I'll not have it!'

She looked at him piteously, the colour gone from her face. 'I – I don't think – I understand, sir,' she quavered.

'Oh, you understand well enough!' he retorted, his suspicions turned to certainty. 'And none of your woman's tricks with me! I've done with Master Arthur, and you've done with him too. If he comes about the place he's to be sent to the right-about. That's my order, and that's all about it. Do you hear?'

She affected to be surprised, and a little colour trickled into her cheeks. But he took this for one of her woman's wiles – they were deceivers, all of them.

'Do you mean, sir,' she stammered, 'that I am not to see Arthur?'

'You're neither to see him nor speak to him nor listen to him! There's to be an end of it. Now, are you going to obey me, girl?'

She looked as if butter would not melt in her mouth. 'Yes, sir,' she answered meekly. 'I shall obey you if those are your orders.'

He was surprised by the readiness of her assent, and he looked at her suspiciously. 'Umph!' he grunted. 'That sounds well, and it will be well for you, girl, if you keep to it. For I mean it. Let there be no mistake about that.'

'I shall do as you wish, of course, sir.'

'He's behaved badly, d—d badly! But if you are sensible I'll say no more. Only understand me, you've got to give him up.'

'Yes, sir.'

'From this day? Now, do you understand?'

'Yes, sir.'

After that he had no more to say. He required obedience, and he should have been glad to receive it. But, to tell the truth, he was a little at a loss. Girls were silly – such was his creed – and it behoved them to be guided by their elders. If they did not suffer themselves to be guided, they must be brought into line, and sharply. But somewhere, far down in the old man's heart, and unacknowledged even by himself, lay an odd feeling – a feeling of something like disappointment. In his young days girls had not been so ready, so very ready, to surrender their lovers. He had even known them to fight for them. He was perplexed.

Chapter Ten

They were standing on the narrow strip of sward between the wood and the stream, which the gun accident had for ever made memorable to them. The stile rose between them, but seeing that his hands rested on hers, and his eyes dwelt unrebuked on her conscious face, the barrier was but as the equator, which divides but does not separate; the sacrifice to propriety was less than it seemed. Spring had come with a rush, the hedges were everywhere bursting into leaf. In the Thirty Acres which climbed the hill above them, the thrushes were singing their May-day song, and beside them the brook rippled and sparkled in the sunshine. All Nature rejoiced, and the pulse of youth leapt to the universal rhythm. The maiden's eyes repeated what the man's lips uttered, and for the time to love and to be loved was all in all.

'To think,' he murmured, 'that if I had not been so awkward we should not have known one another!' And, silly man, he thought this the height of wisdom.

'And the snowdrops!' She, alas, was on the same plane of sapience. 'But when – when did you first, Clem?'

'From the first moment we met! From the very first, Jos!'

'When I saw you standing here? And looking—'

'Oh, from long before that!' he declared. And his eyes challenged denial. 'From the hour when I saw you at the Race Ball in the Assembly Room – ages, ages ago!'

She savoured the thought and found it delicious, and she longed to hear it repeated. 'But you did not know me then. How could you – love me?'

'How could I not? How could I see you and not love you?' he babbled. 'How was it possible I should not? Were we not made for one another? You don't doubt that? And you,' jealously, 'when, sweet, did you first – think of me?'

Alas, she could only go back to the moment when she had tripped heart-whole round the corner of the wood, and seen him standing, solitary, wrapped in thought, a romantic figure. But though, to her shame, she could only go back to that, it thrilled her, it made her immensely happy, to think that he had loved her first, that his heart had gone out to her before she knew him, that he had chosen her even before he had spoken to her. Ay, chosen her, little regarded as she was, and shabby, and insignificant amid the gay throng of the ballroom! She had been Cinderella then, but she had found her glass slipper now – and her Fairy Prince. And so on, and so on, with sweet and foolish repetitions.

For this was the latest of a dozen meetings, and Love had long ago challenged Love. Many an afternoon had Clement waited under the wood, and with wonder and reverence seen the maid come tripping along the green towards him. Many a time had he thought a seven-mile ride a small price to pay for the chance, the mere chance, of a meeting, for the distant glimpse of a bonnet, even for the privilege of touching the pebble set for a token on the stile. So that it is to be feared that, if market days had found him more often at his desk, there had been other days, golden days and not a few, when the bank had not held him, when he had stolen away to play truant in this enchanted country. But then, how great had been the temptation, how compelling the lure, how fair the maid!

No, he had not played quite fairly with his father. But the thought of that weighed lightly on him. For this that had come to him, this love that glorified all things, even as Spring the face of Nature, that filled his mind with a thousand images, each more enchanting than the last, and inspired his imagination with a magic not its own, – this visited a man but once; whereas he would have long years in which he might redeem the time, long years in which he might warm his father's heart by an attendance at the desk that should shame Rodd himself! Ay, and he would! He would! Even the sacrifice of his own tastes, his own wishes seemed in his present mood a small surrender, and one he owed and fain would pay.

For he was in love with goodness, he longed to put himself right with all. He longed to do his duty to all, he who walked with a firmer step, who trod the soil with a conquering foot, who found new beauties in star and flower, he, so happy, so proud, so blessed!

But this being his mood, there was a burden which did weigh on him, and weighed on him more heavily every day, and that was the part which he was playing towards the Squire. It had long galled him, when absent from her; of late it had begun to mar his delight in her presence. The rôle of secret lover had charmed for a time – what more shy, more elusive, more retiring than young love? And what more secret? Fain would it shun all eyes. But he had now reached a farther stage, and being honest, and almost quixotic by nature, he could not without pain fall day by day below the ideals which his fancy set up. Today he had come to meet Josina with a fixed resolve, and a mind wound to the pitch of action; and presently into the fair pool of her content – yet quaking as he did so lest he should seem to hint a fault – he cast the stone.

'And now, Jos,' he said, his eyes looking bravely into hers, 'I must see your father.'

'My father!' Fear sprang into her eyes. She stiffened.

'Yes, dear,' he repeated. 'I must see your father – and speak to him. There is no other course possible.'

Colour, love, joy, all fled from her face. She shivered. 'My father!' she stammered, pale to the lips. 'Oh, it is impossible! It is impossible! You would not do it!' She would have withdrawn her hands if he had not held them. 'You cannot, cannot mean it! Have you thought what you are saying?'

'I have, indeed,' he said, sobered by her fear, and full of pity for her. 'I lay awake for hours last night thinking of it. But there is no other course, Jos, no other course – if we would be happy.'

'But, oh, you don't know him!' she cried. And her terror wrung his heart. 'You don't know him! Or what he will think of me!'

'Nothing very bad,' he rejoined. But more than ever, more than before, his conscience accused him. He felt that the shame which burned her face and in a moment gave way to the pallor of fear was the measure of his guilt; and in proportion as he winced under that knowledge, and under the knowledge that it was she who must pay the heavier penalty, he took blame to himself and was strengthened in his resolve. 'Listen, Jos,' he said bravely. 'Listen! And let me tell you what I mean. And, dearest, do not tremble as you are trembling. I am not going to tell him today. But tell him I must some day – and soon, if we do not wish him to learn it from others.'

She shuddered. All had been so bright, so new, so joyous; and now she was to pay the price. And the price had a very terrible aspect for her.

Fate, a cruel, pitiless fate, was closing upon her. She could not speak, but her eyes, her quivering lips, pleaded with him for mercy.

He had expected that, and he steeled himself, showing thereby the good metal that was in him. 'Yes,' he said firmly, 'we must, Jos. And for a better reason than that. Because if we do not, if we continue to deceive your father, he will have reason to be angry with you, but to despise me; to look upon me as a poor unmanly thing, Jos, a coward who dared not face him, a craven who dared not ask him for what he valued above all the world! Who stole it from him in the dark and behind his back! As it is he will be angry enough. He will look down upon me, and with justice. And at first he will say 'No,' and I fear he will separate us, and there will be no more meetings, and we may have to wait. But if we are brave, if we trust one another and are true to one another – and, alas, you will have to bear the worst – if we can bear and be strong, in the end, believe me, Jos, it will come right.'

'Never,' she cried, despairing, 'never! He will never allow it!'

'Then—'

'Oh,' she prayed, 'can we not go on as we are?'

'No, we cannot.' He was firm. 'We cannot. By and by you would discover that for yourself, and you, as well as he, would have cause to despise me. For consider, Jos. Think, dear. If I do not seek you for my wife, what is before us? To what can we look forward? To what future? What end? Only to perpetual alarms, and some day, when we least expect it, to discovery – to discovery that will cover me with disgrace.'

She did not answer. She had taken her hands from him, she had taken herself from him. She leant on the stile, her face hidden. But he dared not give way, nor would he let himself be repulsed. And very tenderly he laid his hand on her shoulder. 'It is natural that you should be frightened,' he said. 'But if I, too, am frightened; if, seeing the proper course, I do not take it, how can you ever trust me or depend on me? What am I then but a coward? What is the worth of my love, Jos, if I have not the courage to ask for you?'

'But he will want to know—' her shoulders heaved in her agitation, 'he will want to know—'

'How we met? I know. And how we loved? Yes, I am afraid so. And he will be angry with you, and you will suffer, and I shall be God knows how wretched! But if I do not go to him, how much more angry will he be! And how much more ground for anger will he have! If we continue to meet, it cannot be long kept from him, and then how much worse will it be! And I, with not a word to say for myself, with no defence, no plea! I, who shall not then seem to him to be even a man.'

'But he is so – so hard!' she whispered, her face still hidden.

'I know, dear. And so firmly set in his prejudice and his pride. I know. He will think me so far below you; he hates the bank and all connected with it. He holds me a mere clerk, not one of his class, and low, dear, I know it. But' – his voice rose a tone – 'I am not low, Jos, and you have discovered it. And now I must prove it to him. I must prove it. And to make a beginning, I must be no coward. I must not be afraid of him. For you, the times are past when he could ill-treat you. And he loves you.'

'He is very hard,' she murmured. It was his punishment throughout, that though his heart was wrung for her he could not bear her share of the suffering. But he dared not and he would not give way. 'He will make me give you up.'

He had thought of that and he was ready for it. 'That must depend upon you,' he said very soberly. 'For my part, dear – but my part is easy – I shall never give you up. Never! But if the trial be too sore for you who must bear the heavier burden, if you feel that our love is not worth the price you must pay, then I will never reproach you, Jos, never. If you decide on that I will not say one word against it; no, nor think one harsh thought of you. And then we need not tell him. But we must not meet again.'

She trembled, and it was natural, it was very natural, that she should tremble. It was an age when discipline was strict and even harsh, and she had been bred up in awe of her father, and in that absolute subjection to him of which the women about her set the example. Children were then to be seen and not heard. Girls were expected to have neither wills nor views of their own. And in her case this was not all. The Squire was a hard man. He was a man of whom those about him stood in awe, and who, if he had any of the softer affections, hid them under a mask of unpleasing reserve. Proud as he was of his caste, he kept his daughter short of money, and short of clothes. He saw her go shabby without a qualm, and penniless, and rejoiced that she could not get into mischief. If she lost a shilling on an errand or overpaid a bill, he stormed and raved at her. Had she run up a debt he would have driven her from the room with oaths. So that if, under the dry husk, there was any kernel, any softer feeling – either for her or for the young boy who had died in his first uniform at Alexandria – she had no clue to the fact, and certainly no suspicion of it.

Nor was even this the whole. One thing was known to Josina which was not known to Clement. Garth was entailed upon her. Even the Squire could not deprive her of the estate, and in the character of his heir she wore for the old man a preciousness with which affection had nothing to do. What he might have permitted to his daughter was matter for grim conjecture. But that he would ever let his heiress, her whose hand was weighted with the rents of Garth, and with the wide lands he loved – that he would ever let her wed at her pleasure or out of her class, – this appeared to Josina of all things the most unlikely.

It was no wonder then that the girl hesitated before she answered, or that Clement's face grew grave, his heart heavy, as he waited. But he had that insight into the feelings of others which imagination alone can give, and while she wavered or seemed to waver, he felt none of the resentment which comes of wounded love. Rather he was filled with a great pity for her, a deep tenderness. For it was he who was in fault, he told himself. It was he who had made the overtures, he who had wooed and won her fancy, he who had done this. It was his selfishness, his thoughtlessness, his imprudence which had brought them to this pass, a pass whence they could neither advance without suffering nor draw back with honour. So that if she who must encounter a father's anger proved unequal to the test, if the love, which he did not doubt, was still too weak to face the ordeal, it did not lie with him to blame her – even on this day when bird and flower and leaf sang love's pæan. No, perish the thought! He would never blame her. With infinite tenderness, forgiving her beforehand, he touched her bowed head.

And at that, at that touch, she looked up at last, and with a leap of the heart he read her answer in her eyes. He read there a love and a courage equal to his own; for, after all, she was her father's daughter, she too came of an old proud race. 'You shall tell him,' she said, smiling through her tears. 'And I will bear what comes of it. But they shall never separate us, Clem, never, never, if you will be true to me.'

'True to you!' he cried, worshipping her, adoring her. 'Oh, Jos!'

'And love me a little always?'

'Love you? Oh, my darling!' The words choked him.

'It shall be as you say! It shall be always as you say!' She was clinging to him now. 'I will do as you tell me! I will always – oh, but you mustn't, you mustn't,' between tears and smiles, for his arms were about her now, and the poor ineffectual stile had ceased to be even an equator. 'But I must tell you. I love you more now, Clement, more, more because I can trust you. You are strong and will do what is right.'

'At your cost!' he cried, shaken to the depths – and he thought her the most wonderful, the bravest, the noblest woman in the world. 'Ah, Jos, if I could bear it for you!'

'I will bear it,' she answered. 'And it will not last. And see, I am not afraid now – or only a little! I shall think of you, and it will be nothing.'

Oh, but the birds were singing now and the brook was sparkling as it rippled over the shallows towards the deep pool.

Presently, 'When will you tell him?' she asked; and she asked it with scarce a quaver in her voice.

'As soon as I can. The sooner the better. This is Saturday. I will see him on Monday morning.'

'But isn't that – market-day?' faintly. 'Can you get away?'

'Does anything matter beside this?' he replied. 'The sooner, dear, the tooth is pulled, the better. There is only one thing I fear.'

'I think you fear nothing,' she rejoined, gazing at him with admiring eyes. 'But what is it?'

'That someone should be before us. That someone should tell him before I do. And he should think us what we are not, Jos – cowards.'

'I see,' she answered thoughtfully. 'Yes,' with a sigh. 'Then, on Monday. I shall sleep the better when it is over, even if I sleep in disgrace.'

'I know,' he said; and he saw with a pang that her colour ebbed. But her eyes still met his and were brave, and she smiled to reassure him.

'I will not mind what comes,' she whispered, 'if only we are not parted.'

'We shall not be parted for ever,' he assured her. 'If we are true to one another, not even your father can part us – in the end.'

Chapter Eleven

Josina had put a brave face on the matter, but when she came down to breakfast on the Monday, the girl was almost sick with apprehension. Her hands were cold, and as she sat at table she could not raise her eyes from her plate. The habit of years is not to be overcome in an hour, and that which the girl had to face was beyond doubt formidable. She had passed out of childhood, but in that house she was still a child. She was expected to be silent, to efface herself before her elders, to have no views but their views, and no wishes that went beyond theirs. Her daily life was laid out for her, and she must conform or she would be called to heel. On love and marriage she must have no mind of her own, but must think as her father permitted. If he chose she would be her cousin's wife, if he did not choose the two would be parted. She could guess how he would treat her if she resisted his will, or even his whim, in that matter.

And now she must resist his will in a far worse case. Arthur was her cousin. But Clement – she was not supposed even to know him. Yet she must own him, she must avow her love for him, she must confess to secret meetings with him and stolen interviews. She must be prepared for looks of horror, for uplifted hands and scandalised faces, and to hear shameful things said of him; to hear him spoken of as an upstart, belonging to a class beneath her, a person with whom she ought never to have come in contact, one whom her father would not think of admitting to his table!

And through all, she who was so weak, so timid, so subject, must be firm. She must not flinch.

As she sat at table she was conscious of her pale cheeks, and trembled lest the others should notice them. She fancied that her father's face already wore an ominous gloom. 'If you've orders for town,' he flung at Miss Peacock as he rose, 'you'll need be quick with them. I'm going in at ten.'

Miss Peacock was all of a flutter. 'But I thought, sir, that the Bench did not sit—'

'You'd best not think,' he retorted. 'Ten, I said.'

That seemed to promise a blessed respite, and the colour returned to Josina's cheeks. Clement could hardly arrive before eleven, and for this day she might be safe. But on the heels of relief followed reflection. The respite meant another sleepless night, another day of apprehension, more hours of fear. The girl was glad and she was sorry. The spirit warred with the flesh. She did not know what she wished.

And, after all, Clement might appear before ten. She watched the clock and watched her father and in returning suspense hung upon his movements. How he lingered, now hunting for a lost paper, now grumbling over a seed-bill, now drawing on his boots with the old horn-handled hooks which had been his father's! And the clock – how slowly it moved! It wanted eight, it wanted five, it wanted two minutes of ten. The hour struck. And still the Squire loitered outside, talking to old Fewtrell – when at any moment Clement might ride up!

The fact was that Thomas was late, and the Squire was saying what he thought of him. 'Confound him, he thinks, because he's going, he can do as he likes!' he fumed. 'But I'll learn him! Let me catch him in the village a week after he leaves, and I'll jail him for a vagrant! Such impudence as he gave me the other day I never heard in my life! He'll go wide of here for a character!'

'I dunno as I'd say too much to him,' the old bailiff advised. 'He's a queer customer, Squire, as you'd ought to have seen before now!'

'He'll find me a queer customer if he starts spouting again! Why, damme,' irritably, 'one might almost think you agreed with him!'

Old Fewtrell screwed up his face. 'No,' he said slowly, 'I'm not saying as I agree with him. But there's summat in what he says, begging your pardon, Squire.'

'Summat? Why, man,' in astonishment, 'are you tarred with the same brush?'

'You know me, master, better'n that,' the old man replied. 'An' I bin with you fifty years and more. But, certain sure, times is changed and we're no better for the change.'

'But you get as much?'

'Mebbe in malt, but not in meal. In money, mebbe – I'm not saying a little more, master. But here's where 'tis. We'd the common before the war, and run for a cow and geese, and wood for the picking, and if a lad fancied to put up a hut on the waste 'twas five shillings a year; and a rood o' potato ground – it wasn't missed. 'Twas neither here nor there. But 'tisn't so now. Where be the common? Well, you know, Squire, laid down in wheat these twenty years, and if a lad squatted now, he'd not be long of hearing of it. We've the money, but we're not so well off. There's where 't is.'

The Squire scowled. 'Well, I'm d—d!' he said. 'You've been with me fifty years, and—' and then fortunately or unfortunately the curricle came round and the Squire, despising Fewtrell's hint, turned his wrath upon the groom, called him a lazy scoundrel, and cursed him up hill and down dale.

The man took it in silence, to the bailiff's surprise, but his sullen face did not augur well for the day, and when he had climbed to the back-seat – with a scramble and a grazed knee, for the Squire started the horses with no thought for him – he shook his fist at the old man's back. Fewtrell saw the gesture, and felt a vague uneasiness, for he had heard Thomas say ugly things. But then the man had been in liquor, and probably he didn't mean them.

The Squire rattled the horses down the steep drive with the confidence of one who had done the same thing a thousand times. Turning to the left a furlong beyond the gate, he made for Garthmyle where, at the bridge, he fell into the highway. He had driven a mile along this when he saw a horseman coming along the road to meet him, and he fell to wondering who it was. His sight was good at a distance, and he fancied that he had seen the young spark before, though he could not put a name to him. But he saw that he rode a good nag, and he was not surprised when the other reined up and, raising his hat, showed that he wished to speak.

It was Clement, of course, and with a little more wisdom or a little less courage he would not have stopped the old man. He would have seen that the moment was not propitious, and that his business could hardly be done on the highway. But in his intense anxiety lest chance should forestall him, he dared not let the opportunity pass, and his hand was raised before he had well considered what he would say.

The Squire pulled up his horses. 'D'you want me?' he asked, civilly enough.

'If I may trouble you, sir,' Clement answered as bravely as he could. 'It's on important business, or – or I wouldn't detain you.' Already, his heart in his mouth, he saw the difficulty in which he had placed himself. How could he speak before the man? Or on the road?

The Squire considered him. 'Business, eh?' he said. 'With me? Well, I know your face, young gentleman, but I can't put a name to you.'

'I am Mr Ovington's son, Clement Ovington, sir.'

All the Squire's civility left him. 'The devil you are!' he exclaimed. 'Well, I'm going to the bank. I like to do my business across the counter, young sir, to be plain, and not in the road.'

'But this is business – of a different sort, sir,' Clement stammered, painfully aware of the change in the other's tone, as well as of the servant, who was all a-grin behind his master's shoulder. 'If I could have a word with you – apart, sir? Or perhaps – if I called at Garth tomorrow?'

'Why?'

'It is upon private business, Mr Griffin,' Clement replied, his face burning.

'Did your father send you?'

'No.'

'Then I don't see,' the Squire replied, scowling at him from under his bushy eyebrows, 'what business you can have with me. There can be none, young man, that can't be done across the counter. It is only upon business that I know your father, and I don't know you at all. I don't know why you stopped me.'

Clement was scarlet with mortification. 'If I could see you for a few minutes – alone, sir, I think I could explain what it is.'

'You will see me at the bank in an hour,' the old man retorted. 'Anything you have to say you can say there. As it is, I am going to close my account with your father, and after that the less I hear your name the better I shall be pleased. At present you're wasting my time. I don't know why you stopped me. Good morning.' And in a lower tone, but one that was perfectly audible to Clement, 'D—d young counterskipper,' he muttered, as he started the horses. 'Business with me, indeed! Confound his impudence!'

He drove off at speed, leaving Clement seated on his horse in the middle of the road, a prey to feelings that may be imagined. He had made a bad beginning, and his humiliation was complete.

'Young counterskipper!' That rankled – yet in time he might smile at that. But the tone, and the manner, the conviction that under no circumstances could there be anything between them, any relations, any equality – this bit deeper and wounded more permanently. The Squire's view, that he addressed one of another class and another grade, one with whom he could have no more in common than with the servant behind him, could not have been made more plain if he had known the object of the lad's application.

If he had known it! Good heavens, if he said so much now, what would he have said in that case? Certainly, the task which love had set this young man was not an easy one. No wonder Josina had been frightened.

He had – he had certainly made a mess of it. His ears burned, as he sat on his horse and recalled the other's words.

Meanwhile the Squire drove on, and with the air and movement he recovered his temper. As he drew near to the town the market-traffic increased, and sitting high on his seat he swept by many a humble gig and plodding farm-cart, and acknowledged with a flicker of his whip-hand many a bared head and hasty obeisance. He was not loved; men who are bent on getting a pennyworth for their penny are not loved. But he was regardful of his own people, and in all companies he was fearless and could hold his own. And he was Griffin of Garth, one of the few in whose hands were all county power and all county influence. As he drove down the hill toward the West Bridge, seeing with the eye of memory the airy towers and lofty gateways of the older bridge that had once stood there and for centuries had bridled the wild Welsh, his bodily eyes noted the team of the out-going coach which he had a share in horsing. And the coachman, proudly and with respect, named him to the box-seat.

From the bridge the town, girdled by the shining river, climbs pyramid-wise up the sides of a cleft hill, an ancient castle guarding the one narrow pass by which a man may enter it on foot. The smiling plain, in the midst of which it rises, is itself embraced at a distance by a ring of hills, broken at one point only, which happens to correspond with the guarded isthmus; on which side, and some four miles away, was fought many centuries ago a famous battle. It is a proud town, looking out over a proud county, a county still based on ancient tradition, on old names and great estates, standing solid and four-square against the invasion that even in the Squire's day threatened it – the invasion of new men and new money, of Birmingham and Liverpool and Manchester. The airy streets and crowded shuts run down on all sides from the Market Place to the green meadows and leafy gardens that the river laps: green meadows on which the chapels and cloisters of religious houses once nestled under the shelter of the walls.

The Squire could remember the place when his father and his like had had their town houses in it, and in winter had removed their families to it; when the weekly Assemblies at the Lion had been gay with cards and dancing, and in the cockpit behind the inn mains of cocks had been fought with the Gentlemen of Cheshire or Staffordshire; when fine ladies with long canes and red-heeled shoes had promenaded in the fields beside the river, and the town in its season had been a little Bath. Those days, and the lumbering coaches-and-six which had brought in the families, were gone, and the staple of the town, its trade in woollens and Welsh flannels, was also on the decline. But it was still a thriving place, and if the county people no longer filled it in winter, their stately houses survived, and older houses than theirs, of brick and timber, quaint and gabled, that made the streets a joy to antiquaries.

The Squire passed by many a one, with beetling roof and two-storied porch, as he drove up Maerdol. His first and most pressing business was at the bank, and he would not be himself until he had got it off his mind. He would show that d—d Ovington what he thought of him! He would teach him a lesson – luring away that young man and pouching his money. Ay, begad he would!

Chapter Twelve

But as the Squire turned to the left by the Stalls he saw his lawyer, Frederick Welsh – rather above most lawyers were the Welsh brothers, by-blows it was said of a great house – and Welsh stopped him. 'You're wanted at the Bench, Squire, if you please,' he said. 'His lordship is there, and they are waiting for you.'

'But it's not time – by an hour, man!'

'No, but it's a special case, and will take all day, I'm afraid. His lordship says that he won't begin until you come. It's that case of—' the lawyer whispered a few words. 'And the Chief Constable does not quite trust – you understand? He's anxious that you should be there.'

The Squire resigned himself, 'Very well, I'll come,' he said.

He could go to the bank afterwards, but he might not have complied so readily if his vanity had not been tickled. The Justices of that day bore a heavier burden than their successors – *hodie nominis umbrae*. With no police force they had to take the initiative in the detection as well as in the punishment of crime. Marked men, belonging to a privileged class, they had to do invidious things and to enforce obnoxious laws. They represented the executive, and they shared alike its odium and its fearlessness. For hardly anything is more remarkable in the history of that time than the courage of the men who held the reins. Unpopular, assailed by sedition, undermined by conspiracy, and pressed upon by an ever-growing public feeling, the few held on unblenching, firm in the belief that repression was the only policy, and doubting nothing less than their right to rule. They dined and drank, and presented a smiling face to the world, but great and small they ran their risks, and that they did not go unscathed, the fate of Perceval and of Castlereagh, the collapse of Liverpool, and the shortened lives of many a lesser man gave proof.

But even among the firm there are degrees, and in all bodies it is on the shoulders of one or two that the onus falls. Of the one or two in Aldshire, the Squire was one. My lord might fill the chair, Sir Charles might assent, but it was to Griffin that their eyes wandered when an unpleasant decision had to be taken or the public showed its teeth. And the old man knew that this was so, and was proud of it.

Today, however, as he watched the long hand move round the clock, he had less patience than usual. Because he must be at the bank before it closed, everything seemed to work against him. The witnesses were sullen, the evidence dragged, Acherley went off on a false scent, and being whipped back, turned crusty. The Squire fidgeted and scowled, and then, twenty minutes before the bank closed, and when with his eyes on the clock he was growing desperate, the chairman suggested that they should break off for a quarter of an hour. 'Confound me, if I can sit any longer,' he said. 'I must have a mouthful of something, Griffin.'

The Squire seldom took more than a hunch of bread at midday and could do without that, but he was glad to agree, and a minute later he was crossing the Market Place towards the bank. It happened that business was brisk at the moment. Rodd, at a side desk, was showing a customer how to draw a cheque. At the main counter a knot of farmers were producing, with protruding tongues and hunched shoulders, something which might pass for a signature. Two clerks were aiding them, and for a moment the Squire stood unseen and unregarded. Impatiently he tapped the counter with his stick, on which Rodd saw him, and, deserting his task, came hurriedly to him.

The Squire thrust his cheque across the counter. 'In gold,' he said.

The cashier scanned the cheque, his hand in the till. 'Four, seven, six-ten,' he murmured. Then his face grew serious, and without glancing at the Squire he consulted a book which lay beside him. 'Four, seven, six-ten,' he repeated. 'I am afraid – one moment, if you please, sir!' Breaking off he made two steps to a door behind him and disappeared through it.

He returned a moment later, followed by Ovington himself. The banker's face was grave, but his tone retained its usual blandness. 'Good-day, Mr Griffin,' he said. 'You are drawing the whole of your balance, I see. I trust that that does not mean that you are – making any change?'

'That is what it does mean, sir,' the Squire answered.

'Of course, it is entirely your affair—'

'Entirely.'

'But we are most anxious to accommodate you. If there is anything that we can put right, any cause of dissatisfaction—'

'No,' said the Squire grimly. 'There is nothing that you can put right. It is only that I do not choose to do business with my family.'

The banker bowed with dignity. The incident was not altogether unexpected. 'With most people, a connection of the kind would be in our favour,' he said.

'Not with me. And as my time is short—'

The banker bowed. 'In gold, I think? May we not send it for you? It will be no trouble.'

'No, I thank you,' the Squire grunted, hating the other for his courtesy. 'I will take it, if you please.'

'Put it in a strong bag, Mr Rodd,' Ovington said. 'I shall still hope, Mr Griffin, that you will think better of it.' And, bowing, he wished the Squire 'Good-day,' and retired.

Rodd was a first-class cashier, but he felt the Squire's eyes boring into him, and he was twice as long in counting out the gold as he should have been. The consequence was that when the Squire left the bank, the hour had struck, Dean's was closed, and the Bench was waiting for him. He paused on the steps considering what he should do. He could not leave so large a sum unguarded in the Justices' room, nor could he conveniently take it with him into Court.

At that moment his eyes fell on Purslow, the draper, who was standing at the door of his shop, and he crossed over to him. 'Here, man, put this in your safe and turn the key on it,' he said. 'I shall call for it in an hour or two.'

'Honoured, sir, I am sure,' said the gratified tradesman, as he took the bag. But when he felt its weight and guessed what was in it, 'Excuse me, sir. Hadn't you better seal it, sir?' he said. 'It seems to be a large sum.'

'No need. I shall call for it in an hour. Lock it up yourself, Purslow. That's all.'

Purslow, as pleased as if the Squire had given him a large order, assured him that he would do so, and the old man stalked across to the court, where business kept him, fidgeting and impatient, until hard on seven. Nor did he get away then without unpleasantness.

For unluckily Acherley, who had been charged to approach him about the Railroad, had been snubbed in the course of the day. Always an ill-humoured man, he saw his way to pay the Squire out, and chose this moment to broach the delicate subject. He did it with as little tact as temper.

"Pon my honour, Griffin, you know – about this Railroad,' he said, tackling the old man abruptly, as they were putting on their coats. 'You really must open your eyes, man, and move with the times. The devil's in it if we can stand still always. You might as well go back to your old tie-wig, you know. You are blocking the way, and if you won't think of your own interests, you ought to think of the town, I can tell you,' bluntly, 'you are making yourself d—d unpopular there.'

Very seldom of late had anyone spoken to the Squire in that tone, and his temper was up in a minute. 'Unpopular?' he snapped. 'I don't understand you.'

'Well, you ought to!'

'Unpopular? What's that? Unpopular, sir! What the devil have we in this room to do with popularity? I make my horse go my way, I don't go his, nor ask if he likes it. Damn your popularity!'

Acherley had his answer on his tongue, but Woosenham interposed. 'But, after all, Griffin,' he said mildly, 'we must move with the times – even if we don't give way to the crowd. There's no man whose opinion I value more than yours, as you know, but I think you do us an injustice in this matter.'

'An injustice?' The Squire sneered. 'Not I! The fact is, Woosenham, you are letting others use you for a stalking horse. Some are fools, and some – I leave you to put a name to them! If you'd give two thoughts to this Railroad yourself, you'd see that you have nothing to gain by it, except money that you can do without! While you stand to lose more than money, and that's your good name!'

Sir Charles changed colour. 'My good name?' he said, bristling feebly. 'I don't understand you, Griffin.'

One of the others, seeing a quarrel in prospect, intervened. 'There, there,' he said, hoping to pour oil on the troubled waters. 'Griffin doesn't mean it, Woosenham. He doesn't mean—'

'But I do mean it,' the old man insisted. 'I mean every word of it.' He felt that the general sense was against him, but that was nothing to him. Wasn't he the oldest present, and wasn't it his duty to stop this folly if he could? 'I tell you plainly, Woosenham,' he continued, 'it isn't only your affair, if you lend your name to this business. You take it up, and a lot of fools who know nothing about it, who know less, by G–d, than you do, will take it up too! And will put their money in it and go daundering up and down, quoting you as if you were Solomon! And that tickles you! But what will they say of you if the affair turns out to be a swindle – another South Sea Bubble, by G—d! And half the town and half the country are ruined by it! What'll they say of you then – and of us?'

Acherley could be silent no longer. 'Nobody's going to be ruined by it!' he retorted – he saw that Sir Charles looked much disturbed. 'Nobody! If you ask me, I think what you're saying is d—d nonsense.'

'It may be,' the Squire said sternly. 'But just another word, please. I want you to understand, Woosenham, that this is not your affair only. It touches every one of us. What are we in this room? If we are those to whom the administration of this county is entrusted, let us act as such – and keep our hands clean. But if we are a set of money-changers and bill-mongers,' with contempt, 'stalking horses for such men as Ovington the banker, dirtying our hands with all the tricks of the money market – that's another matter. But I warn you – you can't be both. And for my part – we don't any longer wear swords to show we are gentlemen, but I'm hanged if I'll wear an apron or have anything to do with this business. A railroad? Faugh! As if horses' legs and Telford's roads aren't good enough for us, or as if tea-kettles will ever beat the Wonder coach – fifteen hours to London.'

Acherley had been restrained with difficulty, and he now broke loose. 'Griffin,' he cried, 'you're damned offensive! If you wore a sword as you used to—'

'Pooh! Pooh!' said the Squire and shrugged his shoulders; while Sir Charles, terribly put out both by the violence of the scene and by the picture which the Squire had drawn, put in a feeble protest. 'I must say,' he said, 'I think this uncalled for, Griffin. I think you might have spared us this. You may not agree with us—'

'But damme if he shall insult us!' Acherley cried, trembling with passion.

'Pooh, pooh!' said the Squire again. 'I'm an old man, and it is useless to talk to me in that strain. I've spoken my mind, and—'

'And you horse two of the coaches!' Acherley retorted. 'And make a profit by that, dirty or no! But where'd your profit be, if your father who rode post to London had stood pat where he was? And set himself against coaches as you set yourself against the railroad?'

That was a shrewd hit and the Squire did not meet it. Instead, 'Well, right or wrong,' he said, 'that's my opinion. And right or wrong, no railroad crosses my land, and that's my last word!'

'We'll see about that,' Acherley answered, bubbling with rage. 'There are more ways than one of cooking a goose.'

'Just so. But—,' with a steady look at him, 'which is the cook and which is the goose, Acherley? Perhaps you'll find that out some day.' And the Squire clapped on his hat – he had already put on his shabby old driving coat. But he had still a word to say. 'I'm the oldest man here,' he said, looking round upon them, 'and I may take a liberty and ask no man's pleasure. You, Woosenham, and you gentlemen, let this railroad alone. If you are going to move at twenty-five miles an hour, then, depend upon it, more things will move than you wot of, and more than you'll like. Ay, you'll have movement – movement enough and changes enough if you go on! So I say, leave it alone, gentlemen. That's my advice.'

He went out with that and stamped down the stairs. He had not sought the encounter, and, now that he was alone, his knees shook a little under him. But he had held his own and spoken his mind, and on the whole he was content with himself.

The same could not be said of those whom he had warned. Acherley, indeed, abused him freely, but the majority were impressed, and Sir Charles, who respected his opinion, was sorely shaken. He put no trust in Acherley, whose debts and difficulties were known, and Ovington was not there to reassure him. He valued the good opinion of his world, and what, he reflected, if the Squire were right? What if in going into this scheme he had made a mistake? The picture that Griffin had drawn of town and country pointing the finger at him rose like a nightmare before him, and would, he knew, accompany him home and darken his dinner-table. And Ovington? Ovington was doubtless a clever man and, as a banker, well versed in these enterprises. But Fauntleroy – Fauntleroy, with whose name the world had rung these twelve months past, he, too, had been clever and enterprising and plausible. Yet what a fate had been his, and what losses had befallen all who had trusted him, all who had been involved with him!

Sir Charles went home an unhappy man. He wished that Griffin had not warned him, or that he had warned him earlier. Of what use was a warning when his lot was cast and he was the head and front of the matter, President of the Company, Chairman of the Board?

Meanwhile the Squire stood on the steps of the Court House, cursing his man. The curricle was not there, Thomas was not there, it was growing dark, and a huge pile of clouds, looming above the roofs to westward, threatened tempest. The shopkeepers were putting up their shutters, the packmen binding up their bundles, stall-keepers hurrying away their trestles, and the Market Place, strewn with the débris of the day, showed dreary by the failing light. In the High Street there was still some traffic, and in the lanes and alleys around candles began to shine out. A one-legged sailor, caterwauling on a crazy fiddle, had gathered a small crowd before one of the taverns.

'Hang the man! Where is he?' the Squire muttered, looking about him with a disgusted eye, and wishing himself at home. 'Where is the rogue?'

Then Thomas, driving slowly and orating to a couple of men who walked beside the carriage, came into view. The Squire roared at him, and Thomas, taken by surprise, whipped up his horses so sharply that he knocked over a hawker's basket. Still storming at him the old man climbed to his seat and took the reins. He drove round the corner into Bride Hill, and stopped at Purslow's door.

The draper was at the carriage wheel before it stopped. He had the bag in his hand, but he did not at once hand it up. 'Excuse me, excuse the liberty, sir,' he said, lowering his voice and glancing at Thomas, 'but it's a large sum, sir, and it's late. Hadn't I better keep it till morning?'

The Squire snapped at him. 'Morning? Rubbish, man! Put it in.' He made room for the bag at his feet.

But the draper still hesitated. 'It will be dark in ten minutes, sir, and the road – it's true, no one has been stopped of late, but—'

'I've never been stopped in my life,' the Squire rejoined. 'Put it in, man, and don't be a fool. Who's to stop me between here and Garth?'

Purslow muttered something about the safe side, but he complied. He handed in the bag, which gave out a clinking sound as it settled itself beside the Squire's feet. The old man nodded his thanks and started his horses.

He drove down Bride Hill, and by the Stalls, where the taps were humming, and the inns were doing a great business. Passing one or two belated carts, he turned to the right and descended to the bridge, the old houses with their galleries and gables looming above him as for three centuries they had loomed above the traveller by the Welsh road. He rumbled over the bridge, the wide river flowing dark below him. Then he trotted sharply up Westwell, passing by the inns that in old days had served those who arrived after the gates were closed.

Now he faced the open country and the wet west wind, and he settled himself down in his seat and shook up his horses. As he did so his foot touched the bag, and again the gold gave out a clinking sound.

Chapter Thirteen

The Squire, if the truth be told, had not derived much satisfaction from his visit to the bank. He had left it with an uneasy feeling that the step he had taken had not produced the intended effect. Ovington had accepted the loss of his custom, not with indifference, but with dignity, and in a manner which left the old man little upon which to plume himself. The withdrawal of his custom wore in the retrospect too much of the look of spite, and he came near to regretting it, as he drove along.

Had he been present at an interview which took place after he had retired, he might have been better pleased. The banker had not been many minutes in the parlour, chewing the cud of the affair, before he was interrupted by his cashier. In this there was nothing unusual; routine required Rodd's presence in the parlour several times in the day. But his manner on the present occasion, and the way in which he closed the door, prepared Ovington for something new, and 'What is it, Rodd?' he asked, leaning back in his chair, and disposing himself to listen.

'Can I have a word with you, sir?'

'Certainly.' The banker's face told nothing. Rodd's was that of a man who had made up his mind to a plunge. 'What is it?'

'I have been wishing to speak for some time, sir,' Rodd faltered. 'This—' Ovington understood at once that he referred to the Squire's matter – 'I don't like it, sir, and I have been with you ten years, and I feel – I ought to speak.'

Ovington shrugged his shoulders. 'I don't like it either,' he said. 'But it is of less importance than you think, Rodd. I know why Mr Griffin did it. And we are not now where we were. The withdrawal of a few hundreds or the loss of a customer—' again he shrugged his shoulders.

'No,' Rodd said gravely. 'If nothing more follows, sir.'

'Why should anything follow? I know his reasons.'

'But the town doesn't. And if it gets about, sir?'

'It won't do us much damage. We've lost customers before, yet always gained more than we lost. But there, Rodd, that is not what you came in to say. What is it?' He felt, indeed, more surprise than he showed. Rodd was a model cashier, performing his duties in a precise, plodding fashion that had often excited Arthur's ridicule, but hitherto he had never ventured an opinion on the policy of the bank, nor betrayed the least curiosity respecting its secrets. 'What is it?' Ovington repeated. 'What has frightened you, man?'

'We've a lot of notes out, sir!'

The banker looked thoughtfully at the glasses he held in his hand. 'True,' he said. 'Quite true. But trade is brisk, and the demand for credit is large. We must meet the demand, Rodd, as far as we can – with safety. That's our business.'

'And we've a lot of money out – that could not be got in in a hurry, sir.'

'Yes,' the banker admitted, 'but that is our business, too. If we did not put our money out we might close the bank tomorrow. That much of the money cannot be got in at a minute's notice is a thing we cannot avoid.'

The perspiration stood on Rodd's forehead, but he persisted. 'If it were all on bills, sir, I would not say a word. But there is a lot on overdraft.'

'Well secured.'

'While things are up. But if things went down, sir? There's Wolley's account. I suspect that the last bills we discounted for him were accommodation. Indeed, I am sure of it. And his overdraft is heavy.'

'We hold the lease of his mill.'

'But you don't want to run the mill!' Rodd replied, putting his finger on the weak point.

The banker reflected. 'That's the worst account we have. The worst, isn't it?'

'Mr Acherley's, sir.'

'Well, yes. There might be a sounder account than that. But what is it?' He looked directly at the other. 'I want to know what has opened your mouth? Have you heard anything? What makes you think that things are going down?'

'Mr Griffin—'

'No.' The banker shook his head. 'That won't do, Rodd. You had this in your mind before he came in. You are pat with Wolley and Mr Acherley; bad accounts both, as all banks have bad accounts here and there. But it's true – we've been giving our customers rope, and they have bought things that may fall. Still, they've made money, a good deal of money, and we've kept a fair margin and obliged them at the same time. All legitimate business. There must be something in your mind besides this, I'm sure. What is it, lad?'

The cashier turned a dull red, but before he could answer the door behind him opened. Arthur came in. He looked at the banker, and from him to Rodd, and his suspicions were aroused. 'It's four o'clock, sir,' he said, and looked again at Rodd as if to ask what he was doing there.

But Rodd held his ground, and the banker explained.

'Rodd is a little alarmed for us,' he said – and it was difficult to be sure whether he spoke in jest or in earnest. 'He thinks we're going too fast. Putting our hand out too far. He mentions Wolley's account, and Acherley's.'

'I was speaking generally,' Rodd muttered. He looked sullen.

Arthur shrugged his shoulders. 'I stand corrected,' he said. 'I didn't know that Rodd went beyond his ledgers.'

'Oh, he's quite right to speak his mind. We are all in the same boat – though we do not all steer.'

'Well, I'm glad of that, sir.'

'Still,' mildly, 'it is a good thing to have an opinion.'

'If it be worth anything.'

'If opinions are going—' Betty had opened the door behind the banker's chair, and was standing on the threshold – 'wouldn't you like to have mine, Father?'

'To be sure,' Arthur jeered. 'Why not, indeed? Let us have it. Why not have everybody's? And send for the cook, sir, and the two clerks – to advise us?'

Betty dropped a curtsy. 'Thank you, I am flattered.'

'Betty, you've no business here,' her father said. 'You mustn't stop unless you can keep your opinions to yourself.'

'But what has happened?' she asked, looking round in wonder.

'Mr Griffin has withdrawn his account.'

'And Rodd,' Arthur added, with more heat than the occasion seemed to demand, 'thinks that we had better put up the shutters!'

'No, no,' the banker said. 'We must do him justice. He thinks that we are going a little too far, that's all. And that the loss of Mr Griffin's account is a danger signal. That's what you mean, man, isn't it?'

Rodd nodded, his face stubborn. He stood alone, divided from the other three by the table, for Arthur had passed round it and placed himself at Ovington's elbow.

'His view,' the banker continued, polishing his glasses with his handkerchief and looking thoughtfully at them, 'is that if there came a check in trade and a fall in values, the bank might find its resources strained – I'll put it that way.'

Arthur sneered. 'Singular wisdom! But a fall – a universal fall at any rate – what sign is there of it?' He was provoked by the banker's way of taking it. Ovington seemed to be attaching absurd weight to Rodd's suggestion. 'None!' contemptuously. 'Not a jot.'

'There's been a universal rise,' Rodd muttered.

'In a moment? Without warning?'

'No, but—'

'But fiddlesticks!' Arthur retorted. Of late it seemed as if his good humour had deserted him, and this was not the first sign he had given of an uncertain temper. Still, the phase was so new that two of those present looked curiously at him, and his consciousness of this added to his irritation.

'Rodd's no better than an old woman,' he continued. 'Five per cent and a mortgage in a strong box is about his measure. If you are going to listen to every croaker who is frightened by a shadow, you may as well close the bank, sir, and put the money out on Rodd's terms!'

'Still Rodd means us well,' the banker said thoughtfully, 'and a little caution is never out of place in a bank. What I want to get from him is – has he anything definite to tell us? Wolley? Have you heard anything about Wolley, Rodd?'

'No, sir.'

'Then what is it? What is it, man?'

But Rodd, brought to bay, only looked more stubborn. 'It's no more than I've told you, sir,' he muttered, 'it's just a feeling. Things must come down some day.'

'Oh, damn!' Arthur exclaimed, out of patience, and thinking that the banker was making altogether too much of it – and of Rodd. 'If he were a weather-glass—'

'Or a woman!' interjected Betty, who was observing all with bright inscrutable eyes.

'But as he isn't either,' Arthur continued impatiently, 'I fail to see why you make so much of it! Of course, things will come down some day, but if he thinks that with your experience you are blind to anything he can see, he's no better than a fool! Because my uncle, for reasons which you understand, sir, has drawn out four hundred pounds, he thinks every customer is going to leave us, and Ovington's must put up the shutters! The truth is, he knows nothing about it, and if he wishes to damage the bank he is going the right way to do it!'

'Would you like my opinion, Father?' Betty asked.

'No,' sharply, 'certainly not, child. Where's Clement?'

'Well, I'm afraid he's away.'

'Again? Then he is behaving very badly!'

'That was the opinion I was going to give,' the girl answered. 'That some were behaving better than others.'

'If,' Arthur cried, 'you mean me—'

'There, enough,' said her father. 'Be silent, Betty. You've no business to be here.'

'Still, people should behave themselves,' she replied, her eyes sparkling.

Arthur had his answer ready, but Ovington forestalled him. 'Very good, Rodd,' he said. 'A word on the side of caution is never out of place in a bank. But I am not blind, and all that you have told me is in my mind. You can go now.'

It was a dismissal, and Rodd took it as such, and felt, as he had never felt before, his subordinate position. Why he did so, and why, as he withdrew under Arthur's eye, he resented the situation, he best knew. But it is possible that two of the others had some inkling of the cause.

When he had gone, 'There's an old woman for you!' Arthur exclaimed. 'I wonder that you had the patience to listen to him, sir.'

But Ovington shook his head. 'I listened because there are times when a straw shows which way the wind blows.'

'But you don't think that there is anything in what he said?'

'I shall remember what he said. The time may be coming to take in sail – to keep a good look-out, lad, and be careful. You have been with us – how long? Two years. Ay, but years of expansion, of rising prices, of growing trade. But I have seen other times – other times.' He shook his head.

'Still, there is no sign of a change, sir?'

'You've seen one today. What is in Rodd's head may be in others, and what is in men's heads soon reflects itself in their conduct.'

It was the first word, the first hint, the first presage of evil; of a fall, of bad weather, of a storm, distant as yet, and seen even by the clearest eyes only as a cloud no bigger than a man's hand. But the word had been spoken. The hint had been given. And to Arthur, who had paid a high price for prosperity – how high only he could say – the presage seemed an outrage. The idea that the prosperity he had bought was not a certainty, that the craft on which he had embarked his fortune was, like other ships, at the mercy of storm and tempest, that like other ships it might founder with all its freight, was entirely new to him. So new that for a moment his face betrayed the impression it made. Then he told himself that the thing was incredible, that he started at shadows, and his natural confidence rebounded. 'Oh, damn Rodd!' he cried – and he said it with all his heart. 'He's a croaker by nature!'

'Still, we won't damn him,' the banker answered mildly. 'On the contrary, we will profit by his warning. But go now. I have a letter to write. And do you go, too, Betty, and make tea for us.'

He turned to his papers, and Arthur, after a moment's hesitation, followed Betty into the house. In the hall, 'Betty, what is the matter?' he asked. And when the girl took no notice, but went on with her chin in the air as if he had not spoken, he seized her arm. 'Come,' he said, 'I am not going to have this. What is it?'

'What should it be! I don't know what you mean,' she retorted.

'Oh yes, you do. What took you – to back up that ass in the bank just now?'

Then Betty astonished him. 'I didn't think he wanted any backing,' she said, her eyes bright. 'He seemed to me to talk sense, and someone else nonsense.'

'But you're not—'

'A partner in Ovington's? No, Mr Bourdillon, I am not – thank heaven! And so my head is not turned, and I can keep my temper and mind my manners.'

'Oh, it's Mr Bourdillon now, is it?'

'Yes – if you are going to behave to my friends as you did this afternoon.'

'Your friends!' scornfully. 'You include Rodd, do you? Rodd, Betty?'

'Yes, I do, and I am not too proud to do so. Nor too proud to be angry when I see a man ten years younger than he is slap him in the face! I am not so spoiled that I think everyone beneath me!'

'So it's Rodd now?'

'It's as much Rodd now,' her cheeks hot, her eyes sparkling, 'as it was anyone else before! Just as much and just as little. You flatter yourself, sir!'

'But, Betty,' in a coaxing tone, 'little spitfire that you are, can't you guess why I was short with Rodd? Can't you guess why I don't particularly love him? But you do guess. Rodd is what he is – nothing! But when he lifts his eyes above him – when he dares to make eyes at you – I am not going to be silent.'

'Now you are impertinent!' she answered. 'As impertinent as you were mean before. Yes, mean, mean! When you knew he could not answer you! Mean!'

And without waiting for a reply she ran up the stairs.

He went to one of the windows of the dining-room and looked across Bride Hill and along the High Street, full at that hour of market people. But he did not see them, his thoughts were busy with what had happened. He could not believe that Betty had any feeling for Rodd. The man was dull, commonplace, a plodder, and well over thirty. No, the idea was preposterous. And it was still more absurd to suppose that if he, Arthur, threw the handkerchief – or even fluttered it in her direction, for dear little thing as she was, he had not quite made up his mind – she would hesitate to accept him, or would let any thought of Rodd weigh with her.

True he believed that she had captivated Rodd, for he had noticed the cashier's eyes following her on the rare occasions when she had shown herself in the bank. But that was another matter, and that the clerk's feeling was returned, or that Betty thought of him, this he could not believe. It would be too ridiculous.

Still, he would let her temper cool, he would not stay to tea. Instead, he would by and by ride his new horse out to the Cottage. He had not been home for the week-end. He had left Mrs Bourdillon to come to herself and recover her good humour in solitude. Now he would make it up with her, and while he was there he might as well get a peep at Josina – it was a long time since he had seen her. If Betty chose to adopt this unpleasant line, why, she could not blame him if he amused himself.

Chapter Fourteen

For a time after the Squire had driven away, Clement had sat his horse, and stared after him, and in his rage had wished him dead. He had prepared himself for opposition, he had looked to be repulsed – he had expected nothing else. But in the scene which his fancy had pictured, his part had been one of dignity; he had owned his aspirations like a man, he had admitted his insufficiency with modesty, he had pleaded the power of love with eloquence, he had won even from the Squire a meed of unwilling approbation.

But the scene, as played, had run on other lines. The old man had crushed him. He had sworn at him, refused to listen to him, had insulted him, had treated him as no better than a shop-boy. And all this had cut to the quick. For Clement, born after Ovington had risen from the ranks, had his pride and his self-respect, and humiliated, he cursed with all his soul the prejudice and hide-bound narrowness of the Squire and his whole caste. For the time he was more than a radical, he was a republican. If by a gesture he could have swept away King and Commons, lords and justices, he would not have held his hand.

It took him some time to recover, and it was only when he found himself, he hardly knew how, upon the bridge at Garthmyle that he grew more cool. Even then he was not quite himself. He had vowed that he would not see Josina again until he had claimed her from her father, but the Squire's treatment, he now felt, had absolved him from this, and the temptation to see her was great. He longed to pour out his mind to her, and to tell her how he had been insulted, how he had been treated. Perhaps, even, he must say farewell to her – he must give her up.

For he was not all hero, and the task before him seemed for the time too prodigious, the labour too little hopeful. The Hydra had so many heads, and roared so fearfully that for a moment Clement's courage sank before it – and his love. He felt that he must yield, that he must see Josina and tell her so. In any event she ought to know what had happened, and presently he put up his horse at the inn and made by a roundabout road for their meeting-place by the brook.

There was but a chance that she would visit it, and in the meantime he had to exercise what patience he might. His castles in the air had fallen and he had not the spirit to rebuild them. He sat gazing moodily on the rippling face of the water, or watched the pied wagtail jerking its tail on its stone; and he almost despaired. He had known the Squire to be formidable, he now knew him to be impossible. He looked down the stream to where Garth, lofty and fortress-like, raised its twisted chimneys above the trees, and he shook his fist at it. Remote and islanded on its knoll, rising amid ancestral trees, it stood for all that the Squire stood for – governance, privilege, tradition, the past – all the things he had not, all the things that mocked him.

He lingered there, savouring his melancholy, until the sun went down behind the hills, and then, attacked by the pangs of hunger, he made his way back to the village inn. Here he satisfied his appetite on such home-baked bread and yellow butter and nut-brown ale as are not in these degenerate times; and for well-nigh an hour he sat brooding in the sanded parlour surrounded by china cats and dogs – they too, would be of value nowadays. At length with a heavy heart – for what was he to do next? – he rode out of the yard, and crossing the bridge under the shadowy bulk of the squat church tower, he set his horse's head for home. It was nearly dark.

What was he to do next? He did not know, but as he rode through the gloom, the solemn hills falling back on either side and the dark plain widening before him, he took courage; he began to consider, with some return of hope, what lay before him, and how he must proceed – if he were not to give up. Clearly he must face the Squire, but it must be in the Squire's own house, where the Squire must hear him. The old man might insult him, rave at him, order him out, but before he was put out he would speak and ask for Josina, though the roof fell. There should be no further mistake. And he would let the Squire know, if it came to that, that he was a man, as good as other men. By heaven he would!

He was not all hero. But there were some heroic parts about him, and he determined that the very next morning he would ride out and would beard the Hydra in its den, be its heads ever so many. He would win his lady-love or perish!

By this time he was half-way home. The market traffic on the road had ceased, the moon had not yet risen, the night lay quiet about him. Presently as he crossed a wet, rushy flat, one of the loneliest parts of the way, he saw the lights of a vehicle coming towards him. The road at that point had not been long enclosed, and a broad strip of common still survived on either hand, so that moving on this his horse's hoofs made no sound save a soft plop–plop where the ground was wettest. He could hear, therefore, while still afar off, the tramp of a pair of horses driven at a trot, and it occurred to him that this might be the Squire returning late. If he could have avoided the meeting he would have done so, though it was unlikely that the Squire would recognise him in the dark. But to turn aside would be foolish. 'Hang me if I am going to be afraid of him!' he thought. And he touched up his horse with his heel.

Then an odd thing happened. While the carriage was still fifty yards from him, one of the lights went out. His eyes missed it, but his brain had barely taken in the fact when the second vanished also, as if the vehicle had sunk into the ground. At the same moment a cry reached his ears, followed by a clatter of hoofs on the road as if the horses were being sharply pulled up.

Clement took his horse by the head and bent forward, striving to make out what was passing. A dull sound, as of a heavy body striking the road reached him, followed by a silence that seemed ominous. Even the wind appeared to have hushed its whisper through the rushes.

'Hallo!' he shouted. 'What is it? Is anything the matter?' He urged his horse forward.

His cry was lost in the crack of a whip, he heard the horses break away, and without further warning they came down upon him at a gallop, the carriage bounding wildly behind them. He had just time to thrust his nag to the side, and they were on him and past him, and whirling down the road – a mere shadow, but as perilous and almost as noisy as a thunderbolt. There was no doubt now that an accident had happened, but before he could give help he had to master his horse, which had wheeled about; and so a few seconds elapsed before he reached the scene – reached it with his heart in his mouth, for who could say with what emergency he might not have to deal?

Certainly with a tragedy, for the first thing that he made out was the form of a man stooping over another who lay in the road. Clement drew a breath of relief as he slipped from his saddle – he would not have to meet the crisis alone. But as his foot touched the ground, he saw the stooping man raise his hand with something in it, and he knew instinctively that it was raised not to help but to strike.

He shouted, and the blow hung in the air. The man, taken by surprise, straightened himself and turned. He saw Clement at his elbow. He hesitated, then, with an oath, he aimed his blow at the newcomer.

Clement parried it, rather by instinct than with intention, and so weakly, that the other's weapon beat down his guard and cut his cheek-bone. He staggered back and the villain raised his cudgel again. Had the second blow fallen where it was aimed, it would have finished the business. But Clement, aware now that he fought for his life, sprang within the other's guard, and before the cudgel alighted, gripped him by the neckcloth. The man gave ground, tripped backwards over the body that lay behind him, and in a twinkling the two were rolling together on the road, Clement striving to beat in the ruffian's face with the butt-end of his whip, while the man tried vainly to shorten his weapon and use it to purpose.

It was a desperate struggle, in the mire, in the darkness – a struggle for life carried on in a silence that was broken only by the combatants' breathing and a rare oath. Twice each rolled over the other, and once Clement, having the upper hand, became aware that the fight had its spectator. He had a glimpse of a ghastly face, one side of which had been mangled by a murderous blow, a face that glared at them with its remaining eye. He guessed that the man lying in the road had raised himself on an elbow, and he heard a gasping 'At him, lad! Well done, lad!' then in a turn of the struggle he lost the vision. His opponent had him by the throat, he was undermost again – and desperate. His one thought now was to kill – to kill the brute-beast whose teeth threatened his cheek, whose hot breath burned his face, whose hands gripped his throat. He struck again and again, and eventually, supple and young, and perhaps the stronger, he freed himself and staggered to his feet, raising his whip to strike.

But the same thing happened to him which had happened to his assailant. As he stepped back to give power to the blow, he fell over the third man. He came down heavily, and for a moment he was at the other's mercy. Fortunately the rascal's courage was at an end. He got to his feet, but instead of pursuing his advantage, he snatched up something that lay on the ground, and sped away down the road, as quickly as his legs could carry him.

Clement recovered his feet, but more slowly, for the fall had shaken him. Still, his desire for vengeance was hot, and he set off in pursuit. The man had a good start, however, and presently, leaving the road and leaping the ditch, made off across the open common. To follow farther promised little, for in a few seconds his figure, already shadowy, melted into the darkness of the fields. Clement gave up the chase, and turned back, panting and out of breath.

He did not feel his wound, much less did he feel the misgivings which had beset him when he came upon the scene. Instead, he experienced a new and thrilling elation. He had measured his strength against an enemy, he had faced death in fight, he felt himself equal to any and every event. Even when, stooping over the prostrate figure, he saw the bleeding face turned up to the sky it did not daunt him, nor the darkness, nor the loneliness. The injured man seemed to be aware of his presence for he made an attempt to rise; but he failed, and would have fallen back on the road if Clement, dropping on one knee, had not sustained his head on the other. It was the Squire. So much he saw; but it was a Squire past not only scolding but speech, whom he held in his arms. To all Clement's questions he made no answer. It was much if he still breathed.

Clement glanced about him, and his confidence began to leave him. What was he to do? He could not go for help, leaving the old man lying in the road; yet it was impossible to do much in the dark, either to ascertain the extent of the Squire's hurt, or to use means to stanch it. The moon had not yet risen, the plain stretched black about them, no sound except the melancholy whisper of the wind in the rushes came to his ear. There was no house near and it was growing late. No one might pass for hours.

Fortunately when he reached this stage he remembered that he had his tinder box and matches in his pocket, and he fumbled for them and got them out with his disengaged hand. But to strike a light and catch it in the huddled posture in which he knelt was difficult, and it was only after a score of attempts that the match caught the flame. Even so, the light it gave was faint, but it revealed the Squire's face, and Clement saw, with a shudder, that the left eye and temple were terribly battered. But he saw, too, that the old man was conscious, for he uttered a groan, and peered with his uninjured eye at the face that bent over him. 'Good lad!' he muttered, 'good lad!' and he added broken words which conveyed to Clement's mind that it was his man who had attacked him. Then – his face was so turned that it was within a few inches of Clement's shoulder – 'You're bloody, lad,' he muttered. 'He's spoiled your coat, the d—d rascal!'

With that he seemed to slip back into unconsciousness and the light went out. It left Clement in a strait to know what he ought to do, or rather what he could do. Help he must get, if he would save the Squire's life, but his horse was gone, and to walk away for help, leaving the old man lying in the mud of the way seemed inhuman. He must at least carry him to the side of the road.

The task was no light one, for the Squire was tall, though not stout; and before Clement stooped to it he cast a last look round. But silence still wrapped all, and he was gathering his strength to lift the dead weight, when a sound caught his ear, and he raised himself. A moment, and he caught the far-off beat of hoofs on the turf. Someone was coming, approaching him from the direction of Aldersbury. He shouted, shouted his loudest and waited. Yes, he was not mistaken. The soft plop-plop of hoofs grew louder, two forms loomed out of the darkness, a horse shied, a man swore.

'Here!' Clement cried. 'Here! Take care! There's a man in the road.'

'Where?' Then, 'Confound you, you nearly had me down! Are you hurt?'

'No, but—'

'I've got your horse. I met him a couple of miles this side of the town. What has—'

Clement broke in. 'There's bad work here!' he cried, his voice shaky. Now that help was at hand and the peril was over, he began to feel what he had gone through. 'For God's sake get down and help me. Your uncle's man has robbed him and, I fear, murdered him.'

'The Squire?'

'Yes, yes. He's lying here, half dead. We must get him to the side of the road at once.'

Arthur slipped from his saddle, and holding the reins of the two horses, approached the group as nearly as the frightened beasts would let him. 'Quiet, fools!' he cried angrily. And then, 'Good heavens!' in a whisper, as he peered awe-stricken at the injured man. 'Is he dead?'

'No, but he's terribly mauled. And we must get help. Help, man, and quickly, if it is to be of any use. Shall I go?'

'No, no, I'll go,' Arthur answered, recoiling. What he had seen had given him no desire to take Clement's place. 'Garthmyle is the nearer, and I shall not be long. I'll tie up your horse – that'll be best.'

There was an old thorn-tree standing solitary in the waste not many yards away: a tree destined to be pointed out for years to come as marking the spot where the old Squire was robbed. Arthur tied Clement's horse to this, then together they lifted the old man and carried him to the side of the road. The moment that this was done, Arthur sprang on his horse and started off. 'Back soon,' he shouted.

Clement had not seen his way to object, but it was with a heavy heart that he resigned himself to another period of painful waiting. He was cold, his face smarted, and at any moment the old man might die on his hands. Meantime he could do nothing but wait. Or yes, he could do something; chilled as he was, he took off his coat, and rolling it up, he slipped it under the insensible head.

Little had he thought that morning that he would ever pity the Squire. But he did. The man who had driven away from him, hard, aggressive, indomitable, asking no man's help and meeting all men's eyes with the gaze of a master, now lay at his feet, crushed and broken; lay with his head on the coat of the man he had despised, dependent on him for the poor service that still might avail him. Clement felt the pathos of it, and the pity. And his heart was sore for Josina. How would she meet, how bear the shock that a short hour must inflict on her?

He was thinking of her, when, long before he had dared to expect relief, he heard a sound that resolved itself into the rattle of wheels. Yes, there was a carriage coming along the road.

Arthur had been fortunate. He had come upon the Squire's horses, which had been brought to a stand with the near wheels of the curricle wedged in the ditch. He had found them greedily feeding, and he had let his own nag go, and had captured the runaways. He had drawn the carriage out of the ditch, and here he was.

'Thank God!' Clement cried. 'I think that he is still alive.'

'And we've got to lift him in,' said Arthur, more practical. 'He's a big weight.'

It was not an easy task. But they tied up the horses to the thorn-tree, and lifting the old man between them, they carried him with what care they might to the carriage, raised him, heavy and helpless as he was, to the step, and then, while one maintained him there, the other climbed in and lifted him to the front seat. Clement got up behind and supported his shoulders and head, while Arthur, first tying the saddle-horse behind the carriage, released the pair, and with the reins in his hands scrambled to his place.

The thing was done and cleverly done, and they set off. But they dared not travel at more than a walk, and never had the three miles to Garthmyle seemed so long or so tedious.

They were both anxious and both excited. But while in Clement's mind pity, a sense of the tragedy before him, and thought for Josina contended with an honest pride in what he had done, the other, as they drove along, was already calculating chances and busy with contingencies. The Squire's death – if the Squire died – would work a great change, an immense change. Things which had yesterday been too doubtful and too distant to deserve much thought would be within reach, would be his for the asking. And he was the more inclined to consider this because Betty – dear little creature as she was – had shown a spirit that day that was not to his liking. Whereas Josina, mild and docile – it might be that after all she would suit him better. And Garth – Garth with its wide acres and its rich rent-roll would be hers; Garth that would give any man a position to be envied. Its charms, while uncertain and dependent on the whim and caprice of an arbitrary old man, had not fixed him, for to attain to them he must give up other things, equally to his mind. But now the case was or might be altered. He must wait and watch events, and keep an open mind. If the Squire died—

A word or two passed between the couple, but for the most part they were silent. Once and again the Squire moaned, and proved that he still lived. At last, where the road to Garth branched off, at the entrance to the village, they saw a light in front, and old Fewtrell carrying a lanthorn met them. The Squire's absence had alarmed the house, and he had come thus far in quest of news.

'Oh, Lord, ha' mercy! Lord, ha' mercy!' the old fellow quavered as he lifted his lanthorn and the light disclosed the group in the carriage, and his master's huddled form and ghastly visage. 'Miss Jos said 'twas so! Said as summat had happened him! Beside herself, she be! She've been down at the gate this half-hour waiting on him!'

'Don't let her see him,' Clement cried. 'Go, man, and send her back.'

But, 'That's no good,' Arthur objected, with more sense but less feeling. 'She must see him. This is women's work, we can do nothing. Let Fewtrell take your place and do you go for the doctor. You know where he lives, and you'll go twice as quick as he will, and there's no more that you can do here. Take your horse.'

Clement was unwilling to go, unwilling to have no further part in the matter. But he could not refuse. Things were as they were; in spite of all that he had done and suffered, he had no place there, no standing in the house, no right beside his mistress or call to think for her. He was a stranger, an outsider, and when he had fetched the doctor, there would, as Arthur had said, be nothing more that he could do.

Nothing more, though as he rode over the bridge and trotted through the village his heart was bursting with pity for her whom he could not comfort, could not see; from whose side in her troubles and her self-arraignment – for he knew that she would reproach herself – he must be banished. It was hard.

Chapter Fifteen

The Squire was late.

A hundred years ago night fell more seriously. It closed in on a countryside less peopled, on houses and hamlets more distant, and divided by greater risks of flood and field. The dark hours were longer and haunted by graver apprehensions. Every journey had to be made on horses or behind them, roads were rough and miry, fords were plenty, bridges scarce. Sturdy rogues abounded, and to double every peril it was still the habit of most men to drink deep. Few returned sober from market, fewer from fair or merrymaking.

For many, therefore, the coming of night meant the coming of fear. Children, watching the great moths fluttering against the low ceiling, or round the rush-light that cast such gloomy shadows, thought that their elders would never come up to bed. Lone women, quaking in remote dwellings, remembered the gibbet where the treacherous inn-keeper still mouldered, and fancied every creak the coming of a man in a crape mask. Thousands suffered nightly because the good-man lingered abroad, or the son was absent, and in many a window the light was set at dusk to guide the master by the pool. On market evenings women stole trembling down the lane that the sound of wheels might the sooner dispel their fears.

At Garth it was youth not age that first caught the alarm. For Josina's conscience troubled her, and before even Miss Peacock, most fidgety of old maids, had seen cause to fear, the girl was standing in the darkness before the door, listening and uneasy. The Squire was seldom late; it could not be that Clement had met him and there had been a – but no, Clement was not the man to raise his hand against his elder – the thought was dismissed as soon as formed. Yet why did not her father come? Lights began to shine through the casements, she saw the candles brought into the dining-room, the darkness thickened about her, only the trunks of the nearer beeches gave back a gleam. And she felt that if anything had happened to him she could never forgive herself. Shivering, less with cold than with apprehension, she peered down the drive. He had been later than this before, but then her conscience had been quiet, she had not deceived him, she had had nothing with which to reproach herself on his account.

Presently, 'Josina, what are you doing there?' Miss Peacock cried. She had come to the open door and discovered the girl. She began to scold. 'Come in this minute, child! What are you starving the house for, standing there?'

But Josina did not budge. 'He is very late,' she said.

'Late? What nonsense! And what if he is late? What good can you do, standing out there? I declare one might suppose your father was one of those skimble-skambles that can't pass a tavern door, to hear you talk! And Thomas with him! Come in at once when I tell you! As if I should not be the first to cry out if anything were wrong. Late, indeed – why, goodness gracious, I declare it's nearly eight. What can have become of him, child? And Calamy and those good-for-nothing girls warming their knees at the fire, and no more caring if their master is in the river than – Josina, do you hear? Do you know that your father is still out? Calamy!' ringing a hand-bell that stood on the table in the hall, 'Calamy! Are you all asleep? Don't you know that your master is not in, and it is nearly eight?'

Calamy was the butler. A tall, lanthorn-jawed man, he would have looked lugubrious in the King's scarlet, which he had once worn; in his professional black, or in his shirt sleeves, cleaning plate, he was melancholy itself. And his modes and manners were at least as mournful as his aspect – no man so sure as 'Old Calamity' to see the dark side of things or to put it before others. It was whispered that he had been a Dissenter, and why the Squire, who hated a ranter as he hated the devil, had ever engaged him, much less kept him, was a puzzle to Garthmyle. That he had been his son's servant and had been with the boy when he died, might have seemed a sufficient reason, had the Squire been other than he was. But no one supposed that such a thing weighed with the old man – he was of too hard a grain. Yet at Garth, Calamy had lived for a score of years, and been suffered with a patience which might have stood to the credit of more reasonable men.

'Nearly eight!' Miss Peacock flung at him, and repeated her statement.

'We've put the dinner back, ma'am.'

'Put the dinner back! And that's all you think of, when at any minute your master – oh, dear, dear, what can have happened to him?'

'Well, it's a dark night, ma'am, to be sure.'

'Gracious goodness, can't I see that? If Thomas weren't with him—'

The butler shook his head. 'Under notice, ma'am,' he said. 'I think the worst of Thomas. On a dark night, with Thomas—'

Miss Peacock gasped.

'I should say my prayers, ma'am,' the butler murmured softly.

Miss Peacock stared, aghast. 'Under notice?' she cried. 'Well, of all the – 'deed, and I wish you were all under notice, if that is the best you've got to say.'

'Hadn't you better,' said Josina from the darkness outside, 'send Fewtrell to meet him with a lanthorn?'

'And get my nose bitten off when your father comes home! La, bless me, I don't know what to do! And no one else to do a thing!'

'Send him, Calamy,' said Josina.

Calamy retired. Miss Peacock looked out, a shawl about her head. 'Jos! Where are you?' she cried. 'Come in at once, girl. Do you think I am going to be left alone, and the door open? Jos! Jos!'

But Josina was gone, groping her way down the drive. When Fewtrell followed with his lanthorn he came on her sitting on the bridge, and he got a rare start, thinking it was a ghost. 'Lord A'mighty!' he cried as the light fell on her pale face. 'Aren't you afraid to sit there by yourself, miss?'

But Josina was not afraid, and after a word or two he shambled away, the lanthorn swinging in his hand. The girl watched the light go bobbing along as far as the highway fifty yards on, saw it travel to the left along the road, lost it for some moments, then marked it again, a faint blur of light, moving towards the village.

Presently it vanished and she was left alone with her fears. She strained her ears to catch the first sound of wheels. The stream murmured beneath her, a sick sheep coughed, the breeze whispered in the hedges, the cry of an owl, thrice repeated, sank into silence. But that was all, and in the presence of the silent world about her, of the all-enveloping night, of the solemn stars shining as they had shone from eternity, the girl knew herself infinitely helpless, without remedy against the stroke of impending fate.

She recognised that lighted rooms and glowing fires and the indoor life did but deceive; that they did but blind the mind to the immensity of things, to the real issues, to life and death and eternity. Anguished, she owned that a good conscience was the only refuge, and that she had it not. She had deceived her father, and it would be her fate to endure a lasting remorse. At last, her eyes opened, she fancied that she detected behind the mask a father's face. But too late, for the bridge which he had crossed innumerable times, the drive, rough and rutted, yet the harbinger of home, which he had climbed from boyhood to age, the threshold which he had trodden so often as master – they would know him no more. At the thought she broke down and wept, feeling all its poignancy, all its pitifulness, and finding for the moment no support in Clement, no recompense in a love which deceit and secrecy had tainted.

Doubtless she would not have taken things so hardly had she not been overwrought; and, as it was, the first sound that reached her from the Garthmyle road brought her to her feet. A light showed, moving from that direction, travelling slowly through the darkness. It vanished, and she held her breath. It came into view again, and she groped her way forward until she stood in the road. The light was close at hand now, though viewed from the front it moved so little that her worst forebodings were confirmed. But now, now that she saw her fears justified, the woman's fortitude, that in enduring is so much greater than man's, came to her aid, and it was with a calmness that surprised herself that she awaited the slow procession, discerned by the lanthorn-light her father's huddled form, and in a trembling voice asked if he still lived.

'Yes, yes!' Arthur cried, and hastened to reassure her. 'He will do yet, but he is hurt. Go back, Jos, and get his bed ready, and hot water, and some linen. The doctor will be here in a minute.'

His voice, firm and collected, struck the right note, and the girl answered to it bravely. She made no lamentation, shed no tears – there would be time for tears later – but gathering up her skirts she sped up the drive, and before the carriage had passed the bridge she had given the alarm in the house. There, in a moment, all was confusion. Miss Peacock, whatever fears she had expressed, was ill prepared for the fact, and it was Josina, who, steadied by that half-hour of self-examination, stilled the outcry of the maids, gave the needful orders, and seconded Calamy in carrying them out, had candles placed on the stairs, and with her own hand brought out a stout chair. When the carriage, the lanthorn gleaming sombrely on the shining trunks, drew slowly out of the darkness, she was there with lights and brandy. For her the worst was over. The scared faces of the women, their stifled cries and confused hovering, were but a background to her steady courage.

Still, even she yielded the first place to Arthur. Whatever pity or horror he had felt, he had had time to overcome, and to think both of the present and the future. And he rose to the occasion. He directed, arranged, and was himself the foremost worker. By the time Mr Farmer, the village doctor, arrived, he had done much which had to be done. The Squire had been carried upstairs, and lay, breathing stertorously, on his great four-post bed with the dingy drab curtains and the two watch-pockets at the head. And everything which could be of use had been brought to hand.

The doctor shut out the frightened maids and shut out Miss Peacock. But Arthur was only at the beginning of his resources. His nerve was good and he aided Farmer in his examination, while Jos, standing out of sight behind the curtain, calm but quivering in every nerve, handed to him or to Calamy what they needed. Even then, however, and while he was thus employed, Arthur found occasion to whisper a cheering word to the girl, to reassure her and give her hope. He forced her to take a glass of wine, and when Calamy, shaking his head, muttered that he had known a man to recover who had been worse hurt – but he was a strong young fellow – he damned the butler for an old fool, regardless of the fact that coming from Calamy this was a cheerful prognostic.

Presently he made her go downstairs. 'Nothing more can be done now,' said he. 'The doctor thinks well of him so far. He and I will stay with him tonight. You must save yourself, Jos. You will be needed tomorrow.'

He left the room with her, and as she would not go to bed he made her lie down on a couch, and covered her with a cloak. He had dropped the tone of patronage, almost of persiflage, which he had used to her of late, and he was kindness itself, behaving to her as a brother; so that she did not know how to be thankful enough for his presence, or for the relief from responsibility which it afforded.

Afterwards, looking back on that long, strange night, during which lights burned in the rooms till dawn, and odd meals were served at odd times, and stealthy feet trod the stairs, and scared faces peeped in only to be withdrawn – looking back on that strange night, and its happenings, it seemed to her that without him she could not have lived through the hours.

In truth there was not much sleep for anyone. The village doctor, who lived in top-boots, and went his rounds on horse-back, and by old-fashioned people was called the apothecary, could say nothing for certain; in the morning he might be able to do so. But in the morning – well, perhaps by night, when the patient came to himself, he might be able to form an opinion. To Arthur he was more candid. The eye was beyond hope – it could not be saved, and he feared that the other eye was injured; and there was serious concussion. He played with his fob seals and looked sagely over his gold-rimmed spectacles as he mouthed his phrases. Whether there was a fracture he could not say at present.

He had seen in a long life and a country practice many such cases, and was skilful in treating them. But – no active measures. 'Dr Quiet,' he said, 'Dr Quiet, the best of the faculty, my dear. If he does not always effect a cure, he makes no mistakes. We must leave it to him.'

So morning came, and passed, and noon; and still nothing more could be done. With the afternoon reaction set in, the house resigned itself to rest. Two or three stole away to sleep. Arthur dozed in an armchair. The clock struck with abnormal clearness, the cluck of a hen in the yard was heard in the attics. So the hours passed until sunset surprised a yawning house, and in the parlour they pressed one another to eat, and in the kitchen unusual luxuries were consumed with a ghoulish enjoyment, and no fear of the housekeeper. And still Farmer could add nothing. They must wait and hope. Dr Quiet! He praised him afresh in the same words.

Some hours earlier, and before Josina, after much scolding by Miss Peacock, had retired to her room to lie down, Arthur had told his story.

He did not go into details. 'It would only shock you, Jos,' he said. 'It was Thomas, of course, and I hope to heaven he'll swing for it. I suppose he knew that your father was carrying a large sum, and he must have struck him, possibly as he turned to say something, and then thrown him out. We must set the hue and cry after him, but Clement will see to that. It was lucky that he turned up when he did.'

She drew a sharp breath; this was the first she had heard of Clement. And in her surprise 'Clement?' she exclaimed. Then, covering her confusion as well as she could, 'Mr Ovington? Do you mean – he was there, Arthur?'

'By good luck just when he was wanted. Poor chap. I can tell you it knocked him fairly down. All the same, I don't know what might not have happened if he had not come up. I sent him for Farmer, and it saved time.'

'I did not know that he had been there,' she murmured, too self-conscious to ask further questions.

'Well, you wouldn't, of course. He'd been fishing, I fancy, and came along just when it made all the difference. I don't know what I should have done without him.'

'And Thomas? You are sure that it was Thomas? What became of him?'

'He made off across the fields. It was dark and useless to follow him – we had other things to think of, as you may imagine. Ten to one he has made for Manchester, but Clement will see to that. Oh, we'll have him! But there, I'll not tell you any more, Jos. You look ill as it is, and it will only spoil your sleep. Do you go upstairs and lie down, or you will never be able to go on.' And, Miss Peacock seconding his advice, Jos consented and went.

Arthur's manner had been kind, and Jos thought him kind. A brother could not have been more anxious to spare her unpleasant details. But, told as he had told it, the story left her under the impression that Clement's part had been secondary, and that if there were a person to whom she owed the preservation of her father's life, it was Arthur, and Arthur only. Which she was the more ready to believe, in view of the masterly way in which he had managed all at the house, had taken the upper hand in all, and saved her, and spared her.

Yet Arthur had been careful to state no facts which could be contradicted by evidence, should the whole come out – at an inquest, for instance. He had foreseen the possibility of that, and had been careful. Indeed, it was with that in his mind that he had – well, that he had not gone into details.

Chapter Sixteen

Clement had walked with the doctor to the door and had secured a last word with Arthur outside, but he had not ventured to enter the house, much less to ask for Josina. He knew how heavily the shock would fall on her, and his heart was wrung for her. But he knew also that the poignancy of her grief would be sharpened by remorse, and he felt that in the first outburst of self-reproach his presence would be the last she would welcome.

It was not a pleasant thought for a lover; but then how much worse, he reflected, would it have been for her, had she never made up her mind to confession. And in his own person how much better he now stood. He had saved the Squire's life, and had saved it in circumstances that must do him credit. He had run his risks, and been put to the test, and he had come manfully out of it; and he still felt that elation of spirit, that readiness to do and dare, to meet fresh ventures, which attends on a crisis successfully encountered.

He was not in a mood to be dashed by trifles therefore, or Arthur, when he came out to speak to him, would have dashed him, for Arthur was rather short with him. 'You can do nothing here,' he said. 'We are tumbling over one another. Get after that rascal. He has got away with four hundred in gold and we must recover it. Watkins at the Griffin may know where he'll make for.'

'He's in livery, isn't he?'

'Begad, so he is! I'd not thought of that! I'll have his place watched in case he steals back to change. But do you see Watkins.'

Clement took his dismissal meekly and went to Watkins. He soon learned all that the inn-keeper knew, which amounted to no more than a conviction that Thomas would make for Manchester. Watkins shook his head over the livery. The rascal was no fool; he'd have got rid of that. 'Oh, he's a clever chap, sir, and a gallus bad one,' he continued. 'He'd talk here that daring that he'd lift the hair on my head. But I never thought that he'd devil enough,' in a tone of admiration, 'to attack the Squire! Well, he'll swing this time, if he's taken! You're not in very good fettle yourself, sir. You know that your cheek's bleeding?'

'It's nothing. And you think he'll make for Manchester!'

'As sure as sure! He's done that this time, sir, as he never can be safe but in a crowd. And where'd he go but where he knows? He'll be in Manchester before tomorrow night, and it'll take you all your time, sir, finding him there! It's a mortal big place, I understand, and he'll have got rid of his livery, depend on it!'

'I'll find him,' Clement said. And he meant it. His blood was hot, he had tasted of adventure and he found it more to his liking than day-books and ledgers. And already he had made up his mind that it was his business to pursue Thomas. He was angered by the rascal's cowardly attack upon an old man, and were it only for that he would take him. But apart from that he saw that if he recovered the Squire's money it would be another point to his credit – if the Squire recovered. If the old man did not, well, still he would have done something. As he rode home, and passed the scene of the robbery, he laid his plans.

He would leave the search in that district to the Head Constable at Aldersbury. But he expected little from this. In those days if a man was robbed it was the man's own business and that of his friends to follow the thief and seize him if they could. In London the Bow Street Runners saw to it, and in one or two of the big cities there were police officers organised on similar lines. But in the country there were only parish constables, elderly men, often chosen because they were past work.

Clement knew, then, that he must rely on himself, and he tried to imagine what Thomas would do, and what route he would take if he made for Manchester. Not through Aldersbury, for there he would run the risk of recognition. Nor would he venture into either of the direct roads thence – through Congleton or by Tarporley; for it was along these roads that he would be likely to be followed. How, then? Through Chester, Clement fancied. The man was already on the Chester side of Aldersbury, and he could make at once for that place, while in the full stream of traffic between Chester and Manchester his traces would be lost. Travelling on foot and by night, he might reach Chester about ten in the morning, and probably, having money and being footsore, he would take the first Manchester coach that left after ten.

At this point Clement found himself crossing the West Bridge, the faint scattered lights of the town rising to a point before him. His first business was to knock up the constable and tell his tale. This done, he made for the bank, where he found the household awaiting his coming in some alarm, for it was close on midnight. Here he had to tell his story afresh, amid expressions of wonder and pity, while Betty fetched sponge and water and bathed his cheek; nor, modestly as he related his doings, could he quite conceal the part that he had played. The banker listened, approved, and for once experienced a new sensation. He was proud of his son. Moreover, as a dramatic sequel to the Squire's withdrawal of the money, the story touched him home.

Then Clement, as he ate his supper, came to his point. 'I'm going after him,' he said.

The banker objected. 'It's not your business, my lad,' he said. 'You've done enough, I'm sure.'

'But the point is' – Clement had grown cunning – 'it's bank money, sir.'

'It was – this morning.'

'And he was a client this morning – and may be tomorrow.'

The banker considered. There was something in that; and this sudden interest in the bank was gratifying. Yet – yet he did not quite understand it. 'You seem to be confoundedly taken up with this,' he said, 'but I don't see why you need mix yourself up with it further. The scoundrel's neck is in a halter and he won't be taken without a struggle. Have you thought of that?'

'I'd take him if he were ten,' Clement said – and blushed at his own enthusiasm. He muttered something about the man being a villain, and the sooner he was laid by the heels the better.

'Yes, by someone. But I don't see why you need be the one.'

'Anyway, I'm going to do it, sir,' Clement replied with unexpected independence. 'I shall go by the Nantwich coach at half-past five, drop off at Altringham, and catch him as he goes through. True, if he goes by Frodsham I may miss him, but I fancy that the morning coach by Frodsham leaves Chester too early for him. And, after all, I can't stop every bolt-hole.'

Ovington wondered anew, seeing his son in a new light. This was not the idler with his eyes on the ledger and his thoughts abroad, whom he had known in the bank, but a young man with purpose in his glance and a cut on his cheek-bone, who looked as if he could be ugly if it came to a pinch. A quite new Clement – or new at any rate to him.

He reflected. The affair would be talked of, and certainly it would be a feather in the bank's cap if the money, which the Squire had withdrawn, were recovered through the bank's exertions. Viewed in that light there was method in the lad's madness, whatever had bitten him. 'Well, I think it is a dangerous business,' he said at last, 'and it is not your business. But go, if you will, only you must take Payne with you.'

Payne was the bank man-of-all-work, but Clement would not hear of Payne. If he could be called at five, he asked no more. Even if all the seats on the Victory were booked, they would find room for him somewhere.

'But your face?' Betty said. 'Isn't it painful? It's turning black.'

'I'll bet that villain's is as black!' he retorted. 'I know I got home on him once. Only let me be called.'

But his father saw that, as he passed through the hall, he took one of the bank pistols out of the case in which they were kept, and slipped it into his pocket. The banker wondered anew, and felt perhaps more anxiety than he showed. At any rate, it was he who called the lad at five and saw that he drank the coffee that Betty had prepared, and that he ate something. At the last, indeed, Clement feared that his father might offer to accompany him, but he did not. Possibly he had decided that if his son was bent on proving his mettle in this odd business, it was wisest not to balk him.

The sun was rising as Clement's coach rattled down the Foregate between the old Norman towers that crown the Castle Hill, and the long austere front of the school, with its wide low casements twinkling in the first beams. Early milk-carts drew aside to give the coach passage, white-eyed sweeps gazed enviously after it, mob-caps at windows dreamt of holidays and sighed to be on it and away. Soon it burst merrily from the crowded houses and met the morning freshness and the open country and the rolling fields. The mists were rising from the valley behind, as the horses breasted the ascent above the old battle-field, swept down the farther slope, and at eight miles an hour climbed up Armour Hill between meadows sparkling with dew and coverts flickering with conies. Down the hill at a canter, which presently carried it rejoicing into Wem. There the first relay was waiting, and away again they went, bowling over the barren gorse-clad heath that brought them presently through narrow twisting streets to the White Lion at Whitchurch. Again, 'Horses on!' and merrily they travelled down the gentle slope to the Cheshire plain, where miles of green country spread themselves in the sunshine, a land of fatness and plenty, of cheese and milk and slow-running brooks. The clock on Nantwich church was showing a half after eight, as with a long flourish on the bugle they passed below it, and halted for breakfast at the Crown, in the stubborn old Roundhead town.

Half an hour to refresh, topping up with a glass of famous Nantwich ale, and away again. But now the sun was high, the world abroad, the roads were alive with traffic. Onwards from Nantwich, where they began to run alongside the Ellesmere Canal, with its painted barges and gay market boats, the road took on a new importance, and many a smiling wayside house, Lion or Swan, cheered the travellers on their way. Spanking four-in-hands, handled by lusty coachmen, the autocrats of the road, chaises-and-four with postboys in green or yellow, white-coated farmers and parsons on hackneys, commercials in gigs, and publicans in tax-carts, pedlars, packmen, the one-legged sailor, and Punch and Judy – all these met or passed them; and huge wains laden with Manchester goods and driven by teamsters in smocks with long whips on their shoulders. And the inns! The inns, with their swaying signs and open windows, their benches crowded with loungers and their yards echoing with the cry of 'Next team!' – the inns, with their groaning tables and huge joints and gleaming silver, these came so often, swaggered so loudly, imposed themselves so royally, that half the life of the road seemed to be in and about them.

And Clement saw it all and rejoiced in it all, though his eyes never ceased to search for a dour-looking man with a bruised face. He rejoiced in the cantering horses and the abounding life, in the freedom of it and the joyousness of it, his pulses leaping in tune with it; and not the less in tune, so splendid a thing is it to be young and in love, because he had fought a fight and slept only three hours. He watched it all pass before him, and if he had ever believed in his father's scheme of an iron way and iron horses he lost faith in it now. For it was impossible to believe that any iron road running across fields and waste places could vie with this splendid highway, this orderly procession of coaches, travelling and stopping and meeting with the regularity of a weaver's shuttle, these long lines of laden waggons, these swift chaises horsed at every stage! He saw stables that sheltered a hundred roadsters and were not full; ostlers to whom a handful of oats in every peck gave a gentleman's income; teams that were clothed and curried as tenderly as children; mighty caravanserais full to the attics. A whole machinery of transport passed under his wondering eyes, and the railway, the Valleys Railway – he smiled at it as at the dream of a visionary.

They swept through Northwich before eleven, and an hour later Clement dropped off the coach in front of the Bowling Green Inn at Altringham, and knew that his task lay before him. The little town had no church, but it boasted for its size more bustle than he had expected, and as he eyed its busy streets and its flow of traffic his spirits sank; it did not call itself one of the gates of Manchester for nothing. However, he had not come to stand idle, and the first step, to seek out a constable, was easy. But to secure that worthy's aid – he was but a deputy, a pot-bellied, dirty-faced shoemaker – was another matter. The man rolled up his leather apron and pushed his horn-rimmed glasses on to his forehead, but he shook his head. 'A very desperate villain,' he said, 'a very desperate villain! But lor', master, a dark sullen chap with a black eye and legs a little bandy? Why, I be dark and I be bandy, and for black eyes – I'm afeard there's more than one o' that cut on the road.'

'But not today,' Clement urged. 'He'll come through today or tonight.'

'Ay, and more likely night than day. But how be I to see if he's a blackened peeper in the dark! I can't haul a gentleman off a coach to ask the colour of his eyes.'

'Well, anyway, do your best.'

'We might bill him and cry him?'

'That's it! Do that!' Clement saw that that was about the extent of the help he would get in this quarter. 'Send the crier to me at the Bowling Green, and I'll write a bill – Five pounds reward for information!'

The constable's eyes twinkled. 'Now you're on a line, master,' he said. 'Now we'll do summat, maybe!'

Clement took the hint and bettered the line with a crown-piece, and hastening back to his inn he took seisin of a seat in the coffee room which commanded the main street. Here he wrote out a bill, and bribed a waiter to keep the place for him: and in it he sat patiently, scanning every person who passed. But so many passed that an hour had not elapsed before he held his task hopeless, though he continued to perform it. The constable had undertaken to go round the inns and to set a watch on a side street; and the bill might do something. But his fancy pictured half a dozen byways through the town, or the man might avoid the town, or he might go by another route. Altogether it began to seem a hopeless task, his fancied sagacity a silly conceit. But he had undertaken the task, and as he had told his father he could not close all holes. He could only set his snare across the largest and hope for the best.

Presently he heard the crier ring his bell and cry his man. 'Oh yes! Oh yes! Oh yes!' and the rest of it, ending with 'God save the King!' And that cheered him for a while. That was something. But as hour after hour went by and coaches, carriages, and postchaises stopped and started before the door, and pedestrians passed, and still no Thomas appeared – though half a dozen times he ran out to take a nearer view of some traveller, or to inspect a slumberer in a hay-cart – he began to despair. There were so many chances against him. So many straws floated by, half seen in the current.

But Clement was dogged. He persisted, though hope had almost abandoned him, and it was long after mid-night before, sinking with fatigue, he left his post. Even so he was out again by six, but if there was anything of which he was now certain, it was that the villain had gone by in the night. Still he remained, his eyes roving ceaselessly over the passers-by, who were now few, now many, as the current ran fast or slow, as some coach high-laden drew up before the door with a noisy fanfaronade, or some heavy waggon toiled slowly by.

It was in one of these slack intervals, when the street was tolerably empty, that his eyes fell on a man who was loitering on the other side of the way. The man had his hands in his pockets and a straw in his mouth, and he seemed to be a mere idler; but as his eyes met Clement's he winked. Then, with an almost imperceptible gesture of the head, he lounged away in the direction of the inn yard.

Clement doubted if anything was meant, but grasping at every chance he hurried out and found the man standing in the yard, his hands still in his pockets, the straw in his mouth. He was staring at an object, which, to judge from his aspect, could have no possible interest for him – a pump. 'Do you want me?' Clement asked.

'Mebbe, mister. Do you see that stable?'

'Well?'

'D'you go in there and I'll – mebbe I'll join you.'

But Clement was suspicious. 'I am not going out of sight of the street,' he said.

'Lord!' contemptuously. 'Your man's gone these six hours. He's many a mile on by now! You come into the stable.'

The fellow's looks did not commend him. He was blear-eyed and under-sized, wearing a mangy rabbit-skin waistcoat, and no coat. He had the air of a post-boy run to seed. Still, Clement thought it better to go with him, and in the stable, 'Be you the gent that offered five pounds?' the man asked, turning upon him.

'I am.'

'Then fork out, squire. Open your purse, and I'll open my mouth.'

'If you'll come with me to the constable—'

'Not I. I ben't sharing with no constable. That is flat.'

'Well, what do you know?'

'What you want to know. Howsumdever, if you'll give me your word you'll act the gentleman?'

'Who are you, my lad?'

'Ostler at the Barley Sheaf in Malthouse Lane. You're on? Right. I see, you're a gentleman. Well, your chap come in 'bout eleven last night on an empty dray from Chester. He had four sacks of corn with him.'

'Oh, but that can't be the man!' Clement exclaimed, his face falling.

'You listen, mister. He had four sacks of corn with him, and waggoner, he'd bargained to carry him to Manchester. But they had quarrelled, and t'other chucked off his sacks in our yard, and there was pretty nigh a fight. Waggoner he went off and left him cursing, and he offered me a shilling to find him a lift to Manchester first thing i' the morning. 'Bout daylight there come in a hay-cart, but driver'd only take the man and not the forage. Howsumdever, he said at last he'd take one sack, and your chap up and asked me would I take care of t'other three till he sent for 'em. I see he was mighty keen to get on, and I sez, 'No,' sez I, 'but I'll buy 'em cheap.' 'Right,' sez he, and surprising little bones about it, and lets me have 'em cheap! So thinks I, who's this as chucks away money, and as he climbed up I managed to knock off his tile and see his eye was painted, and he the very spot of your bill! I'd half a mind to stop him, but he was overweight for me – I'm a little chap – and I let him go.' He added some details which satisfied Clement that the traveller was really Thomas.

'Did you hear where he was going to in Manchester?'

'Five pound, mister!' The man held out his grimy paw.

Clement did not like the cunning in the bleary eyes, but he had gone so far that he could hardly draw back. He counted out four one-pound notes. 'Now then?' he said, showing the fifth, but keeping a firm hold on it.

'The lad that took him is Jerry Stott – of the Apple-Tree Inn in Fennel Street. You go to him, mister. One of these will do it.'

Clement gave him the other note. 'He didn't tell you where he was going?'

'He very particlar did not. But I'm thinking you'll net him at Jerry's. Do you take one of Nadin's boys. He's a desperate-looking chap. He gave you that punch in the face, I guess?' with interest.

'He did.'

'Ah, well, you marked him. But you get one of Nadin's boys. You'll not take him easy.'

Chapter Seventeen

Clement did not let the grass grow under his feet. An hour later he was rattling over the stony pavements and through the crowded streets of the busy town, which had grown in a short hundred years from something little more than a village, to be the second centre of wealth and population, of poverty and crime, within the seas; a centre on which the eye of Government rested with unwinking vigilance, for without a voice in Parliament and with half of its citizens deprived of civic rights – since half were Nonconformists – it was the focus of all the discontent in the country. In Manchester, if anywhere, flourished the agitation against the Test Acts and the movement for Reform. Thence, had started the famous Blanketeers, there six years before had taken place the Peterloo massacre. Thence as by the million filaments of some great web, was roused or calmed the vast industrial world of Lancashire. The thunder of the power-loom that had created it, the roar of the laden drays that shook it, deafened the wondering stranger. But more formidable and momentous than either, had he known it, was the half-heard murmur of an underworld striving to be free.

Clement had never visited the cotton-town before, and on a more commonplace errand he might have allowed himself to be daunted by a turmoil and bustle as new to him as it was uncongenial. But with his mind set on one thing, he heeded his surroundings only as they threatened to baulk his aim, and he had himself driven directly to the Police Office, over which the notorious Nadin had so lately presided that for most people it still went by his name. Fearless, resolute, and not too scrupulous, the man had through twenty troublous years combated the forces alike of disorder and of liberty; and before London had yet acquired an efficient police, he had gathered round him a body of men equal at least to the Bow Street Runners. He had passed, but his methods survived; and half an hour after

Clement had entered the office he issued from it accompanied by a hard-bitten, sharp-eyed man in a tall beaver hat and a long wide-skirted coat.

'The Apple Tree? Oh, the Apple Tree's on the square,' he informed Clement. 'And Jerry Stott? No harm in him, sir, either. He'll speak when he sees me.'

'You don't think we need another man?'

'There's one following. No use to go in a bunch. He'll watch the front, and we'll go in by the yard. Got a barker, sir?'

'Yes.'

''Fraid so. Well, don't use it – show it if you like. Law's law, and a live dog's worth more than its hide. Ay, that's Chetham's. Queer old place, and – sharp's the word, here we are,' as they turned off Long Mill Gate, and entered the yard of an old-fashioned house, over the door of which hung the sign of an apple-tree. The place was quiet, in comparison with the street they had left, and 'Here's Jerry,' the officer added, as they espied a young fellow, who in a corner of the enclosure was striving to raise to his shoulder a truss of hay. He ceased his efforts when he saw them.

'We want a word with you,' said the officer.

The man eyed them with dismay. 'I never thout 'at he'd come to thee,' he said.

'The chap you brought in this morning?'

'Ay, sure.'

'Happen yes and happen no,' the policeman replied. 'What's it all about?'

'If he says I took his eauts he be a leear. I wurna wi' the sack, not to say alone 'at is, not five minutes, and yo' may look at t' sack and see all's theer as ever was! Never a handfu' missing, tho' the chap he cursed and swore an' took on, the mout ha' been eauts o' gowd! He's a leear iv he says I tetched 'em, but I never thout he'd t' brass to come to thee.'

'Why not, lad?'

''Cause i' the end he let up and steared at t' sack leek a steck pig, and then he fell a shriking i' worse shap than ever, and away he goes as iv a dog had bit him and down t' Long Gate hell for leather!'

'Which way? I see. Did he take the oats?'

'Not he, nor t' bag. An after mekking setch a din about his eauts! I war no wi' 'em five minutes.'

The officer declined to commit himself. 'Let us see them,' he said.

Jerry led them to a tumble-down, black and white building at the rear of the yard, with lattice work in its crazy windows and an old date over the door. They followed him up a ladder and into a loft, where were a frowsy bed or two, some old pack-saddles, and two or three stools made out of casks sawn in two. On the floor in one place lay a heap of oats trampled this way and that, and beside the heap an empty sack. The officer picked up the sack, shook it and examined it.

'What do you make of it?' Clement asked.

'I don't know what to make of it. Here, you, Jerry, fetch me a corn measure!' And when he had thus rid them of the lad, 'He may be carrying out orders and telling a flash tale to put us off. Or he may be telling the truth, and in that case it looks as if someone had been a mite brighter than your man and cleared his stuff.'

'But where is it?'

'Ah! Just so, I'd like to know,' shaking his head. 'Yes, Jerry, measure it back into the sack. How much is there?'

The lad began to gather up the oats and replace them in the bag, while the two men looked on, perplexed and undecided. Suddenly Clement stooped – a scrap of cord, doubtless the cord which had tied the neck of the sack, had caught his eye. He picked it up, looked at it, then, with a word, he handed it to the officer. 'I think that settles it,' he said, his eyes shining. There was a tiny twist of straw-plait, like a rosette, knotted about the cord and still adhering to it.

Nadin's man looked at the plait and for a moment did not understand. Then his face cleared. 'By Joseph! You're right, sir!' he exclaimed, and slapped his thigh. 'And sharp, sharp too. You'd ought to be one of us! That settles it, it's the back-track we've to look to, but I'll take no chances.' And turning to the lad and addressing him in his harshest voice, 'See here, in an hour we shall know if you've told us the truth. If you've not it will be the New Bailey and a pair of iron garters for you. So if you've aught to add, out with it! It's your last chance, Jerry Stott.'

But the lad protested that he'd told all the truth. It had happened just as he had told them.

The officer turned to Clement. 'I think he's on the square,' he said, 'but I'll have him watched.' And he led the way down the ladder. When they reached the street, he stepped out smartly, making nothing of the crowd and bustle, the lumbering drays and overhanging cranes through which they had to thread their way. 'We'll catch the Altringham stage at the Cross if we're sharp,' he said. 'It'll be quicker than getting out a po'chay and a lot cheaper.'

They caught the stage, and alighted in Altringham before five. A walk of as many minutes brought them to the Barley Sheaf, a waggoners' house at the corner of a lane in the poorest part of the town. The ostler, from whom Clement had so lately parted, stood leaning against a post at the entrance to the yard, his hands still in his pockets and the straw still in his mouth. When he saw them a grin broke up his ugly face. 'He's been here,' he cried, 'but,' triumphantly, 'I've routed him, mister! I sent him all ways!'

The officer did not respond. 'Why the devil didn't you seize him?' he growled.

'What, me? And him double my size? And a desperate villain? 'Deed, I'd to save my skin, mister, and only yon lad and a couple of childer in the yard when he come. I see him first, sneaking a look round this yere post, and thinks I, it'll be a knife in the back or a punch in the face for me if he's heard I've rapped. So, first's better than last, thinks I, and seeing as he hung back I up to him bold as brass, but with one eye on the lad too, and sez I, 'Can you read?' sez I. He looked at me 's if he'd have my blood, but there was the lad and the childer a-staring, so "Ay, I can," says he, "and can read you, you thieving villain!" "Well, if you can, read that," sez I, and pointed to a bill as was posted on the gate. "I can't," sez I, "and, happen you can tell me what 'tis all about." He looks, and he sees 'tis the bill about he, and painting him to the life. Anyways, he turns the colour o' whey and he gives me a look as if he'd cut out my innards, but he sees it's no good, for there was the lad and the childer, and he slinks off. Ay, I routed him, I did, little as I be, mister!'

'Right!' said Nadin's man. 'And now do you show us the sack as you changed for his.'

The man's face fell amazingly, but Clement noted that he looked surprised rather than frightened. 'Eh?' he exclaimed. 'Lord, now, who told you, mister? He didn't know.'

'Never mind who told us. We know, and that's enough. There was a twist o' plait round the cord?'

'There were.'

'You said nothing about it before. But out with it now, and do you take care, my lad.'

'Well, who axed me? Exchange is no robbery and I ain't afeard. 'Twas just this way. He sold me three sacks, 's I told you, squire, and I was hauling 'em off to stable when "Not that one!" says he sharp. So then I looked at t' one he was so set on keeping, and when his back was turned I hefted it sly-like, and it seemed to me a good bit heavier than t' others. Then I spied the bit o' plait about the cord, and thinks I, being no fule, 'tis a mark. And when he went in for a squib o' cordial wi' Jerry Stott I shifted t' mark to another sack and loaded up, and off he goes and he none the wiser, and no harm done. Exchange is no robbery and you can't do nowt to me for that.'

'I don't know,' said the officer darkly. 'Let us see the sack.'

'You're not agoing—'

'Do you hear? Jump, unless you want to get into trouble. You show us that sack, and be quick about it, my lad.'

Grumbling, but not daring to refuse, the old man led the way into the stables, and there in an empty stall the three sacks stood upright. 'Which is the one you filched?' asked the man from Manchester.

Reluctantly the ostler pointed it out. 'Then you get me a horse-cloth.'

'You're not going – well, a wilful man must have his way. Will that serve you? But if my oats is spilled and spiled—'

Nadin's man paid no heed to his remonstrance, but in a trice cut the cord that tied the sack's mouth, tipped it on its side, and let the grain pour out in a golden stream. A golden stream it proved to be, for in a twinkling something sparkled amid the corn, and here and there a sovereign glittered. To Clement and the officer who had read the riddle, this was no great surprise, though they viewed it with smiling satisfaction. But the old man, struck dumb by the sight of the treasure that had been for a time in his power, turned a dirty white. He stood gazing at the vision of wealth, greed in his eyes, his hands working convulsively. And presently in a choked voice, "O, Lord! O, Lord!" he muttered. "You'll not take t' all! You'll not take t' all! It were mine. I bought it."

'You came nigh to buying a pair o' bracelets,' the officer replied grimly. 'You with stolen property in your possession to talk o' – thank your stars your neck's not to answer for it! No, we don't need your help. You sheer off. We can count it without you. You've done pretty well as it is. Sheer off, unless you want the handcuffs on you!'

The old ostler went, measuring the five pounds which he had made by the treasure he had lost, and finding no comfort in the possession of that which only an hour before had been a fortune to gloat over. But there was no help for it. He had to swallow his rage. The officer called after him to bring a sieve. He brought it sullenly, and his part was done. All that was left to him was a vision of gold that grew more dazzling with each telling of the tale. And very, very often he told it.

When he was gone they gathered up the oats and riddled them through the sieve and recovered four hundred and thirty pounds. Thomas had taken a mere handful for his spending. As Clement counted it, sovereign by sovereign, into a knotted handkerchief which the other held, he, too, gloated over it, for it spelled success. But the money reckoned and the handkerchief knotted up, 'And now for the man,' he said.

But Nadin's man shook his head. 'We'd be weeks and not get him,' he said. 'You'd best leave him to us, sir. We'll bill him in Manchester and make the flash kens too hot for him. But there's no knowing which way he'll turn. May be to Liverpool, or as like as not to Aldersbury. Chaps like him are pigeons for homing. Back they go, though they know they'll be taken.'

In the end Clement decided to stand content, and having given his assistant a liberal fee, he took his seat next morning on the Victory coach, travelling by Chester to Aldersbury. He was not vain, but it was with some exultation that he faced again the free-blowing winds and the open pastures, heard the cheery notes of the bugle, and viewed the old-fashioned marketplaces and roistering inns, some of which he had passed three days before. He had not failed. He had done something; and he thought of Jos, and he thought of the Squire, and he thanked Providence that had put it in his power to turn the tables on the old man. Surely after what he had done the Squire must consider him. Surely after services so notable – and Lord, what luck he had had – the Squire would be willing to listen to him? He recalled the desperate struggle in the road, and the old man's 'At him, good lad! At him!' and he thought of the sum – no small sum, and the old man was avaricious – which his promptness had recovered. His hopes ran high.

To be sure, there was another side to it. The Squire might not recover, and then – but he refused to dwell on that contingency. No, the Squire must recover, must receive and reward him, must own that after all he was something better than a clerk or a shopboy. And all things would be well, all roads be made smooth, all difficulties be cleared away.

And in time he and Jos – his eyes shone.

Of course in the elation of the hour, and flushed by success, he ignored facts which he would have been wiser to remember, and over-leapt obstacles which were not small. A little thought would have taught him, that the Squire was not the man to change his views in an hour, or to swallow the prejudices of a life-time because a young chap had done him a service. To be beholden to a man, and to give him your daughter, are things far apart.

And this Clement in cooler moments would have seen. But he was young and in love, and he had done something; and the sun shone and the air was sweet, and if, as the coach swung gaily up the Foregate between School and Castle, his heart beat high and he already foresaw a triumphant issue, who shall blame him? At any rate his case was altered, and in comparison with his position a few days before, he stood well.

He alighted at the door of the Lion, and by a coincidence which was to have its consequences the first person he met in the High Street was Arthur Bourdillon. 'Hallo!' Arthur cried, his face lighting up. 'Back already, man? Have you done anything?'

'I've got the money,' Clement replied. And he waved the bag.

'And Thomas?'

'No, he gave us the slip for the time. But I've got the money, except a dozen pounds or so.'

'The deuce you have!' the other answered – and it was not quite clear whether he were pleased or not. 'How did you do it? Tell us all about it.' He drew Clement aside on to some steps at the foot of St. Juliana's church.

Clement ran briefly over his adventures. When he had done, 'Deuced sharp of you,' Arthur said. 'Devilish sharp, I must say! Now, if you'll hand over I'll take it out to Garth, I am on my way there, am just starting, and I haven't a moment to spare. If you'll hand over—'

But Clement made no move to hand over. Instead, 'How is he?' he asked.

'Oh, pretty bad.'

'Will he get over it?'

'Farmer thinks so. But there's no hope for the eye, and he doubts about the other eye. He's not to use it for six weeks at least.'

'He's in bed?'

'Lord, yes, and will be in bed for heaven knows how long – if he ever gets up from it. Why, man, he's had the deuce of a shake. The wonder is that he's alive, and it's long odds that he'll never be the same man again.'

'That's bad,' Clement said. 'And how is—' He was going to inquire after Miss Griffin, but Arthur broke in on him.

'Ask the rest another time,' he said. 'I can't stay now. I'm taking out things that are wanted in a hurry and the curricle is waiting. This is the first day I've been in town, for there's no one there to do anything except my cousin and the old Peahen. So hand over, old chap, and I'll take the stuff out. It will do the old man more good than all the doctor's medicine.'

Clement hesitated. If he had not been carrying the money, he might have made an excuse. He might at any rate have delayed the act. But the money was the Squire's, he could give no reason for taking it to the bank, and he had not that hardness of fibre, that indifference to the feelings of others which was needed if he was to say boldly that it was he who had recovered the money and he who was going to hand it over. Still he did hesitate, something telling him that the demand was unreasonable. Then Arthur's coolness, his assumption that what he proposed was the natural course did its work. Clement handed over the bag.

'Right,' Arthur said, weighing it in his hand. 'You counted it, I suppose? Four hundred and thirty, or thereabouts?'

'That's it.'

'Good! See you soon. Good-bye!' And well pleased with himself, chuckling a little – for Clement's discomfiture had not escaped him – Arthur hurried away.

And Clement went his way. But reality had touched his golden dreams, and they had melted. The sun still shone, but it did not shine for him, and he no longer walked with his head in the air. It was not only that, by resigning the money and entrusting its return to another, he had lost the advantage on which he had counted, but he had been worsted. He had failed, in the contest of wits and wills, and, abuse his ill-luck as he might, he owed the failure to himself – to his own weakness. He saw it.

It was possible that Arthur had acted in innocence. But Clement doubted this, and he doubted it the more the longer he thought of it. He fancied that he recognised a thing which had happened before: that this was not the first time that Arthur had taken the upper hand with him and jockeyed him into the worse position. As he crossed the threshold of the bank, his self-confidence fell from him, he felt himself slip into the old atmosphere, he became once more the inefficient.

Nor was it any comfort to him that his father saw the matter in the same light and after listening with an appreciative face and some surprise to his earlier adventures, made no effort to hide the chagrin that he felt at the *dénouement*. 'But why – why in the world did you do that?' he exclaimed. 'Give up the money after you had done the work? And to Bourdillon, who had no more right to it than you had? Good heavens, lad, it was the act of a fool! I'd not be surprised if old Griffin never heard your name in connection with it!'

'Oh, I don't think Arthur—'

'Well, I do.' The banker was vexed. 'It's clear that Arthur is a deal sharper than you. As for the Squire, I hear that he is only half-conscious, and what he hears, if he ever hears the tale at all, will make little impression on him. Now if he had seen you, and you'd handed over the money – if he had seen you, then the bank and you would have got the credit.'

'Still, Clem did recover it,' Betty said.

'Ay, but who will ever know that he did?'

'Still he did, and I believe that he'll get a message from Garth tomorrow. Now, see if you don't, Clem. Or the next day.'

But no message came on the morrow, or on the next day. No message came at all; and though it was possible to attribute this to the Squire's condition – for he was reported to be very ill – and Clement did his best to attribute it to that and to keep up his spirits, the tide of time wears away even hope, and presently he began to see that he had built on the sand.

At any rate no message and no acknowledgment came, unless a perfunctory word of thanks dropped by Arthur counted as such. And Clement had soon to recognise that what he had done, he might as well, for any good it was likely to do him, have left undone. His father, who had no thought of anything but his son's credit, was merely chagrined. But with Clement, who had built high hopes upon the event, hopes of which his father and Betty little dreamed, the wound went far deeper.

Chapter Eighteen

The Squire raised himself painfully on his elbow and hid the bag between pillow and tester, where he could assure himself of its presence by a touch. Then he sank back with a grunt of relief and his hand went to the keys, which also had their home under his pillow. He clung to them – they were his badge of authority, of power. While he had them, sightless as he was, he was still master; about his room, the oak-panelled chamber, spacious but shabby, with the uneven floor and the low wide casement, the life of the house still circled.

'Good lad!' he muttered. 'Good lad! Jos?'

'Yes, Father.' She rose and came towards him.

'Where's Arthur?'

'He went out with your message.'

'To be sure! To be sure! I'm forgetting.'

But, once started on the road to recovery, he did not forget much. From his high, four-post bed with the drab hangings in which his father and grandfather had died, he gripped house and lands in a firm grip. Morning by morning he would have his report of the lambs, of the wheat, of the hay-crops, of the ploughing on the eight acres where the Swedish turnips were to go. He would know what corn went to the mill, what mutton to the house. The bounds fence that Farmer Bache had neglected was not forgotten, nor the young colt that he had decided to take against Farmer Price's arrears, nor the lease for lives that involved a knotty point of which he proved himself to be in complete possession.

Indeed, he showed himself indomitable, the old heart in him still strong; so that neither the shock that he had borne, nor the pain that he had suffered, nor the possibility of permanent blindness which they could not wholly hide from him, sufficed to subdue or unman him.

Only in one or two things was a change apparent. He reverted to an older and ruder form of speech familiar to him when George the Third was young, but which of late he had only used when talking with his tenants. He said 'Dunno you do this' and 'I wunt ha' that!' used 'ship' for sheep, and 'goold' for gold, called Thomas a 'gallus bad rascal,' and the like.

And in another and more important point he was changed. For eyes he must now depend on someone, and though he showed that he liked to have Jos about him and bore with her when the Peahen's fussiness drove him to bad words, it was soon clear that the person he chose was Arthur. Arthur was restored, and more than restored to favour. It was 'Where's Arthur?' a score of times a day. Arthur must come, must go, must be ever at his elbow. He must check such and such an account, see the overseers about such an one, speak to the constable about another, go into Aldersbury about the lease. Even when Arthur was absent the Squire's thoughts ran on him, and often he would mutter 'Good lad! Good lad!' when he thought himself alone.

It was a real *bouleversement*, but Josina, supposing that Arthur had saved her father's life at the risk of his own, and had then added to his merit by recovering the lost money, found it natural enough. For the full details of the robbery had never been told to her. 'Better leave it alone, Jos,' Arthur had said when she had again shown a desire to know more. 'It was a horrid business and you won't want to dream of it. Another minute and that d—d villain would have – but there, I'd advise you to leave it alone.'

Jos, suspecting nothing, had not persisted, but on the contrary had thought Arthur as modest as he was brave. And the doctor, with an eye to his patient's well-being, had taken the same view. 'Put no questions to him,' he said, 'and don't talk to him about it. Time enough to go into it by and by, when the shock's worn off. The odds are that he will remember nothing that happened just before the scoundrel struck him – that's the common thing – and so much the better, my dear. Let sleeping dogs lie, or, as we doctors say, don't think about your stomach till your victuals trouble you.'

So Josina knew no particulars except that Arthur had saved his uncle's life, and Clement – she shuddered as she thought of it – had come up in time to be of service. And no one at Garth knew more. But, knowing so much, it was not surprising to her that Arthur should be restored to favour, and, lately forbidden the house, should now rule it as a master. And clearly Arthur, also, found the position natural, so easily did he fall into it. He was up and down the old shallow stairs – which the Squire, true to the fashions of his youth, had never carpeted – a dozen times a day. He was as often in and out of his uncle's bedroom, or sitting on the deep window-seat on which generations of mothers had sunned their babes; and all this with a laugh and a cheery word that wondrously brightened the sick room. Alert, quick, serviceable, and willing to take any responsibility, he made himself a favourite with all. Even Calamy, who shook his head over every improvement in the Squire, and murmured much of the 'old lamp flickering before it went out,' grew hopeful in his presence. Miss Peacock adored him. He put Josina's nose out of joint.

Of the young fellow, whose moodiness had of late perplexed his companions in the bank, not a trace remained. Had they seen him now they might have been tempted to think that a weight had been lifted from him. But he seemed, for the time, to have forgotten the bank. He rarely mentioned the Ovingtons.

There was one at Garth, however, who had not forgotten either the bank or the Ovingtons, and who proved it presently to Arthur's surprise. 'Jos,' said the Squire one afternoon. And when she had replied that she was there, 'Where is Arthur?'

'I think he has just come in, sir.'

'Prop me up. And send him to me. Do you leave us.'

She went, wondering a little for she had not been dismissed before. She sent Arthur, who, after his usual fashion, scaled the stairs at three bounds. He found the old man sitting up in the shadow of the curtains, a grotesque figure with his bandaged head. The air of the room was not so much musty as ancient, savouring of worm-eaten wood and long decayed lavender, and linen laid by in presses. On each side of the drab tester hung a dim flat portrait, faded and melancholy, in a carved wooden frame, unglazed; below each hung a sampler. 'You sent for me, sir?'

'Ay. When's that money due?'

The question was so unexpected that for a moment Arthur did not understand it. Then the blood rushed to his face. 'My mother's money, sir?'

'What else? What other money is there, that's due? I forget things but I dunno forget that.'

'You don't forget much, sir,' Arthur replied cheerfully. 'But there's no hurry about that.'

'When?'

'Well, in two months from the twenty-first, sir. But there is not the least hurry.'

'This is the seventeenth?'

'Yes, sir.'

'Well, I'll pay and ha' done with it. But I'll ha' to sell stock. East India Stock it is. What are they at, lad?'

'Somewhere about two hundred and seventy odd, I think, sir.'

'And how do you sell 'em?' The Squire knew a good deal about buying stock but little about selling it, and he winced as he put the question. But he bore the pang gallantly, for had not the boy earned his right to the money and to his own way? Ay, and earned it by a service as great as one man could perform for another? For the Squire had no more reason than those about him to doubt that he owed his life to his nephew. He had found him beside his bed when he had recovered his senses, and putting together this and that, and adding his own hazy impressions of the happenings of the night, and of the young man on whose shoulder he had leant, he had never questioned the fact. 'How do you go about to sell 'em?' he repeated. 'I suppose you know?'

'Oh, yes, sir, it's my business,' Arthur replied. 'You have to get a transfer – they are issued at the India House. You've only to sign it before two witnesses, It is quite simple, sir.'

'Well, I can do that. Do you see to it, lad.'

'You wouldn't wish to do it through Ovington's?'

'No!' the Squire rapped out. 'Do it yourself. And lose no time. Write at once.'

'Very well, sir. I suppose you have the certificates?'

'Course I have,' annoyed. 'Isn't the stock mine?'

'Very good, sir. I'll see to it.'

'Well, see to it. And, mark ye, when you're in Aldersbury see Welshes, and tell them I'm waiting for that lease o' lives. I signed the agreement for the new lease six weeks ago and I should ha' had the lease by now. Stir 'em up, and say I must have it. The longer I'm waiting the longer the bill will be! I know 'em, damn 'em, though Welshes are not the worst.'

When he had settled this he wanted a letter written, and Arthur sat down at the oaken bureau that stood between the windows, its faded green lining stained with the ink of a century and its pigeon-holes crammed with receipts and sample-bags. While he wrote his thoughts were busy with the matter that they had just discussed, but it was not until he found himself standing at a window outside the room, staring with unseeing eyes over the green vale, that he brought his thoughts to a head, and knew that at the eleventh hour he hesitated.

Yes, he hesitated. The thing that he had so much desired, that had presented itself to him in such golden hues, that had dazzled his ambition and absorbed his mind, was within his grasp now, ready to be garnered – and yet he hesitated. Ovington was a just man and beyond doubt would release him and cancel the partnership agreement, if he desired to have it cancelled. And he was very near to desiring it at this moment.

For he saw now that there were other things to be garnered – Garth, its broad acres, its fine rent-roll, the old man's savings, Josina. Secure of the Squire's favour, he had but to stretch out his hand and all these things might be his; might certainly be his if he gave up the bank and his prospects there. That step, if he took it, would remove his uncle's last objection; it would bind him to him by a triple bond. And it would do more. It would ease his own mind, by erasing from the past – for he would no longer need the five thousand – a thing which troubled his conscience and harassed him when he lay awake at night. It would erase that blot, it would make all clean behind him, and it would at the same time remove the impalpable barrier that had risen between him and his mother.

It was still in his power to do all this. A word would do it. He had only to go back to the Squire and tell him that he had changed his mind, that he no longer wanted the money, and was not going into the bank.

He hesitated, standing at the window, looking on the green vale and the hillside beyond it. Yes, he might do it. But what if he repented later? And what security had he for those other things? His uncle might live for years, long years, might live to quarrel with him and discard him. Did not the proverb say that it was ill-work waiting for dead men's shoes? And Josina? Doubtless he might win Josina, for the wooing; he had no doubt about that. But he was not sure that he wanted Josina.

He decided at last that the question might wait. Until he had written the letter to the brokers, until then, at any rate, either course was open to him. He went downstairs. In the wainscoted hall, small and square, with a high narrow window on each side of the door, his mother and Josina were sitting on one of the window seats. The door stood open, the spring air and the sunshine poured in. 'I'm telling her that she's not looking well,' his mother said, as he joined them.

'She spends too much time in that room,' he answered. Then, after a moment's thought, rattling the money in his fob, 'Is Farmer coming today?'

'No.' The girl spoke listlessly. 'I don't think he is.'

'He's made a wonderful recovery,' his mother observed.

'Yes – if it's a real recovery.'

'At any rate, the doctor hopes that he may come downstairs in ten days. And then, I'm afraid, we shall have Josina to nurse.'

The girl protested that she was well, quite well. But her heavy eyes and the shadows under them belied her words.

'Well, I'm off to town,' he said. 'I have to see Welshes for him.'

He left them, and ten minutes later he was on the road to Aldersbury, still undecided, still uncertain what course he would pursue, and at one moment accusing himself of a weakness that deserved the contempt of every strong man, at another praising moderation and a country life. Had he had eyes and ears for the things about him as he rode, he might have found much to support the latter view. The cawing of rooks, the murmur of wood-doves, the scents of late spring filled the balmy air. The sky was pure blue, and beneath it the pastures shone yellow with buttercups. Tree and field, bank and hedgerow rioted in freshest green, save where the oak wood, slow to change and careless of fashion, clung to its orange garb, or the hawthorn stood out, a globe of snow. The cuckoo and the early corncrake told of coming summer, and behind him the Welsh hills simmered in the first heat of the year. Clement, had he passed that way, would have noted it all, and in the delight of the eye and the spring-tide of all growing things would have found ground to rejoice, whatever his trouble.

But Arthur, wrapt in his own thoughts, barely noticed these things. He rode with his eyes fixed on his horse's ears, and only roused himself when he saw the very man whom he wished to see coming to meet him. It was Dr Farmer, in the mahogany-topped boots, the frilled shirt, and the old black coat – shaped as are our dress coats but buttoned tightly round the waist – which the dust of a dozen summers and every road in the district had whitened.

'Hallo, doctor!' Arthur cried as they met. 'Are you going up to the house today?'

'No, Mr Bourdillon. But I can if necessary. How is he?'

'That is what I want you to tell me. One can't talk freely at the house and I have a reason for wishing to know. How is he, doctor?'

'Do you mean—'

'Has this really shaken him? Will he be the same man again?'

'I see.' Farmer rubbed his chin with the horn-handle of his riding-crop. 'Well – I see no reason at present why he should not be. He's one in a hundred, you know. Sound heart, good digestion, a little gouty – but tough. Tough! You never know, of course. There may be some harm we haven't detected, but I should say that he had a good few years of life in him yet.'

'Ah!'

'Of course, an unusual recovery – from such injuries. And I say nothing about the sight. I'm not hopeful of that.'

'Well,' said Arthur. 'I'll tell you why I asked. There's a question arisen about a lease for lives – his is one. But you won't talk, of course.'

Farmer nodded. He found it quite natural. Leases for lives were still common, and doctors were often consulted as to the value of lives which survived or which it was proposed to insert. With another word or two they parted and Arthur rode on.

But he no longer doubted. To wait for eight or ten years, dependent on the whims of an arbitrary and crotchety old man? No! Only in a moment of imbecility could he have dreamed of resigning for this, the golden opportunities that the new world, opening before him, extended to all who had the courage to seize them. He had been mad to think of it, and now he was sane. Garth was worth a mass. He might have served a year or two for it. But seven, or it might be ten? No. Besides, why should he not take the Squire at his word and make the best of both worlds, and availing himself of the favour he had gained, employ the one to exploit the other? He had his foot in at Garth and he was no fool, he could make himself useful. Already, he was well aware, he had made himself liked.

It was noon when he rode into Aldersbury, the town basking in the first warmth of the year, the dogs lying stretched in the sunshine. And he was in luck, for, having met Farmer, he now met Frederick Welsh coming down Maerdol. The lawyer, honestly concerned for his old friend, was urgent in inquiry, and when he had heard the news, 'Thank God!' he said. 'I'm as pleased to hear that as if I'd made a ten-pound note! Aldshire without the Squire – things would be changing, indeed!'

Arthur told him what the Squire had said about the lease. But that was another matter. The Squire was too impatient. 'He's got his agreement. We'll draw the lease as soon as we can,' the lawyer said. 'The office is full, and more haste less speed. We'll let him know when it's ready.' Like all old firms he was dilatory. There was no hurry. All in good time.

They parted, and Arthur rode up the street, alert and smiling, and many eyes followed him – followed him with envy. He worked at the bank, he had his rooms on the Town Walls, he chatted freely with this townsman and that. He was not proud. But they never forgot who he was. They did not talk to him as they talked even to Ovington. Ovington had risen and was rich, but he came as they came, of common clay. But this young man, riding up the street in the sunshine, smiling and nodding this way and that, his hand on his thigh, belonged to another order. He was a Griffin – a Griffin of Garth. He might lose his all, his money might fly from him, but he would still be a Griffin, one of the caste that ruled as well as reigned, that held in its grasp power and patronage. They looked after him with envy.

Chapter Nineteen

The week in early June which witnessed Arthur's return to his seat at the bank – that and the following week which saw his mother's five thousand pounds paid over for his share in the concern – saw the tide of prosperity which during two years had been constantly swelling, reach its extreme point. The commerce and wealth of the country, as they rose higher and higher in this flood-time of fortune, astonished even the casual observer. Their increase seemed to be without limit; they answered to every call. They not only filled the old channels, but over-ran them, irrigating, in appearance at least, a thousand fields hitherto untilled. Abroad, the flag of commerce was said to fly where it had never flown before; its clippers brought merchandise not only from the Indies, East and West, and tea from China, and wool from Sydney, and rich stuffs from the Levant, but Argosies laden with freight still more precious were – or were reported to be – on their way from that new Southern continent on the opening of which to British trade so many hopes depended. The gold and silver of Peru, the diamonds of Brazil, the untapped wealth of the Plate were believed to be afloat and ready to be exchanged for the produce of our looms and spindles, our ovens and forges.

Nor was that produce likely to fail, for at home the glow of foundries, working night-shifts, lit up the northern sky, and in many a Lancashire or Yorkshire dale, old factories, brought again into service, shook, almost to falling, under the thunder of the power-loom. Mills and mines, potteries and iron-works changed hands from day to day, at ever-rising prices. Men who had never invested before, save in the field at their gate, or the house under their eyes, rushed eagerly to take shares in these ventures, and in thousands of offices and parlours conned their securities, summed up the swelling total of their gains, and rushed to buy and buy again, with a command of credit which seemed to have no bottom.

To provide that credit, the banks widened their operations, increased, on the security of stocks ever rising in value, their overdrafts, issued batch after batch of fresh notes. The most cautious admitted that accommodation must keep step with trade, and the huge strides which this was making, the changed conditions, the wider outlook, the calling in of the New World to augment the wealth of the Old – all seemed to demand an advance which promised to be as profitable as it was warranted.

To the ordinary eye the sun of prosperity shone in an unclouded sky. Even the experienced, though they scanned the heavens with care, saw nothing to dismay them. Only here and there an old fogey whose memory went back to the crisis of '93, or to the famous Black Monday of twenty years earlier, uttered a note of warning; or some mechanical clerk, of the stamp of Rodd, sunk in a rut of routine, muttered of Accommodation Bills where his employer saw only legitimate trade. But their croakings, feeble at best, were lost in the joyous babble of an Exchange enriched by commissions and drunk with success.

It was a new era. It was the age of gold. It was the fruit of conditions long maturing. Men's labour, aided by machinery, was henceforth to be so productive that no man need be poor, all might be rich. Experts, reviewing the progress which had been made and the changes which had been wrought during the last fifty years, said these things; and the vulgar took them up and repeated them. The Bank of England acted as if they were true. The rate of discount was low.

And while all men thus stretched out their hands to catch the golden manna, Aldersbury was not idle. The appetite for gain grows by what it feeds upon and Aldersbury appetites had been whetted by early successes in their own field. The woollen mills, sharing in the general prosperity of the last two years, had done well, and more than one mill had changed hands at unheard-of prices. The Valleys were said to be full of money which, or part of it, trickled into the town, improving a trade already brisk.

Many had made large gains by outside speculations and had boasted of them. Report had multiplied their profits, others had joined in and they too had gained, and their gains had fired the greed of their neighbours. Some had followed up their first successes. Others prepared to extend their businesses, built new premises, put in newfangled glass windows, and by their action gave an impetus to subordinate trades, and spread still further the sense of well-being.

On the top of all this had come the Valleys Railroad Scheme, backed by Ovington's Bank, and offering to everyone a chance of speculating on his door-step: a scheme which, while it appealed to local pride, had a specious look of safety, since the railway was to be built under the shareholders' own eyes, across the fields they knew, and by men whom they saw going in and out every day.

There was a great run on it. Some of the gentry, following the old Squire's example, held aloof, but others put their hundreds into it, not much believing in it but finding it an amusing gamble. The townsfolk took it more seriously, with the result that a week after allotment the shares were changing hands at a premium of thirty shillings and there was still a busy market in them. Some who, tempted by the premium, sold at a profit suspected as soon as they had sold that they had thrown away their one chance of wealth, and went into the market and bought again, and so the rise was maintained and even extended. More than once Ovington put in a word of caution, reminding his customers that the first sod was not yet cut, that all the work was to do, that even the Bill was not yet passed. But his warnings were disregarded.

To the majority it seemed a short and easy way to fortune, and they wondered that they had been so simple in the past as to know nothing of it. It was by this way, they now saw, that Ovington had risen to wealth, while they, poor fools, not yet admitted to the secret, had gaped and wondered. And what a secret it was! To rise in the morning richer by fifty pounds than they had gone to bed! To retire at night with another fifty as good as in the bank, or in the old and now despised stocking! The slow increment of trade seemed mean and despicable beside their hourly growing profits, made while men slept or dined, made, as a leading tradesman pithily said, while they wore out their breeches on their chairs! Few troubled themselves about the Bill, or the cutting of the first sod, or considered how long it would be before the railroad was at work. Fewer still asked themselves whether this untried scheme would ever pay. It was enough for them that the shares were ever rising, that men were always to be found to buy them at the current price, and that they themselves were growing richer week by week.

For the directors these were great days! They walked Bride Hill and the Market Place with their heads high and their toes turned out. They talked in loud voices in the streets. They got together in corners and whispered, their brows heavy with the weight of affairs. They were great men. The banker, it is true, did not like the pitch to which the thing was being carried; but it was his business to wear a cheerful face, and he had no misgivings to speak of, though he knew that success was a long way off. And even on him the prosperity of the venture had some effect. Sir Charles and Acherley, too, were not of those who openly exulted; it is possible that the latter sold a few shares, or even a good many shares.

But Purslow and Grounds and Wolley? Who shall describe the importance which sat upon their brows, the dignity of their strut, the gravity of their nod, the mock humility of their reticence? Never did they go in or go out without the consciousness that the eyes of passers-by were upon them! Theirs to make men's fortunes by a hint – and their bearing betrayed that they knew it. Purslow's apron was discarded, no longer did he come out to customers in the street; if he still rubbed one hand over the other it was in self-content. Grounds was dazzled, and wore his Sunday clothes on week-days. Wolley, always a braggart, swaggered and talked, closed his eyes to his commitments and remembered only his gains. He talked of buying another mill, he even entered into a negotiation with that in view. He was convinced that safety lay in daring, and that this was the golden moment, if he would free himself from the net of debt that for years had been weaving itself about him.

He assumed the airs of a rich man, but he was not the worst. The draper, if more honest, had less brains, and success threw him off his balance. 'A little country 'ouse,' he said, speaking among his familiars. 'I'm thinking of buying a little country 'ouse. Two miles from town. A nice distance.' He recalled the fact that the founder of Sir Charles' family had been Mayor of Aldersbury in the days of Queen Bess, and had bought the estate with money made in the town, 'Who knows,' with humility – 'my lad's a good lad – what may come of it? After all there is nothing like land.'

Grounds shook his head. 'I don't know. It doesn't double—'

'Double itself in a month, Grounds? No. But all in good time. All in good time. 'Istory repeats itself. My lad may be a parliament-man, yet. I saw Ovington this morning.' Two months before it would have been 'Mr Ovington.' 'He's sold those Anglo-Mexicans for me and it beats all! A gold-mine! Bought at forty, sold at seventy-two! He wanted me to pay off the bank, but not I, Grounds. When you can borrow at seven and double the money in a month! No, no! Truth is, he's jealous. He gets only seven per cent, and sees me coining! Of course he wants his money. No, no, I said.'

Grounds looked doubtful. He was too cautious to operate on borrowed money. 'I don't know. After all, enough is as good as a feast, Purslow.'

Purslow prodded him playfully, 'Ay, but what is enough?' he chuckled. 'No. We've been let in and I mean to stay in. There's plenty of fools grubbing along in the old way, but you and me, we are inside now, Grounds, and I mean to stay in. The days of five per cent are gone for you and me. Gone! 'Twarn't by five per cent that Ovington got where he is.'

'My wife wants a silk dress.'

'Let 'er 'ave it! And come to me for it! You can afford it!' He strutted off. 'Grounds all over!' he muttered. 'Close, d—d close! Hasn't the pluck of a mouse – and a year ago he could buy me twice over!' In fancy he saw his Jack a college-man and counsellor, and by and by he passed various parks and halls before his mental vision and saw Jack seated in them, saw him Sir John Purslow, saw him Member for Aldersbury. He held his head high as he marched across the street to his shop, jingling the silver in his fob. Queen Bess, indeed! What were Queen Bess' days to these?

But a man cannot talk big without paying for the luxury. The draper's foreman asked for higher wages; his second hand also. Purslow gave the rise, but, reminded that their pay was in arrear, 'No, Jenkins, no,' he said. 'You must wait. Hang it, man, do you think I've nothing better to do with my money in these days than pay you fellows to the day? 'Ere! 'ere's a pound on account. Let it run! Let it run! All in good time, man. Fancy my credit's good enough!'

And instead of meeting the last acceptance that he'd given to his cloth-merchant, he took it up with another bill at two months – a thing he had never done before. 'Credit! Credit's the thing in these days,' he said, winking. 'Cash? Excuse me! Out of date, man, with them that knows. Credit's the 'orse!'

Arthur Bourdillon wore his honours more modestly, and courted the mean with success. But even he felt the intoxication of this noontide prosperity. At Garth he had doubted, and suffered scruples to weigh with him. But no sooner had he returned to the bank than the atmosphere of money enveloped him, and discerning that it was now in his power to make the best of two worlds, hitherto inconsistent, he plunged with gusto into the business. As secretary of the company he was a person to be courted; as a partner, now recognised, in the bank, he was more. He felt himself capable of all, for had not all succeeded with him? And awake to the fact that the times were abnormal – though he did not deduce from this the lesson he should have drawn – he thanked his stars that he was there to profit by them, and to make the most of them.

He was beyond doubt an asset to the bank. His birth, his manners, his good looks, the infection of his laugh, made him a favourite with gentle and simple. And then he worked. He had energy, he was tireless, no task was too hard or too long for him. But he laboured under one disadvantage, though he did not know it. He had had experience of the rise, not of the fall. As far back as he had been connected with Ovington's, trade had continued to expand, things had gone well; and by nature he was sanguine and leant towards the bold policy. He threw his weight on that side, and, able and self-confident, he made himself felt. Even Ovington yielded to the thrust of his opinion, was swayed by him, and at times, perhaps, put a little out of his course.

Not that Arthur was without his troubles. Naturally and inevitably a cloud had fallen on the relations, friendly hitherto, between him and Clement. Clement had grown cool to him, and the change was unwelcome, for it was in Arthur's nature to love popularity and to thrive and to bask in the sunshine of it. But it could not be helped. Without breaking eggs one could not make omelettes. Clement blamed him, he knew, feeling, and with reason, that what he had done deserved acknowledgment, and that it lay with Arthur to see that justice was done. And Arthur, for his part, would have gladly acquitted himself of the debt had it consisted with his own interests. But it did not.

Had he suspected the tie between Clement and Josina he might have acted otherwise. He might have foreseen the possibility of Clement's gaining the old man's ear, might have scented danger, and played a more cautious game. But he knew nothing of this. Garth and Clement stood apart in his mind. Clement and Josina were as far as he knew barely acquainted. He was aware, therefore, of no special reason why Clement should desire to stand well at Garth, while he felt sure that his friend was the last person to push a claim, or to thrust himself uninvited on the Squire's gratitude.

Accordingly, and the more as the banker had not himself taken up the quarrel, he put it aside as of no great importance. He shrugged his shoulders and told himself that Clement would come round. The cloud would pass, and its cause be forgotten.

In the meantime he ignored it. He met Clement's hostility with bland unconsciousness, smiled and was pleasant. He was too busy a man to be troubled by trifles. He was not going to be turned from his course by the passing frown of a silly fellow, who could not hold an advantage when he had won it.

Betty was another matter. Betty was behaving ill and showing temper, in league apparently with her brother and sympathising with him. She was changed from the Betty of old days. He had lost his hold upon her, and though this fell in well enough with the change in his views – or the possible change, for he had not quite made up his mind – it pricked his conceit as much as it surprised him. Moreover, the girl had a sharp tongue and was not above using it, so that more than once he smarted under its lash.

'Fine feathers make fine birds!' she said, as Arthur came bounding into the house one day and all but collided with her. 'Only they should be your own, Mr Daw!'

'Oh, I give your father all the credit,' he replied, 'only I do some of the work. But you used not to be so critical, Betty.'

'No? Well, I'll tell you why if you like.'

'Oh, I don't want to know.'

'No, I don't think you do!' the girl retorted. 'But I'll tell you. I thought your feathers were your own then. Now – I should be uneasy if I were you.'

'Why?'

'You might fall among crows and be plucked. I can tell you, you'd be a sorry sight in your own feathers!'

He turned a dusky red. The shaft had gone home, but he tried to hide the wound. 'A dull bird, eh?' he said, affecting to misunderstand her. 'Well, I thought you liked dull birds. I couldn't be duller than Rodd, and you don't find fault with him.'

It was a return shot, aimed only to cover his retreat. But the shot told in a way that surprised him. Betty reddened to her hair, and her eyes snapped.

'At any rate, Mr Rodd is what he seems!' she cried.

'Oh! oh!'

'He's not hollow!'

'No! Of course not! A most witty, bright, amusing gentleman, the pink of fashion, and – what is it? – the mould of form! Hollow? Oh, no, Betty, very solid, I should say – and stolid!' with a grin. 'Not a roaring blade, perhaps – I could hardly call him that, but a sound, substantial, wooden – gentleman! I am sure that your father values him highly as a clerk, and would value him still more highly as—'

'What?'

'I need not put it into words – but it lies with you to qualify him for the post. Rodd? Well, well, times are changed, Betty! But we live and learn.'

'You have a good deal to learn,' she cried, bristling with anger, 'about women!'

He got away then, retiring in good order and pleased that he had not had the worst of it; hoping, too, that he had closed the little spitfire's mouth. But there he found himself mistaken. The young lady was of a high courage, and perhaps had been a little spoiled. Where she once felt contempt she made no bones about showing it, and whenever they met, her frankness, sharpened by a woman's intuition, kept him on tenterhooks.

'You seem to think very ill of me,' he said once. 'And yet you trouble yourself a good deal about me.'

'You make a mistake!' she replied. 'I am not troubling myself about you. I'm thinking of my father.'

'Ah! Now you are out of my reach. That's beyond me.'

'I wish he were!'

'He knows his own business.'

'I hope he does!' she riposted. And though it was the memory of Rodd's warning that supplied the dart, the animosity that sped it had another source. The truth was that Clement had at last taken her into his confidence.

It was not without great unhappiness that he had seen all the hopes which he had built upon the Squire's gratitude come to nothing. He had hoped, and for a time had been even confident. But nothing had happened, no message, no summons had reached him. The events of that night might have been a dream, as far as he was concerned. Yet he could not see his way to blow his own trumpet, or proclaim what he had done. He stood no better than before, and indeed his position was worse.

For as long as the Squire lay bedridden and ill he could not go to him. Even when the report came that he was mending, Clement hesitated. To go to him, basing his claim on what had happened, to go to him and tell the story, as he must, with his own lips – this presented difficulties from which a man with delicate feelings might well shrink!

Meanwhile a veil had fallen between him and Josina. He had sworn that he would not see her again until he could claim her, and he supposed her to be engrossed by her father's illness and tied to his bedside. He even with a lover's insight inferred the remorse which she felt and her recoil from a continuance of their relations. Meanwhile he did not know what to do. He did not see any outlet. He was in an impasse with no prospect of delivery. And while he felt that Arthur had behaved ungenerously, while he even suspected that his friend had taken the credit which was his own due, he had no clue to his motives, or his schemes.

It was Betty who first saw into the dark place. For one day, longing as lovers long for a confidante, he had told her all, from the first meeting with Josina to his final parting from the girl by the brook, and his brief and unfortunate interview with her father on the road. The romance charmed Betty, the audacity of it dazzled her, for, a woman, she perceived more clearly than Clement the gulf between the town and the country, the new and the old. She listened to his tale with sighs and tears and little endearments, and led him on from one thing to another. She could not hear too much of a story that hardly a woman alive could have heard with indifference. She praised Josina to the top of his bent, and if she could not give him much hope, she gave him sympathy.

And, shrewdly, in her own mind she put things together. 'Arthur is off with the old love,' she thought, 'and on with the new.' He had changed sides, and that explained many things. So, with hardly any premises, she jumped to a conclusion so nearly correct that, could Arthur have read her mind, he would have winced even more than he did under the thrusts of her satire.

But she did not tell Clement. Her suspicions were not founded on reason, and they would only alarm him, and he was gloomy enough as it was. Instead, she cheered him and bade him be patient. Something might turn up, and in no case could much be done until the Squire was well enough to leave his room.

At bottom she was not hopeful. She saw arrayed between Clement and his love a host of difficulties, apart from Arthur's machinations. The pride of class, the old man's obstinacy, the young girl's timidity, Josina's wealth – these were obstacles hard to surmount. And Arthur was on the spot ready to raise new barriers, should these be overcome.

Chapter Twenty

The money for Arthur's share in the bank had been paid over in the early part of June, but the transaction had not gone through with the smoothness which he had anticipated. He had found himself up against a thing which he had not taken into his reckoning: the jealousy with which the old and the rich are apt to guard the secret of their wealth, a jealousy in the Squire's case aggravated by his blindness. Arthur had felt the check and was forced to own, with some alarm, that high as he stood in favour, a little thing might upset him.

He had written to the brokers, requesting them to sell sufficient India Stock to bring in a sum of six thousand pounds. They had replied that they could not carry out the order unless they had the particulars of the Stock standing in the Squire's name at the India House. But when Arthur took the letter to the Squire's room and read it to him, the outcome surprised him. The old man sat up in bed and confounded him by the vigour of his answer. 'Want to know how much I hold?' he cried. 'D—n their impudence! Then they'll not know! Want to look at my books and see what I'm worth! What next? What is it to them what I hold? You bid 'em sell' – beating the counterpane with his stick – 'you bid 'em sell two thousand two hundred pounds – at two hundred and seventy-five, that's near the mark! That's all they've got to do, the impudent puppies! Do you write, d'you hear, and tell 'em to do it!'

Arthur cursed the old man's unreasonableness, and wondered what he was to do. If there was going to be all this difficulty about the particulars, what about the certificates? How was he to get them? For the Squire as he sat erect, thrusting forward his bandaged head, and clutching the stick that lay beside him, grew almost threatening. He was in arms in defence of his money-bags and his secrets, and his nephew saw that it would take a bolder man than himself to cross him.

He hesitated. 'I am afraid, sir,' he ventured at last, 'there's a difficulty here that I had not foreseen. The certificates—'

'They don't want the certificates – yet! Don't they say so? Plain as a pikestaff!'

'Perhaps, sir,' doubtfully, 'if Welshes have got them—'

'Welshes have not got them!'

Arthur did not know what to say to that. At last, in a tone as reasonable as he could compass, 'I am afraid the difficulty is, sir,' he said, 'that they cannot make out a transfer until they have the particulars. Which I fancy we can only get from the certificates.'

'Then they may go to blazes!' the Squire replied, and he lay down with his face to the wall. Not he! There might be officials at the India House who knew this or that, and Welshes, who had acted for him in making one purchase or another, might know a part. But to no living man had he ever entrusted the secret of his fortune, or the result of those long years of stinting and sparing and saving that had cleared the mortgaged estate and had been continued because habit was strong and age is penurious. No, to no man living! That was his secret while the breath was in him. Afterwards – but he was not going to give it up yet.

Presently he bade Arthur go, and Arthur went, troubled in his mind, and much less assured of his position than he had been an hour before. He thanked his stars that he had not given way to the temptation to cut loose from the bank. It would never have done, he saw that now. And how was he going to extract his money, his six thousand, from this unreasonable old dotard? For so he styled him in his wrath.

However, the riddle solved itself before many hours had passed.

That afternoon he was absent, and Jos, about whom Miss Peacock was growing anxious, had gone out to take the air. The butler, left on guard, occupied himself with laying the table in the dining-room, where, if the Squire tapped the floor, he could hear him. He heard no summons, but presently as he went about his work he heard someone moving upstairs and he pricked up his ears. Surely the Squire was not getting out of bed? Weak and blind as he was – but again he heard heavy footsteps, and, thoroughly alarmed, the man lost no time. He hurried up the stairs, and entered his master's room. The Squire was out of bed. He was on his feet, clinging to the post at the foot of the bed, and feeling helplessly about him with the other hand.

'Lord, ha' mercy!' Calamy cried, eyeing the gaunt figure with dismay. He hastened forward to support it.

The Squire collapsed on the bed as soon as he was touched. 'I canna do it,' he groaned, 'I canna do it. It's going round wi' me. Who is it?'

'Calamy, sir,' the butler answered, and added bluntly, 'If you want to get into your coffin, master, you're going the right way to do it!'

'Anyway, I canna do it,' the Squire repeated, and remained motionless for a moment. 'I couldn't manage the stairs if 'twere ever so.'

'You'd manage 'em one way. You'd fall down 'em. You get to bed, sir. You get to bed. There, I'll heave you up.'

'I'm weaker than I thought,' the Squire muttered. He suffered himself to be put into bed.

'You've lost blood, sir, that's what it is,' the butler said. 'And at your age it's not to be replaced in a week, nor a fortnight. You lie still, sir. Maybe in a month you'll be tramping the stairs. But blindfold – it's the Lord's mercy as you didn't fall and only stop in Kingdom Come! For if fall you did, I don't know where else you'd stop.'

'I'm afraid so. Anyway I canna do it!'

'Only feet foremost.'

The Squire sighed and turned himself to the wall, perhaps to hide the tear that helplessness forced from old eyes. He couldn't do it, and he must put up with the consequences. He could not any longer be sufficient to himself. It was a sad thought, but apparently he made up his mind to it, for twenty-four hours later, when Jos and Arthur were with him, he sent the girl away. When she had gone he sought under the pillow for his keys, and after handling them for a time, 'Is the door shut? No one here but you? Are you sure?'

'We are quite alone, sir.'

'No one within hearing, lad?'

'Not a soul, sir.'

'It's not that I mistrust the wench,' the Squire muttered. 'She's a Griffin and a good girl, a good girl. But she's a tongue like other women.' By this time he had found what he wanted, and holding the bunch by one of the keys he offered it to Arthur. 'That's the key. Now you listen to me. Go down to the dining-room, and don't you do anything till you've locked the door and seen there's no one at the windows. The panel, right side of the fireplace – are you minding me? Ay? Well, pass your hand down the moulding next the hearth and you'll feel a crack across it, and, an inch below, another. They're so small you as good as can't see them, when you know they're there. Twist that bit, top part to the right, and you'll see a key-hole. Turn the key and pull, and the panel comes open, and you'll see a cupboard door behind it. Same key unlocks it. Are you minding me?'

'I am, sir, I quite understand.'

'Well, on the middle shelf – you'll see a box. The key to that box is the next on the bunch. Open it and you will have the India Stock Certificates.' The Squire sighed and for a moment was silent. 'There's one for two thousand two hundred, which will do it. Bring it here. You needn't,' drily, 'go routing among the others, once you've found it. Then lock up, and slip the moulding into place. But be sure, lad, before you do aught, that the door is locked.'

'I will be careful,' Arthur assured him. 'I quite understand, sir.'

'It's not that I distrust Jos,' the Squire repeated – as if he defended himself against an accusation. 'But tell a secret to a woman, and you tell it to the parish.'

'Shall I do it now, sir?'

'Ay, and bring back the keys. Don't let 'em out of your hands.'

Arthur went downstairs, and as he descended the shallow steps he smiled. Men, even the sharpest of men, were easy to manage if you had patience.

The afternoon was drawing in. The corners in the hall were growing dim. The sky seen through the open door was pale green. The air came in from the garden, sweet but chilly, laden with the scent of lilac and gilly flowers. A single rook cawed. The peace of the country was upon all. He could hear his mother and Josina talking somewhere within the house.

He slipped into the dining-room and, locking himself in, he looked round him. The paint on the panelled walls was faded, blistered in places by the sun, or soiled where elbows had rubbed it, or the butler's tray, standing against it through long years, had marked it. The panels were large, dating from Dutch William or Anne, of chestnut and set in heavy mouldings.

Arthur glanced at the windows to make sure that he was unseen, then he stepped to the hearth and felt for and found the bit of moulding, in front of which, though he had forgotten to mention it, the Squire had hung an old almanack. Arthur twisted the upper end to the right, uncovered the key-hole, and within a minute had the inner door open.

It masked a cupboard, contrived in the thickness of the chimney-breast, perhaps at the time when the open shaft had been closed and a smaller fireplace had been inserted. Inside, two shelves formed three receptacles. In the uppermost were parcels of old letters secured with dusty and faded ribands, and piled at random one on another – the relics of the love-letters or law-letters of past generations. In the lowest compartment were bigger bundles secured with straps, which Arthur judged to contain leases and farm agreements, and the like. Some were of late date – he took up one or two bundles and looked at the endorsements – none of them appeared to be very old.

The middle space displayed a row of old ledgers and farm books, and standing alone before them a small iron box. It was with this no doubt that his business lay, and he tried his key in it. The key fitted. He opened the box.

It contained three certificates and, though he had been bidden not to rout among them, he felt it his duty to ascertain – for he would probably have to inform the brokers – what was the total of the Squire's holding. They all three represented India Stock, and Arthur's eyes glistened as he noted the amount and figured up the value in his mind. One, as the Squire had said, was for two thousand two hundred, the other two were for two thousand five hundred each. Arthur calculated that at the price of the day they were worth little short of twenty thousand pounds. He withdrew the smallest certificate and locked the box. He had done his errand, but as he went about to close the cupboard-door he paused. He had seen old letters, and modern agreements and the like. But no old deeds. Where did the Squire keep the title-deeds of Garth? They were not here.

Arthur glanced at the other side of the fireplace. There, precisely corresponding with the almanack which he had removed, hung an old-fashioned silver sconce with a flat back serving for a reflector. A pair of snuffers flanked the candle-holder on one side, an extinguisher on the other. It was a piece which Arthur had admired for its age but had never seen in use. He stared at it, and as he closed the cupboard and panel by which he stood, and replaced the bit of moulding, he hesitated. With the keys in his hand he cast a glance at the windows, then he crossed the hearth, took down the sconce, and ran his fingers down the moulding.

Yes, here were the cracks, barely to be discovered by the fingers and not at all by the eye. The bit of moulding, when he twisted it, moved stiffly, but it moved. With another glance over his shoulder he inserted the key, then he listened. All was quiet in the house. Outside, a wood-pigeon coo'd in a neighbouring tree while a solitary rook uttered a shrill 'Bah-doo! Bah-doo!' – not the common caw, but a cry that he had often heard.

Something in the stealthiness of his movements and the stillness of the house whispered a warning to him, and he paused, his arm raised. Yet – why not? What could come of it? Knowledge was always useful, and if his business had lain with this second cupboard his uncle would have sent him to it as freely as to the other. With an effort he shook off his scruples, and to satisfy himself that he was doing no wrong he laughed. He turned the key and swung back the panel. He unlocked and opened the inner door.

Here there were but two divisions. The lower one was piled high with plate; with a part, if not the whole, of a dinner-service, cups, bowls, candlesticks, wine-jugs, salt-cellars – a collection that, tarnished and dull as the pieces were, made Arthur's mouth water. Among them lay half a dozen leather cases which he fancied held jewellery, and more than a dozen bulky parcels – spoons and forks and the like. They had not been disturbed, it was plain, for years, and he dared not touch them.

On the shelf were two iron boxes, and arrayed before them four parcels of deeds, old and discoloured, with ends of green riband hanging from them, and here and there a great seal – one seal was of lead. They gave out a damp, sour smell, the odour of slowly decaying sheepskins. Three of the parcels related to farms which the Squire had bought within Arthur's memory. The fourth and largest bundle, in a coarse wrapper, neatly bound about with straps, had a label attached to it, 'The Title Deeds of the Garth Estate,' and thrust under one of the straps was a folded slip of parchment. Arthur opened this and saw that it was a memorandum, dated fifty years before, of the deposit of the deeds to secure the repayment of thirty-eight thousand pounds and interest. Below were receipts for instalments repaid at intervals of years, and opposite the last receipt appeared, in the Squire's hand 'Cancelled and deeds returned – Thank God for His mercies!'

Arthur felt a thrill of sympathy as he read the words. He returned the slip to its place and softly closed the door, he swung back the panel and secured it. He replaced the silver sconce.

But though two inches of wood now intervened, he retained a vision of the bundle of deeds. It was not large, he could have carried it under his arm. But it meant, that little parcel, power, wealth, position, the Garth Estate! It spoke to Arthur the banker – for whom wealth lay in pieces of paper, not in gold and silver – as eloquently as the broad acres themselves, the farms and water-mills, the coverts and dingles, the wide-flung hill-side that he loved, spoke to the Squire. For the first time Arthur coveted Garth, valuing it not as the Squire did for what it was, hill and dale spread under heaven, but for what it was worth, for what might be made of it, for the use to which it might be put.

'He has added to it. One could raise fifty thousand on it,' he thought. And with fifty thousand what could one not do? With fifty thousand pounds, free money, added to the bank's resources, what might not be done? It was a golden vision that he saw, as he stood in the evening stillness with the scent of roses stealing into the room, and the wood-pigeon cooing softly in the tree outside.

Ay, what might he not do?

But the Squire might be growing suspicious. He roused himself, saw that all was as he had found it, and unlocking the door, he went upstairs.

'You've been a long time about it, young man,' the Squire grumbled. 'What's amiss?'

But Arthur was ready with his answer. 'You told me to go about it quietly, sir. So I waited until the coast was clear. It's a capital hiding-place. It's not to be found in a minute even when you know where it is.'

'Ay, ay. It would take a clever rogue to find it,' complacently.

'I suppose it's old, sir?'

'My grandfather put it in when the Scots were at Derby. And, mark ye, no one knows of it but Frederick Welsh – and now you. D'you be careful and keep your mouth shut, lad. You ha' got the certificate?'

'Yes, sir.'

'Well, go about the business and get it done. And now do you send Jos to me.'

Arthur made a mental note that the old man was changing at last – was losing that hard grip on all about him which he had maintained for half a century; and he was confirmed in this idea by the ease with which the India Stock transaction presently went through. The brokers showed themselves unusually complaisant. They wrote that, as the matter was personal to him, they were anxious that nothing should go wrong; and, as his customer was blind, they were forwarding with the transfer on which the particulars had been inserted a duplicate in blank, in order that if the former were spoiled in the execution delay might be avoided. This was irregular, but if the duplicate were not needed, it could be returned and no harm done.

Arthur thought this polite of them, and was flattered; he felt that he was a client of value. But as it turned out the duplicate was not needed; the Squire made nothing of the formality. His hand once directed to the proper place, he signed his name boldly and plainly – as he did most things; and Arthur and Jos added their signatures as witnesses. Ten days later the money was received, and five-sixths of it was paid over to the bank. The duplicate transfer, overlooked at the moment, lay on the Squire's bureau until it did not seem worth while to return it. Then Arthur, tired of coming upon it every day, thrust it out of sight in a pigeon-hole.

He had other things to think of, indeed, for he was in high feather in these days, while the summer sun climbed slowly to the zenith and began again to sink. He had two-fold interests. After a long day spent in the bank he would ride out of town in the cool of the evening, and passing down the winding streets under the gables of the old black and white houses, he would cross the West Bridge. Bucketing his horse up the rise that led from the river, he would leave the town behind and see before him the road running straight and dusty towards the sunset-glow, which still shone above the Welsh hills. From the fields on either side came the sharp sound of the scythe-stone, the laughter of haymakers, the call of the waggoner to his team, the creaking of the laden wheels over the turf. Partridges dusting themselves in the road scuttled out of his way and presently took wing; rabbits watched him from the covert-edge. The corncrake's persistent note spoke rather of the hot hours that were past than of the evening air that cooled his cheek. An aged simpleton in a smocked frock, the clown of the countryside, danced a jig before an ale-house; a stray bullock gazed patiently at him from a pound. The countryside lay quiet about him, and despite himself he owned the charm of peace, the fall of night, the end of labour.

But his thoughts still dwelt on the day's work. There had been a discussion over Wolley's account. Wolley had been behaving ill. Ignoring the claim of the bank he had assigned a number of his railway shares to meet a bill discounted elsewhere. The natural course would have been to insist on the lien and to retain the shares. But the consequences, as

Ovington saw, might be serious. The step might not only involve the bank in a loss, which he still hoped to avoid, but it might imply taking over the mill – and it is not the business of bankers to run mills. Arthur, on the other hand, who did not like the man, would have cut the knot at once and sent him to the devil.

In the end Ovington had decided against Arthur. 'We must be careful,' the banker said. 'Credit is like a house of cards. You take one card away, you do not know how many may fall.'

'But if we don't teach him a lesson now?'

'Quite true, lad. But – well, I will see him. If, as Rodd thinks, he is drawing on men of straw, whose acceptances are worthless—'

'That would be the devil!'

'There will be an end of him – but not of him only. We must go warily, lad. To throw him down now' – the banker shook his head. 'No, we will give him one more chance. I will talk to him.'

'I should not have the patience.'

'That is one of the things you have to learn.'

Arthur reviewed the conversation as he rode, and retained his own opinion. He thought Ovington too apprehensive. He would himself have played a bolder game and cut Wolley and his losses, if losses there must be. Then, shrugging his shoulders, he dismissed the matter and allowed his thoughts to go before him to Garth, to the old man, to his favour, and the path it opened to Josina. Yes, Josina. He was not doing much there, but there was no hurry, and despite the charms of Garth he had not quite made up his mind. When he did, he anticipated no difficulty.

Still something was due to her, were it only as a matter of form; and she was pale and sweet and appealing. A little love-making would not be unpleasant these summer evenings, though he had so far held off, haunted by a foolish hankering after Betty; Betty with her sparkle and colour, her wit and high spirit, ay, and her very temper, mutinous little rebel as she was – her temper which, manlike, he longed to tame.

Ten minutes later saw him in the Squire's room, entertaining him with scraps of county gossip and the latest news from town. Into the dull room, with its drab hangings and shadowy portraits, where the old man sat by his fireless grate, he came like a gleam of sunshine, his laugh lighting up the dim places, his voice expelling the tedium of the long day. He brought with him the new *Quarterly*, or the last *Morning Post*. He had news of what

Sir Harry had lost at Goodwood, of Mytton's last scrape, of the poaching affray at my lord's. He had a joke for Josina and a teasing word for Miss Peacock – who idolised him.

And he had tact. He could listen as well as talk. He heard with interest who had called to ask after the Squire, whose landau and outriders had turned on the narrow sweep, and whose curricle; what humbler visitors had left their respects at the stables or the back-door, and what was Calamy's last scrap of dolefulness.

He was the universal favourite. He had taken the length of the Squire's foot; it had been an easier matter than he had anticipated. But even in his cup there was a sour drop. He had his occasional misgivings and now and then he suffered a shock. One day it was, 'What about your coat, lad?'

'My coat?' Arthur stared at the old man. He did not understand.

'Ay. You thought that I'd forgotten it. But I'm not that shaken. What about it?'

Now, between the darkness of the night and the confusion, Arthur had not noticed the damage done to Clement's overcoat. Consequently he could make nothing of the Squire's words and he tried to pass the matter off. 'Oh, it's all right, sir,' he said. He waited for something to enlighten him.

'Can you wear it?'

'Oh yes.'

'The deuce you can!' The Squire was surprised. 'Then all I can say is, you've found a d—d good cleaner, lad. If you got that blood off – but as you did, all's well. I was afeared I'd owe you a new coat, my boy. I'd not forgotten it, but I knew that you'd not be wearing it this weather, and I thought in another week or two I'd be getting this bandage off. Then I'd see how it was, and what we could do with it.'

Arthur understood then, and a thrill of alarm ran through him. What if the Squire began – but no, the danger was over, and as quickly as possible he rid himself of fear. He was not a fool to start at shadows. Things were going so well with him that he had no mind to spare for trifles, and no time to look aside.

Chapter Twenty-One

July had passed into August. Who was it who whispered the first word of doubt? Of misgiving? Where was felt the first shiver of distrust? What lips first let drop the fatal syllables, a fall? Who in the secrecy of some bank-parlour or some discounter's office, sitting at the centre of the spider's web of credit, felt a single filament, stretched it may be across half a world, shiver, and relax? And, refusing to draw the unwelcome inference, sceptical of danger, felt perhaps a second shock, ever so slight and ever so distant; and then, reading the message aright, began to narrow his commitments, to draw in his resources, to call in his money, to turn into gold his paper wealth? And so from that dark office or parlour in Fenchurch Street or Change Alley, set in motion, obscurely, imperceptibly at first, the mighty impetus that was to reach to such tremendous ends?

Who? Probably no one knew then, and certainly no one can say now. But it is certain that in the late summer of that year, while the Squire sat blinded in his drab-hued room at Garth, and Ovington's hummed with business, and Arthur rode gaily to and fro between the two, the thing happened. Someone, some bank, perhaps some great speculator with irons in many fires and many lands, took fright and acted on his fears – but silently, stealthily, as is the manner of such. Or it may have been a manufacturer on a great scale who looked abroad and fancied that he saw, though still a long way off, that bugbear of manufacturers, a glut.

At any rate there came a check, unmarked by the vast majority, but of which a whisper began to pass round the inner recesses of Lombard Street – a fall, such as there had been a few months earlier, but which then had been speedily made good. Aldersbury lay far beyond the warning, or if a hint of it reached Ovington, it did not go beyond him. He did not pass it on, even to Arthur, much less did it reach others. Sir Charles, secluded within his park walls, was not in the way of hearing such things, and Acherley and his like were busy with preparations for autumn sport, getting out their guns and seeing that their pink coats were aired and their mahogany tops were brought to the right colour. Wolley had his own troubles, and dealt with them after his own reckless fashion, which was to retire one bill by another; he found it all he could do to provide for today, without thinking what tomorrow might bring forth, should his woollen goods become unsaleable, or his bills fail to find discounters. And the multitude, Grounds and Purslow and their followers, were happy, secure in their ignorance, foreseeing no evil.

This was the state of things at Aldersbury, as summer passed into autumn. Men still added up their investments, and chuckled over what they had made, and added to the sum what they were sure of making, when the shares of this mine or that canal company rose another five or ten points. Their wealth on paper was still, to them, solid, abiding wealth, to be garnered and laid by and enjoyed when it pleased them. And trade seemed still to flourish, though not quite so briskly. There was still a demand for goods, though not quite so urgent a demand – and the price stuck a little. The railway shares still stood at the high premium to which they had risen, though for the moment they did not seem to be inclined to go higher.

But about the end of September – perhaps someone in London or Birmingham or Liverpool had twitched the filament which connected it with Aldersbury – Ovington called Arthur back as he was leaving the parlour at the close of the day's business. 'Wait a moment,' he said, 'I want you. I have been thinking things over, lad, and I am not quite comfortable about them.'

'Is it Wolley?' Wolley's case had been before them that morning and sharp things had been said about his trading methods.

'No, it's not Wolley.' Having got so far Ovington paused, and Arthur noticed that his face was grave. 'No, though Wolley is a part of it. I am always uneasy about him. But—'

'What is it, sir?'

'It is the general situation, lad. I don't like it. I've an impression that things have gone farther than they should. There is an amount of inflation that, if things go smoothly, will be gradually reduced and no harm done. But we have a large sum of money out' – he touched the pile of papers before him – 'and I should like to see it lessened. I hardly know why, but I do not feel that the position is healthy.'

'But our money is well covered.'

'As things are.'

'And we are as solvent, sir, as—'

'As need be, with the ordinary time to meet the calls that may be made upon us. But in the event of a sudden fall, of one big failure leading to another – in the event of a sudden rush to present our notes?'

'Even then, sir, we are well secured. We should have no difficulty in finding accommodation.'

'In ordinary circumstances, no – and if we alone needed it. We could go to A. or B. or C., and there would be no difficulty. We have the money's worth and a good margin. But if A. and B. and C. were also short, what then, lad?'

Arthur felt something approaching contempt. The banker seemed to him to be inventing bogies, imagining dangers, dreaming of difficulties where none existed. He saw him in a new light, and discovered him to be timorous. 'But that state of things is not likely to occur,' he objected.

'Perhaps not, but if it did?'

'Have you had any hint?'

'No. But I see that iron is down – since Saturday. And the Manchester market was flat yesterday.'

'Things that have happened before,' Arthur said. 'I think, sir, it is really Wolley's affair that is troubling you.'

'If it ended with Wolley it would be a small matter. No, I am not thinking of that.' He looked before him and drummed upon the table with his fingers. 'But the position calls for – caution. We must go no farther. We must be careful how we grant accommodation, no matter who applies for it. We must raise our reserve. See, if you please, that we do not discount a single bill without recourse to me – though, of course, you will let nothing be noticed on the other side of the counter.'

'Very good,' Arthur said. But he thought that the other's caution was running away with him. The sky seemed clear to him; He could discern no signs of a storm, and he did not reflect that, as he had never been present at a storm, the signs might escape him. 'Very good,' he said, 'I'll tell Rodd. I am sure it will please him,' and with that tiny sting he went out.

The conversation had been held behind closed doors, yet it had its effect. A chill seemed to fall upon the bank. The air became less genial. Ovington's face was both keen and watchful. Arthur, perplexed and puzzled, grew more brusque, his speech shorter, while Rodd's face reflected his superiors' gravity. Only Clement, going about his branch of the work with his usual stolid indifference, perceived no change in the temperature, and, depressed before, was only a degree nearer to the mean level.

Poor Clement! There are situations in which it is hard to play the hero, and he found himself in one of them. He had vowed that there should be no more meetings and no more love-making until he had faced and conquered his dragon. But meanwhile the dragon lay sick and blind at the bottom of its den, out of reach, and guarded by its very weakness from attack, while every hour and every day that saw nothing done seemed to remove Clement farther from his mistress, seemed to set a greater distance between them, seemed to blacken his face in her eyes.

Yet what could he do? How could he wrest himself from the inaction – it must seem to her the ignoble inaction – which pressed upon him? She watched – he pictured her watching from her tower, or more precisely from the terraced garden at Garth, for the deliverance which did not come, for the knight whose trumpet never sounded! She watched, while he, weak and shiftless, hung back in uncertainty, the inefficient he had ever been!

Ay, that he had ever been! It was that which hurt him. It was the sense of that which wasted his spirits as sorely as the impatience, the fever, of thwarted love. The spell of vigour which had for a few days lifted him out of himself, and given him the force to meet and to impress his fellows, had not only failed to win any real advantage, but, failing, had left him less self-reliant than before. For he saw now where he had failed. He saw that with the winning-card in his hand he had allowed himself to be defeated by Arthur, and to be jockeyed out of the fruits of his labour, simply because he had lacked the moral courage, the hardness of fibre, the stiffness to stand by his own!

And he feared that it would ever be so. Arthur had got the better of him, and the knowledge depressed him to the ground. He was not a man. He was a weakling, a dreamer, good for neither one thing nor another! As useless outside the bank as at his desk, below and not above the daily tasks that he secretly despised.

Yet what could he do? What was it in his power to do? He asked himself that question a hundred times. He could not force himself on the Squire, ill and confined to his bed as he was – and be sure, Arthur did not make the best of his uncle's condition. He could only wait, though to wait was intolerable. He could only wait, while poor Josina first doubted, then despaired! Wait while first hope, and then faith, and in the end love died in her breast! Wait, till she thought herself abandoned!

Of course in his impatience and his humility Clement exaggerated both the delay and its results. The days seemed weeks to him, the weeks months. He fancied it a year since he had seen Josina. He did not consider that she was no stranger to his difficulties, nor reflect that though his silence might try her, and his absence cause her unhappiness, she might still approve both the one and the other. As a fact, the lesson which he had taught her at their last meeting had been driven home by the remorse that had tortured her on that dreadful night; and lonely hours in the sick room, much watching, and many a thought of what might have been, had strengthened the impression.

But Clement did not know this. He pictured the girl as losing all faith in him, and as the weeks ran on, the time came when he could bear the delay no longer, when he felt that he must either act, that he must either do something, or write himself down a coward. So one day, after hearing in the town that the Squire was able to leave his room, he wrote to Josina. He told her that he should call on the morrow and see her father.

And on the morrow he rode over, blind for once to the changes of nature, of landscape and cloudscape that surrounded him. But he never reached the house, for at the little bridge at the foot of the drive Josina met him, and eager as he had been to see his sweetheart and to hear her voice, he was checked by the change in her. It was a change which went deeper than mere physical alteration, though that, too, was there. The girl was paler, finer, more spiritual. Trouble and anxiety had laid their mark on her. He had left her girl, he found her woman. A new look, a look of purpose, of decision, gave another cast to her features.

She was the first to speak, and her words bore out the change in her. 'You must come no farther, Clement,' she said. And then as their hands met and their eyes, the colour flamed in her cheeks, her head drooped flower-like, she was for an instant the old Josina, the girl he had wooed by the brook, who had many a time fallen on his breast. But for a moment only. Then, 'You cannot see him yet,' she announced. 'Not yet, for a long time, Clem. I met you here that I might stop you, and that there might be no misunderstanding – and no more secrets.'

And this she had certainly secured, for the place which she had chosen for their meeting was overlooked, though at a distance, by the doorway of the house, and by all the walks about it.

But he was not to be so put off. 'I must see him,' he said, and he told himself that he must not be moved by her pleadings. It was natural that she should fear, but he must not fear – and indeed he had passed beyond fear. 'No, dear,' as she began to protest, 'you must let me judge of this.' He held her hands firmly as he looked down at her. 'I have suffered enough, I have suffered as much as I can bear. I have had no sight of you and no word of you for months, and I cannot endure this longer. Every hour of every day I have felt myself a coward, a deserter, a do-nothing! I have had to bear this, and I have borne it. But now – now that your father is downstairs—'

'You can still do nothing,' she said. 'Believe, believe me,' earnestly, 'you can do nothing. Dear Clement,' and the tenderness which she strove to suppress betrayed itself in her tone, 'you must be guided by me, you must indeed. I am with my father, and I know, I know that he cannot bear the disclosure now. I know that it would be cruel to tell him now. He is blind. Blind, Clement! And he trusts me, he has to trust me. To tell him now would be to destroy his faith in me, to shock him and to frighten him – irreparably. You must go back now – now at once.'

'What? And do nothing?' he cried. 'And lose you?' The pathos of her appeal had passed him by, and only his love and his jealousy spoke.

'No,' she answered soberly, 'you will not lose me, if you have patience.'

'But have you patience?'

'I must have.'

'And I am to do nothing?' He spoke with energy, almost with anger. 'To go on doing nothing? I am to stand by and – and play the coward still – go on playing it?'

Her face quivered, for he hurt her. He was selfish, he was cruel; yet she understood, and loved him for his cruelty. But she answered him firmly. 'Nothing until I send for you,' she said. 'You do not think, Clem. He is blind! He is dependent on me for everything. If I tell him in his weakness that I have deceived him, he will lose faith in me, he will distrust me, he will distrust everyone. He will be alone in his darkness.'

It began to come home to him. 'Blind?' he repeated.

'Yes.'

'But for good? Do you mean – quite blind?'

'Ah, I don't know!' she cried, unable to control her voice. 'I don't know.

Dr Farmer does not know, the physician who came from Birmingham to see him does not know. They say that they have hopes – and I don't know! But I fear.'

He was silent then, touched with pity, feeling at length the pathos of it, feeling it almost as she felt it. But after a pause, during which she stood before him watching his face, 'And if he does not recover his sight?'

'God forbid!'

'I say God forbid too, with all my heart. Still, if he does not – what then? When may I—'

'When the time comes,' she answered, 'and of that I must be the judge. Yes, Clement,' with resolution. 'I must be the judge, for I alone know how he is, and I alone can choose the occasion.'

The delay was very bitter to him. He had ridden out determined to put his fate to the test, to let nothing stand between him and his love, to override excuses; and he could not in a moment make up his mind to be thwarted.

'And I must wait? I must go on waiting? Eating my heart out – doing nothing?' he protested.

'There is no other way. Indeed, indeed there is not.'

'But it is too much. It is too much, Jos, that you ask!'

'Then, Clement—'

'Well?'

'You must give me up.' She spoke firmly but her lips quivered, and there were tears in her eyes.

He was silent. At last, 'Do you wish me to do that?' he said.

She looked at him for answer, and his doubts, if he had doubted her, his distrust, if it had been possible for him to distrust her, vanished. His heart melted. They were a very simple pair of lovers, moved by simple impulses.

'Forgive me, oh, forgive me, dear!' he cried. 'But mine is a hard task. You do not know what it is to wait, to wait and to do nothing!'

'Do I not?' Her eyes were swimming. 'Is it not that which I am doing every day, Clem? But I have faith in you, and I believe in you. I believe that all will come right in the end. If you trust me, as I trust you, and have to trust you—'

'I will, I will,' he cried, repentant, remorseful, recognising in her a new decision, a new sweetheart, and doing homage to the strength that suffering had given her. 'I will trust you, trust you for ever – and wait!'

Her eyes thanked him, and her hands; and after this there was little more to be said. She was anxious that he should go, and they parted. He rode back to Aldersbury, thinking less of himself and more of her, and something too of the old man, who, blind and shorn of his strength, had now to lean on women, and suspicious by habit must now trust others, whether he would or no. Clement had imagination, and by its light he saw the pathos of the Squire's position; of his helplessness in the midst of the great possessions he had gathered, and the acres that he had added, acre to acre. He who had loved to look on hill and covert and know them his own, to whom every copse and hedgerow was a friend, who had watched his marches so jealously and known the rotation of every field, must now fume and fret, thinking them neglected, suspecting waste, doubting everyone, lacking but a little of doubting even his daughter.

'Poor chap!' he muttered, 'poor old chap!' He was sorry for the Squire, but he was even more sorry for himself. Any other, he felt, would have surmounted the obstacles that stopped him, or by one road or another would have gone round them. But he was no good, he was useless. Even his sweetheart – this in a little spirit of bitterness – took the upper hand and guided him and imposed her will on him. He was nothing.

In the bank he grew more taciturn, doing his business with less spirit than before, suspecting Arthur and avoiding speech with him, meeting his careless smile with a stolid face. His father, Rodd too, deemed him jealous of the new partner, and his father, growing in these days a little sharp in temper, spoke to him about it.

'You took no interest in the business,' he said, 'and I had to find someone who would take an interest and be of use to me. Now you are making difficulties and causing unpleasantness. You are behaving ill, Clement.'

But Clement only shrugged his shoulders. He had become indifferent. He had his own burden to bear.

Chapter Twenty-Two

Arthur, on the other hand, felt that things were going well with him. A few months earlier he had decided that a partnership in Ovington's would be cheaply bought at the cost of a rupture with his uncle. Now he had the partnership, he could look forward to the wealth and importance which it would bring – and he had not to pay the price. On the contrary, his views now took in all that he had been prepared to resign, as well as all that he had hoped to gain. They took in Garth, and he saw himself figuring not only as the financier whose operations covered many fields, and whose riches were ever increasing, but as the landed Squire, the man of family, whose birth and acres must give him a position in society which no mere wealth could confer. The unlucky night which had cost the old man so much, had been for Arthur the birth-night of fortune. He could date from it a favour, proof, as he now believed, against chance and change, a favour upon which it seemed unlikely that he could ever overdraw.

For since his easy victory on the question of the India Stock, he had become convinced that the Squire was failing. The old man, once so formidable, was changed; he had grown, if not weak, yet dependent. And it could hardly be otherwise, Arthur reflected. The loss of sight was a paralysing deprivation, and it had fallen on the owner of Garth at a time of life when any shock must sap the strength and lower the vitality. For a while his will had reacted, he had seemed to bear up against the blow, but age will be served, and of late he had grown more silent and apathetic. Arthur had read the signs and drawn the conclusion, and was now sure that, blind and shaken, the old man would never again be the man he had been, or assert himself against an influence which a subtler brain would know how to weave about him.

Arthur was thinking of this as he rode into town one morning in

November, his back turned to the hills and the romance of them, his face to the plain. It was early in the month. St. Luke's summer, prolonged that year, had come to an end a day or two before, and the air was raw, the outlook sombre. Under a canopy of grey mist, the thinning hedgerows and dripping woods showed dark against clear blue distances. But in the warmth of his thoughts the rider was proof against weather, and when he came to the sedgy spot, never more dreary to the view than today, which Thomas had chosen for his attack on the Squire, he smiled. That little patch of ground had done much for him, but at a price, of course – for there he had lost a friend, a good easy friend in Clement. And Betty – Betty, whose coolness had caused him more than one honest pang – he had no doubt that there had come a change in her, too, from that date.

But one had to pay a price for everything, and these were but small spots on the sun of his success. Soon he had put the thought of them from him, and, abreast of the first houses of the town, began to employ his mind on the work of the day – revolving this and that, matters outside routine which would demand his attention. He knew what was likely to arise.

Rarely in these days did he enter Aldersbury without a feeling of elation. The very air of the town inspired him. The life of the streets, the movement of the markets, the sight of the shopkeepers at their doors, the stir and bustle had their appeal for him. He felt himself on his own ground; it was here and not in the waste places that his work lay, here that he was formed to conquer, here that he was conquering fortune. Garth was very well – a grand, a splendid reserve; but as he rode up the steep streets to the bank, he felt that here was his vocation. He sniffed the battle, his eyes grew brighter, his figure more alert. From some Huguenot ancestor had descended the Huguenot appetite for business, the Huguenot ability to succeed.

This morning, however, he did not reach the bank in his happiest mood. Purslow, the irrepressible Purslow, stopped him, with a long face and a plaint to match. 'Those Antwerp shares, Mr Bourdillon! Excuse me, have you heard? They're down again – down twenty-five since Wednesday! And that's on to five, as they fell the week before! Thirty down, sir! I'm in a regular stew about it! Excuse me, sir, but if they fall much more—'

'You've held too long, Purslow,' Arthur replied. 'I told you it was a quick shot. A fortnight ago you'd have got out with a good profit. Why didn't you?'

'But they were rising – rising nicely. And I thought, sir—'

'You thought you'd hold them for a bit more? That was the long and short of it, wasn't it? Well, my advice to you now is to get out while you can make a profit.'

'Sell?' the draper exclaimed. 'Now?' It is hard to say what he had expected, but something more than this. 'But I should not clear more than – why, I shouldn't make—'

'Better make what you can,' Arthur replied, and rode on a little more cavalierly than he would have ridden a few months before.

He did not reflect how easy it is to sow the seeds of distrust. Purslow, left alone to make the best of cold comfort, felt for the first time that his interests were not the one care of the bank. For the first time he saw the bank as something apart, a machine, cold, impassive, indifferent, proceeding on its course unmoved by his fortunes, good or bad, his losses or his gains. It was a picture that chilled him, and set him thinking.

Arthur, meantime, left his horse at the stables and let himself into the bank by the house-door. As he laid his hat and whip on the table in the hall, he caught the sound of an angry voice. It came from the bank parlour. He hesitated an instant, then he made up his mind, and stepping that way he opened the door.

The voice was Wolley's. The man was on his feet, angry, protesting, gesticulating. Ovington, with set lips, the pallor of his handsome face faintly tinged with colour, sat behind his table, his elbows on the arms of his chair, his finger-tips meeting.

Arthur took it all in. Then, 'You don't want me?' he said, and he made as if he would close the door again. 'I thought that you were alone, sir.'

'No, stay,' Ovington answered. 'You may as well hear what Mr Wolley has to say, though I have told him already—'

'What?' the clothier cried rudely. 'Come! Let's have it in plain words!'

'That we can discount no more bills for him until the account against him is reduced. You know as well as I do, Mr Wolley, that you have been drawing more bills and larger bills than your trade justifies.'

'But I have to meet the paper I've accepted for wool, haven't I? And if my customers don't pay cash – as you know it is not the custom to pay – where am I to get the cash to pay the wool men?'

The banker took up one of two bills that lay on the table before him.

'Drawn on Samuel Willis, Manchester,' he said. 'That's a new name. Who is he?'

'A customer. Who should he be?'

'That's the point,' Ovington replied coldly. 'Is he? And this other bill. A new name, too. Besides, we've already discounted your usual bills. These bills are additional. My own opinion is that they are accommodation bills, and that you, and not the acceptors, will have to meet them. In any case,' dropping the slips on the table, 'we are not going to take them.'

'You won't cash them? Not on no terms?'

'No, we are going no further, Wolley,' the banker replied firmly. 'If you like I will send for the bill-book and ledger and tell you exactly what you owe, on bills and overdraft. I know that it is a large amount, and you have made, as far as I can judge, no effort to reduce it. The time has come when we must stop the advances.'

'And you'll not discount these bills?'

'No!'

'Then, by G—d, it's not I will be the only one to be ruined!' the man exclaimed, and he struck the table with his fist. The veins on his forehead swelled, his coarse mottled face became disfigured with rage. He glared at the banker. But even as Ovington met his gaze, there came a change. The perspiration sprang out on his forehead, his face turned pale and flabby, he seemed to shrink and wilt. The ruin, which recklessness and improvidence had hidden from him, rose before him, certain and imminent. He saw his mill, his house, his all gone from him, saw himself a drunken, ruined, shiftless loafer, cadging about public-houses! 'For God's sake!' he pleaded. 'Do it this once, Mr Ovington. Meet just these two, and I'll swear they'll be the last. Meet these.'

'No,' the banker said. 'We go no farther.'

Perhaps the thought that he and Ovington had risen from the ranks together, that for years they had been equals, and that now the one refused his help to the other, rose and mocked the unhappy man. At any rate, his rage flared up anew. He swore violently. 'Well, there's more than I will go down, then!' he said. 'And more than will suit your book, banker! Wise as you think yourself, there's more bills out than you know of!'

'I am sorry to hear it.'

'Ay, and you'll be more sorry by and by!' viciously. 'Sorry for yourself and sorry that you did not give me a little more help, d—n you! Are you going to? Best think twice about it before you say no!'

'Not a penny,' Ovington rejoined sternly. 'After what you have admitted I should be foolish indeed to do so. You've had my last word, Mr Wolley.'

'Then damn your last word and you too!' the clothier retorted, and went out, cursing, into the bank, shouting aloud as he passed through it, that they were a set of blood-suckers and that he'd have the law of them! Clement from his desk eyed him steadily. Rodd and the clerks looked startled. The customers – there were but two, but they were two too many for such a scene – eyed each other uneasily. A moment, and Clement, after shifting his papers uncertainly, left his desk and went into the parlour.

Ovington and Arthur had not moved. 'What's the matter?' Clement asked. The occurrence had roused him from his apathy. He looked from the one to the other, a challenge in his eyes.

'Only what we've been expecting for some time,' his father answered. 'Wolley has asked for further credit and I've had to say, no. I've given him too much rope as it is, and we shall lose by him. He's an ill-conditioned fellow, and he is taking it ill.'

'He wants a drubbing,' said Clement.

'That is not in our line,' Ovington replied mildly. 'But,' he continued – for he was not sorry to have the chance of taking his son into his confidence – 'we are going to have plenty to think of that is in our line. Wolley will fail, and we shall lose by him; and I have no doubt that he is right in saying that he will bring down others. We must look to ourselves and draw in, as I warned Bourdillon some time ago. That noisy fellow may do us harm, and we must be ready to meet it.'

Arthur looked thoughtful. 'Antwerps have fallen,' he said.

'I wish it were only Antwerps!' the banker answered. 'You haven't seen the mail? Or Friday's prices? There's a fall in nearly everything. True,' looking from one to the other, 'I've expected it – sooner or later, and it has come, or is coming. Yes, Rodd? What is it?'

The cashier had opened the door. 'Hamar,' he said in a low voice, 'wants to know if we will buy him fifty of the railroad shares and advance him the face value on the security of the shares. He'll find the premium himself. He thinks they are cheap after the drop last week.'

The banker shook his head. 'No,' he said. 'We can't do it, tell Mr Hamar.'

'It would support the shares,' Arthur suggested.

'With our money. Yes! But we've enough locked up in them already. Tell him, Rodd, that I am sorry, but it is not convenient at present.'

'They are still at a premium of thirty shillings,' Arthur put in.

'Is the door shut, Rodd?'

'Yes, sir.'

'Thirty shillings? That might run off in a week, Mr Secretary. No, Bourdillon, the time is come when we must not shilly-shally. I see your view and the refusal may do harm. But we have enough money locked up in the railway, and with the outlook such as it is, I will not increase the note-issues. They are already too large, as we may discover. We must say no, Rodd, but tell him to come and see me this evening, and I will explain.'

The cashier nodded and went out.

Ovington gazed thoughtfully at his joined finger-tips. 'Is the door closed?' he asked again, and assured that it was, he looked thoughtfully from one to the other of the young men. He seemed to be measuring them, considering how far he could trust them, how far it would be well to take them into his confidence. Then, 'We are going to meet a crisis,' he said. 'I have now no doubt about that. All over the country the banks have increased their issues, and hold a vast quantity of pawned stock. If the fall in values is continued, the banks must throw the stock on the market, and there will be a general fall. At the same time they will be obliged to restrict credit and refuse discounts, which will force traders to throw goods on the market to meet their obligations. Goods as well as stocks will fall. Alarm will follow, and presently there will be a run on a weak bank and it will close its doors. Then there will be a panic, and a run on other banks – a run proportioned in violence to the amount of credit granted in the last two years. We may have to meet a run on deposits at the same time that we may be called upon to cash every note that we have issued.'

'Impossible!' Arthur cried. 'We could not do it.'

'If you mean that the run is impossible,' the banker answered quietly, 'I much fear that events will confute you. If you mean that we could not meet our obligations, well, we must strain every nerve to do so. We must retain all the cash that comes in, and we must issue no more notes, create no more credit. But even this we must do with discretion, and above all not a whisper must pass beyond this room. I will speak to Rodd. Hamar I will see this evening, and do what I can to sweeten the refusal. We must wear confident faces. We are solvent, amply solvent, if time be given us to realise our resources. But time may not be given us, and we may have to make great sacrifices. You may be inclined to blame me—' he paused, and looked from one to the other – Arthur stood frowning, his eyes on the carpet – 'that I did not take the alarm earlier? Well, I ought to have done so, perhaps. But—'

'Nobody blames you, sir!' It was Clement who spoke – the last few minutes had wrought a marked change in him. His dullness and listlessness had fallen from him, he stood upright and alert. The imagination which had balked at the routine of banking faced a crisis with interest, and conscious that he had hitherto failed his father, he welcomed the opportunity of proving his loyalty, 'Nobody blames you, sir!' he repeated firmly. 'We are here to stand by you, and I am confident that we shall win through. If any bank can stand, Ovington's will stand. And if we don't win through, if the public insists on cutting its own throat, well' – a little ashamed of his own enthusiasm – 'we shall still believe in you, sir, you may be sure of that!'

'But isn't – isn't all this a little premature?' Arthur asked, his tone cold and business-like. 'I don't understand why you think that all this is coming upon us at a moment's notice, sir? Without warning?'

'Not quite without warning,' the banker rejoined with patience. Clement's declaration of faith had moved him more deeply than he showed, and, having that, he could bear a little disappointment. 'I have hinted more than once, Arthur, that I was uneasy. But why, you ask, this sudden alarm – now? Well, look at Richardson's list of last Friday's prices. Exchequer Bills that a week ago were at par are at a discount. India Stock are down five points on the day – a large fall for such a stock. New Four per Cents, have fallen 3, Bank Stock that stood at 224 ten days ago is 214. These are not panic falls, but they are serious figures. With Bank Stock falling ten points in as many days, what will happen to the immense mass of speculative securities held by the public and on much of which calls are due? They will be down this week; next week the banks will have to throw them out to save their margins, and customers to pay their calls. They will fall, and fall. The week after, perhaps, panic! A rush to draw deposits, or a rush to cash notes, or, probably, both.'

'Then you think – you must think' – Arthur's voice was not quite under his control – 'that there is danger?'

'It would be as foolish in me to deny it here,' the banker replied gravely, 'as it would be reckless in me to affirm it outside. There is danger. We shall run a risk, but I believe that we shall win through, though, it may be, by a narrow margin. And a little thing might upset us.'

Arthur was not of an anxious temperament – far from it. But he had committed himself to the bank. He had involved himself in its fortunes in no ordinary way. He had joined it against the wishes of his friends and in the teeth of the prejudices of his caste. He had staked his reputation for judgment upon its success, and assured that it would give him in the future all for which he thirsted, he had deemed himself far-sighted, and others fools. In doing this he had never dreamt of failure, he had never weighed the possibility of loss. Not once had he reflected that he might turn out to be wrong and robbed of the prize – might in the end be a laughing-stock!

Now, as the possibility of this, as the thought of failure, complete and final, flooded his mind and shook his self-confidence, he flinched. Danger! Danger, owned to by Ovington himself! Ah, he ought to have known! He ought to have suspected that fortunes were not so easily made! He ought to have reflected that Ovington's was not Dean's! That it was but a young bank, ill-rooted as yet – and speculative! Ay, speculative! Such a bank might fall, he was almost certain now that it would fall, as easily as it had risen!

It was a nerve-shaking vision that rose before him, and for a moment he could not hide his disorder. At any rate, he could not hide it from two jealous eyes. Clement saw and condemned – not fully understanding all that this meant to the other or the sudden strain which it put upon him. A moment and Arthur was himself again, and his first words recovered for him the elder man's confidence. They were practical.

'How much – I mean, what extra amount of reserve,' he asked, 'would make us safe?'

'Just so,' and in the banker's eyes there shone a gleam of relief. 'Well, if we had twelve thousand pounds, in addition to our existing assets, I think – nay, I am confident that that would place us out of danger.'

'Twelve thousand pounds.'

'Yes. It is not a large sum. But it might make all the difference if it came to a pinch.'

'In cash?'

'In gold, or Bank paper. Or in such securities as could be realised even in a crisis. Twelve thousand added to our reserve – I think I may say with confidence that with that we could meet any run that could be made upon us.'

'There is no doubt that we are solvent, sir?'

'You should know that as well as I.'

'We could realise the twelve thousand eventually?'

'Of course, or we should not be solvent without it.' For once Ovington spoke a little impatiently.

'Then could we not,' Arthur asked, 'by laying our accounts before our London agents obtain the necessary help, sir?'

'If we were the only bank in peril, of course we could. And even as it is, you are so far right that I had already determined to do that. It is the obvious course, and my bag is being packed in the house – I shall go to town by the afternoon coach. And now,' rising to his feet, 'we have been together long enough – we must be careful to cause no suspicion. Do you, Clement, see Massy, the wine-merchant, today, and tell him that I will take, to lay down, the ten dozen of '20 port that he offered me. And ask the two Welshes to dine with me on Friday – I shall return on Thursday. And get some oysters from Hamar's – two barrels – and have one or two people to dine while I am away. And, cheerful faces, boys – and still tongues. And now go. I must put into shape the accounts that I shall need in town.'

He dismissed them with calmness, but he did not at once fall to work upon the papers. His serenity was that of the commander who, on the eve of battle, reviews the issues of the morrow, and habituated to the chances of war, knows that he may be defeated, but makes his dispositions, folds his cloak about him, and lies down to sleep. But under the cloak of the commander, and behind the mask that deceives those about him, is still the man, with the man's hopes and fears, and cares and anxieties, which habit has rendered tolerable, and pride enables him to veil. But they are there. They are there.

As he sat, he thought of his rise, of his success, of step won after step; of the praise of men and the jealousy of rivals which wealth had won for him; and of the new machine that he had built up – Ovington's. And he knew that if fate went against him, there might in a very short time be an end of all. Yesterday he and Wolley had been equals. They had risen from obscurity together. Today Wolley was a bankrupt. Tomorrow – they might be again equal in their fall, and Ovington's a thing to wonder at. Dean's would chuckle, and some would call him a fool and some a rogue, and all an upstart – one who had not been able to keep his head. He would be ruined, and they would find no name too bad for him.

He thought of Betty. How would she bear it? He had made much of her and spoiled her, she had been the apple of his eye. She had known only the days of his prosperity. How would she bear it, how take it? He sighed.

He turned at last to the papers.

Chapter Twenty-Three

It was with a firmer tread that Clement went back to his desk in the bank. He had pleased his father and he was pleased with himself. Here at last was something to do. Here at last was something to fight. Here at last was metal in the banking business that suited him; and not a mere counting of figures and reckoning of pennies, and taking in at four per cent and putting out at eight. His gaze, passing over the ledger that lay before him, focused itself on the unconscious customers beyond the counter. He had the air of challenging them, of defying them. They were the enemy. It was their folly, their greed, their selfishness, their insensate desire to save themselves, let who would perish, that menaced the bank, that threatened the security, the well-being, the happiness of better men. It was a battle and they were the enemy. He scowled at them. Supposing them to have sense, patience, unselfishness, there would be no battle and no danger. But he knew that they had it not in them. No, they would rush in at the first alarm, like a flock of silly sheep, and thrusting and pushing and trampling one another down, would run, each bent on his own safety, blindly on ruin.

From this moment the bank became to him a place of interest and colour, instead of that which it had been. Where there was danger there was romance. Even Rodd, adding up a customer's pass-book, his face more thoughtful than usual, wore a halo, for he stood in peril. If the shutters went up Rodd would suffer with his betters. He would lose his place, he would be thrown on the world. He would lose, too, the trifle which he had on deposit in the bank. And even Rodd might have his plans and aims and ambitions, might be hoping for a rise, might be looking to marry some day – and someone!

Pheugh! Clement's mouth opened, he stared aghast – stared at the wire blind that obscured the lower half of the nearer window, as if all his faculties

were absorbed in reading the familiar legend, OVINGTON'S BANK
that showed darkly upon it. Customers, Rodd, the bank, all vanished. For
he had forgotten! He had forgotten Josina! In contemplating what was
exciting in the struggle before him he had forgotten that his stake was
greater than the stake of others – that it was immeasurably greater. For it
was Josina. He stood far enough below her as it was, separated from her
by a height of pride and prejudice and convention, which he must scale if
he would reach her. But he had one point in his favour – as things were.
His father was wealthy, and standing a-tiptoe on his father's money-bags
he might possibly aspire to her hand. So uplifted, so advantaged he might
hope to grasp that hand, and in the end, by boldness and resolution, to
make it his own.

That was the position as long as all went well at the bank: and it
was a position difficult enough. But if the money-bags crumbled and sank
beneath his feet? If in the crisis that was coming they toppled over, and his
father failed, as he might fail? If he lost the footing, the one footing that
money now gave him? Then her hand would be altogether out of his reach,
she would be far above him. He could not hope to reach her, could not
hope to gain her, could not in honour even aspire to her?

He saw that now. His stake was Josina, and the battle lost, he lost
Josina. He had been brave enough until he thought of that, reckless even,
welcoming the trumpet call. But seeing that, and seeing it suddenly, he
groaned.

The sound recalled him to himself, and he winced, remembering his
father's injunction to show a cheerful front. That he should have failed so
soon! He looked guiltily at Arthur. Had he heard?

But Arthur had not heard. He was standing at a desk attached to
the wall, his back towards Clement, his side-face to the window. He had
not heard, because his thoughts had been elsewhere, and, strange to say,
the subject which had engaged them had been also Josina. The banker's
warning had been a sharp blow to him. He was practical, he prided himself
on the quality, and he foresaw no pleasure in a contest in which the success
that was his be-all and end-all would be hazarded.

True, his mercurial spirit had already begun to rise, and with
every minute he leant more and more to the opinion that the alarm was
groundless. He thought that the banker was scaring himself, and seeing
bogies where no bogies were – as if forsooth a little fall meant a great

catastrophe, or as if all the customers would leave the bank because Wolley did! But he none the less for that looked abroad. Prudently he reviewed the resources that would remain to him in the event of defeat, and like a cautious general he determined beforehand his line of retreat.

That line was plain. If the bank failed, if a thing so cruel and incredible could happen, he still had Garth. He still had Garth to fall back upon, its lands, its wealth, its position. The bank might go, and Ovington – confound him for the silly mismanagement that had brought things to this! – might go into limbo with it, and Clement and Rodd and the rest of them – after all, it was their native level! But for him, born in the purple, there would still be Garth.

Only he must be quick. He must not lose a day or an hour. If he waited too long, word of the bank's embarrassments might reach the old man, re-awaken his prejudices, and warp his mind, and all might be lost. The influence on which he counted for success might cease to be his, and in a moment he might find himself out in the cold. Weakened as the Squire was, it would not be wise to trust too much to the change in him!

No, he must do it at once. He would ride out that very day, and gain, as he did not doubt that he would gain, the Squire's permission to speak to Josina. He would leave no room for accidents, and, setting these aside, he did not doubt the result.

He carried out his intention in spite of some demur on Clement's part, who in his new-born zeal thought that in his father's absence the other ought to remain on the spot. But Arthur had the habit of the upper hand, and with a contemptuous fling at Clement's own truancies, took it now. He was at Garth before sunset of the short November day, and he had not sat in the Squire's room ten minutes before chance gave him the opening he desired.

The old man had been listening to the town news, and apparently had been engrossed in it. But suddenly he leant forward, and poked Arthur with the end of his stick. 'Here, you tell me!' he said. 'What ails the girl? I've no eyes, but I've ears, and there's something. What's amiss with her, eh?'

'Do you mean Josina, sir?'

'Who else? I asked you what's the matter with her. D'you think I don't know that there is something? I've all my senses but one, thank God, and I can hear if I can't see! What is it?'

Arthur saw in a moment that here was the opportunity he needed, and he made haste to seize it. 'The truth is, sir,' he avowed with a candour which was attractive, 'I was going to speak to you about Josina. I have been wishing to do so for some time.'

'Well?'

'I have said nothing to her. But it is possible that she may be aware of my feelings.'

'Oh, that's it, is it?' It was impossible to say whether the Squire was pleased or not.

'If I had your permission to speak to her, sir?' Arthur felt, now that he had come to the point, just the amount of nervousness which was becoming. 'We have been brought up together, and I don't think that I can be taking you by surprise.'

'And you think it will be no surprise to her?'

'Well, sir,' modestly, 'I think it will not.'

'More ways of killing a cat than drowning it, eh? That's it, is it? Haven't spoken, but let her know? And you want my leave?'

'Yes, sir, to ask her to be my wife,' Arthur said frankly. 'It has been my wish for some time, but I have hesitated. Of course, I am no great match for her, but I am of her blood, and—'

He paused. He did not know what to add, and the Squire did not help him, and for the first time Arthur felt a pang of uneasiness. This was not lessened when the old man asked, 'How long has this been going on, eh?'

'Oh, for a long time, sir – on my side,' Arthur answered. And on that followed an ominous silence. The Squire might be taking it well or ill – it was impossible to judge. He had not changed his attitude and still sat, leaning forward, his hands on his stick, impenetrable behind his bandages. It struck Arthur that he might have been premature; that he might have put his favour to too high a test. It might have been wiser to work upon Josina, and wait and see how things turned out.

At last. 'She'll not go out of this house,' the Squire said. And he sighed in a way unusual with him, even when he had been at his worst. 'That's understood. There's room for you here, and any brats you may have. That's understood, eh?'

'Willingly, sir,' Arthur answered. A great weight had been lifted from him.

'And you'll take her name, do you hear?'

'Of course, sir. I shall be proud to do so.'

The Squire sighed, and again he was silent.

'Then – then I may speak to her, sir?'

'Wait a bit! Wait a bit!' The Squire had more to say, it appeared. 'You'll leave the bank, of course?'

Arthur's mind, trained to calculation, reviewed the position. Most heartily he wished – though he thought that Ovington's views were unnecessarily dark – that he could leave the bank. But he could not. The moment when Ovington might have released him, when the cancellation of the articles had been possible, was past. The banker could no longer afford to cancel them, or to lose the five thousand pounds that Arthur had brought in.

He hesitated, and the old man read his hesitation, and was wroth. 'You heard what I said?' he growled, and he struck his stick upon the floor. 'Do you think I am going to have my daughter's husband counterskipping in Aldersbury? Cheek by jowl with every grocer and linen-draper in the town? Bad enough as it is, bad enough, but when you're Jos' husband – no, by G–d, that's flat! You'll leave the bank, and you'll leave it at once, or you're no son-in-law for me. I'll not have the name of Griffin dragged in the dirt.'

Arthur had not anticipated this, though he might easily have foreseen it; and he cursed his folly. He ought to have known that the old question would be raised, and that it would revive the Squire's antagonism. He was like a fox caught in a trap, nay, like a fox that has put its own foot in the trap; and he had no time to give any but a candid answer. 'I am afraid, sir,' he said. 'I mean – I am quite willing to comply with your wishes. But unfortunately there's a difficulty. I am tied to the bank for three years. At the end of three years—'

'Three years be d—d!' In a passion the Squire struck his stick on the floor. 'Three years! I'm to sit here for three years while you go in and out, partner with Ovington! Then my answer is, No! No! D'you hear? I'll not have it.'

The perspiration stood on Arthur's brow. Here was a *débâcle*! An end, crushing and complete, to all his hopes! Desperately he tried to explain himself and mend matters. 'If I could act for myself, sir,' he said, 'I would leave the bank tomorrow. But the agreement—'

'Don't talk to me of agreements! You could ha' helped it!' the Squire snarled. 'Only you would go on! You went in against my advice! And for the agreement, who but a fool would ha' signed such an agreement? No, you may go, my lad. As you ha' brewed you may bake! You may go! If I'd known this was going on, I'd not ha' seen so much of you, you may be sure of that! As it is, Good-day! Good-day to you!'

It was indeed a *débâcle*; and Arthur could hardly believe his ears, or that he stood in his own shoes. In a moment, in one moment he had fallen from the height of favour and the pinnacle of influence, and disowned and defeated, he could hardly take in the mischance that had befallen him. Slowly he got to his feet, and as soon as he could master his voice, 'I'm grieved, sir,' he answered, 'more grieved than I can say, that you should take it like this – when I have no choice. I am sorry for my own sake.'

'Ay!' with grim irony. 'I can believe that.'

'And sorry for Josina's.'

He could think of no further plea at the moment – he must wait and hope for the best; and he moved towards the door, cursing his folly, his all but incredible folly, but finding no remedy. His hand was on the latch of the door when 'Wait!' cried the old man.

Arthur turned and waited; wondering, even hoping. The Squire sat, looking straight before him, if that might be said of a blind man, and presently he sighed. Then, 'Here, come back!' he ordered. But again for awhile he said no more, and Arthur waited, completely in the dark as to what was working in the other's mind. At last. 'There, maybe I've been hasty,' the old man muttered, 'and not thought of all. Will you leave the bank when you can, young man?'

'Of course, I will, sir!' Arthur cried.

'Then – then you may speak to her,' the Squire said reluctantly, and he marked the reluctance with another sigh.

And so, as suddenly as he had raised the objection, he withdrew it, to Arthur's intense astonishment. Only one conclusion could he draw – that the Squire was indeed failing. And on that, with a hastily murmured word of thanks, he escaped from the room, hardly knowing whether he walked on his head or his feet.

Lord, what a near thing it had been. And yet – no! The Squire – it must be that – was a failing man. He had no longer the strength or the stubbornness to hold to the course that his whims or his crabbed humour suggested. The danger might not have been so real or substantial, after all.

Yet the relief was great, and coming on Miss Peacock, who was crossing the hall with a bowl in her hand, he seized her by the waist and whirled her round, bowl and all. 'Hallo, Peacock! Hallo, Peacock!' he cried in the exuberance of his joy. 'Where's Jos?'

'Let go!' she cried. 'You'll have it over! What's come to you?'

'Where's Jos? Where's Jos?'

'Good gracious, how should I know? There, be quiet,' in pretended anger, though she liked it well enough. 'What's come to you? If you must know, she's moping in her room. It's where I find her most times when she's not catching cold in the garden-house, and her father's noticed it at last. He's in a pretty stew about her, and if you ask me, I don't think that she's ever got over that night.'

'I'll cure her!' Arthur cried in a glow, and he gave Miss Peacock another twirl.

But he had no opportunity of trying his cure that evening, for Jos, when she came downstairs, kept close to her father, and it was not until after breakfast on the morrow that he saw her go into the garden through the side-door, a relic of the older house that had once stood there. To frame it a stone arch of Tudor date had been filled in, and on either side of this, outlined in stone on the brick wall, was a pointed window of three lights. But Arthur's thoughts as he followed Jos into the garden were far from such dry-as-dust matters. The reaction after fear, the assurance that all was well, intoxicated him, and in a glow of spirits that defied the November day he strode down the walk under boughs that half-bare, and over leaves that half-shrivelled, owned alike the touch of autumn. He caught sight of a skirt on the raised walk at the farther end of the garden and he made for it, bounding up the four steps with a light foot and a lover's haste. A handsome young fellow, with a conquering air!

Jos was leaning on the wall, a shawl about her shoulders, her eyes bent on the mill and the Thirty Acres; and her presence in that place on that not too cheerful morning, and her pensive stillness, might have set him wondering, had he given himself time to think. But he was full of his purpose, he viewed her only as she affected it, and he saw nothing except what he wished to see. When, hearing his footsteps, she turned, her colour did not rise – and that too might have told him something. But had he spared this a thought, it would only have been to think that her colour would rise soon enough when he spoke.

'Jos!' he cried, while some paces still separated them. 'I've seen your father! And I've spoken to him!' He waved his hand as one proclaiming a victory.

But what victory? Jos was as much in the dark as if he had never paid court to her in those far-off days. 'Is anything the matter?' she asked, and she turned as if she would go back to the house.

But he barred the way. 'Nothing,' he said. 'Why should there be? On the contrary, dear. Don't I tell you that I've spoken to the Squire! And he says that I may speak to you.'

'To me?' She looked at him candidly, with no inkling in her mind of what he meant.

'Yes! My dear girl, don't you understand? He has given me leave to speak to you – to ask you to be my wife?' And as her lips parted and she gazed at him in astonishment, he took possession of her hand. The position was all in favour of a lover, for the parapet was behind her, and she could not escape if she would; while the ordeal through which he had passed gave this lover an ardour that he might otherwise have lacked. 'Jos, dear,' he continued, looking into her eyes, 'I've waited – waited patiently, knowing that it was useless to speak until he gave me leave. But now' – after all, love-making with that pretty startled face before him, that trembling hand in his, was not unpleasant – 'I come to you – for my reward.'

'But, Arthur,' she protested, almost too much surprised for words, 'I had no idea—'

'Come! Don't say that! Don't say that, Jos dear?' he protested in his turn. 'No idea? Why, hasn't it always been this way with us! Since the day that we cut our names on the old pew? Haven't I seen you blush like a rose when you looked at it – many and many a time? And if I haven't dared to make love to you of late, surely you have known what was in my mind? Have we not always been meaning this – you and I?'

She was thunder-struck. Had it been really so? Could he be right? Had she been blind, and had he been feeling all this while she guessed nothing of it? She looked at him in distress, in increasing distress. 'But indeed, indeed,' she said, 'I have not been meaning it, Arthur, I have not, indeed!'

'Not?' incredulously. 'You've not known that I—'

'No!' she protested. 'And I don't think that it has always been so with us.' Then, collecting herself and in a firmer voice, 'No, Arthur, not lately, I am sure. I don't think that it has been so on your side – I don't, indeed. And I'm sure that I have not thought of this myself.'

'Jos!'

'No, Arthur, I have not, indeed.'

'You haven't seen that I loved you?'

'No. And,' looking him steadily in the face, 'I am not sure that you do.'

'Then let me tell you that I do. I do!' And he tried to possess himself of her other hand, and there was a little struggle between them. 'Dear, dear girl, I do love you,' he swore. 'And I want you, I want you for my wife. And your father permits it. Do you understand – I don't think you do? He sanctions it.'

He would have put his arm round her, thinking to overcome her bashfulness, thinking that this was but maidenly pride, waiting to be conquered. But she freed herself with unexpected vigour and slipped from him. 'No, I don't wish it!' she said. And her attitude and her tone were so resolute, that he could no longer deceive himself. 'No! Listen, Arthur.' She was pale, but there was a surprising firmness in her face. 'Listen! I do not believe that you love me. You have given me no cause to think so these many months. Such a boy and girl affection as was once between us might have grown into love in time, and had you wished it. But you did not seem to wish it, and it has not. What you feel is not love.'

'You know so much about love!' he scoffed. He was taken aback, but he tried to laugh – tried to pass it off.

But she did not give way. 'I know what love is,' she answered firmly. And then, without apparent cause, a burning blush rose to her very hair. Yet, in defiance of this, she repeated her words. 'I know what love is, and I do not believe that you feel it for me. And I am sure, quite sure, Arthur,' in a lower tone, 'that I do not feel it for you. I could not be your wife.'

'Jos!' he pleaded, earnestly. 'You are joking! Surely you are joking.'

'No, I am not joking. I do not wish to hurt you. I am grieved if I do hurt you. But that is the truth. I do not want to marry you.'

He stared at her. At last she had compelled him to believe her, and he reddened with anger; only to turn pale, a moment later, as a picture of himself humiliated and rejected, his plans spoiled by the fancy of this foolish girl, rose before him. He could not understand it; it seemed incredible. And there must be some reason? Desperately he clutched at the thought that she was afraid of her father. She had not grasped the fact that the Squire had sanctioned his suit, and, controlling his voice as well as he could, 'Are you really in earnest, Jos?' he said. 'Do you understand that your father is willing? That it is indeed his wish that we should marry?'

'I cannot help it.'

'But – love?' Though he tried to keep his temper his voice was growing sharp. 'What, after all, do you know of – love?' And rapidly his mind ran over the possibilities. No, there could be no one else. She knew few, and among them no one who could have courted her without his knowledge. For, strange to say, no inkling of the meetings between Clement and his cousin had reached him. They had all taken place within a few weeks, they had ceased some months back, and though there were probably some in the house who had seen things and drawn their conclusions, the favourers of young love are many, and no one save Thomas had tried to make mischief. No, there could be no one, he decided; it was just a silly girl's romantic notion. 'And how can you say,' he persisted, 'that mine is not real love? What do you know of it? Believe me, Jos, you are playing with your happiness. And with mine.'

'I do not think so,' she answered gravely. 'As to my own, I am sure, Arthur. I do not love you and I cannot marry you.'

'And that is your answer?'

'Yes, it must be.'

He forced a laugh. 'Well, it will be news for your father,' he said. 'A clever game you have played, Miss Jos! Never tell me that it is not in women's nature to play the coquette after this. Why, if I had treated you as you have treated me – and made a fool of me! Made a fool of me!' he reiterated passionately, unable to control his chagrin – 'I should deserve to be whipped!'

And afraid that he would break down before her and disgrace his manhood, he turned about, sprang down the steps and savagely spurning, savagely trampling under foot the shrivelled leaves, he strode across the garden to the house. 'The little fool!' he muttered, and he clenched his hands as if he could have crushed her within them. 'The little fool!'

He was angry, he was very angry, for hitherto fortune had spoiled him. He had been successful, as men with a single aim usually are successful. He had attained to most of the things which he had desired. Now to fail where he had deemed himself most sure, to be repulsed where he had fancied that he had only to stoop, to be scorned where he had thought that he had but to throw the handkerchief, to be rejected and rejected by Jos – it was enough to make any man angry, to make any man grind his teeth and swear! And how – how in the world was he to explain the matter to his uncle? How account to him for his confidence in the issue? His cheeks burned as he thought of it.

He was angry. But his wrath was no match for the disappointment that warred with it and presently, as passion waned, overcame it. He had to face and to weigh the consequences. The loss of Jos meant much more than the loss of a mild and biddable wife with a certain charm of her own. It meant the loss of Garth, of the influence that belonged to it, the importance that flowed from it, the position it conferred. It meant the loss of a thing which he had come to consider as his own. The caprice of this obstinate girl robbed him of that which he had bought by a long servitude, by much patience, by many a tiresome ride between town and country.

There, in that loss, was the true pinch! But he must think of it. He must take time to review the position and consider how he might deal with it. It might be that all was not yet lost – even at Garth.

In the meantime he avoided seeing his uncle, and muttering a word to Miss Peacock, he had his horse saddled. He mounted in the yard and descended the drive at his usual pace. But as soon as he had gained the road, he lashed his nag into a canter, and set his face for town. At worst the bank remained, and he must see that it did remain. He must not let himself be scared by Ovington's alarms. If a crisis came he must tackle the business as he alone could tackle business, and all would be well. He was sure of it.

Withal he was spared one pang, the pang of disappointed love.

Chapter Twenty-Four

Arthur was at the bank by noon, and up to that time nothing had occurred to justify the banker's apprehensions or to alarm the most timid. Business seemed to be a little slack, the bank door had a rest, and there was less coming and going. But in the main things appeared to be moving as usual, and Arthur, standing at his desk in an atmosphere as far removed as possible from that of Garth, had time to review the check that he had received at Josina's hands, and to consider whether, with the Squire's help, it might not still be repaired.

But an hour or two later a thing occurred which might have passed unnoticed at another time, but on that day had a meaning for three out of the five in the bank. The door opened a little more abruptly than usual, a man pushed his way in. He was a publican in a fair way of business in the town, a smug ruddy-gilled man who, in his younger days, had been a pugilist at Birmingham and still ran a cock-pit behind the Spotted Dog, between the Foregate and the river. He stepped to the counter, his small shrewd eyes roving slyly from one to another.

Arthur went forward to attend to him. 'What is it, Mr Brownjohn?' he asked. But already his suspicions were aroused.

'Well, sir,' the man answered bluntly, 'what we most of us want, sir. The rhino!'

'Then you've come to the right shop for that,' Arthur rejoined, falling into his humour. 'How much?'

'How's my account, sir?'

Arthur consulted the book which he took from a ledge below the counter. In our time he would have scribbled the sum on a scrap of paper and passed the paper over in silence. But in those days many customers would have been none the wiser for that, for they could not read. So,

'One, four, two, and three and sixpence,' he said.

'Well, I'll take it,' the publican announced, gazing straight before him.

Arthur understood, but not a muscle of his face betrayed his knowledge. 'Brewers' day?' he said lightly. 'Mr Rodd, draw a cheque for Mr Brownjohn. One four two, three and six. Better leave five pounds to keep the account open?'

'Oh, well!' Mr Brownjohn was a little taken aback. 'Yes, sir, very well.'

'One three seven, Rodd, three and six.' And while the customer, laboriously and with a crimsoning face, scrawled his signature on the cheque, Arthur opened a drawer and counted out the amount in Ovington's notes. 'Twenty-seven fives, and two, three, six,' he muttered, pushing it over. 'You'll find that right, I think.'

Brownjohn had had his lesson from Wolley, who put up at his house, but he had not learnt it perfectly. He took the notes, and thumbed them over, wetting his thumb as he turned each, and he found the tale correct. 'Much obliged, gentlemen,' he muttered, and with a perspiring brow he effected his retreat. Already he doubted – so willingly had his money been paid – if he had been wise. He was glad that he had left the five pounds.

But the door had hardly closed on him before Arthur asked the cashier how much gold he had in the cash drawer.

'The usual, sir. One hundred and fifty and thirty-two, thirty-three, thirty-four – one hundred and eighty-four.'

'Fetch up two hundred more before Mr Brownjohn comes back,' Arthur said. 'Don't lose time.'

Rodd did not like Arthur, but he did silent homage to his sharpness. He hastened to the safe and was back in two minutes with twenty rouleaux of sovereigns. 'Shall I break them, sir?' he asked.

'Yes, I think so. Ah!' as the door swung open and one of the Welsh brothers entered. It was Mr Frederick. Arthur nodded. 'Good-day, Welsh, I was thinking of you. I fancy Clement wants to see you.'

'Right – in one moment,' the lawyer replied. 'Just put that—'

But Arthur saw that he had a cheque to pay in – he banked at Dean's but had clients' accounts with them – and he broke in on his business. 'Clement,' he said, 'here's Welsh. Just give him your father's message.'

Clement came forward with his father's invitation – oysters and whist at five on Friday – and his opinion on a glass of '20 he was laying down? He kept the lawyer in talk for a minute or two, and then, as Arthur had shrewdly calculated, the door opened and Brownjohn slid in. The man's face was red, and he looked heartily ashamed of himself, but he put down his notes on the counter. He was going to speak when, 'In a moment, Brownjohn,' Arthur said. 'What is it, Mr Welsh?'

'Just put this to the Hobdays' account,' the lawyer answered recalled to his business. 'Fifty-four pounds two shillings and fivepence. And, by the way, are you going to Garth on Saturday?'

'On Saturday, or Sunday, yes. Can I do anything for you?'

'Will you tell the Squire that that lease will be ready for signature on Saturday week. If you don't mind I'll send it over by you. It will save me a journey.'

'Good. I'll tell him. He has been fretting about it. Good-day! Now, Mr Brownjohn?'

'I'd like cash for these,' the innkeeper mumbled, thrusting forward the notes, but looking thoroughly ill at ease.

'Man alive, why didn't you say so?' Arthur answered, good-humouredly, 'and save yourself the trouble of two journeys? Mr Rodd, cash for these, please. I've forgotten something I must tell Welsh!' And flinging the cash drawer wide open, he raised the counter-flap and hurried after the lawyer.

Rodd knew what was expected of him, and he took out several fistsful of gold and rattled it down before him. Rapidly, as if he handled so many peas, he counted out and thrust aside Mr Brownjohn's portion, swiftly reckoned it a second time, then swept the balance back into the open drawer. 'I think you'll find that right,' he said. 'Better count it. How's your little girl that was ailing, Mr Brownjohn?'

Brownjohn muttered something, his face lighting up. Then he counted his gold and sneaked out, impressed, as Arthur had intended he should be, with his own unimportance, and more inclined than before to think that he had made a mistake in following Wolley's advice.

But before the bank closed that day two other customers came in and drew out the greater part of their balances. They were both men connected in one way or another with the clothier, and the thing stopped there. The following day was uneventful, but the drawings had been unusual, and the two young clerks might have exchanged notes upon the subject if their

elders had not appeared so entirely unconscious. As it was it was impossible
for them to think that anything out of the common had happened.

Worse, and far more important, than this matter was the fact that
stocks and shares continued to fall rapidly all that week. Night after night
the arrival of the famous 'Wonder,' the fast coach which did the journey
from London in fifteen hours, was awaited by men who thought nothing
of the wintry weather if they might have the latest news. Afternoon after
afternoon the journals brought by the mail were fought for and opened
in the street by men whose faces grew longer as the week ran on. Some
strode up jauntily, and joined themselves to the group of loungers before
the coach-office, while others sneaked up privily, went no farther than the
fringe of the crowd, and there, gravitating together by twos and threes,
conferred in low voices over prices and changes. Some, until the coach
arrived, lurked in a neighbouring churchyard, raised above the street, and
glancing suspiciously at one another affected to be immersed in the study
of crumbling gravestones; while a few made a pretence of being surprised,
as they passed, by the arrival of the mail, or hiding themselves in doorways
appeared only at the last moment, and when they believed that they might
do so unobserved.

One thing was noticeable of most of these; that they avoided one
another's eyes, as if, declining to observe others, they became themselves
unseen. Once possessed of the paper, they behaved in different ways,
according as they were of a sanguine or despondent nature. Some tore the
sheet open at once, devoured a particular column and stamped or swore, or
sometimes flung the paper underfoot. Others sneaked off to the churchyard
or to some neighbouring nook, and there, unable to wait longer, opened
the journal with shaking fingers; while a few – and these perhaps had the
most at stake – dared not trust themselves to learn the news where they
might by any chance be overlooked, but hurried homewards through 'shuts'
and by-lanes, and locked themselves in their offices, afraid to let even their
wives come near them.

For the news was very serious to very many; the more so as,
inexperienced in speculation, they clung for the most part to the hope of
a recovery, and could not bring themselves to sell at a lower figure than
that which they might have got a week before. Much less could they bring
themselves to sell at an actual loss. They had sat down to play a winning
game, and they could not now believe that the seats were reversed, and

that they were liable to lose all that they had gained, nay, in many cases much more than their stake. Amazed, they saw stocks falling, crumbling, nay, sinking to a nominal value, while large calls on them remained to be paid, and loans on them to be repaid. No wonder that they stared aghast, or that many after a period of stupefaction at a state of things so new and so paralysing, began to feel that it was neck or nothing with them, and bought when they should have sold, seeing that in any case the price to which stock was falling meant their ruin.

For a time indeed there was no public outcry and no great excitement on the surface. For a time men kept their troubles to themselves, jealous lest they should get abroad, and few suspected how common was their plight or how many shared it. Men talk of their gains but not of their losses, and the last thing desired by a business man on the brink of ruin is that his position should be made public. But those behind the scenes feared only the more for the morrow, for with this ferment of fear and suspense working beneath the surface it was impossible to say at what moment an eruption might not take place or where the ruin would stop. One thing was certain, that it would not be confined to the speculators, for many a sober trader, who had never bought shares in his life, would fail, beggared by the bankruptcy of his debtors.

Ovington returned on the Friday, and Arthur met him at the Lion, as he had met him eleven months before. They played their parts well – so well that even Arthur did not learn the news until the door of the bank had closed behind them and they were closeted with Clement in the dining-room. Then they learned that the news was bad – as bad as it could be.

The banker retained his composure and told his story with calmness, but he looked very weary. Williams' – Williams and Co. were Ovington's correspondents in London – would do nothing, he told them. 'They would not re-discount a single bill nor hear of an acceptance. My own opinion is that they cannot.'

Arthur looked much disturbed. 'As bad as that,' he said, 'is it?'

'Yes, and I believe, nay, I am sure, lad, that they fear for themselves. I saw the younger Williams. He gave me good words, but that was all; and he looked ill and harassed to the last degree. There was a frightened look about them all. I told them that if they would re-discount fifteen thousand pounds of sound short bills, we should need no further help, and might by and by be able to help others. But he would do nothing. I said I should go to the Bank. He let out – though he was very close – that others had done so, and that the Bank would do nothing. He hinted that they were short of gold there, and saw nothing for it but a policy of restriction. However, I went there, of course. They were very civil, but they told me frankly that it was impossible to help all who came to them; that they must protect their reserve. They were inclined to find fault, and said it was credit recklessly granted that had produced the trouble, and the only cure was restriction.'

'But surely,' Arthur protested, 'where a bank is able to show that it is solvent?'

'I argued it with them. I told them that I agreed that the cure was to draw in, but that they should have entered on that path earlier; that to enter on it now suddenly and without discrimination after a period of laxity was the way to bring on the worst disaster the country had ever known. That to give help where it could be shown that moderate help would suffice, to support the sound and let the rotten go was the proper policy, and would limit the trouble. But I could not persuade them. They would not take the best bills, would in fact take nothing, discount nothing, would hardly advance even on government securities. When I left them—'

'Yes?' The banker had paused, his face betraying emotion.

'I heard a rumour about Pole's.'

'Pole's? Pole's!' Arthur cried, astounded; and he turned a shade paler. 'Sir Peter Pole and Co.? You don't mean it, sir? Why, if they go scores of country banks will go! Scores! They are agents for sixty or seventy, aren't they?'

The banker nodded. His weariness was more and more apparent. 'Yes, Pole's,' he said gloomily. 'And I heard it on good authority. The truth is – it has not extended to the public yet, but in the banks there is panic already. They do not know where the first crash will come, or who may be affected. And any moment the scare may spread to the public. When it does it will run through the country like wild-fire. It will be here in twenty-four hours. It will shake even Dean's. It will shake us down. My God! when I think that for the lack of ten or twelve thousand pounds – which a year ago we could have raised three times over with the stroke of a pen – just for the lack of that a sound business like this—'

He broke off, unable to control his voice. He could not continue. Clement went out softly, and for a minute or so there was silence in the room, broken only by the ticking of the clock, the noise of wheels in the street, the voices of passers-by – voices that drifted in and died away again, as the speakers walked by on the pavement. Opposite the bank, at the corner of the Market Place, two dogs were fighting before a barber's shop. A woman drove them off with an umbrella. Her 'Shoo! Shoo!' was audible in the silence of the room.

Before either spoke again, Clement returned. He bore a decanter of port, a glass, a slice of cake. 'D'you take this, sir,' he said. 'You are worn out. And never fear,' cheerily, 'we shall pull through yet, sir. There will surely be some who will see that it will pay better to help us than to pull us down.'

The banker smiled at him, but his hand shook as he poured out the wine. 'I hope so,' he said. 'But we must buckle to. It will try us all. A run once started – have there been any withdrawals?'

They told him what had happened and described the state of feeling in the town. Rodd had been going about, gauging it quietly. He could do so more easily, and with less suspicion, than the partners. People were more free with him.

Ovington held his glass before him by the stem and looked thoughtfully at it. 'That reminds me,' he said, 'Rodd has some money with us – three hundred on deposit, I think. He had better have it. It will make no difference one way or the other, and he cannot afford to lose it.'

Arthur looked doubtful. 'Three hundred,' he said, 'might make the difference.'

'Well, it might, of course,' the banker admitted wearily. 'But he had better have it. I should not like him to suffer.'

'No,' Clement said. 'He must have it. Shall I see to it now? The sooner the better.'

No one demurred, and he left the room. When he had gone Arthur rose and walked to the window. He looked out. Presently he turned. 'As to that twelve thousand?' he said. 'That you said would pull us through? Is there no way of getting it? Can't you think of any way, sir?'

'I am afraid not,' Ovington answered, shaking his head. 'I see no way. I've strained our resources; I've tried every way. I see no way unless—'

'Yes, sir?'

'Unless – and I am afraid that there is no chance of that – your uncle could be induced to come forward and support us – in your interest.'

Arthur laughed aloud, but there was no mirth in the sound. 'If that

is your hope, if you have any idea of that kind, sir,' he said, 'I am afraid you
don't know him yet. I know nothing less likely.'

'I am afraid that you are right. Still, your future is at stake. I am sorry
that it is so, lad, but there it is. And if it could be made clear to him that
he ran no risk?'

'But could it? Could it?'

'He would run no risk.'

'But could he be brought to see that?' Arthur spoke sharply, almost
with contempt. 'Of course he could not! If you knew what his attitude is
towards banks generally, and bankers, you would see the absurdity of it!
He hates the very name of Ovington's.'

The other yielded. 'Just so,' he said. Even to him the idea was
unpalatable. 'It was only a forlorn hope, a wild idea, lad, and I'll say no
more about it. It comes to this, that we must depend on ourselves, show a
brave face, and hope for the best.'

But Arthur, though he had scoffed at the suggestion which Ovington
had made, could not refrain from turning it over in his mind. He had
courage enough for anything, and it was not the lack of that which hindered
him from entertaining the project. The storm which was gathering ahead,
and which threatened the shipwreck of his cherished ambition and his
dearest hopes, was terrible to him, and to escape from its fury he would
have faced any man, had that been all. But that was not all. He had other
interests. If he applied to the Squire and the Squire took it amiss, as it was
pretty certain that he would, then not only would no good be done and no
point be gained, but the life-boat, on which he might himself escape, if
things came to the worst, would be shipwrecked also.

For that life-boat consisted in the Squire's influence with Josina. The
Squire's word might still prevail with the girl, silly and unpractical as she
was. It was a chance; no more than a chance, Arthur recognised that. But
at Garth the old man's will had always been law, and if he could be brought
to put his foot down, Arthur could not believe that Josina would resist
him. And amid the wreck of so many hopes and so many ambitions, every
chance, even a desperate chance, was of value.

But if he was to retain the Squire's favour, if he was to fall back on his
influence, he must do nothing to forfeit that favour. Certainly he must not
hazard it by acting on a suggestion as ill-timed and hopeless as that which
the banker had put forward. Not to save the bank, not to save Ovington,

not to save anyone! The more, as he felt sure that the application would do none of these things.

Ovington did not know the old man. He did, and he was not going to sink his craft, crank and frail as it already was, by taking in passengers.

Chapter Twenty-Five

While the leaven of uneasiness, fermenting into fear, and liable at any moment to breed panic, worked in Aldersbury, turning the sallow bilious and the sanguine irritable – while the contents of the mail-bag and the *Gazette* were awaited with growing apprehension, and inklings of the truth, leaking out, were turning to water the hearts of those who depended on the speculators, life at Garth was proceeding after its ordinary fashion. No word of what was impending, or might be impending, travelled so far. No echo of the alarm that assailed the ears of terrified men, forced on a sudden to face unimagined disaster, broke the silence of the drab room, where the Squire sat brooding, or of the garden where Josina spent hours, pacing the raised walk and looking down on that strip of sward where the water skirted the Thirty Acres wood.

That strip of sward where she had met him, that view from the garden were all that now remained to her of Clement, all that proved to her that the past was not a dream; and they did much to keep hope alive in her breast, and to hold her firm in her resolve. So precious indeed were the associations they recalled, that while, with the hardness of a woman who loves elsewhere, she felt little sympathy with Arthur in his disappointment, she actively resented the fact that he had chosen to address her there, and so had profaned the one spot, on which with some approach to nearness, she could dream of Clement.

Living a life so retired, and with little to distract her, she gave herself to long thoughts of her lover, and lived and lived again the stolen moments which she had spent with him. It was on these that she nourished her courage and strengthened her will; for, bred to submission and educated to obey, it was no small thing that she contemplated. Nor could she have raised herself to the pitch of determination which she had reached had she not gained elevation from the thought that the matter now rested in her own hands, and that all Clement's trust and all his dependence were on her. She must be true to him or she would fail him indeed. Honour no less than love required her to be firm, let her timid heart beat as it might.

On wet days she sat in the Dutch summer-house, the squat tower with the pyramidal roof and fox-vane on top, which flanked the raised walk, and had, when viewed from below, the look of a bastion. But the day after Ovington's return happened to be fine. It was one of those days of mild sunshine and soft air, which occur in late autumn or early winter and, by reason of their rarity, linger in the memory; and she was walking in the garden when, an hour before noon, Calamy came to tell her that 'the master' was asking for her. 'And very peevish,' he added, shaking his head as he stalked away under the apple-trees, 'as he's like to be, more and more till the end.'

She overtook the man in the hall. 'Is he alone, Calamy?' she asked.

'Ay, but your A'nt's been with him. He's for going up the hill.'

'Up the hill?'

'Ay, he's one that will walk while he can. But the next time, I'm thinking,' shaking his head again, 'it won't be his feet he'll go out on.'

'Mrs Bourdillon has gone?'

'Ay, miss, she's gone – as we're all going,' despondently, 'sooner or later. She brought some paper, for I heard her reading to him. It would be his will, I expect.'

Josina thought the supposition most unlikely, for, if her father was close with his money, he was at least as close with his affairs. As long as she could remember he had held himself in a crabbed reserve, he had moved a silent master in a dependent world, even his rare outbursts of anger had rather emphasised than broken his reticence.

And since the attack which had consigned him to darkness he had grown even more taciturn. He had not repelled sympathy; he had rendered it impossible by ignoring the existence of a cause for it. While all about him had feared for his sight and, as hope faded, had dreaded the question which they believed to be trembling on his lips, he had either never hoped, or, drawing his own conclusions, had abandoned hope. At any rate, he had never asked. Instead he had sat – when Arthur was not there to enliven him or Fewtrell to report to him – wrapped in his own thoughts, too proud to complain or too insensible to feel, and silent. Whatever he thought, whatever he feared, he hid all behind an impenetrable mask; and whether pride or patience or resignation were behind that mask, none knew. Complaint, pity, sympathy, these, he seemed to say, were for the herd. He had ruled; darkness and helplessness had come upon him, but he was still the master.

Arthur might think that he failed, but those who were always about him saw few signs of it. Today, when Josina entered his room she found him on his feet, one hand resting on the table, the other on his cane. 'Get your hat and cloak,' he said. 'I am going up the hill.'

So far his longest excursion had been to the mill, and Josina thought that she ought to remonstrate. 'Won't it be too far, sir?' she said.

'Do as I say, girl. And tell Calamy to bring my hat and coat.'

She obeyed him, and a minute later they left the house by the yard door. He walked with a firm step, his hand sometimes on her shoulder, sometimes on her arm, but, aware how easily she might forget to warn him of an obstacle, or to allow for his passage, she accompanied him with her heart in her mouth. Yet she owned a certain sweetness in his dependence on her, in the weight of his hand on her shoulder, in his nearness.

Before they left the yard he halted. 'Look in the pig-styes,' he said. 'Tell me if that idle dog has cleaned them?'

She went and looked, and assured him that they were in their usual state. He grunted, and they moved on. Passing beneath the gable end of the summer-house they descended the steep, rutted-lane which led to the mill. 'The first day of the year was such a day,' the Squire muttered, and raised his face that the sun might fall upon it.

When they came to the narrow bridge beside the mill, with its roughened causeway eternally shaken by the roar and wet with the spray of the overshot wheel, she trembled. There was no parapet, and the bridge was barely wide enough to permit them to pass abreast. But he showed no fear, he stepped on to it firmly, and on the crown he halted. 'Look what water is in the pound,' he said.

'Had I not better wait – till you are over, sir?'

'Do as I say, girl! Do as I say!' He struck his cane impatiently on the stones.

She left him unwillingly, and more than once looked back, but always to see him standing, gaunt and slightly stooping, his sightless eyes bent on the groaning, labouring wheel, on the silvery cascade that poured over its black flanges, on the fragment of rainbow that glittered where the sun shot the spray with colours. He was seeing it all, as he had seen it a thousand times: in childhood, when he had lingered and wondered before it, fascinated by the rush and awed by the thunder of the falling water; in youth, when with gun or rod he had just glanced at it in passing; in manhood, when it had come to be one of the amenities of the property, and he had measured its condition with an owner's eye; ay, and in later life, when to see it had been rather to call up memories, than to form new impressions. Now, he would never see it again with his eyes, and he knew it. And yet he had never seen it more clearly than he did today, as he stood in darkness, with the cold breath of the water-fall on his cheek.

She grasped something of this as she hurried back, and satisfied as to the pound he went on. They ascended the lane which, on the farther side of the brook, led to the highway, and crossing the road began to climb the rough track, that wound up through that part of the covert which was above the road.

Here and there a clump of hollies, a spreading yew, a patch of young beech to which the leaves still clung, blocked the view, but for the most part the eye passed unobstructed amid trees stripped of foliage, and disclosing here a huge boulder, there a pile of moss-grown stones. A climb of a third of a mile, much of it steep, brought them without mishap – though a hundred times she trembled lest he should trip – to the abrupt glacis of sward that fringed, and in places ran up into, the limestone face.

It was broken by huge stones, precariously stayed in their descent, or by outcrops of rock from which sprang slender birches, light, graceful, their white bark shining.

'Are we clear of the wood?' he asked, lifting his face to meet the breeze.

'Yes, sir.'

He turned leftwards. 'There's a flat stone with a holly to north of it. D'you see it? I'll sit there.'

She led him to it and he sat down on the stone, his stick between his knees, the sunshine on his face. She sat beside him, and as she looked over the expanse of pleasant vale and the ring of hills that compassed it about, the sense of his blindness moved her almost to tears. At their feet Garth, its red walls, its buildings and yards and policies, lay as on a plan. Beyond it, the tower of Garthmyle Church rose in the middle distance, a few thatched roofs peeping through the half-leafless trees about it. Leftwards the valley narrowed as the Welsh hills closed in, while to their right it melted into the smiling plain with its nestling villages, its rows of poplars, its shining streams. She fancied that he had been in the habit of coming to this place, and the thought that he saw no more from it now than when he sat in his room below, that he viewed nothing of the bright landscape spread beneath her own eyes, swelled her breast with pity. She could have cast her arms about him and wept as she strove to comfort him – could have sworn to him that while he lived her eyes should be his! Ay, she could have done this, all this – if he had been other than he was!

Perhaps it was as well – or perhaps it was not as well – that she did not give way to the impulse. For presently in a voice as dry as usual, 'Do you see the gable of Wolley's Mill, girl? Carry your eyes right of the hill, over the coppice at the corner of Archer's Leasow?'

She told him that she could see it.

'That's two miles away. It's the farthest I own in that direction, but there's a slip of Acherley's land between us and it. Now look down the valley – d'you see five poplars in a row?'

'Yes, sir, I see them.'

'That's our boundary towards the town. Behind us we march with the watershed. Facing us – the boundary is the far fence of Whittall's farm at the foot of the hills.'

'The black and white house, sir?'

'Ay. Well, look at it, girl. There's five thousand acres and a bit over; and there's two hundred and ninety people living on it – there's barely one of them I don't know. I've looked after them, but I've not cosseted them, and don't you cosset them. And it's not only the people; there's not a field I don't know nor a bit of coppice that I can't see, nor a slate roof that I have not slated, and the Lord knows how much of it I've drained. It's been ours, the heart of it since Queen Bess, and part of it since Mary; sometimes logged with debt, and then again cleared. I came into it logged, and I've cleared it. It's come down, sometimes straight, sometimes sideways, but always in a man's hands. Well, it will soon be in a girl's. In two or three years, more or less, it will be yours, my girl. And do you mark what I say to you this day. You're the heir of tail, and I couldn't take it from you, if I would – but do you mark me!' He found her hand and gripped it so hard as to give her pain, but she would not wince. 'Don't you part with an acre of it! Not with an acre of it! Not with an acre of it! Do you hear me, girl; or I think I'll turn in my grave! If you are bidden to do it when your son comes of age, you think of me and of this day, and don't put your hand to it! Hold to the land, hold to the land, and they as come after you shall hold up their heads as we have held ours! It isn't money, it isn't land bought with money, it's the land that's come down, that will keep Griffins where Griffins have been. When I am gone do you mark that! Whatever betide, let 'em say what they like, don't you be one of those that sell their birthright, the right to govern, for a mess of pottage!'

'I will remember, sir!' she said with tears. 'I will, I will indeed!'

'Ay, never forget it, don't you forget this day. I ha' brought you up the hill on purpose to show you that. For fifty years I have spared and lived niggardly and put shilling to shilling to clear that land and to drain it and round it – and may be, for Acherley is a random spendthrift, I'll yet add that strip of his to it! I've lived for the land, that those who come after me may govern their corner as Griffins have governed it time out of mind. I've done my duty by the people and the land. Don't you forget to do yours.'

She told him earnestly that she never would – she never would. After that he was silent awhile. He let her hand go. But presently, and without warning, 'Why don't you ha' the lad?'

Josina was surprised and yet not surprised; or if surprised at all, it was at her own calmness. Her colour ebbed, but she neither trembled nor faltered. She had not even to summon up the thought of Clement. The charge to which she had just listened clothed her with a dignity which the prospect, spread before her eyes and insensibly raising her mind to higher issues, helped to support. 'I couldn't, sir,' she said quietly, 'I do not love him.'

'Don't love him?' the Squire repeated – yet not half so angrily as she expected. 'What's amiss with him?'

'Nothing, sir. But I do not love him.'

'Love? Bah! Love'll come! Maids ha' naught to do with love! When they're married love'll come fast enough, I'll warrant! The lad's straight and comely and a proper age – and what else do you want? What else do you want, eh? He's of your own blood, and if he's wild ideas 'tis better than wild oats, and he'll give them up. He's promised me that, or I'd never ha' said yes to him! Why, girl!' with sudden exasperation, ''twas only the other day you were peaking and puling for him! Peaking and puling like a sick sparrow, and I was saying, no! And now – why, damme, what do you mean by it?'

'It was all a mistake, sir,' she said with dignity. 'I never did think of him, or wish for him. It was a mistake.'

'A mistake! What do you mean?'

'You bade me think no more of him, and I obeyed; But I – I never had any thought of him.'

That did irritate the old man; it seemed to him that she played with him. In a rage he struck his cane on the ground. 'Damme!' he exclaimed. 'That's womankind all over! Give her what she wants and she doesn't want it. But, see here, I'll not have it, girl. I know your flimsies and you've got to have him! Do you hear?'

He was enraged by this queer twist in her, and he blustered. But his anger – and he felt it – lacked something of force. He did not know how to bring it to bear. And when she did not reply to him at once, 'Do you forget that he saved my life?' he cried, dropping to a lower level. 'D'you forget that, you ungrateful wench?'

'But he did not save mine, sir!' she answered, with astonishing spirit. 'Yet it is mine that you ask me to give him. And indeed, indeed, sir, he does not love me.'

'Then why should he want you?' he retorted. 'But he'll soon make you sure of that, if you'll let him. And you've got to take him. You've got to take him. Let's ha' no more words about it. I've said the word.'

'But I've not, sir,' she replied, that new and astonishing courage of hers still supporting her. 'And I cannot say it. I am grateful to him, I shall ever be grateful to him for saving you – and he is my cousin. But he does not love me, he has never made love to me. And am I, your daughter, to – to accept him, the moment it suits him to marry me?'

That touched the Squire's pride. It gave him to think. 'Never made love to you?' he explained. 'What do you mean, girl?'

'Until he came to me in the garden on Tuesday he never – he never gave me cause to think that he would come. Am I,' with a tremor of indignation in her voice, 'of so little account, is that which you have just told me that I may some day bring to him so little, that I must put all in his hand the moment he chooses to lift it?'

The Squire was bothered by that, and 'You are like all women!' he exclaimed. 'I don't know where to ha' you. That's where it is. You twist and you turn, and you fib—'

'I am not fibbing, sir.'

'And you've as many quirks as – as a hunted hare. There's no holding you! My father would ha' locked you up with bread and water till you did what you were told, and my mother 'd ha' boxed your ears till she put some sense into you. But we're a d—d silly generation. We're too soft!'

She minded this little, as long as he did not put her to the supreme test; as long as he did not ask her if there was anyone else, any other lover. But his mind was now busy with Arthur. Was it true that the young spark was thinking more of Garth than of the girl? More of the heiress than of the sweetheart? More of lucre than of love? If so, d—n his impudence! He deserved what he had got! From which point it was but a step to thoughts of the bank. Ay, Arthur was certainly one who had his plans for getting on, and getting on in ways to which no Griffin had stooped before. Was this of a piece with them?

The doubt had a cooling effect upon him. While Josina trembled lest the fateful question should be put, and clenched her little hands as she summoned up fortitude to meet it – while she tried to still the fluttering of her heart, the old man relapsed into thought, muttered inarticulately, fell silent.

She would have given much to know the direction of his thoughts.

At last, 'Well, you're so clever you must settle your own affairs,' he grumbled. 'I'm d—d if I understand either of you, girl or man. In my time if a wench said No, we took her and hugged her till she said Yes! We didn't go to her father. But since the old king died there's no red blood in the country – it's all telling and no kissing. There, I've done with it. Maybe when he turns his back on you, you'll be wanting him fast enough.'

'No, sir, never!' she answered, overwhelmed by a victory so complete.

'Anyway, don't come fretting to me if you do! Your aunt told me that you were pining for him, but I'm hanged if she knows more than I do – or happen you don't know your own mind. Now look out, and tell me if they've finished thatching that waggoner's cottage at the Bache?'

'Yes, sir. I can see the new straw from here,' she said.

'Have they brought it down over the eaves?'

'I'm afraid I can't see that. It's too far.'

''Mind me to ask Fewtrell. Now get me home. Where's your arm? I'll go down through the new planting.'

'But it's not so safe, sir,' she remonstrated. 'There's the stone stile, and—'

'When I canna get over the stone stile I'll not come up the hill. I want to see the planting. D'you take me that way and tell me if the rabbits ha' got in. March, girl!'

She obeyed him, but in fear and trembling, for there was not only the awkward stile to climb, but the track ran over outcrops of rock on which even a careful walker might slip. However, he crossed the stile with ease, aided less by her arm than by his own memory of its shape, and of every stone that neighboured it; and it was only over the treacherous surface of the rock that he showed himself really dependent on her care. Memory could not help him there, and here it was, as he leant on her shoulder, that she felt, her breast swelling with pity, the real, the blood tie between them. Her heart went out to him, and her eyes were dim with tears when at length they stood again on the high road, and viewed, on a level with themselves but divided from them by the trough of green meadows in which the brook ran, the gables and twisted chimneys, the buttressed walls, that gave to Garth its air of a fortress.

The girl gazed at it, the old man's hand still on her shoulder. It was her home: she knew no other, she had never been fifty miles from it. It stood for peace, safety, protection. She loved it – never more than now, and never as much as now. And never as much as now had she loved her father; never before had she understood him so well. The last hour had wrought a change, dimly suspected by both, in their relations. They stood on a level – more on a level, at any rate; with no gulf between them but the natural interval of years, a green valley, which the eyes of understanding and the light foot of love could cross at will.

Chapter Twenty-Six

A week and a day went by after the banker's return and there was no run upon the bank. But afar off, in London and Manchester and Liverpool, and even in Birmingham, there were shocks and upheavals, failures and talk of failures, fear in high places, ruin in low. For there was no doubt about the crisis now. The wheels of trade, which had for some time been running sluggishly, stopped. It was impossible to sell goods, for the prudent and foreseeing had already flung their products upon the market, and glutted it, and later, others had come in and, forced to find money, had sold down and down, procuring cash at any sacrifice. Now it was impossible to sell at all. Men with the shelves of their warehouses loaded with goods, men whose names in ordinary times were good for thousands, could not find money to meet their trade bills, to pay their wages, to discharge their household accounts.

And it was still less possible to sell shares, for shares, even sound shares, had on a sudden become waste paper. The bubble companies, created during the frenzy of the past two years, were bursting on every side, and the public, unable to discriminate, no longer put faith in anything. Rudely awakened, they opened their eyes to reality. They saw that they had dreamed, and been helped to dream. They discovered that skates and warming pans were in no great request in the tropics, and could not be exported thither at a profit of five hundred per cent. They saw that churns and milkmaids, freighted to lands where the cattle ran wild on the pampas and oil was preferred to butter, were no certain basis on which to build a fortune. Their visions of South American argosies melted into thin air. The silver from La Plata which they had pictured as entering the mouth of the Thames, or at worst as within sight from the Lizard, was discovered to be reposing in the darkness of unopened seams. The pearling ships were yet to build, the divers to teach, and, for the diamonds of the Brazils which this man or that man had seen lying in skin packages at the door of the Bank of England, they now twinkled in a cold and distant heaven, as unapproachable as the Seven Stars of Orion. The canals existed on paper, the railways were in the air, the harbours could not be found even on the map.

The shares of companies which had passed from hand to hand at fourfold and tenfold their face value fell with appalling rapidity. They fell and fell until they were in many cases worth no more than the paper on which they were printed. And the bursting of these shams, which had never owned the smallest chance of success, brought about the fall of ventures better founded. The good suffered with the bad. Presently no man would buy a share, no man would look at a share, no bank advance on its security. Men saw their fortunes melt day by day as snow melts under an April sun. They saw themselves stripped, within a few weeks or even days, of wealth, of a competence, in too many cases of their all.

And the ruin was widespread. It reached many a man who had never gambled or speculated. Business runs on the wheels of credit, and those wheels are connected by a million unseen cogs. Let one wheel stop and it is impossible to say where the stoppage will cease, or how many will be affected by it. So it was now. The honest tradesman and the manufacturer, striving to leave a competence to a family nurtured in comfort, were involved in one common ruin with the spendthrift and the speculator. The credit of all was suspect; from all alike the sources of accommodation were cut off. Each in his turn involved his neighbour, and brought him down.

There was a great panic. The centres of commerce and trade were convulsed. The kings of finance feared for themselves and closed their pockets. The Bank of England would help no one. Men who had never sought aid before, men who had held their heads high, waited, vain petitioners, at its doors.

Fortunately for Ovington's, Aldersbury lay at some distance from the centres of disturbance, and for a time, though the storm grumbled and crackled on the horizon, the town remained calm. But it was such a calm as holds the tropic seas in a breathless grip, before the typhoon, breaking from the black canopy overhead, whirls the doomed bark away, as a leaf is swept before our temperate blasts. Throughout those six days, though little happened, anything, it was felt, might happen. The arrival of every coach was a thing to listen for, the opening of every mail-bag a terror, the presentation of every bill a pang, the payment of every note a thing at which to wince; while the sense of danger, borne like some infection on the air, spread mysteriously from town to village, and village to hamlet, to penetrate at last wherever one man depended on another for profit or for subsistence. And that was everywhere.

A storm impended, and no man knew where it would break, or on whom it would fall. Each looked in his neighbour's face and, seeing his fear reflected, wondered, and perhaps suspected. If so-and-so failed, would not such-an-one be in trouble? And if such-an-one 'went,' what of Blank – with whom he himself had business?

The feeling which prevailed did not in the main go beyond uneasiness and suspicion. But, in quarters where the facts were known and the peril was clearly discerned, these days of waiting were days – nay, every day was a week – of the most poignant anxiety. In banks, where those behind the scenes knew that not only their own stability and their own fortunes were at stake, but that if they failed there would be lamentation in a score of villages and loss in a hundred homes, endurance was strained to the breaking point. To show a cheerful face to customers, to chat over the counter with an easy air, to smile on a visitor who might be bringing in the bowstring, to listen unmoved to the murmur in the street that might presage bad news – these things made demands on nerve and patience which could not be met without distress. And every hour that passed, every post that came in, added to the strain.

Under this burden Ovington's bearing was beyond praise. The work of his life – and he was over-old to begin it again – was in danger, and doubtless he thought of his daughter and his son. But he never faltered. He had, it is true, to support him the sense of responsibility, which steels the heart of the born leader, even as it turns to water that of the pretender; he knew, and doubtless he was strengthened by the knowledge, that all depended on him, on his calmness, his judgment, his resources; that all looked to him for guidance and encouragement, watched his face and marked his demeanour.

But even so, he was the admiration of those in the secret. Not even Napoleon, supping amid his marshals, and turning over to sleep beside the watch-fire on the night before a battle, was more wonderful. His son swore fealty to him a dozen times a day. Rodd, who had received his money in silence, and now stood to lose no more than his place, followed him with worshipping eyes and, perhaps, an easier mind. The clerks, who perforce had gained some inkling of the position, were relieved by his calmness, and spread abroad the confidence that they drew from him. Even Arthur, who bore the trial less well, admired his leader, suspected at times that he had some secret hope or some undisclosed resources, and more than once suffered himself to be plucked from depression by his example.

The truth was that while financial ability was common to both, their training had been different. The elder man had been always successful, but he had been forced to strive and struggle; he had climbed but slowly at the start, and there had been more than one epoch in his career when he had stood face to face with defeat. He had won through, but he had never shut his eyes to the possibility of failure, or to the fact that in a business, which in those days witnessed every twenty years a disastrous upheaval, no man could count on, though with prudence he might anticipate, a lasting success. He had accepted his profession with its drawbacks as well as its advantages. He had not closed his eyes to its risks. He had viewed it whole.

Arthur, on the other hand, plunging into it with avidity at a time when all smiled and the sky was cloudless, had supposed that if he were once admitted to the bank his fortune was made, and his future secured. He knew indeed, and if challenged he would have owned, that banking was a precarious enterprise; that banks had broken. He knew that many had closed their doors in '16, still more on one black day in '93. He was aware that in the last forty years scores of bankers had failed, that some had taken their own lives, that one at least had suffered the last penalty of the law. But he had taken these things to be exceptions – things which might, indeed, recur, but not within his experience – just as in our day, though railway accidents are not uncommon, no man for that reason refrains from travelling.

At any rate the thought of failure had not entered into Arthur's mind, and mainly for this reason he, who in fair weather had been most confident and whose ability had shone most brightly, now cut an indifferent figure. It was not that his talent or his judgment failed; in these he still threw Clement and Rodd into the shade. But the risk, suddenly disclosed, was too much for him. It depressed him. He grew crabbed and soured, his temper flashing out on small provocation. He sneered at Rodd, he snubbed the clerks. When it was necessary to refuse a request for credit – and the necessity arose a dozen times a day – his manner lacked the suavity that makes the best of a bad thing.

In very truth they were trying times. Men who had bought shares through Ovington's, and might have sold them at a profit but had not, could not understand why the bank would not now advance money on the security of the shares, would not even pay calls on them, and had only advice, and that unpalatable, at their service. They came to the parlour and argued, pleaded, threatened, stormed. They would close their accounts, they would remove them to Dean's, they would publish the treatment that they had received. Again, there were those who had bought railway shares, which were now at a considerable discount and looked like falling farther; the bank had issued them – they looked to the bank to take them off their hands. More trying still were the applications of those who, suddenly pressed for money, came, pallid and wiping their foreheads with bandanna handkerchiefs, to plead desperately for a small overdraft, for twenty, forty, seventy pounds – just enough to pay the weekly wage-bill, or to meet their household outgoings, or to settle with some pressing creditor. For all creditors were now pressing. No man gave time, no man trusted another, and for those in the bank the question was, How long would they trust Ovington's? For every man who left the doors of the bank after a futile visit, every man who went away with his request declined, became a potential enemy, whose complaint or chance word might breed suspicion.

'Still, every day is a day gained,' the banker said as he dropped his mask on the Friday afternoon and sank wearily into a chair. It was closing time, and the clerks could be heard in the outer room, putting away books, counting the cash, locking the drawers. Another day had passed without special pressure. 'Time is everything.'

Arthur shrugged his shoulders. 'It would be, if it were money.'

'Well, I think that we are doing capitally – capitally so far,' said Clement.

'I am glad you are satisfied,' Arthur retorted. 'We are four hundred down on the day! I can't think, sir' – peevishly – 'why you let Purslow have that seventy pounds.'

'Well, he is a very old customer,' the banker replied patiently, 'and he's hard hit – he wanted it for wages, and I fear that he's behindhand with them. And if we withhold all help, my boy, we shall certainly precipitate a run. On Monday those bills of Badger's fall due, and I think will be met. We shall receive eleven hundred from them. On Tuesday another bill for three hundred and fifty matures, and I think is good. If we can go on till Wednesday we shall be a little stronger to meet the crisis than we are today. And we can only live from day to day' – wearily. 'If Pole's bank goes' – he glanced doubtfully at the door – 'I fear that Williams' will follow. And then—'

'There will be the devil to pay!'

'Well, we must try to pay him!'

'Bravo, sir!' Clement cried. 'That's the way to talk.'

'Yes, it is no use to dwell on the dark side,' his father agreed. 'All the same' – he was silent a while, reviewing the position and making calculations which he had made a hundred times before – 'all the same, it would make all the difference if we had that additional twelve thousand.'

'By Jove, yes!' Arthur exclaimed. For a moment hope animated his face. 'Can you think of no way – no way of getting it, sir?'

The banker shook his head. 'I have tried every quarter,' he said, 'and strained every resource. I cannot. I'm afraid we must fight our battle as we are.'

Arthur gazed at the floor. The elder man looked at him and thought again of the Squire. But he would not renew his suggestion. Arthur knew better than he what was possible in that quarter, and if he saw no hope, there doubtless was no hope. At best the idea had been fantastic, in view of the prejudice which the Squire entertained against the bank.

While they pondered, the door opened, and all three looked sharply round, the movement betraying the state of their nerves. But it was only Betty who entered – a little graver and a little older than the Betty of eight or nine months before, but with the same gleam of humour in her eyes. 'What a conclave!' she cried. She looked round on them.

'Yes,' Arthur answered dryly. 'It wants only Rodd to be complete.'

'Just so.' She made a face. 'How much you think of him lately!'

'And unfortunately he's taken his little all and left us.'

The shot told. Her eyes gleamed, and she coloured with anger. 'What do you mean? Dad' – brusquely – 'what does he mean?'

'Only that we thought it better,' the banker explained, 'to make Rodd safe by paying him the little he has with us.'

'And he took it – of course?'

The banker smiled. 'Of course he took it,' he said. 'He would have been foolish if he had not. It was only a deposit, and there was no reason why he should risk it with us – as things are.'

'Oh, I see. Things are as bad as that, are they? Any other rats?' – with a withering look at Arthur.

'I am afraid that there is no one else who can leave,' her father answered. 'The gangway is down now, my dear, and we sink or swim together.'

'Ah! Well, I fancy there's one of the rats in the dining-room now. That is what I came to tell you. He wants to see you, Dad.'

'Who is it?'

'Mr Acherley.'

Ovington shrugged his shoulders. 'Well, it is after hours,' he said, 'but – I'll see him.'

That broke up the meeting. The banker went out to interview his visitor, who had been standing for some minutes at one of the windows of the dining-room, looking out on the slender stream of traffic that passed up and down the pavement or slid round the opposite corner into the Market Place.

Acherley was not of those who go round about when a direct and more brutal approach will serve. Broken fortunes had soured rather than tamed him, and though, when there had been something to be gained by it, he had known how to treat the banker with an easy familiarity, the contempt in which he held men of that class made it more natural to him to bully than to fawn. Before he had turned to the street for amusement he had surveyed the furniture of the room with a morose eye, had damned the upstart's impudence for setting himself up with such things, and consoled himself with the reflection that he would soon see it under the hammer. 'And a d—d good job, too!' he had muttered. 'What the blazes does he want with a kidney wine-table and a plate-chest! It will serve Bourdillon right for lowering himself to such people!'

When the banker came to him he made no apology for the lateness of his visit, but 'Hallo!' he said bluntly, 'I want a little talk with you. But short's the word. Fact is, I find I've more of those railway shares than it suits me to keep, Ovington, and I want you to take a hundred off my hands. I hear they're fetching two-ten.'

'One-ten,' the banker said. 'They are barely that.'

'Two-ten,' Acherley repeated, as if the other had not spoken. 'That's my price. I suppose the bank will accommodate me by taking them?'

Ovington looked steadily at him. 'Do you mean the shares you pledged with us? If so I am afraid that in any event we shall have to put them on the market soon. The margin has nearly run off.'

'Oh, hang those!' – lightly. 'You may as well account for them at the same price – two and a half. I'll consider that settled. But I've a hundred more that I don't want to keep, and it's those I am talking about. You'll take them, I suppose – for cash, of course! I'm a little pressed at present, and want the money.'

'I am afraid that I must say no,' Ovington said. 'We are not buying any more, even at thirty shillings. As to those we hold, if you wish us to sell them at once – and I am inclined to think that we ought to—'

'Steady, steady! Not so fast!' Acherley let the mask fall, and, drawing himself to his full height – and tall and lean, in his long riding coat shaped to the figure, he looked imposing and insolent enough – he tapped his teeth with the handle of his riding whip. 'Not so fast, man! Think it over!' – with an ugly smile. 'I've been of use to you. It is your turn to be of use to me. I want to be rid of these shares.'

'Naturally. But we don't wish to take them, Mr Acherley.'

Acherley glowered at him. 'You mean,' he said, 'that the bank can't afford to take them? If that's your meaning—'

'It does not suit us to take them.'

'But by G–d you've got to take them! D'you hear, sir? You've got to take them, or take the consequences! I went into this to oblige you.'

'Not at all,' Ovington said. 'You came into it with your eyes open, and with a view to the improvement of your property, if the enterprise proved a success. No man came into it with eyes more open! To be frank with you—'

But Acherley cut him short. 'Oh, d—n all that!' he cried. 'I did not come here to palaver. The long and short of it is you've got to take the shares, or, by Gad, I go out of this room and I say what I think! And you'll take the consequences. There's talk enough in the town already, as you know. It only needs another punch, one more good punch, and you're out of the ring and in the sponging house. And your beautiful bank you know where. You know that as well as I do, my good man. And if you want a friend instead of an enemy you'll oblige me, and no words about it. That's flat!'

The room was growing dark. Ovington stood facing such light as there was. He looked very pale. 'Yes, that's quite flat,' he said.

'Very good. Then what do you say to it?'

'What I said before – No! No, Mr Acherley!'

'What? Do you mean it? Why, if you are such a fool as not to know your own interests—'

'I do know them – very well,' Ovington said, resolutely taking him up. 'I know what you want and I know what you offer. It is, as you say, quite flat, and I'll be equally – flat! Your support is not worth the price. And I warn you, Mr Acherley, and I beg you to take notice, that if you say a word against the solvency of the bank after this – after this threat – you will be held accountable to the law. And more than that, I can assure you of another thing. If, as you believe, there is going to be trouble, it is you and such as you who will be the first to suffer. Your creditors—'

'The devil take them! And you!' the gentleman cried, stung to fury. 'Why, you swollen little frog!' losing all control over himself, 'you don't think my support worth buying, don't you? You don't think it's worth a dirty hundred or two of your scrapings! Then I tell you I'll put my foot on you – by G–d, I will! Yes! I'll tread you down into the mud you sprang from! If you were a gentleman I'd shoot you on the Flash at eight o'clock tomorrow, and eat my breakfast afterwards! You to talk to me! You, you little spawn from the gutter! I've a good mind to thrash you within an inch of your life, but there'll be those ready enough to do that for me by and by – ay, and plenty, by God!'

He towered over the banker, and he looked threatening enough, but Ovington did not flinch. He went to the door and threw it open. 'There's the door, Mr Acherley!' he said.

For a moment the gentleman hesitated. But the banker's firm front prevailed, and with a gesture, half menacing, half contemptuous, Acherley stalked out. 'The worse for you!' he said. 'You'll be sorry for this! By George, you will be sorry for this next week!'

'Good evening,' said the banker – he was trembling with passion. 'I warn you to be careful what you say, or the law will deal with you.' And he stood his ground until the other, shrugging his shoulders and flinging behind him a last curse, had passed through the door. Then he closed the door and went back to the fireplace. He sat down.

The matter was no surprise to him. He knew his man, and neither the demand nor the threat was unexpected. But he knew, too, that Acherley was shrewd, and that the demand and the threat were ominous signs. More forcibly than anything that had yet occurred, they brought before him the desperate nature of the crisis, and the likelihood that, before a week went by, the worst would happen. He would be compelled to put up the shutters. The bank would stop. And with the bank would go all that he had won by a life of continuous labour: the position that he had built up, the status that he had gained, the reputation that he had achieved, the fortune which he had made and which had so much exceeded his early hopes. The things with which he had surrounded himself, they too, tokens of his success, the outward and handsome signs of his rise in life, many of them landmarks, milestones on the path of triumph – they too would go. He looked sadly on them. He saw them, he too, under the hammer: saw the mocking, heedless crowd handling them, dividing them, jeering at his short-lived splendour, gibing at his folly in surrounding himself with them.

Ay, and one here and there would have cause to say more bitter things. For some – not many, he hoped, but some – would be losers with him. Some homes would be broken up, some old men beggared; and all would be laid at his door. His name would be a byword. There would be little said of the sufferers' imprudence or folly or rashness; he would be the scapegoat for all, he and the bank he had founded. Ovington's Bank! They would tell the story of it through years to come – would smile at its rise, deride its fall, make of it a town tale, the tale of a man's arrogance, and of the speedy Nemesis which had punished it!

He was a proud man, and the thought of these things, the visions that they called up, tortured him. At times, he had borne himself a little too highly, had presumed on his success, had said a word too much. Well, all that would be repaid now with interest, ay, with compound interest.

The room was growing dark, as dark as his thoughts. The fire glowed, a mere handful of red embers, in the grate. Now and again men went by the windows, talking – talking, it might be, of him: anxious, suspicious, greedy, ready at a word to ruin themselves and him, to cut their own throats in their selfish panic. They had only to use common sense, to control themselves, and no man would lose a penny. But they would have no common sense. They would rush in and destroy all, their own and his. For no bank called upon to pay in a day all that it owed could do so, any more than an insurance office could at any moment pay all its lives. But they would not blame themselves. They would blame him – and his!

He groaned as he thought of his children. Clement, indeed, might and must fend for himself. And he would – he had proved it of late days by his courage and cheerfulness, and the father's heart warmed to him. But Betty? Gay, fearless, laughing Betty, the light of his home, the joy of his life! Who, born when fortune had already begun to smile on him, had never known poverty or care or mean shifts! For whom he had been ambitious, whom he had thought to see well married – married into the county, it might be! Poor Betty! There would be an end of that now. Past his prime and discredited, he could not hope to make more than a pittance, happy if he could earn some two or three pounds a week in some such situation as Rodd's. And she must sink with him and accept such a home as he could support, in place of this spacious old town-house, with its oaken wainscots and its wide, shallow stairs, and its cheerful garden at the back.

His love suffered equally with his pride.

He was thinking so deeply that he did not hear the door open, or a light foot cross the room. He did not suspect that he was observed until a pair of warm young arms slid round his neck, and Betty's curls brushed his cheek. 'In the dumps, Father?' she said. 'And in the dark – and alone? Poor Father! Is it as bad as that? But you have not given up hope? We are not ruined yet?'

'God forbid!' he said, hardly able, on finding her so close to him, to control his voice. 'But we may be, Betty.'

'And what then?' She clasped him more closely to her. 'Might not worse things happen to us? Might you not die and I be left alone? Or might I not die, and you lose me? Or Clement? You are pleased with Clement, Father, aren't you? He may not be as clever as – as some people. But you know he's there when you want him. Suppose you lost us?'

'True, child. But you don't know what poverty is – after wealth, Betty – how narrowing, how irksome, how it galls at every point! You don't know what it is to live on two or three pounds a week, in two or three rooms!'

'They will bring us the closer together,' said Betty.

'And to be looked down upon by those who have been your equals, and shunned by those who have been your friends!'

'Nice friends! We shall do better without them!'

'And things will be said of me, things it will be hard to listen to!'

'They won't say them to me,' said Betty. 'Or look out for my nails, ma'am! Besides, they won't be true, and who cares, Father! Lizzie Clough said yesterday I'd a cast in one eye, but does it worry me? Not a scrap. And we'll shut the door on our two or three rooms and let them – go hang! As long as we are together we can face anything, Father – we can live on two pounds or two shillings or two pence. And consider! You might never have known what Clement was, how lively, how brave, how' – with a funny little laugh – 'like me,' hugging him to her, 'if this had not happened – that's not going to happen after all.'

He sighed. He dealt with figures, she with fancy. 'I hope not,' he said, 'At any rate I've two good children, and if it does come to the worst—'

'We'll lock ourselves in and our false friends out!' she said; and for a moment after that she was silent. Then, 'Tell me, Father, why did Mr Rodd take that money – when you need all that you can get together, and he knows it? For he's taking the plate to Birmingham to pledge, isn't he? So he must know it.'

'He is, if—'

'If it comes to the worst? I know. Then why did he take his money, when he knew how things stood?'

'Why did he take his own when we offered it?' the banker replied. 'Why shouldn't he, child? It was his own, and business is business. He would have been very foolish if he had not taken it. He's not a man who can afford to lose it.'

'Oh!' said Betty. And for some minutes she said no more. Then she roused herself, poked the fire, and rang for the lamp.

Chapter Twenty-Seven

'Well,' said the Squire peevishly, 'I can do no more. Girls ha' their whimsies, and it's much if you can hinder 'em running after Mr Wrong without forcing 'em to take Mr Right. At any rate I've said what I could for you, lad, and the end was as if I hadn't. You must fight your own battles. Jos hasn't' – this would never have occurred to the Squire in his seeing days – 'too gay a life of it, and if you're not man enough to get on the soft side of her, with a clear field, why, damme, you don't deserve to have her.'

'I was well enough with her,' Arthur said resentfully, 'till lately. But she is changed, sir.'

'Well, like enough. Girls are like that.'

'There may be – someone else.'

The Squire snorted. 'Who?' he said. 'Who?' – more roughly. 'You're talking nonsense.'

Arthur could not say who. He could not name anyone. So far as he knew there could not be anyone. But his temper, chafed by a week of suspense and anxiety, was not smoothed by the old man's refusal to do more. And then to fail with Josina! To be rejected by Josina, the simple girl whom, in his heart, he had regarded as a *pis aller*, on whom he had deigned to confer a half-contemptuous affection, on whose youthful fancy he had played for his pastime! This was enough to try him, apart from the fact that things in Aldersbury looked black, and that, losing her, he lost the consolation prize to which he had looked forward to make all good. So, taken to task by the Squire, he did not at once assent. 'Who?' he repeated gloomily. 'Ah, I don't know.'

'Nor I!' the Squire retorted. 'There is nobody. Truth is, my lad, the man who has been robbed sees a face in every bush. However, there 'tis.

I've said my say, and I've done with it. Did you bring those deeds from Welsh's?'

Arthur swallowed his mortification as best he might – fortunately the old man could not see his face. 'Yes,' he said. 'I left them downstairs.' The Squire had caught a cold, sitting out on the hill on the Saturday, and had been for some days in his bedroom.

'Well, I'm going to pay wages now,' the other rejoined. 'Bring 'em up after dinner and I'll sign 'em. You and the girl or Peacock can witness them. And hark you – here, wait a minute!' – irascibly, for Arthur, giving as much rein to his temper as he dared, had turned on his heel and was marching off. 'Take my keys and open the safe-cupboard downstairs, and bring me up the agreement. I've got to compare it with the lease – I shan't sign it without! Lock the door, d'you hear, before you open the cupboard, and have a care no one sees you.'

'Very well,' Arthur said, and was half-way to the door when again, as if to try his patience, the old man stopped him. 'What's this they're saying about Ovington's, eh? 'Bout the bank? Pretty thing, if he's let you in and your money too! But I'm not surprised. I told you you were a fool, young man, to dirty your hands in that bag, whatever you thought to get out of it. And if you're not going to get anything out of it, but to leave your own in, as I hear talk of – what then? Come, let's hear what you have to say about it! I'd like to know.'

'I don't know what you've heard, sir,' Arthur answered, sparring for time. For self-control, provoking as the old man was, he had no longer need to fight. For he had seen, the moment the Squire spoke, that here, here if he chose to avail himself of it, was his chance of the twelve thousand! Here was an opening, if he had the courage to seize it. Granted the chance was desperate, and the opening unpromising – a poorer or less promising could hardly be. And the courage necessary was great. But here it was. The Squire himself had brought up the subject. He knew of the rumours; he had broken the ice. Here it was, and for a moment, uncertain, wavering, giddy with the swift interchange of *pros* and *cons*, Arthur tried for time – time to think. 'What was it? What did you hear, sir?' he asked.

'What did I hear?' the Squire answered. 'Why, that they're d—d suspicious of them in the town. And I don't wonder. Up in a night, and cut off in a day, like a rotten mushroom!' He spoke with gusto, forgetting for the moment what this might mean to his listener; who, on his side, hardly heeded the brutality, so absorbed was he in the question which he must answer – the question whether it would be wise or foolish, ruin or salvation, to ask the Squire for help. 'He'll be another Fauntleroy, 'fore he's done,' the old man went on with relish. 'He'll stretch a rope, you'll see if he won't! I told him as much myself. I told him as much in those very words the day he came here about his confounded silly toy of a railroad. He might take in Woosenham and a lot of other fools, I told him, but he did not deceive me. Now I hear that he's going to burst up, and where'll you be, my lad? Where'll you be? By Gad, you may be in the dock with him!'

Certainly he might speak on that. The old man was harsh and hard-fisted, but he was also hard-headed and very shrewd; and conceivably the case might be so put to him that he might see his profit in it. Certainly it might be so put that he might see a fair prospect of saving his nephew's five thousand at no great risk to himself. The books might be laid before him, the figures be taken out, the precise situation made clear. There was – it could not be put higher than this – just a slender chance that he would listen, prejudiced as he was.

But twelve thousand! It was such a stupendous sum to name. It needed such audacity to ask for it. And yet it was that or nothing. Less might not serve; while to ask for less, to ask for anything at all, might cost the petitioner the favour he had won, his standing in the house, and all the advantages which the Squire's support might still gain for him. And then it was such a forlorn hope, such a desperate, feckless venture! No, he would be a fool to risk it. He dared not do it. He had not the face.

Yet, for a few seconds after the Squire had ceased to speak, Arthur hesitated, confession trembling on his lips. The twelve thousand would make all good, save all, redeem all – ay, and bind Ovington to him in bonds of steel. But no, he dared not. He would be a fool to speak. And instead of the words that had risen to his lips, 'I think you mistake, sir,' he said coldly. 'I think you'll find that this is all cry and little wool! Of course money is tight, and there is trouble in the City. I've heard talk of two or three weak banks being in difficulties, and I should not wonder if one or two of them stopped payment between this and Christmas. We are told that it is likely. But we are perfectly solvent. It will take more than talk to bring Ovington's down.'

'Umph!' the Squire grumbled. 'Well, maybe. You talk as if you knew, and you ought to know. I hope you do know. After all – I don't want you to lose your money – Gad, a pretty fool you'd look, my lad! A pretty fool, indeed! But as for Ovington, a confounded rascal, who thinks himself a gentleman because he has filled his purse at some poor devil's expense – I'd see him break with pleasure.'

'I don't think you'll have the pleasure this time!' Arthur retorted with a bitterness which he could not repress – a bitterness caused as much by his own doubts as by the other's harshness. He left the room without more, the keys in his hand, and went downstairs.

It wanted about an hour of the Squire's dinner-time, but Calamy had laid the table early, and the dining-room was dark. Arthur carried in a lamp from the hall, and himself closed the shutters. He locked the door. Then he opened the nearer panel and the cupboard behind it, and sought for and found the agreement – but all mechanically, his mind still running on the Squire's words, and now approving of the course he had taken, now doubting if he had not missed his opportunity. The agreement in his hand, his errand done, he closed the cupboard door, and was preparing to close the panel, when, with his hand still on it, he paused. More clearly than when his bodily eyes had rested upon them he saw the contents of the cupboard.

And one thing in particular, a small thing, but it was on this that his mind focused itself – the iron box containing the India Stock. He saw it before him; it stood out dark, its every outline sharp. And with equal clearness he saw its contents, the two certificates that remained in it. He recalled the value of them, and almost against his will he calculated their worth at the price of the day. India Stock, sound and safe security as it was, had fallen more than thirty points since the Squire had sold. It stood today, he thought, at two hundred and forty or a little over or a little under – somewhere about that. At the lowest figure five thousand pounds would fetch – just twelve thousand, he calculated.

Twelve thousand!

He stood staring at the door, and even by the yellow light of the lamp his face looked pale. Twelve thousand! And upstairs in a pigeon-hole of the old bureau, where he had carelessly thrust it, was the blank transfer.

It seemed providential. It seemed as if the stock – stock to the precise amount he required – had been placed there for a purpose. Twelve thousand! And realisable, no matter what the pinch. If he borrowed it for a month, what harm would there be? Or what risk? The bank was solvent, he knew that; give it time, and it would stand as strong as ever. Within a month, or two months at the most, he could replace the stock, and no one would be the wiser. And the bank and his own fortune would be saved.

Whereas – whereas, if the bank failed, he lost everything. And what was it his uncle had said? 'A pretty fool you will look!' It was true, it was horribly true. He would be the laughing stock of the county. Men of his own class would say with a sneer that it served him right. And the Squire – what would he say? His life would be a hell!

Still he hesitated, though he told himself that it was not by boggling at trifles that men arrived at great ends – nor by poltroonery. And who would be the loser? No one. It would be all gain. The Squire, if he had common sense, would be the first to wish it done.

Yet, as he felt through the bunch, with fingers that shook a little, for the small key that opened the box, he glanced fearfully over his shoulder. But the door of the room was locked, the windows were shuttered: no one could see him. No one could ever say what he had done in that room. And he was lawfully there, at the Squire's own request, on his errand.

Five minutes later he closed the cupboard, closed the panel. He took up the lamp with a steady hand and left the room. He went into the Squire's bedroom to return the keys, loitered a minute or two at the bureau, then he went to his own room. On the table lay the lease and the counterpart that he had brought from Aldersbury for the old man's signature. He closed and locked the door.

It was some hour and a half later that, having finished dinner – and he had talked more fluently at the meal, and with less restraint than of late – he rose from the table with Miss Peacock and Josina. 'I'll come with you,' he said. 'I shall have my wine upstairs.' And then, turning to the Peacock, 'The Squire will want you to witness his signature,' he said. 'Will you come? He has to sign some deeds that Welsh's have sent.'

Miss Peacock bewailed herself. She was in a flurry at the prospect. 'Oh, dear, dear,' she said, 'I wish he didn't! I am all of a twitter, and then he scolds me. I am sure to put my name in the wrong place, or write his or something.'

Josina laughed. 'What will you give me to go instead?' she asked. 'Come? But, there, I'll go. In fact, he told me before dinner that I was to go.' She moved towards the door.

But Arthur did not move. He looked disturbed. 'I don't think that

that will do,' he said slowly. 'Considering what it is – I think the Peahen would be the better.'

'But if she doesn't like it?' Jos objected. 'And I must go, Arthur, for he told me to go. So the sooner the better. We have sat longer than usual, and, though Calamy is with him, he won't like to be kept waiting.'

Arthur seemed to consider it. 'Oh, very well,' he said at last. He followed her from the room.

The Squire was sitting before the fire, at the small round table at which he had eaten his meal. A decanter of port and a couple of glasses stood at his elbow. Two candles in tall silver candlesticks shed a circle of light on the table, and showed up his white head and his hands, but failed to illumine the larger part of the room. The great bed with its drab hangings, the lofty press with its brass handles, the dark Windsor chairs, now lurked in and now sprang from the shadows, as the fire flickered up or sank. On the verge of the circle of light the butler moved mysteriously, now appearing, now disappearing; now coming forward to set an inkstand and goose-quills beside the decanter, now withdrawing to pile unseen plates upon an unseen tray.

The Squire was tapping impatiently on the table when they entered. 'Well, you're in no hurry for your wine tonight,' he said. 'Have you brought the papers? You might have a'most written them in the time you've been.'

'Sorry, sir,' said Arthur. 'They are here. Will you sit here, Jos?'

'Nay, nay, she must be near by,' the old man objected. His hearing was still good. 'Close up! Close up, girl! I want her eyes. And do you fill your glass. Now have you all ready? Then do you read me the agreement first, that I may see if the lease tallies. And read slowly, lad, slowly. Calamy?'

'I am here, sir,' lugubriously. 'Where we'll be tomorrow—'

'D – n you, don't whine, man, but snuff the candles. And then get out. Do you hear?'

Calamy mumbled that it would be all the same at the latter end. He went out with his tray, and closed the door behind him.

'Now!' said the Squire, 'we're ready.' And obedient to the word Arthur began to read. Once or twice his voice failed him, and he had to clear his throat. Josina would have thought that he was nervous, had she ever known him nervous. Fortunately, the document was short, as legal documents go, and some five minutes, during which the Squire sat listening intently to it, saw it at an end.

'Umph! Sounds all right,' he commented. 'Sight o' words! But there, they've got to charge. Now do you give the girl the counterpart, and do you read the lease, lad, and read it slowly, so as I may understand. And hark you, Jos, speak up if there is any differ – nail it like a rat, girl, and don't go to sleep over it! Don't you let me be cheated. Welsh is as honest, and I'd as lief trust him, as another, but if aught's amiss it's not he that will suffer, nor the confounded scamp of a clerk that made the mistake. And see you there's no erasures; I'm lawyer enough to know that. Now, slow, lad, slow,' he commanded, 'so that I can take it in.'

Arthur complied, and began to read slowly and carefully. But again he had more than once to stop, his voice failing. He explained it by saying that the light was not good, and he rose to snuff the candles. The lease, too, was longer than the agreement, and was full of verbiage, and it took some time to read, and some patience. But at long last the delivery clause was reached. No discrepancy or erasure had been discovered, and the Squire, whose attention had never faltered – he was an excellent man of affairs – declared himself satisfied.

'Well, there,' he said, in a tone of relief, 'that's done! Drink up, lad, and wet your throttle.' He turned himself squarely to the table. 'Give me the pen I used last,' he continued. 'And do you guide my hand to the right place.'

'I am afraid your pen was left to dry,' Arthur said, 'and the nib has opened. You'll have to use a new one, sir, and try it first. And – the sand? We shall want that. I am afraid it is downstairs. If Josina would not mind running down for it?'

'Pooh! pooh! Never mind the sand! Let 'em dry o' themselves. Less chance of blotting. Where's the pen?' – holding out his hand for it.

'Here, sir. Will you try it on this? If you'll write your name in full, as if you were signing the deeds' – he guided the Squire's hand to the place – 'I shall see if it is right – and straight.'

'Ay, ay, best be careful,' the Squire agreed, squaring himself to his task. ''Twon't do to spoil 'em. Here?'

'Yes – just as you are now.'

The old man bent over the table, his white hair shining in the centre of the little circle of light cast by the candles. Slowly and laboriously, in a tense silence, while Arthur, leaning over his shoulder, followed each movement of the pen, and Josina, half in light, half in shadow, watched them both from the farther side of the table, he wrote his name.

It was a perfect signature, though rather bolder and larger than usual, and 'Excellent!' Arthur cried in a tone of relief, which betrayed the anxiety he had felt. 'Good! It could not be better! Well done, sir!' He removed the paper as he spoke, but in the act looked sharply across at Josina. The girl's eyes were upon him, but her face was in shadow, and he could not read its expression. He hesitated a moment, the paper in his hand, then he laid it on the table beside him – and out of her reach.

'Right!' said the Squire. 'Then, now for business. Let's have the lease. My hand's in now.'

Arthur laid it before him, and guided his hand to the place. 'Is there ink enough in the pen?' the old man asked.

'Quite enough, sir. It won't do to blot it.'

'Right, lad, right!' The Squire wrote his name. 'Now the counterpart!' he continued briskly, holding the quill suspended.

Arthur put it before him. He signed it, steadily and clearly. 'All right?' he asked.

'Quite right. Couldn't be better, sir.'

'Then, thank God that's done!' He sank back in his chair, and raised his hand to take off his glasses, then remembered himself. 'Pheugh!' he said, 'it's a job when you can't see.' But it was plain that he was pleased with himself.

Arthur turned to Josina. 'Your turn next!' he said; and he gave her the pen. He put the lease before her, and pointed to the place where she was to sign.

She was not as nervous as Miss Peacock, but she was anxious to make no mistake. 'Here?' she asked.

'Yes, there. Be careful.' Arthur snuffed the candles, and as he did so he glanced over his shoulder, his eyes searching the shadows. Then he leant over her, watching her pen.

She wrote her name, slowly and carefully. 'Good!' he said, and he removed the document. He set another before her, and silently showed her with his finger where to write. She wrote her name.

'Now here,' he said. 'Here! But wait! Is there enough ink in the pen?'

She dipped the pen in the inkpot to make sure, and shook it, that there might be no danger of a blot. Again she wrote her name.

'Capital!' he said. His voice betrayed relief. 'That's done, and well done! Couldn't be better. Now it's my turn.'

'But' – Jos looked up in doubt, the pen still in her hand – 'but I've signed three, Arthur! I thought there were but two.'

'Three!' exclaimed the Squire, turning his head, his attention caught. 'Damme!' – peevishly – 'what mess has the girl made now?' It was part of his creed that in matters of business no woman was to be trusted to do the smallest thing as it should be done.

But Arthur only laughed. 'No mess, sir,' he said. 'Only a goose of herself! She has witnessed your trial signature as well as the others. That's all. I thought I could make her do it, and she did it as solemnly as you like!' He laughed a little loudly. 'I shall keep that, Jos.'

The Squire, pleased with himself, and glad that the business was over, was in a good humour, and he joined in the laugh. 'It will teach you not to be too free with your signature, my girl,' he said. 'When you come some day to have a cheque book, you'll find that that won't do! Won't do, at all! Well, thank God, that's done.'

Arthur, who was stooping over the table, adding his own name, completed his task. He stood up. 'Yes, sir, that's done. Done!' he repeated in an odd, rising tone. 'And now – the lease goes back to Welsh's. Shall I lock up the counterpart – downstairs, sir?'

'No, lad,' the Squire announced. 'I'll do that myself o' Monday.'

'But it's no trouble, sir.' He held out his hand for the keys. 'And perhaps the sooner it's locked up – the tenant's signed it, and it is complete now – the safer.'

But 'No, no, time enough!' the Squire persisted. 'I'll put it back on Monday. I am not so helpless now I can't manage that, and I shall be downstairs o' Monday.'

For a moment Arthur hesitated. He looked as if something troubled him. But in the end, 'Very good, sir. Then that's all?' he said.

'Ay, put the counterpart in the old bureau there. 'Twill be safe there till Monday. How's the wine? Fill my glass and fill your own, lad. You can go, Jos. Tell Calamy to come to me at half-past nine.'

Chapter Twenty-Eight

The next day, Sunday, was raw and wet. Mist blotted out the hills, and beneath it the vale mourned. The trees dripped sadly, pools gathered about the roots of the beeches, the down-spouts of the eaves gurgled softly in the ears of those who sat near the windows. Miss Peacock alone ventured to church in the afternoon, Arthur walking with her as far as the door, and then going on to the Cottage to have tea with his mother. Josina stayed at home in attendance on her father, but ten minutes after the others had left the house, he dismissed her with a fractious word.

She went down to the dining-room, where she could hear his summons if he tapped the floor. She poked up the smouldering logs, and looked through the windows at the dreary scene – the day was already drawing in – then, settling herself before the fire, she opened a book. But she did not read, indeed she hardly pretended to read, for across the page of the Sunday volume, in black capitals, blotting out the type, forcing itself on her brain, insistent, inexorable, unavoidable, there printed itself the word 'When?'

Ay, when? When was she going to summon Clement, and give him leave to speak? When was she going to keep her word, to make a clean breast of it to her father and confront the storm, the violence of which her worst fears could not picture or exaggerate?

When?

With every day of the past fortnight the question had confronted her with growing insistence. Now, in this idle hour, with the house silent about her, with nothing to distract her thoughts, it rose before her, grim as the outlook. It would not be denied, it came between her and the page, it forced itself upon her, it called for, nay, it insisted upon, an answer. When?

There was no longer any hope that the Squire would regain his sight, no longer any fear for his general health. He was as well as he ever would be, as well able to bear the disclosure. Delay on that ground was a plea which could no longer avail her or deceive her. Then, when? Or rather, why not now? Her conscience told her that she was playing the coward, proving false to her word, betraying Clement – Clement whom she loved, and whom, craven as she was, she feared to acknowledge.

Then, when? Surely now, or not at all.

Alas, the longer she dwelt on the avowal she must make, the more appalling the ordeal appeared. Her father, indeed, had been more gentle of late; that walk on the hill had brought them closer together, and since then he had shown himself more human. Glimpses of sympathy, even of affection, had peeped through the chinks of his harshness. But how difficult was the position! She must own to stolen meetings, to underhand practices, to things disreputable; she must proclaim, maid as she was, her love. And her love for whom? A stranger, and worse than a stranger – a nobody. Then apart from her father's contempt for the class to which Clement belonged, and with which he was less in sympathy than with the peasants on his lands, his prejudice against the Ovingtons was itself a thing to frighten her! Hardly a day passed that he did not utter some jibe at their expense, or some word that betrayed how sorely Arthur's defection rankled. And then his blindness – that added the last touch of deceit to her conduct, that made worse and more clandestine what had been bad before. As she thought of it, and imagined the avowal and the way in which he would take it, the colour left her cheeks and she shivered with fright. She did not know how she could do it, or how she could live through it. He would lose all faith in her. He would pluck from his heart even that affection for her which she had begun to discern under the mask of his sternness – to discern and to cherish.

Yet time pressed, she could no longer palter with her love, she must be true to Clement now, or false, she must suffer for him now or play the coward. She had given him her word. Was she to go back on it?

Oh, never! never! she thought, and pressed her hands together. Those spring days when she had walked with him beside the brook, when his coming had been sunshine and her pulses had leapt at the sound of his footsteps, when his eyes had lured the heart from her and the touch of his lips had awakened the woman in her, when she had passed whole days and nights in sweet musings on him – oh, never!

No, he had urged her to be brave, to be true, to be worthy of him; and she must be. She must face all for him. And it would be but for a time. He had said that her father might separate them, and would separate them; but if they were true to one another—

'Miss! Miss Josina!'

She turned, her dream cut short, and saw Molly, the kitchenmaid, standing in the doorway. She was surprised, for the stillness of a Sunday afternoon held the house – it was the servants' hour, and one at which they were seldom to be found, even when wanted. 'What is it?' she asked, and stood up, alarmed. 'Has my father called?' He might have rapped, and deep in thought she might not have heard him.

'No, miss,' Molly answered – and heaven knows if Molly had an inkling of the secret, but certainly her face was bright with mischief. 'There is a gentleman asking for you, if you please, miss. He bid me give you this,' She held out a three-cornered note.

Josina's face burned. 'A gentleman?' she faltered.

'Yes, miss, a young gentleman,' Molly answered demurely.

Josina took the note – what else could she do? – and opened it with shaking fingers. For a moment, such was her confusion, she failed to read the few words it contained. Then she collected herself – the words became plain: 'Very urgent – forgive me and see me for ten minutes. – C.'

Very urgent? It must be urgent indeed, or, after all she had said, he would not come to her unbidden. She hesitated, looking shamefacedly at Molly. But the eyes of young kitchen-maids are sharp, and probably this was not the first glimpse Molly had had of the young mistress' love story, or of the young gentleman. 'You can slip out easy, miss,' she said, 'and not a soul the wiser. They are all off about their business.'

'Where is he?'

'He's under the garden wall, miss – down the lane.'

Jos took her courage in her hands. She snatched up a shawl from the hall-table, and with hot cheeks she went out through the back regions, Molly accompanying her as far as the yard. 'I'll be about the place, miss,' the girl said – if no one else was enjoying herself, she was. 'I'll rattle the milk-pail if – if you're wanted.'

Josina drew the shawl about her head, and went down the yard, passing on her right the old stable, which bore over its door the same date as the table in the hall – 1691. A moment, and she saw Clement waiting for her under the eaves of the Dutch summer-house, of which the sustaining wall overhung the lane, and, with the last of the opposing outhouses, formed a sort of entrance to the yard.

She had been red enough under Molly's gaze, resenting the confederacy which she could not avoid. But the colour left her face as her eyes met her lover's, and she saw how sad and downcast he looked, and how changed from the Clement of her meetings. He was shabby, too – he who had always been so neat – so that even before he spoke she divined that there was something amiss, and knew at last, too, that there was nothing that she would not do, no risk that she would not run, no anger or storm that she would not face for this man before her. The mother in her awoke, and longed to comfort him and shield him, to give all for him. 'Clement!' she cried, and, trembling, she held out her hands to him. 'Dear Clement! What is it?'

He took her hands and held them, and if he had taken her in his arms she would have forgiven him and clung to him. But he did not. He seemed even to hold her from him. 'Forgive me, dear, for sending for you,' he said. 'I thought to catch you going into church, but you were not there, and there was nothing for it but this. Jos, I have bad news.'

'Bad news?' she exclaimed. 'What? Don't keep me waiting, Clement! What bad news?'

'The worst for me,' he said. 'For we must part. I have come to say good-bye.'

'Good-bye?' Oh, it was impossible! It was not, it could not be that! 'What do you mean?' she cried, and her eyes pleaded with him to take it back. 'Tell me! You cannot mean that we must part.'

'I do,' he said soberly. 'Something has happened, dear – something that must divide us. Be brave, and I will tell you.'

'You must,' she said.

He told his story – rapidly, in clear short phrases which he had rehearsed many times as he covered the seven miles from Aldersbury on this dreary errand. He told her all, that which no one else must know, that which she must not reveal. They expected a run on the bank. They were sure, indeed, that a run must come, and though the issue was not yet quite certain, though his father still had hope, he had, himself, no hope. Within a week he would be a poor man, little better than a beggar, dependent on his own exertions; with no single claim, no possible pretensions to her hand, no ground on which he could appeal to her father. It must be at an end between them, and he preferred to let her know now rather than to wait until the blow had fallen. He thought himself bound in honour to release her while he still had some footing, some show of equality with her.

She smiled when she had heard him out. She smiled in his face. 'But if I will not be released?' she said. And then, before he could answer her, she bade him tell her more. What was this run? What did it mean? She did not understand.

He told her in detail, and, while he told her, they stood, two pathetic figures in the mist and rain that dripped slowly and sadly from the eaves of the Dutch summer-house. She stood, pressing her hands together, trying to comprehend. And he hid nothing: telling her even of the ten or twelve thousand that, did they possess it, would save them; telling her that which had decided him to bid her farewell – an item of news which had reached the bank on the previous evening, after Arthur had left for Garth. The great house of Poles, with a wide connection among country banks, had closed its doors; and not only that, but Williams', Ovington's agents, had followed suit within six hours. The tidings had come by special messenger, but would be known in the town in the morning, and would certainly cause a panic and a run on both banks. That news had been the last straw, he said. It had pushed him to a decision. He had felt that he must give her back her word, and without the loss of a day must put it in her power to say that there was nothing between them.

Once and again, as he told his tale, she put in a question, or uttered a pitying exclamation. But for the most part she listened in silence, controlling herself, suppressing the agitation which shook her. When he had done, she put a question, but it was one so irrelevant, so unexpected, so far from the mark, that it acted on him like a douche of cold water. 'What have you done to your coat?' she asked.

'My coat?'

'Yes.' She pointed to his shoulder.

He glanced down at his coat, but he felt the check. Surely the ways of women were strange, their manner of taking things past finding out. He explained, but he could not hide his chagrin. 'I wasn't thinking, and took the first that came to hand,' he said, 'an old one. Does it matter?'

But she continued to stare at it. He was wearing a riding coat, high in the collar, long in the skirts, shaped to the figure. On the light buff of the cloth a stain spread downwards from shoulder to breast. The right arm and cuff, too, were discoloured, and it said much for the disorder of his thoughts that he had ridden from town without noticing it. She eyed the stain with distaste, with something like a shudder. 'It is blood,' she said, 'isn't it?'

He shrugged his shoulders, yet himself viewed it askance. 'Yes,' he said. 'I don't know how you knew. I wore it that night, you know. I did not mean to wear it again, but in my hurry—'

'Do you mean the night that my father was hurt?'

'Yes.'

'You held him up in the carriage?'

'Yes, but' – squinting at it – 'I don't think that it was done then. I believe it was done when I was picking him up in the road, Jos, before Bourdillon came. Indeed, I remember that your father noticed it – before he fainted, you know.'

'My father noticed it?'

'Well, oddly enough, he did.'

'While you were supporting him?' There was a strange light in her eyes, and the blood had come back to her cheeks. 'But where was Thomas – the man – then?'

'Oh, he had gone off, across the fields.'

'Before Arthur came up, do you mean?'

'To be sure, some time before. However—'

But, 'No, Clement, I want to understand this,' she insisted, breaking in on him. Her voice betrayed her excitement, and to hold him to the point she laid her hands on his shoulders, standing before him and close to him. 'Tell me again, and clearly. Do you mean that it was you who drove Thomas off? Before Arthur came up?'

He stared. 'Well, of course it was,' he said. 'Didn't you know that? Didn't Arthur tell you?'

She avoided the question, and instead, 'Then it was your coat that was spoiled?' she said. 'This coat?'

'Well, of course it was. You can see that.'

She looked at him, her cheeks flushed, her pride in him showing in her eyes. He had indeed justified her choice of him, her belief in him, her confidence in him. He had done this and had said nothing. The day was cold, and she was not warmly clad, but she felt no cold – now. It was raining, but she was no longer aware of it. There had sprung up in her heart, not only courage, but a faint, a very faint hope.

He had come to dash her down, to fill her cup of sorrow to the brim, to leave her lonely in the world – for never, never could she love another! And instead he had given her hope – a hope forlorn and far off, gleaming faint as the small stars in distant Cassiopeia, and often doubt, like an evening mist, would veil it. But it sparkled, she saw it, she drew courage from it.

Meanwhile, surprised by the turn her thoughts had taken, he was still more surprised by the change in her looks, the colour in her cheeks, the light in her eyes. He did not understand, and for a moment, seeing himself no hope but only sorrow and parting, he was tempted to think that she trifled. What mattered it what coat he wore, or what had stained it, or the details of a story old now, and which he supposed to be as well known to her as to him? Perhaps she did not comprehend, and, 'Jos,' he said, inviting her to be serious, 'do you understand that this is our parting?'

But 'No! no!' she said resolutely. 'We are not going to part.'

'But don't you see,' sadly, 'that I cannot go to your father now? That next week we may be beggars, and my father a ruined man? I could ask no man, even a poor man, for his daughter now. I must work to live, work as a clerk – as, I don't know what, Jos, but in some position far removed from your life, and far removed from your class. I could not speak to your father now, and it is that which has brought me to you to – to say good-bye, dearest – to part, Jos! The gates are closed, we must go out of the garden, dear. And you' – he looked at her with yearning eyes – 'must forgive me, before we part.'

'Perhaps we are not going to part,' she said.

He shook his head. He would not deceive her. 'Nothing else is possible,' he said.

'Perhaps, and perhaps not. At any rate,' putting her hands in his, and looking at him with brave, loving eyes, 'I would not undo one of those days – in the garden! No, nor an hour of them. They are precious to me. And for forgiving, I have nothing to forgive and nothing to regret, if we never meet again, Clement. But we shall meet. What if you have to begin the world again? We are both young. You will work for me. And do you think that I will not wait for you, wait until you have climbed up again, or until something happens to bring us together? Do you not know that I love you more now, far more, in your unhappiness – that you are more to me, a thousand times more today – than in your prosperity?'

'Oh, Jos!' He could say no more, but his swimming eyes spoke for him.

'But you must leave it to me now,' she continued. 'After all, things may turn out better than you think. You may not be ruined. People may not be so foolish as to want all their money at once. Have hope, and – and remember that I am always here, though you do not see me or hear from me; that I am always here, thinking of you, waiting for you, loving you, always yours, Clement, till you come – though it be ten years hence.'

'Oh, Jos!' His eyes were overflowing now.

'You believe me, you do believe me, don't you?' she said, clinging to him. 'And now you must go. But kiss me first. No, I do not mind who sees us, or who knows that I am yours now. I am past that.'

He took her in his arms and kissed her, not as he would have kissed her an hour before, with passion, but in reverence and humility, in love too sacred for words. Never till now had he known what a woman's love was, how much it gave, how little it asked, how pure in its highest form it could be – and how strong! Nor ever till now had he known her, this girl to whom he had once presumed to teach firmness, whose weakness he had taken on himself to guide, whom he had thought to encourage, to strengthen, to arm – he, who had not been worthy to kiss the hem of her robe!

Oh, the wonderful power of love, which had transformed her! Which had made her what she was, and now laid him in the dust before her!

Work for her, wait for her, live for her? Ah, would he not, and deem himself happy though the years brought him no nearer, though the memory of her, transfiguring his whole life, proved his only and full reward!

Chapter Twenty-Nine

An hour after Arthur had left the house on the Monday morning Josina went slowly up the stairs to her father's room. She was young and the stairs were shallow, but the girl's knees shook under her as she mounted them, as she mounted them one by one, while her hand trembled on the banister. Before now the knees of brave men, going on forlorn hopes, have shaken under them, but, like these men, Josina went on, she ascended step by step. She was frightened, she was horribly frightened, but she had made a vow to herself and she would carry it out. How she would carry it out, how she would find words to blurt out the truth, how she would have the courage to live through that which would follow, she did not know, she could not conceive. But her mind was fixed.

She reached the shabby landing on which two or three sheepskins, laid at the doors of the rooms, served for carpet, and there, indeed, she paused awhile and pressed her hand to her side to still the beating of her heart. She gazed through the window. On the sweep below, Calamy was shaking out the cloth, while two or three hens clucked about his feet, and a cat seated at a distance watched the operation with dignity. In the field beyond the brook a dog barked joyously as it rounded up some sheep. Miss Peacock's voice, scolding a maid, came up from below. All was going on as usual, going on callous and heedless; while she – she had that before her which turned her sick and faint, which for her, timid and subject, was almost worse than death.

And with her on this forlorn hope went no comrades, no tramp of marching feet, no watching eyes of thousands, no bugle note to cheer her. Only Clement's shade – waiting.

She might still draw back. But when she had once spoken there could be no drawing back. A voice whispered in her ear that she had better think it over – just once more, better wait a little longer to see if aught would happen, revolve it once again in her mind. Possibly there might be some other, some easier, some safer way.

But she knew what that whisper meant, and she turned from the window and grasped the handle of the door. She went in. Her father was sitting beside the fire. His back was towards her, he was smoking his after-breakfast pipe. She might still retreat, or – or she might say what she liked, ask perhaps if he wanted anything. He would never suspect, never conceive in his wildest moments the thing that she had come to confess. It was not too late even now – to draw back.

She went to the other side of the table on which his elbow rested, and she stood there, steadying herself by a hand which she laid on the table. She was sick with fear, her tongue clung to her mouth, her very lips were white. But she forced herself to speak. 'Father, I have something – to tell you,' she said.

'Eh?' He turned sharply. 'What's that?' She had not been able to control her voice, and he knew in a moment that something was wrong. 'What ha' you been doing?'

Now! Now, or never! The words she had so often repeated to herself rang in her ears. 'Do you know who it was,' she said, 'who saved you that night, sir? The night you were – hurt?'

He turned himself a little more towards her. 'Who? Who it was?' he repeated. 'Why, the lad, to be sure. What art talking about, girl? Who else?'

'No, sir,' she said, shaking from head to foot, so that the table rocked audibly under her hand. 'It was Mr Ovington's son. And – and I love him. And he wishes to marry me.'

The Squire did not say a word. He sat, his head erect, still as a stone.

'And I want – to help him,' she added, her voice dying away with the words. Her knees were so weak, that but for the support of the table she must have sunk on the floor.

Still the Squire did not speak. His jaw had fallen. He sat, arrested in the attitude of listening, his face partly turned from her, his pipe held stiffly in his hand. At last, 'Ovington's son wants to marry you?' he repeated, in a tone so even that it might have deceived many.

'He saved your life!' she cried. She clung desperately to that.

'And you love him?'

'Oh, I do! I do!'

He paused as if he still listened, still expected more. Then, in a low voice, 'The girl is mad,' he muttered. 'My God, the girl is mad! Or I am mad! Blind and mad, like the old king! Ay, blind and mad!' He let the pipe fall from his hand to the floor, and he groped for his stick that he might rap and summon assistance. But in his agitation he could not find the stick.

Then, as he still felt for it with a flurried hand, nature or despair prompted her, and the girl who had never caressed him in her life, never taken a liberty with him, never ventured on the smallest familiarity, never gone beyond the morning and evening kiss, timidly given and frigidly received, sank on the floor and clasped his knees, pressed herself against him. 'Oh, Father, Father! I am not mad,' she cried, 'I am not mad. Hear me! Oh, hear me!' A pause, and then, 'I have deceived you, I am not worthy, but you are my father! I have only, only you, who can help me! Have mercy on me, for I do love him. I do love him! I—' Her voice failed her, but she continued to cling to him, to press her head against his body, mutely to implore him, and plead with him.

'My God!' he ejaculated. He sat upright, stiff, looking before him with sightless eyes; as far as he could withholding himself from her, but not actively repelling her. After an interval, 'Tell me,' he muttered.

That, even that, was more than she had expected from him. He had not struck her, he had not cursed her, and she took some courage. She told him in broken words, but with sufficient clearness, of her first meeting with Clement, of the gun-shot by the brook, of her narrow escape and the meetings that had followed. Once, in a burst of rage, he silenced her. 'The rascal! Oh, the d—d rascal!' he cried, and she flinched. But she went on, telling him of Clement's resolve that he must be told, of that unfortunate meeting with him on the road, and then of that second encounter the same night, when Clement had come to his rescue. There he stopped her.

'How do you know?' he asked. 'How do you know? How dare you say—' And now he did make a movement as if to repel her and put her from him.

But she would not be repulsed. She clung to him, telling him of the coat, of the great stains that she had seen upon it; and at last, 'Why did you hide this?' broke from him. 'Why didn't you tell me?'

She told him that she had not known, that the part which Clement had taken on that night was new to her also.

'But you see him?' he snarled, speaking a little more like himself. 'You see him!'

'Twice only – twice only since that night,' she vowed. 'Indeed, indeed, sir, only twice. Once he came to speak to you and tell you, but you were ill, and I would not let him. And yesterday he came to – to give me up, to say good-bye. Only twice, sir, as God sees me! He would not. He showed me that we had been wrong. He said,' sobbing bitterly, 'that we must be open or – or we must be nothing – nothing to one another!'

'Open? Open!' the Squire almost shouted. 'D—d open! Shutting the stable door when the horse is gone. D—n his openness!' And then, 'Good Lord! Good Lord!' with almost as much amazement as anger in his voice. That all this should have been going on and he know nothing about it! That his girl, this child as he had deemed her, should have been doing this under his very eyes! Under his very eyes! 'Good Lord!' But then rage got the upper hand once more, and he cursed Clement with passion, and again made a movement as if he would rise and throw her off. 'To steal a man's child! The villain!'

'Oh, don't call him that!' she cried. 'He is good, Father. Indeed, indeed, he is good. And he saved your life.'

He sat back at that, as if her words shifted his thoughts to another matter. 'Tell me again,' he said, sternly, yet with more of calmness. 'He told you this tale yesterday, did he? Well, tell me as he told you, do you hear? And mind you, if you're lying, you slut, he or you, 'twill come up! I am blind, and you may think to deceive me now as you have deceived me before—'

'Never, never again, sir!' she vowed. Then she told him afresh, from point to point, what she had learned on the Sunday.

'Then the lad didn't come up till after?'

'Arthur? No, sir. Not till after Thomas was gone. And it was Clement who followed Thomas to Birmingham and got the money back.' For Clement had told her that also.

When she had done, the Squire leant forward and felt again for his stick, as if he were now equipped and ready for action. 'Well, you begone,' he said, harshly. 'You begone, now. I'll see to this.'

But, 'Not till you forgive me,' she entreated, holding him close, and pressing her face against his unwilling breast. 'And there's more, there's more, sir,' in growing agitation, 'I must tell you. Be good to me! Oh, be good to me! Forgive me and help him.'

'Help him!' the Squire cried, and this time he was indeed amazed. 'I help him! Help the man who has gone behind my back and stolen my girl! Help the man who – let me go! Do you hear me, girl! Let me get up, you shameless hussy!' growing moment by moment more himself, as he recovered from the shock of her disclosure, and could measure its extent. 'How do I know what you are? Or what he mayn't have done to you? Help, indeed? Help the d—d rascal who has robbed me? Who has dared to raise his eyes to my girl – a Griffin? Who—'

'He saved your life,' she cried, pleading desperately with him, though he strove to free himself. 'Oh, Father, he saved your life! And I love him! I love him! If you part us I shall die.'

He could not struggle against her young strength, and he gave up the attempt to free himself. He sank back in his chair. 'D – n the girl!' he cried. He sat silent, breathing hard.

And she – she had told him, and she lived! She had told him and he had not cursed her, he had not struck her to the ground, he had not even succeeded in putting her from him! She had told him, and the world still moved about her, his gold watch, which lay on the table on a level with her head, still ticked, the dog still barked in the field below. Miss Peacock's voice could still be heard, invoking Calamy's presence. She had told him, and he was still her father, nay, if she was not deceived, he was more truly her father, nearer to her, more her own, than he had ever been before.

Presently, 'Ovington's son! Ovington's son!' he muttered in a tone of wonder. 'Good God! Couldn't you find a man?'

'He is a man,' she pleaded, 'indeed, indeed, he is!'

'Ay, and you are a woman!' bitterly. 'Fire and tow! A few kisses and you are aflame for him. For shame, girl, for shame! And how am I to be sure it's no worse? Ain't you ashamed of yourself?'

She shivered, but she was silent.

'Deceiving your father when he was blind!'

She clung to him. He felt her violently trembling.

After that he sat for a time as if exhausted, suffering her embrace, and silent save when at rare intervals an oath broke from him, or, in a gust of passion, he struck his hand on the arm of his chair. Once, 'My father would ha' spurned you from the house,' he cried, 'you jade.' She did not answer, and a new idea striking him, he sat up sharply. 'But what – what

the devil is all this about? What's all this, if it's over and – and done with?'
His tone was almost jubilant. 'If he's off with it? Maybe, girl, I'll forgive
you, bad as you've been, if – if that's so. Do you say it's over?'

'No, no!' she cried. 'He came—'

'You told me—'

'He came to say good-bye to me, because—' And then in words the
most moving that she could find, words sped from her heart, winged by
her love, she explained Clement's errand, the position at the bank, the
crisis, the menace of ruin, the need of help.

The Squire listened, his business instincts aroused, until he grasped
her meaning. Then he struck his hand on the table. 'And he thought that I
should help them!' he cried, with grim satisfaction. 'He thought that, did
he?' And he would not listen to her protests that it was not Clement, that
it was not Clement, it was she who – 'He thought that? I see it now, I see
it all! But the fool, the fool, to think that! Why, I wouldn't stretch out my
little finger to save his father from hell! And he thought that? He took me
for as big a fool as the silly girl he had flattered and lured, and thought he
could use, to save them from perdition! As if he had not done me harm
enough! As if he hadn't stolen my daughter from me, he'd steal my purse!
Why, he must be the most d—d impudent, cunning thief that ever trod
shoe leather. He must be a cock of a pretty hackle, indeed. He should go
far, by G—d, with the nerve he has. Far, by G—d! My daughter first and
my purse afterwards! This son of an upstart, whose grandfather would have
sat in my servants' hall, he'd steal my—'

'No, no!' she protested.

'Yes, yes! Yes, yes! But he'll find that he's not got a girl to deal with
now! Help him? Save his bank? Pluck him from the debtors' prison he's
due to rot in! Why, I'll see him in hell first!'

She had risen and moved from him. She was standing on the other
side of the table now. 'He saved your life!' she cried. And she, too, was
changed. She spoke with something of his passion. 'He saved your life!' she
repeated, and she stamped her foot on the floor.

'Well, the devil thank him for it!' the Squire cried with zest. 'And
you,' with fresh anger, 'do you begone, girl! Get out of my room before
you try my patience too far!' He waved his stick at her. 'Go, or I'll call up
Calamy and have you put out! Do you hear? Do you hear? You ungrateful,
shameless slut! Go!'

She had fancied victory, incredible, unhoped-for-victory to be almost within her grasp; and lo, it was dashed from her hand, it was farther from her than ever. And she could do no more. Courage, strength, hope were spent, shaken as she was by the emotions of the past hour. She could do no more; a little more and he might strike her. She crept out weeping, and went, blinded by her tears, up the stairs, up, stair by stair, to hide herself in her room. There had been a moment when she had fancied that he was melting, but all had been in vain. She had come close to him, but in the end he had put her from him. He had thrust her farther from him than before. Her only consolation, if consolation she had, was that she had spoken, that the truth was known, that she had no longer any secret to weigh her down. But she had failed.

Chapter Thirty

Meantime the old man, left to himself, sat for a while, deeply moved. He breathed quickly, wiping his brow from time to time with a hand that trembled, and for some minutes it was upon the last and the least unwelcome aspect of the matter that he dwelt. So that was the point of it all, was it? That was the end and the aim of this clandestine, this disgraceful intrigue! This conspiracy! They had made this silly woman-child, soft like all her sex, their puppet, and using her they had thought that he, too, might be drawn into their game and used and exploited for their profit. But they had been mad, mad, as they would learn, to think it. They must have been mad to dream of it. Or desperate. Ay, that must be it. Desperate!

But as he grew cooler, and the first impulse, so natural in him, to pin his enemies and shake them, began to lose its force, less pleasant aspects of the matter rose before him. For the girl and her nonsense and her bad, bad behaviour, he did not tell himself, he would not allow, that it was that which hurt him most. On the contrary, he affected to put that from him – for the time. He told himself and strove to believe that he could deal with it when it pleased him. He could easily put an end to that folly. Girls were only girls, and she'd forget. He would deal with that later.

But Arthur's five thousand – that would be lost, if the girl's story were true. Five thousand! It was a fine sum and a d—d pity! The Squire's avarice rose in arms as he thought of it. Five thousand! And that silly woman, Arthur's mother – he would have to provide for her. She would be penniless, almost penniless.

And Arthur himself? Confound the lad, what had he been doing? Why had he been silent about the bank's difficulties and the peril in which his money stood? For, it was only two days ago that he had denied the existence of any peril. And then, again, what was this story about that unlucky night which had cost him his sight? If it really was young Ovington who had come to his rescue and beaten off Thomas, why had not Arthur said so? Why had he never let fall a single word about him, never mentioned the young fellow's name, never given him the credit that – that was certainly due to him, rogue as he was, if this story was true. There was something odd about that – the Squire moved uneasily in his chair – something underhand and – and fishy! He had a glimpse of Arthur in a new light, and he did not like what he saw.

He liked it almost less, if that were possible, than he liked another thing – the idea that this young Ovington's silence was creditable to him. If it were indeed he who had done the thing, why had he been quiet all this time, and never even said 'I did it?' If a gentleman had behaved after that fashion, the Squire would have known what to think of it. But that this low-bred young cub, who had behaved so disgracefully to his daughter, should bear himself in that way – no, he was not going to believe it. After all, the world wasn't turned upside down to that extent.

No! For in his connection with the girl the young scamp had shown what he was – a sneaking, underhand, interloping puppy. In connection with his girl! As he thought of it, the veins swelled on the Squire's forehead and he shook with rage. His girl! 'Damn him! Damn him!' he cried, trembling with passion. And again and again he cursed the man who had dared to raise his eyes to a Griffin – who had stolen his child's heart from him. No fate, no punishment, no lot was too bad for such a one. Help him! Help him, indeed!

The Squire laughed mirthlessly at the notion.

And then there remained only his daughter to think of, and as he came back to her and to her share in the matter, more, far more than he wished, recurred to his memory: her prayers and her pleading, her clinging arms and her caresses, the tears that had fallen on his hands, her warm, slender body pressed against his. He could not forget the sound of her voice in his ears, nor the touch of her hand, nor the feel of her body. Words that she had used returned and beat on his old heart, and beat and beat again, tormenting him, trying him, softening, ay, softening him. He thought of the boy, dead these many years ago at Alexandria, and, yes, she was all that he had, all. And he must thwart her, he must make her unhappy. It was his duty. She knew not what she asked. And she had behaved ill, ay, very ill.

But on that, with a vividness which the reflection had never assumed before – for the old man, like other old men, did not feel old – he saw that he had but a very short span to live – a year or two, or it might be three or four years. The last page of his life was all but turned, the book was near its end. Two or three years and all that he treasured would be hers. Even now he was dependent on her for care and affection, and to the last he must be dependent. A little while and she would be alone, her own mistress; and he who had ruled his lands and his people for more than half a century would be a memory. A memory of what?

Again, and yet again, he felt her arms about his knees, her little head pressed against his breast. Again and yet again her tears, her prayers beat upon his heart. She was a silly woman-child, a fool; but a dear fool, made dear to him in the very hour of her misbehaviour. It was his duty to deny her. It was for him to order, for her to obey. And yet, 'He saved your life!' that cry so oft repeated, so often dinned into his ears, that, too, came back to him. And before he was aware of it he was wondering what manner of man this young fellow was, what spell he had woven about the girl, whence his power over her.

And why had the man been silent about that night? Had he in truth intended to beard him and claim her in the road that morning – when they met? He remembered it.

The son of that man, Ovington! Lord Almighty! It could hardly be worse. And yet 'He saved your life!' The Squire could not get over that – if it were true. If it were really true.

He thought upon it long, forced out of the usual current of his life. Miss Peacock, bringing up his frugal luncheon, found him silent, sunk low in his chair, his chin upon his breast. So he appeared when any one stole in during the next two hours to attend to the fire or to light his pipe. Calamy, safe outside the door, uttered his misgivings. 'It's the torpor,' he told Miss Peacock, shaking his head. 'That's how it takes them before the end, miss. I've seen it often. The torpor! He'll not be long now!'

Miss Peacock scolded the butler, but was none the less impressed, and presently she sought Josina, who was lying down in her room with a headache. She imparted her fears to the girl, and unwillingly Jos rose, and bathed her face and tidied her hair, and by and by came out. She must take up the burden of life again.

By that time Miss Peacock had disappeared, and Josina went down alone. Half-way down the upper flight she halted, for she heard a slow, heavy step descending the stairs below her. She looked down the well of the staircase, and to her astonishment she saw her father going down before her, stair by stair, his hand on the rail, a paper and his stick in the other hand. It was not the first time that he had done such a thing, but hitherto someone had always gone with him, to aid him should aid be necessary.

Josina's first impulse was to hurry after him, but seeing the paper in his hand and recognising, as she fancied, the agreement that he had signed on the Saturday, she followed him softly, without letting him know that she was there. He reached the foot of the staircase, and with an accustomed hand he groped for and found the door of the dining-room. He pushed open the door and went in. He closed the door behind him, and distinctly – the house was very quiet, it was the dead of the afternoon – she heard him turn the key in the lock.

That alarmed her, for if he fell or met with an accident, there would be a difficulty in assisting him. She moved to the door and listened. She heard him passing slowly and carefully across the floor, she heard the table creak under his hand, as he reached it. A moment later her ear caught the jingle of a bunch of keys.

His visit had a purpose, then. He might be going to deposit the lease, but she could not imagine where. His papers were in his own room or in his bedroom. And Calamy had the wine, it could not be that he wanted. For a moment her thoughts reverted to her own trouble, and she sighed. Then she caught again the jingle of keys, and she listened, her head bent low. What could he be doing? And would he be able to find the door again?

Presently the silence was broken by an oath, followed by a rustling sound, as if he were handling papers. This lasted for quite a minute, and then there came from the room a strange, half-strangled cry, a cry that stopped the beating of her heart. She seized the handle of the door and turned it, shook it. But the door, as she knew, was locked, and, in terror, she cried, 'Father! Father! What is it? What is it?' She beat on the door.

He did not answer, but she heard him coming towards her, moving at random, striking against the table, overturning a chair. She trembled for him; he might fall at any moment, and the door was locked. But he did not fall. He reached the door and turned the key. The door opened. She saw him.

Her fears had not been baseless. The light in the doorway was poor on that cheerless December day, but it was enough to show her that the Squire's face was distorted and drawn, altered by some strange shock.

And he was shaking in all his limbs. The moment that she touched him he gripped her arm, and, 'Come here! Come here!' he ordered, his voice piping and high. 'Lock the door! Lock the door, girl!' And when she had done this, 'Do you see that cupboard? D'you see it?'

She was alarmed, for, whatever might be its cause, she was sure that the excitement under which he laboured was dangerous for him. But she had her wits about her, and she nerved herself to do what he wanted. She saw the open cupboard, of the existence of which she had not known, but she showed no surprise. 'Yes, I see it, sir,' she said. She put her arm through his, striving to calm him by her presence.

He drew her across the room till they stood before the cupboard. 'Do you see a box?' he demanded, hardly able to articulate the words in his haste. 'Ay? Then do you look in it, girl! Look in it. What is there in it? Tell me, girl. Tell me quick! What is in it?'

The box, its lid raised, stood on the shelf before him, and he laid his trembling hand on it. She looked into it. 'It is empty, sir,' she said.

'Empty? Quite empty?'

'Yes, sir, quite empty.'

'Nothing in it?' desperately. 'Are you sure, girl? Can you see nothing? Nothing?'

'Nothing, sir, I am quite sure,' she said. 'There is nothing in it.'

'No papers?'

'No, sir, no papers.'

An idea seemed to strike him. 'They may ha' fallen on the floor,' he exclaimed. 'Look! Look all about, girl! Look! Ah,' and there was something of agony in the cry, 'curse this blindness! I am helpless, helpless as a child! Can you see no papers – on the floor, wench! Thin papers? No? Nor on the shelves?'

'No, sir. There is the lease you signed on Saturday. That is all.'

'For God's sake, make no mistake, make no mistake, girl!' he cried in irrepressible agitation. 'Look! Look 'em over. Two papers – thin papers – no great size they are.'

She saw that there was something very much amiss, and she searched carefully, but there were no loose papers to be seen. There were books on one shelf and bundles of deeds below them, and a great many packets of letters on a shelf above them, but all tied up. She could see no loose papers. None!

He seemed on the verge of collapse, but a new thought came to his support, and he drew her, almost as if he could see, to the other side of the hearth. There he felt for and found the moulding of the panel, he fumbled for the keyhole. But his shaking hands would not do his will, and with a tremulous curse he gave the key to her, and obeying his half-intelligible directions, she unlocked and threw wide first the panel and then the door of the second cupboard.

'Two small papers! Thin papers!' he reiterated. 'Look! Look, girl! Are they there? Someone may have moved them. He may have put them here. Search, girl, search!'

But though she obeyed him, looking everywhere, a single glance showed her that there were no two papers there, papers such as he had described. She told him what she saw – the bundles of ancient deeds, the tarnished plate, the jewel cases.

'But no – no loose papers?'

'No, sir, I can see none.'

Convinced at last, he uttered an exceeding bitter cry, a cry that went to the girl's heart. 'Then he has robbed me!' he said. 'He has robbed me! A Griffin, and he has robbed me! Get – get me a chair, girl.'

Horrified, she helped him to a chair, and he sank into it, and with a shaking hand he sought for his handkerchief and wiped the moisture from his lips. Then his hands fell until they rested on his lap, his chin dropped on his breast. Two tears ran down his withered cheeks. 'A Griffin!' he whispered. 'A Griffin! And he has robbed me!'

Chapter Thirty-One

In Aldersbury there had been a simmering of excitement through all the hours of that Monday. At the corner of the Market Place on which the little statue of the ancient Prince looked down, in the shops on Bride Hill, in the High Street under the shadow of St. Juliana's, knots of people had gathered, discussing, some with scared faces and low voices, others with the gusto of unconcern, the rumours of troubles that came through from Chester, from Manchester, from the capital; that fell from the lips of guards in inn-yards, and leaked from the boots of coaches before the Lion. Gibbon's, one of the chief banks at Birmingham, had closed its doors, Garrard's had stopped payment at Hereford, there was panic on the stones in Manchester, a bank had failed at Liverpool.

It was reported that a director had hung himself, a score had fled to Boulogne, dark stories of '15 and '93 were revived. It was asserted that the Bank of England had run out of gold, that cash payments would be again suspended. In a dozen forms these and wilder statements ran from mouth to mouth, gathered weight as they went, blanched men's faces and turned traders' hearts to water. But the worst, it was agreed, would not be known until the afternoon coaches came in and brought the mails from London. Then – ah, then, people would see what they would see!

Idle men, with empty pockets, revelled in news which promised to bring all to their level. And malice played its part. Wolley, who had little but a debtor's prison in prospect, was in town and talking, bent on revenge, and the few who had already withdrawn their accounts from Ovington's were also busy; foxes who had lost their tails, they felt themselves marked men until others followed their example. Meanwhile, Purslow and such as were in his case lay low, sweated in their shop-parlours, conned their ledgers with haggard faces, or snarled at their women-folk. Gone now was the pride in stock and scrip, and bounding profits! Gone even the pride in a directorship.

Purslow, perhaps, more than anyone was to be pitied. A year before he had been prosperous, purse-proud, free from debt, with a good business. Now his every penny was sunk in unsaleable securities, his credit was pledged to the bank, his counter was idle, while trade creditors whom in the race for wealth he had neglected were pressing him hard. Worst of all, he did not know where he could turn to obtain even the small sum needed to pay the next month's wages.

But, though the pot was boiling in Aldersbury as elsewhere, it did not at once boil over. The day passed without any serious run on either of the banks. Men were alarmed, they got together in corners, they whispered, they marked with jealous eyes who entered and who left the banks. They muttered much of what they would do on the morrow, or when the London mail came in, or when they had made up their minds. But to walk into Ovington's and face the clerks and do the deed required courage; and for the most part they were not so convinced of danger, or fearful of loss, as to be ready to face the ordeal. They might draw their money and look foolish afterwards. Consequently they hung about, putting off the act, waiting to see what others would do. The hours slipped by and the excitement grew, but still they waited, watching their neighbours, and doing nothing, but prepared at any moment to rush in and jostle one another in their panic.

'By G—d, I'll see I get my money!' said one. 'You wait, Mr Lello! You wait and—'

In another part, 'I'd draw it, I'd draw it, Tom, if I were you! After all, it's your own money. Why, confound it, man, what are you afraid of?'

'I ain't afraid of anything,' Tom replied surlily. 'But Ovington gave me a leg-up last December, and I'm hanged if I like to go in and—'

'And ask for your own? Well, you are a ninny!'

'Maybe. May – be,' jingling the money in his fob. 'But I'll wait. I'll wait till tomorrow. No harm done afore then!'

A third had left Dean's under a cloud, and if he quarrelled with Ovington's, where was he to go? While a fourth had bills falling due, and did not quite see his way. He might be landing a trout and losing a salmon. He would see how things went. Plenty of time!

But though this was the general attitude, and the Monday passed without a run of any consequence, a certain number of accounts were closed, and the excitement boded ill for the morrow. It waxed rather than waned as the day went on, and Ovington's heart would have been heavy and his alarm keen if the one had not been lightened and the other dispersed by the good news which Arthur had brought from Garth that morning – the almost incredibly good news!

Aldersbury, however, was in ignorance of that news, and when Clement issued from the bank a few minutes after the doors had closed, there were still knots of people hanging about the corners of the Market Place, watching the bank. He viewed them with a sardonic eye, and could afford to do so, for his heart was light like his father's, and he could smile at that which, but for the good news of the morning, would have chilled him with apprehension. He turned from the door, intending to seek the Lime Walks by the river, and, late as it was, to get a breath of fresh air after the confinement of the day. But his intention was never carried out. He had not gone half a dozen yards down the street before his ear caught the sound of a horse breasting Bride Hill at an unusual pace, and something in the speed, at which it approached warned him of ill. He waited, and his fears were confirmed. The vehicle, a gig, drew up at the door of the bank, and the driver, a country lad, began to get down. Clement retraced the half-dozen steps that he had taken.

'Who is it you want?' he asked.

The lad sat down again in his seat. 'Be Mr Arthur here, sir?' he inquired.

'Mr Bourdillon?'

'Ay, sure, sir.'

'No, he is not.'

'Well, I be to follow 'ee wheresomever he be, axing your pardon!'

'I'm afraid you can't do that, my lad,' Clement explained. 'He's gone to London. He went by coach this morning.'

The lad scratched his head. 'O Lord!' he said. 'What be I to do? I was to bring him back, whether or no. Squire's orders.'

'Squire Griffin?'

'Ay, sure, sir. He's in a taking, and mun see him, whether or no! Mortal put about he were!'

Clement thought rapidly, the vague alarm which he had felt taking solid shape. What if the Squire had repented of his generosity? What if the help, heaven-sent, beyond hope and beyond expectation, which had removed their fears, were after all to fail them? Clement's heart sank. 'Who sent you?' he asked. 'The young lady?'

'Ay, sure. And she were in a taking, too. Crazy she were.'

Clement leapt to a decision. He laid his hand on the rail of the gig. 'Look here,' he said. 'You'd better take me out instead, and I can explain.'

'But it were Mr Arthur—'

'I know, but he's half-way to London by now. And he won't be back till Thursday.'

He climbed up, and the lad accepted his decision and turned the horse. They trotted down the hill between the dimly lighted shops, past observers who recognised the Garth gig, by groups of men who loitered and shivered before the tavern doors. They swung sharply into Maerdol, where the peaks of the gables on either hand rose against a pale sky, and a moment later they were crossing the bridge, and felt the cold waft of the river breeze on their faces. Two minutes saw them trotting steadily across the open country, the lights of the town behind them.

Clement sat silent, lost in thought, wondering if he were doing right, and fearing much that the Squire had repented of his generosity and was minded to recall it. If that were so, the awakening from the dream of security in which they had lost themselves, would be a cruel shock. Clement shrank from thinking what its effect would be on his father, whose relief had betrayed the full measure of his fears. And his own case was hardly better, for it was not only his fortune that was at stake and that he had thought saved. He had given rein, also, to his hopes. He had let them carry him far into a roseate country where the sun shone and Josina smiled, and all the difficulties that had divided them melted into air. There might be need of time and patience; but with time and patience he had fancied that he might win his way.

It was cruel, indeed, then if the old man at Garth had changed his mind, if he had played with them, only to deceive them, only to disappoint them! And Clement could not but fear that it was so. The closing day, the wintry air, the prospect before him, as they swung across the darkening land, seemed to confirm his fears and oppress him with misgivings. A long cloud, fish-shaped, hung lowering across the western sky; below it, along the horizon, a narrow strip of angry yellow, unnaturally bright, threw the black, jagged outline of the hills into violent contrast, and shed a pale light on the intervening plain. Ay, he feared the worst. He could think of nothing else that could be the cause of this sudden, this agitated summons. The Squire must have repented. He had changed his mind, and—

But here they were at the bridge. The cottages of the hamlet showed now and again a spark of light. They turned to the left, and five minutes later – the horse quickening its pace as they approached its stable – they were winding up the sunken drive under the stark limbs of the beeches. The house stood above them, a sombre pile, its chimneys half obscured by the trees.

Heavily Clement let himself down, to find Calamy at his elbow. The man had been waiting for him in the dimly lighted doorway. 'Mr Bourdillon has gone to London,' Clement explained. 'I have come instead if I can be of any use.' Then he saw that the butler did not know him, and 'I am Mr Clement Ovington,' he added. 'You'd better ask your master if he would like to see me.'

'There's times when the devil 'd be welcome,' the man replied bluntly. 'It's tears and lamentations and woe in the house this night, but God knows what it's all about, for I don't. Come in, come in, sir, in heaven's name, but I'm fearing it's little good. The devil has us in his tail, and if the master goes through the night – but this way, sir – this way!'

He opened a door on the left of the hall, pushed the astonished Clement into the room, and over his shoulder, 'Here's one from the bank, at any rate,' he proclaimed. 'Maybe he'll do.'

Clement took in the scene as he entered, and drew from it an instant impression of ill. The room was in disorder, lighted only by a pair of candles, the slender flames of which were reflected, islanded in blackness, in the two tall windows that, bald and uncurtained, let in the light. The fire, a pile of wood ashes neglected or forgotten, was almost out, and beside it a cupboard-door gaped widely open. A chair lay overturned on the floor, and in another the Squire sat, gaunt and upright, muttering to himself and gesticulating with his stick, while over him, her curls falling about her neck, her face tragic and tear-stained, hung his daughter, her shadow cast grotesquely on the wall behind her. She had a glass in her hand, and by her on the table, from which the cloth had fallen to the floor, stood water and a medicine bottle.

In their absorption neither of the two had heard Calamy's words, and for a moment Clement stood in doubt, staring at them and feeling that he had been wrong to come. The trouble, whatever it was, could not be what he had feared. Then, as he moved, half minded to withdraw, Josina heard him, and turned. In her amazement, 'Clement!' she cried. 'You!'

The Squire turned in his chair. 'Who?' he exclaimed. 'Who's there? Has he come?'

The girl hesitated. The hand that rested on the old man's shoulder trembled. Then – oh, bravely she took her courage in her hands, and 'It is Clement who has come,' she said – acknowledging him so firmly that Clement marvelled to hear her.

'Clement?' The old man repeated the word mechanically, and for a moment he sought in his mind who Clement might be. Then he found the answer, and 'One of them, eh?' he muttered – but not in the voice that Clement had anticipated. 'So he won't face me? Coward as well as rogue, is he? And a Griffin! My God, a Griffin! So he's sent him?'

'Where is Arthur?' Josina asked.

'He left for London this morning – by the coach.'

'Ay, ay,' the Squire said. 'That's it.'

Clement plucked up courage. 'And hearing that you wanted him, I came to explain. I feared from what the messenger said that there was something amiss.'

'Something amiss!' The Squire repeated the words in an indescribable tone. 'That's what he calls it! Something amiss!'

Clement looked from one to the other. 'If there is anything I can do?'

'You?' bluntly. 'Why, you be one of them!'

'No!' Josina interposed. 'No, Father. He has no part in it! I swear he has not!'

But, 'One of them! One of them!' the Squire repeated in the same stubborn tone, yet without lifting his voice.

'No!' Josina repeated as firmly as before; and the hand that rested on her father's shoulder slid round his neck. She held him half embraced. 'But he may tell you what has happened. He may explain, sir?'

'Explain!' the Squire muttered. Contempt could go no farther.

'Shall I tell him, sir?'

'You're a fool, girl! The man knows.'

'I am sure he does not!' she said.

Again Clement thought that it was time to interpose. 'Indeed I do not, sir,' he said. 'I am entirely in the dark.' In truth, looking on what he did, seeing before him the unfamiliar room, the dark staring windows, and the old man so unlike himself and so like King Lear or some figure of tragedy, he was tempted to think the scene a dream. 'If you will tell me what is the matter, perhaps I can help? Arthur left this morning for London. He went to raise the money with which he was entrusted—'

'Entrusted?' the Squire cried, and with something of his old energy. He raised his head and struck the floor with his stick. 'Entrusted? That's what you call it, is it?'

Clement stared. 'I don't understand,' he said.

'What did he tell you?' Josina asked. 'For heaven's sake speak, Clement! Tell us what he told you.'

'Ay,' the Squire chimed in. 'Tell us how you managed it. Now it's done, let's hear it.' For the time scorn, a weary kind of scorn, had taken the place of anger and subdued him to its level.

But Clement was still at sea. 'Managed it?' he repeated. 'What do you—'

'Tell us, tell us – from the beginning!' Jos cried, at the end of her patience. 'About this money? What did Arthur tell you? What did he tell you – this morning?'

Then for the first time Clement saw what was in question, and he braced himself to meet the shock which he foresaw. 'He told us,' he said, 'what Mr Griffin had consented to do – that he had given him securities for twelve thousand pounds for the use of the bank and to support its credit. He had the stock with him, and he received from the bank, in return for it, an undertaking to replace the amount two months after date with interest at seven per cent. It was thought best that he should take it to London himself, as it was so large a sum and time was everything. And he went by the coach this morning – to realise the money.'

Josina shivered. 'He took it without authority,' she said, her voice low.

'He stole it,' the Squire said, 'out of that cupboard.'

'Oh, but that's impossible, sir!' Clement replied with eagerness. He felt an immense relief, for he thought that he saw light. He took note of the Squire's condition, and he fancied that his memory, if not his mind, had given way. He had forgotten what he had done. That was it! 'That's impossible sir.' he repeated firmly. 'He had a proper transfer of the stock – India Stock it was – signed and witnessed and all in order.'

'Signed and witnessed?' the Squire ejaculated. 'Signed and – signed, your grandmother! So that's your story, is it? Signed and witnessed, eh?'

But Clement was beginning to be angry. 'Yes, sir,' he said. 'That is our story, and it is true.' He thought that he had hit on the truth, and he clung to it. The Squire had signed and the next minute had forgotten the whole transaction – Clement had heard of such cases. 'He had the transfer with him,' he continued, 'signed by you and witnessed by himself and – and Miss Griffin. I saw it myself. I saw the signatures, and I have seen yours, sir, often enough on a cheque to know it. The transfer was perfectly in order.'

'In whose favour, young man?'

'Our brokers', sir.'

The Squire flared up. 'I did not sign it!' he cried. 'It's a lie, sir! I signed nothing! Nothing!'

But Josina intervened. She, poor girl, saw light. 'Yes,' she said, 'my father did sign something – on Saturday after dinner. But it was a lease. I and Arthur witnessed it.'

'And what has that to do with it?' the Squire asked passionately. 'What the devil has that to do with it? I signed a lease and – and a counterpart. I signed no transfer of stock, never put hand to it! Never! What has the lease to do with it?'

But Josina was firm. 'I am afraid I see now, sir,' she said. 'You remember that you signed a paper to try your pen? And I signed it too, father, by mistake? You remember? Ah!' – with a gesture of despair – 'if I had only not signed it!'

The Squire groaned. He, too, saw it now. He saw it, and his head sank on his breast. 'Forger as well as thief!' he muttered. 'And a Griffin!'

And Clement's heart sank too as he met the girl's anguished eyes and viewed the Squire's bowed head and the shame and despair that clothed themselves in an apathy so unlike the man. He saw that here was a tragedy indeed, a tragedy fitly framed in that desolate room with its windows staring on the night and its air of catastrophe; a tragedy passing bank failures or the loss of fortune. And in his mind he cursed the offender.

But even as the words rose to his lips, doubt stayed them. There was, there must be, some mistake. The thing could not be. He knew Arthur, he thought that he knew Arthur; he knew even the darker side of him – his selfishness, his lack of thought for others, his desire to get on and to grow rich. But this thing Arthur never could have done! Clement recalled his gay, smiling face, his frank bearing, his care-free eyes, the habit he had of casting back a lock from his brow. No, he could not have done this thing. 'No, sir, no!' he cried impulsively. 'There is some mistake! I swear there is! I am sure of it.'

'You've the securities?'

'Yes, but I am sure—'

'You're all in it,' the Squire said drearily. And then, with energy and in a voice quivering with rage, 'He's learned this at your d—d counter, sir! That's where it is. It's like to like, that's where it is. Like to like! I might ha' known what would happen, when the lad set his mind on leaving our ways and taking up with yours. I might ha' known that that was the blackest day our old house had ever seen – when he left the path his fathers trod and chose yours. You can't touch pitch and keep your hands clean. You ha' stole my daughter – d—n you, sir! And you ha' taught him to steal my money. I mind me I bid your father think o' Fauntleroy, I never thought he was breeding up a Fauntleroy in my house.' And, striking the table with all his old vitality, 'You are thieves! Thieves all o' you! And you ha' taught my lad to thieve!'

'That is not true!' Clement cried. 'Not a word of that is true!'

'You ha' stole my daughter!'

Clement winced. She had told him, then.

'And now you ha' stole my money!'

'That, at least, is not true!' He held up his head. He stepped forward and laid his hand on the table. 'That is not true,' he repeated firmly. 'You do not know my father, Mr Griffin, though you may think you do. He would see the bank break a hundred times, he would see every penny pass from him, before he would do this that you say has been done. Your nephew told us what I have told you, and we believed him – naturally we believed him. We never suspected. Not a suspicion crossed my father's mind or mine. We saw the certificates, we saw the transfer, we knew your handwriting. It was in order, and—'

'And you thought – you ha' the impudence to tell me that you thought that I should throw thousands, ay, thousands upon thousands into the gutter – to save your bank?'

'We believed what we were told,' Clement maintained. 'Why not – as you put the question, sir? Your nephew had five thousand pounds at stake. His share in the bank was at stake. He knew as well as we did that with this assistance the bank was secure. We supposed that for his sake and the sake of his prospects—'

'I don't believe it!' the Squire retorted. 'I'll never believe it. Your father's a trader! I know 'em, and what their notion of honesty is. And you tell me—'

'I tell you that a trader is nothing if he be not honest!' Clement cried hotly. 'Honesty is to him what honour is to you, Mr Griffin. But we'll leave my father's name out of this, if you please, sir. You may say what you like of me. I have deserved it.'

'No,' said Josina.

'Yes, I have deserved it, and I am ashamed of myself – and proud of myself. But my father has done nothing and known nothing. And for this money, when he learns the truth, Mr Griffin, he will not touch one penny of it with one of his fingers. It shall be returned to you, every farthing of it, as soon as we can lay our hands on it. Every penny of it shall be returned to you – at once!'

'Ay,' dryly, 'when you have had the use of it!'

'No, at once! Without the loss of an hour!'

'You be found out,' said the old man bitterly. 'You be found out! That's it!'

Clement read an appeal in Josina's eyes, and he stayed the retort that rose to his lips. 'At any rate the money shall be restored,' he said, 'at once. I will start for town tonight, and if I can overtake' – he paused, unwilling to utter Arthur's name – 'if I can overtake him before he transfers the stock, the securities shall be returned to you. In that case no harm will be done.'

'No harm!' the Squire ejaculated. He raised his hand and let it fall in a gesture of despair. 'No harm?'

But Clement was determined not to dwell on that side of it. 'If I am not able to do that,' he continued, 'the proceeds shall be placed in your hands without the delay of an hour. In which case you must let the signature pass – as good, sir.'

'Never!' the old man cried, and struck his hand on the table.

'But after all it is yours,' Clement argued. 'And you must see, sir—'

'Never! Never!' the Squire repeated passionately.

'You will not say that in cold blood!' Clement rejoined, and from that moment he took a higher tone, as if he felt that, strange as the call was, it lay with him now to guide this unhappy household. 'You have not considered, and you must consider, Mr Griffin,' he continued, 'before you do that, what the consequences may be. If you deny your signature, and anyone, the India House or anyone, stands to lose, steps may be taken which may prove – fatal. Fatal, sir! A point may be reached beyond which even your influence, and all you may then be willing to do, may not avail to save your nephew.'

The Squire groaned. Clement's words called up before him and before Josina, not only the thing which Arthur had done, but the position in which he had placed himself. In this room, in this very room in which men of honour – dull and narrow, perhaps, but men of honour, and proud of their honour – had lived and moved for generations, he, their descendant, had done this thing. The beams had stood, the house had not fallen on him. But to Josina's eyes the candles seemed to burn more mournfully, the windows to stare more darkly on the night, the ashes on the hearth to speak of desolation and a house abandoned and fallen.

Clement hoped that his appeal had succeeded, but he was disappointed. The old man in his bitterness and unreason was not to be moved – at any rate as yet. He would listen to no arguments, and he suspected those who argued with him. 'I'll never acknowledge it!' he said. 'No, I'll never acknowledge it. I'll not lie for him, come what may! He has done the thing and disgraced our blood, and what matter who knows it – he has done it! He has made his bed and must lie on it! He went into your bank and learned your tricks, and now you'd have me hush it up! But I won't, d—n you! I'll not lie for you, or for him!'

Clement had a retort on his lips – for what could be more unfair than this? But again Josina's eyes implored him to be silent, and he crushed back the words. He believed that by and by the Squire would see the thing differently, but for the moment he could do no more, and he turned to the door.

There in the doorway, and for one moment, Josina's hands met his, she had one word with him. 'You will save him if you can, Clement?' she murmured.

'Yes,' he promised her, 'I will save him if I can.'

Chapter Thirty-Two

If the news which Arthur had conveyed to the bank on that Monday morning had been much to Clement, it had been more to his father. It had brought to Ovington immense relief at the moment when he had least reason to expect it. The banker had not hidden the position from those who must needs work with him, but even to them he had not imparted the full measure of his fears, much less the extent of the suffering which those fears occasioned him. The anxiety that kept him sleepless, the calculations that tormented his pillow, the regret with which he reviewed the past, the responsibility for the losses of others that depressed him – he had kept these things to himself, or at most had dropped but a hint of them to his beloved Betty.

But they had been very real to him and very terrible. The spectre of bankruptcy – with all the horror which it connoted for the mercantile mind – had loomed before him for weeks past, had haunted and menaced him; and its sudden exorcism on this Monday morning meant a relief which he dared not put into words to others and shrank from admitting even to himself. He who had held his head so high – no longer need he anticipate the moment when he would be contemned as a reckless adventurer, whose fall had been as rapid as his rise, and whom the wiseacres of Aldersbury had doomed to failure from the first! That had been the bitterest drop in his cup, and to know that he need not drain it, was indeed a blessed respite.

Still, he had received the news with composure, and through the day he had moved to and fro doing his work with accuracy. But it was in a pleasant dream that he had followed his usual routine, and many a time he paused to tell himself that the thing was a fact, that Dean's would not now triumph over him, nor his enemies now scoff at him. On the contrary, he might hope to emerge from the tempest stronger than before, and with his credit enhanced by the stress through which he had ridden. Business was business, but in the midst of it the banker had more than once to stand and be thankful.

And with reason. For if he who has inherited success and lives to see it threatened suffers a pang, that pang is as nothing beside the humiliation of the man who has raised himself; who has outstripped his fellows, challenged their admiration, defied their jealousy, trampled on their pride; who has been the creator of his own greatness, and now sees that greatness in ruins. He had escaped that. He had escaped that, thank God! More than once the two words passed his lips; and in secret his thoughts turned to the great chief of men to whom in his own mind and with a rather absurd vanity he had compared himself. Thank God that his own little star had not sunk like his into darkness!

It was relief, it was salvation. And that evening, as the banker sat after his five o'clock dinner and sipped his fourth and last glass of port and basked in the genial heat of the fire, while his daughter knitted on the farther side of the hearth, he owned himself a happy man. He measured the danger, he winced at the narrow margin by which he had escaped it – but he had escaped! Dean's, staid, long-established, slow-going Dean's, which had viewed his notes askance, had doubted his stability and predicted his failure, Dean's which had slyly put many a spoke in his wheel, would not triumph. Nay, after this, would not he, too, rank as sound and staid and well established, he who had also ridden out the storm? For in crises men and banks age rapidly; they are measured rather by events than by years. Those who had mistrusted him would mistrust him no longer; those who had dubbed him new would now count him old.

As he stretched his legs to meet the genial heat and sank lower in his chair he could have purred in his thankfulness. Things had fallen out well, after all; he saw rosy visions in the fire. Schemes which had lain dormant in his mind awoke. His London agents had failed, but others would compete for his business, and on better terms. The Squire who had so marvellously come to his aid would bring back his account, and his example would be followed. He would extend, opening branches at Bretton and Monk's Castle and Blankminster. And the railroad? He was not quite sure what he would do about the railroad; possibly he might decide that the time was not ripe for it, and in that case he might wind up the company, return the money, and himself meet the expenses incurred. The loss would not be great, and the effect would be prodigious. It would be a Napoleonic stroke – he would consider it. He lost himself in visions of prosperity.

And it would be all for Clement and Betty. He looked across the hearth at the girl who sat knitting under the lamp-light, and his eyes caressed her, his heart loved her. She would make a great match. Failing Arthur – and of late Arthur and she had not seemed to hit it off – there would be others. There would be others, well-born, who would be glad to take her and her dowry. He saw her driving into town in her carriage, with a crest on the panels.

It was she who cut short his thoughts. She looked at the clock. 'I can't think where Clement is,' she said. 'You don't think that there is anything wrong, Dad?'

'Wrong? No,' he answered. 'Why should there be!'

'But he disappeared so strangely. He said nothing about missing his dinner.'

'He was to check some figures with Rodd this evening. He may have gone to his rooms.'

'But – without his dinner?'

But the banker was not in the mood to trouble himself about trifles. The lamp shone clear and mellow, the fire crackled pleasantly, a warm comfort wrapped him round, the port had a flavour that he had not perceived in it of late. Instead of replying to Betty's question he measured the decanter with his eye, decided that it was a special occasion, and filled himself another glass. 'Ovington's Bank,' he said as he raised it to his lips. But that to which he really drank was the home that he saw about him, saved from ruin, made secure.

Betty smiled. 'You're relieved tonight, Dad.'

'Well, I am, Betty,' he admitted. 'Yes, I am – and thankful.'

'And that queer old man! I wonder,' as she turned her knitting on her knee, 'why he did it.'

'For Arthur's sake. He'd have lost pretty heavily – for him.'

'But you didn't expect that Mr Griffin would come forward?'

The banker allowed it. 'No,' he said, 'I don't know that I ever expected anything less. Such things don't happen, my girl, very often. But he will be no loser, and I suppose Arthur convinced him of that. He is shrewd, and, once convinced, he would see that it was the only thing to do.'

'But not many people would have been convinced?'

'No, perhaps not.'

Betty knitted awhile. 'I thought that he hated the bank?' she said, as she paused to rub her chin with a needle.

'He does – and me. But he loves his money.'

'Still, it isn't his. It is Arthur's.'

'True. But he's a man who cannot bear to see money lost. He thinks a good deal of it.'

'He is not alone in that,' Betty exclaimed. 'Sometimes I feel that I hate money! People grow so fond of it. They think only of themselves, even when you've been ever so good to them.'

'Well, it's human nature,' the banker replied equably. 'I don't know who it is that you have in your mind, Betty, but it applies to most people.' He was going to say more when the door opened.

'Mr Rodd is here, asking for Mr Clement, sir,' the maid said. 'He was to meet him at half after six, and—'

'Ask Mr Rodd to come in.'

The cashier entered shyly. In his dark suit, with his black stock and stiff carriage, he made no figure, where Arthur, or even Clement, would have shone. But there were women in Aldersbury who said that he had fine eyes, eyes with something of a dog's gentleness in them; and Arthur so far agreed that he dubbed him a dull, mechanical dog, and often made fun of him as such. But perhaps Arthur did not always see to the bottom of things.

Ovington pushed the decanter and a glass towards him. 'A glass of wine, Rodd,' he said genially. He was not of those who undervalued his cashier, though he knew his limitations. 'The bank!' he said.

'And those who have stood by it!' Betty added softly.

Rodd drank the toast with a muttered word.

'Mr Rodd has not the same reason to be thankful that we have,' Betty continued carelessly, holding her knitting up to the lamp.

'Why not?' Her father did not understand.

'Why,' innocently, as she lowered the knitting again, 'he does not stand to lose anything, does he?'

'Except his place,' the cashier objected, his eyes on his glass.

'Just so,' the banker rejoined. 'And in that event,' moved to unusual frankness, 'we should have been all out together. And Rodd might not have been the worst off, my girl.'

'Exactly,' Betty said. 'I'm sure that he would take care of that.'

The cashier opened his mouth to speak, but checked himself, and drank off his wine. Then, as he rose, 'If you know where Mr Clement is, sir—'

'I don't. I can't think what has become of him,' the banker answered. 'He went out about four, and since then – hallo! That's someone in a hurry. It sounds like a fire.'

A vehicle had burst in on the evening stillness. It came clattering at a reckless pace up Bride Hill. It passed the bank, it rattled noisily round the corner of the Market Place, and pounded away down the High Street.

'More likely someone hastening to get out of danger,' said Betty. '*A sauve qui peut*, Mr Rodd – if you know what that means.'

The clerk, with a flushed cheek, avoided the question. 'It might be someone trying to catch the seven o'clock coach, sir,' he said.

'Very likely. And if so he's failed, for he's coming back again. Ay, here he comes. And he's stopping here, by Jove! I hope that nothing's wrong.'

The vehicle had, indeed, stopped abruptly before the house. They heard someone alight on the pavement, a latchkey was thrust into the door. 'It's Clement!' the banker exclaimed, his eyes on the door. 'I hope he does not bring bad news! Well, lad?' as Clement in his overcoat, his hat on his head, appeared in the doorway. 'What is it? Is anything wrong?'

'Very much wrong!' his son replied, and he closed the door behind him. He was pale, and his splashed coat and neck-shawl tied awry, no less than his agitated face, confirmed their misgivings.

'Out with it, lad! What is it?' his father asked, fearing he knew not what.

'Bad news, sir!' was the answer. 'I'm sorry to say I bring very bad news!'

'What?'

'That loan of Mr Griffin's—'

'The twelve thousand? Yes?' – anxiously – 'well?'

'It's a fraud, sir! A cursed fraud!'

There was a tense silence. Then, 'Impossible!' the banker exclaimed. But he grasped a chair to steady himself. His face had turned grey.

'The Squire knows nothing of it!' Clement struck his open hand on the back of a chair. 'He never signed the transfer! He never gave any authority for the loan!'

'No, no, that's impossible!' Ovington straightened himself with a sigh of relief. What mare's nest, what bee in the bonnet, was this? The lad was dreaming – must be dreaming. 'Impossible!' he repeated. 'I saw it, man, and read it? And I know the old man's signature as well as I know my own. You must be dreaming.'

'I am not, sir!' Clement answered, and added bitterly, 'It was Arthur that was dreaming! Dreaming or worse, d—n him!' – the pent-up excitement of the evening finding vent at last, and the sight of his father's stricken face whetting his rage. 'He has robbed, ay, robbed his uncle, and dishonoured us! That is what he has done, sir. I am not dreaming! I wish to heaven I were!'

The banker no longer protested. 'Well – tell us!' he said weakly.

'It's hard on you, sir—'

'Never mind me! Tell me what you know.'

They stood round Clement, amazed and shocked, fearing the worst and yet incredulous, while he, his weary face and travel-stained figure at odds with the lighted room and the comfort about him, told his story. The banker listened. He still hoped, hoped to detect some flaw, to perceive some misunderstanding – so much, so very much, hung upon it. But even on his mind the truth at last forced itself, and monstrous as the story, incredible as Arthur's action still appeared, he had at last to accept it and its consequences – its consequences!

He seemed to grow years older as he listened.

But when Clement had done, and the whole shameful story was told, he made no comment. The position, indeed, was no worse than it had been twenty-four hours before. He might still hope against hope, that, by putting a bold face on matters, and by a dexterous use of his resources, he might ride out the storm. But the reaction from a triumphant confidence was so sudden, the failure of his recent expectations so overwhelming, that even his firm spirit yielded. He sank into his chair. Betty laid her hand on his shoulder and whispered some word of comfort in his ear, but he said nothing.

It was Clement who spoke the first word. 'I am going after him,' he said, his tone hard and practical. 'I have thought it out, and by posting all night I may be in London by noon tomorrow, and I may intercept him either at the brokers' or at the India House before he has sold the stock. In that case I may be in time to stop him.'

'Why?' the banker asked, looking up. 'What have we to do with him? Why should we stop him?'

'For our own sakes as well as his,' Clement answered firmly. 'For our own good name, which is bound up with his. Think, think, sir, of the harm it will do us if there is a prosecution – and the old man swears that he will not acknowledge the signature! Besides I have promised to stop him – if I can. If I am too late to do that, and he has sold the stock, I can still get possession of the money, and it must be our business to return it to the owner without the loss of an hour. Of an hour, sir!' Clement repeated earnestly. 'We must repudiate this transaction from the outset. We must wash our hands of it at once, if it be only to clear our own name.'

The banker looked dazed. 'But,' he said, as if his mind were beginning to work again, 'why should we – take all this trouble?' He hesitated, then he began again. 'We have done nothing. We are innocent. Why should we—'

'Stop him?'

'Ay, or be in such a hurry to return the money? It is no fault of ours if it comes to our hands. And, remember, if it lies with us only a week' – he looked at his son, his face troubled – 'only a week, the position is such—'

'No! no!' Clement cried, and for once he spoke peremptorily. 'Not for a day, Father, not for an hour! And when you have thought it over as I have, when you have had time to think it over, you will see that. You will be the first, the very first, to see that, and to say that we must have no part or share with Bourdillon in this; that if we must go down we will go down with clean hands. To avail ourselves of this money, even for a day, and though it would save the bank twice over, would be to make us accomplices, ay, partners in the fraud.'

The banker stood up. 'Right!' he said firmly. 'You are right, lad!' He drew a deep breath, the colour returned to his face. He laid his hand on Clement's shoulder. 'You are quite right, my boy, and I wasn't myself when I said that. You shall have no reason to blush for your father. You are quite right. We will repudiate the transaction from the first. We will have neither art nor part in it. We will return the money the moment it comes into your hands!'

'Thank God, sir, that you see it as I do.'

'I do, I do! The money shall be paid over at once, though the shutters go up the next hour. And we will fight our battle as we must have fought it if this had never happened.'

'With clean hands, at any rate, sir.'

'Yes, lad, with clean hands.'

'Oh, Father, that's splendid!' Betty cried, and she pressed herself against him. 'But as for Clement going, he must be worn out. Could not Mr Rodd go?'

'Rodd will be of more use to you here,' Clement said. 'You will be short-handed as it is.'

'We shall pay out the more slowly,' the banker answered with grim humour.

'And I doubt, besides,' said Clement, 'if Bourdillon would listen to Rodd.'

'Will he listen to you?'

'He will have to, or face the consequences!' And Clement looked as if he meant it: a hard Clement this, with a new note in his voice. 'From the India House to Bow Street is not very far, and he will certainly go to Bow Street – or the Mansion House – if he does not see reason. But he will.'

'He may, if you are with him before he parts with the securities. But from this to noon tomorrow – you will not do it in that time, my lad, at night? Winter time, too? You'll never do it!'

But Clement averred that he would – in fourteen hours, with good luck. It was for that reason that he had gone straight to the Lion and ordered a chaise for eight o'clock and sent on word by the seven o'clock coach for a relay to be ready at the Heygate Inn. He had also asked the Lion to pass on word by any chaise starting in front of him. 'So I hope for two or three stages I shall find the horses ready. Betty, pack up some food for me, that's a good girl. I've only twenty minutes.'

'And your travelling cloak?' she cried. 'I'll air it.'

'You must eat something before you start,' said his father.

'Yes, I will. And, Rodd, do you get me the bank pistols – and see that they are loaded!'

The banker nodded. 'Yes, you'd better take them,' he said. 'It's an immense sum – if you bring it back. It would be a terrible business if you were robbed.'

'Ay, for then we should share the blame,' Clement answered drily. 'That wouldn't do, would it? But let me get the money, and I'll not be robbed, sir.'

They parted, hurrying to and fro on their several errands, the banker fetching money for the journey, Rodd loading the pistols, Betty setting food before the traveller and cutting sandwiches for the journey, Clement himself making some change in his dress. For ten minutes a cheerful stir reigned in the house. But Ovington, though he yielded to this and watched his son at his meal and filled his glass, and played his part, did but feign. He knew that within a few minutes the door would close on Clement, the house would relapse into silence, the lights would go out, and he would be left to face the failure of all the hopes, the plans and expectations which he had entertained through the day. The odds against him, which had not seemed overwhelming twenty-four hours before, now appeared to be invincible, irresistible. He felt that the fates were opposed to him. He had had his chance, and it had been withdrawn. As he climbed the stairs to bed, climbed them slowly and with heavy feet, he read ruin in the flame of his candle. As he undressed he heard the voices of revellers passing the house at midnight, on their way from the Raven or the Talbot, and he suspected derision in their tones. He fancied that they were talking of him, jeering at him, rejoicing in his fall. In bed he lay long awake, calculating, and trying to make of four, five. Could he hold out till Wednesday? Till Thursday? Or would panic running through the town on the morrow, like fire amid tinder, kindle the crowd and hurl it, inflamed with greed and fear, upon his slender defences?

He was buying honesty at a great price. But he thought of Clement and Betty, and towards morning he fell asleep.

Chapter Thirty-Three

Travelling in the old coaching days was not all hardship. It had its own, its peculiar pleasures. A writer of that time dwells with eloquence on the rapture with which he viewed a fine sunrise from the outside of a fast coach on the Great North Road, on the appetite with which he fell to upon a five o'clock breakfast at Doncaster, on the delight with which he heard the nightingales sing on a fine night as he swept through Henley, on the satisfaction of seeing old Shoreditch Church, which betokened the end of the journey. Men did not then hurry at headlong speed along iron rails, with their heads buried in a newspaper or in the latest novel. They learned to know and had time to view the objects of interest that fringed the highway – to recognise the farm at which the Great Durham Ox was bred, and the house in which the equally great Sir Isaac Newton was born. If these things were strange to them and their appearance promised a good fee, the coachman condescended from his greatness and affably pointed out the local wonders.

But to sit through the long winter night, changing each hour from one damp and musty post-chaise to another, to stamp and fume and fret while horses were put to at every stage, to scold an endless succession of incoming and fee an endless series of out-going postboys, each more sleepy and sullen than the last – this was another matter. To be delayed here and checked there and overcharged everywhere, to be fobbed off with the worst teams – always reserved for night travellers – and to find, once started on the long fourteen-mile stage, that the off-wheeler was dead lame, to fall asleep and to be aroused with every hour – these were the miseries, and costly miseries they were, of old-world journeying. This was its seamy side. And many a time Clement, stamping his stone-cold feet in wind-swept inn yards, or ringing ostlers' bells in stone-paved passages, repented that he had started, repented that he had ever undertaken the task.

Why had he? he asked himself more than once that bitter night. What was Arthur Bourdillon to him that he should spend himself in an effort as toilsome as it promised to be vain, to hold him back from the completion of his roguery? Would Arthur ever thank him? Far from it. And Josina? Josina, brave, loving Josina, who had risen to heights of which he thrilled to think, she might indeed thank him – and that should be enough for him. But what could she do to requite him, apart from her father? And the Squire at Garth had stated his position, nor even if he relented was he one to pour himself out in gratitude – he who hated the name of Ovington, and laid all this at their door. It would be much if he ever noticed him with more than a grunt, or ever gave one thought to his exertions or their motive.

No, he had let a quixotic, a foolish impulse run away with him! He should have waited until Arthur had brought down the money, and then he should have returned it. That had been the simple, the matter-of-fact course, and all that it had been incumbent on him to do. As it was, for what was he spending himself and undergoing these hardships? To hasten the ruin of the bank, to meet failure half-way, to render his father penniless a few hours earlier, rather than later. To mask a rascality that need never be disclosed, since no one would hear of it unless the Squire talked. Yes, he had been a fool to hurl himself thus through the night, chilled to the bone, with fevered head and ice-cold feet, when he might have been a hundred times better employed in supporting his father in his need, in putting a brave front on things, and smiling in the face of suspicion.

To be sure, it was only as the night advanced, or rather in the small hours of the morning, when his ardour had died down and Josina's pleading face was no longer before him, and the spirit of adventure was low in him, that he entertained these thoughts. For a time all went well. He found his relay waiting for him at the Heygate Inn by Wellington, where the name of the Lion was all-powerful; and after covering at top speed the short stage that followed, he drove, still full of warmth and courage, into Wolverhampton at a quarter before eleven. Over thirty miles in three hours! He met with a little delay there: the horses had to be fetched from another stable, in another street. But he got away in the end, and ten minutes later he was driving over a land most desolate by day, but by night lurid with the flares of a hundred furnace-fires. He rattled up to the Castle at Birmingham at half an hour after midnight, found the house still lighted and lively, and by dint of scolding and bribing was presently on the road again with a fresh team, and making for Coventry, with every inclination to think that the difficulties of posting by night had been much exaggerated.

But here his good luck left him. At the half-way stage he met with disaster. He had passed the up coach half an hour before, and no orders now anticipated him. When he reached the Stone Bridge there were no horses; on the contrary, there were three travellers waiting there, clamorous to get on to Birmingham. Unwarily he jumped out of his chaise, and 'No horses?' he cried. 'Impossible! There must be horses!'

But the ostler gave him no more than a stolid stare. 'Nary a nag!' he replied coolly. 'Nor like to be, master, wi' every Quaker in Birmingham gadding up and down as if his life 'ung on it! Why, if I've—'

'Quakers? What the devil do you mean?' Clement cried, thinking that the man was reflecting on him.

'Well, Quakers or drab-coated gentry like yourself!' the man replied, unmoved. 'And every one wi' pistols and a money bag! Seems that's what they're looking for – money, so I hear. Such a driving and foraging up and down the land these days, it's a wonder the horses' hoofs bean't worn off.'

'Then,' said Clement, turning about, 'I'll take these on to Meriden.'

But the waiting travellers had already climbed into the chaise and were in possession, and the postboy had turned his horses. And, 'No, no, you'll not do that,' said the ostler. 'Custom of the road, master! Custom of the road! You must change and wait your turn.'

'But there must be something on,' Clement cried in despair, seeing himself detained here, perhaps for the whole night.

'Naught! Nary a 'oof in the yard, nor a lad!' the man replied. 'You'd best take a bed.'

'But when will there be horses?'

'Maybe something'll come in by daylight – like enough.'

'By daylight? Oh, confound you!' cried Clement, enraged. 'Then I'll walk on to Meriden.'

'Walk? Walk on to—' the ostler couldn't voice his astonishment. 'Walk?'

'Ay, walk, and be hanged to you!' Clement cried, and without another word plunged into the darkness of the long, straight road, his bag in his hand. The road ran plain and wide before him, he couldn't miss it; the distance, according to Paterson, which he had in his handbag, was no more than two miles, and he thought that he could do it in half an hour.

But, once away, under the trees, under the midnight sky, in the silence and darkness of the countryside, the fever of his spirits made the distance seem intolerable. As he tramped along the lonely road, doubtful of the wisdom of his action, the feeling of strangeness and homelessness, the sense of the uselessness of what he was doing, grew upon him. At this rate he might as well walk to London! What if there were no horses at Meriden? Or if he were stayed farther up the road? He counted the stages between him and London, and he had time and enough to despair of reaching it, before he at last, at a good four miles an hour, strode out of the night into the semicircle of light which fell upon the road before the Bull's Head at Meriden. Thank Heaven there were lights in the house and people awake, and some hope still! And, more than hope, for almost before he had crossed the threshold a sleepy boots came out of the bar and met him, and 'Horses? Which way, sir? Up? I'll ring the ostler's bell, sir!'

Clement could have blessed him. 'Double money to Coventry if I leave the door in ten minutes!' he cried, taking out his watch. And ten minutes later – or in so little over that time as didn't count – he was climbing into a chaise and driving away: so well organised after all – and all defects granted – was the posting system that at that time covered England. To be sure, he was on one of the great roads, and the Bull's Head at Meriden was a house of fame.

He had availed himself of the interval to swallow a snack and a glass of brandy and water, and he was the warmer for the exercise and in better spirits; pluming himself a little, too, on the resolution which had plucked him from his difficulty at the Stone Bridge. But he had lost the greater part of an hour, and the clocks at Coventry were close on three when he rattled through the narrow, twisting streets of that city. Here, early as was the hour, he caught rumours of the panic, and hints were dropped by the night-men in the inn yard – in sly reply, perhaps, to his adjurations to hasten – of desperate men hurrying to and fro, and buying with gold the speed which meant fortune and life to them. Something was said of a banker who had shot himself at Northampton – or was it Nottingham? – of London runners who had passed through in pursuit of a defaulter; of a bank that had stopped, 'up the road.' 'And there'll be more before all's over,' said his informant darkly. 'But it's well to be them while it lasts! They've money to burn, it seems.'

Clement wondered if this was an allusion to the crown piece that he had offered. At any rate the ill-omened tale haunted him as he left the city behind him, and, after passing under the Cross on Knightlow Hill, and over the Black Heath about Dunsmoor, committed himself to the long, monotonous stretch of road that, unbroken by any striking features, and regularly dotted with towns that hardly rose above the rank of villages, extended dull mile after dull mile to London. The rumble of the chaise and the exertions he had made began to incline him to sleep, but the cold bit into his bones, his feet were growing numb, and as often as he nodded off in his corner he slid down and awoke himself. Sleet, too, was beginning to fall, and the ill-fitting windows leaked, and it was a very morose person who turned out in the rain at Dunchurch.

However, luck was with him, and he got on without delay to Daventry, and had to be roused from sleep when his postboy pulled up before the famous old Wheat-sheaf that, wakeful and alight, was ready with its welcome. Here cheerful fires were burning and everything was done for him. A chaise had just come in from Towcester. The horses' mouths were washed out while he swallowed a crust and another glass of brandy and water, the horses were turned round, and he was away again. He composed himself, shivering in the warmer corner, and, thanking his stars that he had got off, was beginning to nod, when the chaise suddenly tilted to one side and he slid across the seat.

He sat up in alarm and felt the near wheels clawing at the ditch, and thought that he was over. A moment of suspense, and through the fog that dimmed the window-panes flaming lights blazed above him and over him, and the down mails thundered by, coach behind coach – three coaches, the road quivering beneath them, the horses cantering, the guards replying with a volley of abuse to the postboy's shout of alarm. Huge, lighted monsters, by night the bullies of the road, they were come and gone in an instant, leaving him staring with dazzled eyes into the darkness. But the shave had not bettered his temper. The stage seemed a long one, the horses slow, and he was fretting and fuming mightily, and by no means as grateful as he should have been for the luck that had hitherto attended him, when at last he jogged into Towcester.

Alas, the inn here was awake, indeed, in a somnolent, grumpy, sullen fashion, but there were no horses. 'Not a chance of them,' said the sleepy boots, flicking a dirty napkin towards the coffee room. 'There are two business gents waiting there to get on – life and death, 'cording to them. They're going up same way as you are, and they've first call. And there's a gentleman and his servant for Birmingham – down, they are, and been waiting since eleven o'clock and swearing tremendous!'

'Then I'll take mine on!' Clement said, and whipped out into the night and ran to his chaise. But he was too late. The gentleman's servant had been on the watch, he had made his bargain and stepped in, and his master was hurrying out to join him. 'The devil!' cried Clement, now wide awake and very angry. 'That's pretty sharp!'

'Yes, sir, sharp's the word,' said the boots. It was evident that night work had made him a misanthrope, or something else had soured him. 'They'd be no good for Brickhill anyway. It's a long stage. You'll take a bed?'

'Bed be hanged!' said Clement, wondering what he should do. This seemed to be a dead stop, and very black he looked. At last, 'I'll go to the yard,' he said.

'There's nobody up. You'd best—' and again the boots advised a bed.

'Nobody up? Oh, hang it!' said Clement, and stood and thought, very much at a standstill. What could he do? There was a clock in the passage. He looked at it. It was close on six, and he had nearly sixty miles to travel. Save for the delay at the Stone Bridge, he had done well. He had kept his postboys up to the mark: he had spared neither money nor prayers, nor, it must be added, curses. He had done a very considerable feat, the difficulties of night posting considered. But he had still fifty-eight miles before him, and if he could not get on now he had done nothing. He had only wasted his money. 'Any up coach due?'

'Not before eight o'clock,' said the boots cynically. 'Reaches the Saracen's Head, Snow-Hill, at three-thirty. You are one of these moneyed gents, I suppose? Things is queer in town, I hear – crashes and what not, something terrible, I am told. Blue ruin and worse. The master here' – becoming suddenly confidential – 'he's in it. It's U-p with him! They seized his horses yesterday. That's why—' he winked mysteriously towards the silent stables. 'Wouldn't trust him, and couldn't send a bailiff with every team. That's why!'

'Who seized them?' Clement asked listlessly. But he awoke a second later to the meaning of his words.

'Hollins, Church Farm yonder. Bill for hay and straw. D'you know him?'

'No, but – here! D'you see this?' Clement plucked out a crown piece, his eyes alight. 'Is there a postboy here? That's the point! Asleep or awake! Quick, man!'

'A postboy? Well, there's old Sam – he can ride. But what's the use of a postboy when there's no horses?'

'Wake him! Bring him here!' Clement retorted, on fire with an idea, and waving the crown piece. 'D'you hear? Bring him here and this is yours. But sharp's the word. Go! Go and get him, man, it will be worth his while. Haul him out! Tell him he must come! It's money, tell him!'

The boots caught the infection and went, and for three or four minutes Clement stamped up and down in a fever of anxiety. By and by the postboy came, half dressed, sulky, and rubbing his eyes. Clement seized him by the shoulders, shook him, pounded him, pounded his idea into him, bribed him. Five minutes later they were hurrying towards the church, passing here and there a yawning labourer plodding through the darkness to his work. The farmer at Hollins' was dressing, and opened his window to swear at them and at the noise the dogs were making. But, 'Three pounds! Three pounds for horses to Brickhill!' Clement cried. The proper charge was twenty-six shillings at the eighteen-penny night scale, and the man listened. 'You can come with me and keep possession!' Clement urged, seeing that he hesitated. 'You run no risk! I'll be answerable.'

Three pounds was money, much money in those days. It was good interest on his unpaid bill, and Mr Hollins gave way. He flung down the key of the stables, and hurrying down after it, helped to harness the horses by the light of a lanthorn. That done, however, the good man took fright at the novelty, almost the impudence of the thing, and demanded his money. 'Half now, and half at Brickhill,' Clement replied, and the sight of the cash settled the matter. Mr Hollins opened the yard gate, and two minutes later they were off, the farmer's wife staring after them from the doorway and, with a leaning to the safe side, shrilly stating her opinion that her husband was a fool and would lose his nags.

'Never fear,' Clement said to the man. 'Only don't spare them! Time is money to me this morning!'

Fortunately, the horses had done no work the previous day and had been well fed. They were fresh, and the old postboy, feeling himself in luck, and exhilarated by what he called 'as queer a start as ever was,' was determined to merit the largest fee. The farmer, as they whirled down Windmill Hill at a pace that carried them over the ascent and past Plum Park, fidgeted uneasily in his seat, fearing broken knees and what not. But seeing then that the postboy steadied his pair and knew his business, he let it pass. As far as Stony Stratford the road was with them, and thence to Fenny Stratford they pushed on at a good pace.

It was broad daylight by now, the road was full of life and movement, they met and passed other travellers, other chaises, one or two of the early morning coaches. Men, topping and tailing turnips, stood and watched them from the fields, a gleam of December sunrise warmed the landscape. To the tedious nightmare of the long, dark hours, with their endless stages and sleepy turn-outs and shadowy postilions, their yawning inns and midnight meals, had succeeded sober daylight, plodding realities, waking life; and Clement should have owned the relief. But he did not, and for a simple reason. During the night the end had been far off and uncertain, a thing not yet to be dwelt upon or considered. Now the end was within sight, a few hours must determine it one way or the other, and his anxiety as the time passed, and the horses now slackened their pace to climb a rise, now were detained by a flock of sheep, centred itself upon it. He had endured so much that he might intercept Arthur before the deed was done and the false transfer used, that to fail Josina now, to be too late now, was a thing not to be considered.

Chapter Thirty-Four

Still, the daylight had one good effect, it completed the reassurance of Mr Hollins. He could see his man now, and judging him to be good for the money, he gave way to greed and proposed to run the horses on to Dunstable. Clement thought that he might do worse and assented, merely halting for five minutes at the George at Brickhill, to administer a quart of ale apiece to the nags, and to take one themselves. Then they pressed on to Dunstable, which they reached at half-past eight.

Even so, Clement had still thirty miles to cover. But the postboy, a sportsman with his heart in the game, had ridden in, waving his whip and shouting for horses, and his good word spread like magic. Two minutes let the yard know that here was a golden customer, an out-and-outer, and almost before Clement could swallow a cup of scalding coffee and pocket a hot roll he had wrung the farmer's hand, fee'd old Sam to his heart's content, and was away again, on the ten-mile down hill stage to St. Albans. They cantered most of the way, the postboy's whip in the air and the chaise running after the horses, and did the distance triumphantly in forty-three minutes. Then on, with the reputation of a good paymaster, to Barnet – Barnet, that seemed to be almost as good as London.

Luck could not have stood by him better, and, now the sun shone, they raced with taxed-carts, and flashed by sober clergymen jogging along on their hacks. The midnight shifts to which he had been put, the despairing struggle about Meriden and Dunchurch, were a dream. He was in the fairway now, though the pace was not so good, and the hills, with windmills atop, seemed to be set on the road at intervals on purpose to delay him. Still he was near the end of his journey, and he began to consider all the alternatives to success, all the various ways in which he might yet fail. He might miss Bourdillon; he began to be sure that he would miss him.

Either he would be at the India Office when Bourdillon was at the brokers', or at the brokers' when he was at the India Office; and, failing the India Office or the brokers', he had no clue to him. Or his quarry would have left town already, with the treasure in his possession. Or they might pass one another in the streets or even on the road. He would be too late and he would fail, after all his exertions! He began to feel sure of it.

Yes, he had certainly been a fool not to think at starting of the hundred chances, the scores of accidents which might occur to prevent their meeting. And every minute that he spent on the road made things worse. He had had yonder windmill in sight this half-hour – and it seemed no nearer. He fidgeted to and fro, lowered a window and raised it again, scolded the postboy, flung himself back in the chaise.

At the Green Man at Barnet he got sulkily into his last chaise, and they pounded down five miles of a gentle slope, then drove stoutly up the easy hill to Highgate. By this time the notion that Bourdillon would pass him unseen had got such hold upon him – though it was the unlikeliest thing in the world that Arthur could have got through his business so early – that his eyes raked every chaise they met, and a crowded coach by which they sped, as it crawled up the southern side of the hill, filled him with the darkest apprehensions. Had he given a moment's thought to the state of the market, to the pressure of business which it must cause, and to the crowd, greedy for transfers, in which Arthur must take his turn, he would have seen that this fear was groundless.

However, the true state of things was by and by brought home to his mind. He had directed the postboy to take him direct to the brokers' in the City, and he had hardly exchanged the pleasant country roads of Highbury and Islington, with their villas and cow-farms, for the noisy, dirty thoroughfares of north London, before he was struck by the evidences of excitement that met his eyes. Lads, shouting raucously, ran about the busier streets, selling broadsheets, which were fought for and bought up with greedy haste. A stream of walkers, with their faces set one way, hastened along almost as fast as his post-chaise. Busy groups stood at the street corners, debating and gesticulating. As he advanced still farther, and crossed the boundary and began to thread the narrow streets of the City – it wanted a half-hour of noon – he found himself hampered and almost stopped by the crowd which thronged the roadway, and seemed in its preoccupation to be insensible to the obstacles that barred its way and into which it cannoned at every stride. And still, with each yard that he advanced, the press increased. The signs of ferment became more evident. Distracted men, hatless and red-hot with haste, regardless of everything but the errand on which they were bent, sprang from offices, hurled themselves through the press, leaped on their fellows' backs, tore on their way, while those whom they had maltreated did not even look round, but continued their talk, unaware of the outrage. Some pushed through the press, so deep in thought that they saw no one and might have walked a country lane, while others, meeting as by appointment, seized one another, shook one another, bawled in each other's faces as if both had become suddenly deaf. And now and again the whole tormented mass, seething in the narrow lanes or narrower alleys, swayed this way or that under the impulse of some unknown mysterious impulse, some warning, some call to action.

Clement had never seen anything like it, and he viewed it with awe, his ears deafened by the babel or pierced by the shrill cries of the news-sellers who constantly bawled, 'Panic! Great panic in the City! Panic! List of banks closed!' He had heard as he changed at Barnet that fourteen houses in the City had shut their doors, but he had not appreciated the fact. Now he was to see with his own eyes shuttered windows and barred doors with great printed bills affixed to them, and huge crowds at gaze before them, groaning and hooting. Even the shops bore singular and striking witness to the crisis, for in Cheapside every other window exhibited a card stating that they would accept bank-notes to any extent and for goods to any amount – a courageous attempt to restore public confidence which deserved more success than it won; while there, and on all sides, he heard men execrating the Bank of England and loudly proclaiming – though this was not the fact – that it had published a notice that it could no longer pay cash.

Here was panic indeed! Here was an appalling state of things! And very low his heart sank, as the chaise gained a few yards, stopped, and advanced again. What chance had Ovington's, what hope of survival had their little venture, when the very credit of the country tottered, and here in the heart of London age-long institutions with vast deposits and forty or fifty branches toppled down on all sides? When merchant princes with tens of thousands in sound but unsaleable securities could do nothing to save themselves, and men of world-wide fame, the giants of finance, went humbly, hat in hand, to ask for time?

Stranded, or moving at a snail's pace, he caught scraps of the talk about him. Smith's in Mansion House Street had closed its doors. Everett and Walker's had followed Pole's into bankruptcy. Wentworth's at York had failed for two hundred thousand pounds. Telford's at Plymouth had been sacked by an angry mob. The strongest bank in Norwich was going or gone. The Bank of England had paid out eight millions in gold within the week – and had no more. They were paying in one-pound notes now, a set found God knows where – in the cellars, it was said. The tellers were so benumbed with terror that they could not separate them or count them.

For the moment he forgot Arthur and Arthur's business, and thought only of his father and of their own plight. 'We are gone!' he reflected, his face almost as pale as the faces in the street. 'We are ruined! There is no hope. When this reaches Aldersbury we must close!' He could no longer bear the inaction. He could not sit still. He paid off the chaise – with difficulty, owing to the press – and pushed forward on foot. But his mind still ran on Aldersbury, was still busy with the fate of their own bank. He felt an immense pity for his father, and recognised that until this moment, when panic in its most dreadful form stared him in the face, he had not realised the catastrophe, or the sadness, or the finality of it. They must close. They must begin the world again, begin it at the bottom, in competition with a multitude of beggared men, of whom three-fourths had never speculated, never touched a share, never left the safe path of industrious commerce, but were now to pay with all they possessed in the world, their daughters' portions and their sons' fortunes, for the recklessness or the extravagance of others.

For a space there was vouchsafed to him the wider vision, and he saw the thing that was passing in its true light. He saw the wave of ruin spread from these crowded streets ever farther and farther, from city to town and town to country; and where it passed it wrecked homes, it made widows, it swept away the dowries of children, it separated lovers, it overwhelmed the happiness of thousands and tens of thousands. He saw the honest trader, whose father's good name was his glory, broken in heart and fortune through the failure of others, his health shattered, his house sold over his head, his pensioners and dependants flung into the workhouse. He saw deluded parsons doomed to spend the close of their lives in a hopeless wrestle with debt, their sons taken from school, their daughters sent out into a cold and unfeeling world. He saw squires, the little gods of their domain, men once wealthy, doomed to drink themselves into forgetfulness of the barred entail and the lost estate; the great house would be closed, the agent would squeeze the tenants, and they in turn the labourers, until the very village shop would feel the pinch. Thousands upon thousands would lose their hoarded savings, and, too old to begin again, would sink, they and their children and their children's children, into the under-world, there to be lost amid the dregs of the population.

And he and his? Why should they escape? How could they escape? It would be much if they could feel, while they shared the common lot, that they had deserved to escape, that they were not of those whose wild speculations had brought this disaster on their kind.

He had by this time fought his way as far as the end of Cheapside, and here, where the roar was loudest and the contending currents mingled their striving masses, where the voices of the news-boys were shrillest, and the timid stood daunted, while even strong men paused, measuring the human whirlpool into which they must plunge, Clement's eye was caught by a side-scene which was passing in the street hard by the Mansion House. Raised above the crowd on the steps of a large building, a haggard man was making an announcement – but in dumb show, for no word could be heard even by those who stood beside him, and his meaning could be deduced only from his gestures of appeal.

The lower windows of the house were shuttered, and the upper exhibited many broken panes; behind these and the cornice of the roof gleamed here and there a pale frightened face, peering down at the proceedings below. From the crowd collected before the haggard man rose a continuous roar of protest, a forest of menacing hands, shrill cries and curses, and now and again a missile, which, falling absurdly short – for in that press no man could swing his arm – still bore witness to the malice that urged it. Nearer to Clement on the skirts of the throng, where they could see little and were perpetually elbowed by impatient passers-by, loitered a few who at a first glance seemed to be uninterested – so apathetic were their attitudes, so absent was their gaze. But a second glance disclosed the truth. They were men whom the tidings of ruin, sudden and unforeseen, had stunned. Spiritless and despairing, seeing only the home they had forfeited and the dear ones they had beggared, they stood in the street, blind and deaf to what was passing about them, and only by the mute agony of their eyes betrayed the truth.

The sight wrung Clement's heart with pity, and he seized a news-lad by the arm. 'What is that place?' he shouted in his ear. In that babel no man could make himself heard without shouting.

The man looked at him suspiciously. 'Yar! Yer kidding!' he said. 'Yer know as well as me!'

Clement shook him in his impatience. 'No, I don't,' he shouted. 'I'm a stranger! What is it, man? A bank?'

'Where d'yer come from?' the lad retorted, as he twisted himself free. 'It's Everitt's, that's what it is! They closed an hour ago! Might as well ha' never opened!'

He went off hurriedly, and Clement went too, plunging into the maelstrom that divided him from Cornhill. But as he buffeted his way through the throng, the faces of the ruined men went with him, coming between him and the street, and with a sinking heart he fancied that he read, written on them, the fate of Ovington's.

Chapter Thirty-Five

It was to Clement's credit that, had his object been to save his father's bank, instead of to do that which might deprive it of its last hope, he could not have struggled onward through the press more stoutly than he did. But though the offices for which he was bound, situate in one of the courts north of Cornhill, were no more than a third of a mile from the point at which he had dismissed his chaise, the city clocks had long struck twelve before, wresting himself from the human flood, which panic and greed were driving through the streets, he turned into this quiet backwater.

He stood for a moment to take breath and adjust his dress, and even in that brief space he discovered that the calm was but comparative. Many of the windows which looked on the court were raised, as if the pent-up emotions of their occupants craved air and an outlet even on that December day; and from these and from the open doors below issued a dropping fire of sounds, the din of raised voices, of doors recklessly slammed, of feet thundering on bare stairs, of harsh orders. Clerks rushing into the court, hatless and demented, plunged into clerks rushing out equally demented, yet flew on their course without look or word, as if unconscious of the impact. From a lighted window – many were lit up, for the court was small and the day foggy – a hat, even as Clement paused, flew out and bounded on the pavement. But no one heeded it or followed it, and it was a passing clerk who came hurrying out a little less recklessly than his fellows, whom Clement, after a moment's hesitation, seized by the arm. 'Mr Bourdillon here?' he asked imperatively – for he saw that in no other way could he gain attention.

'Mr Bourdillon!' the man snapped. 'Oh, I don't know! Here, Cocky Sands! Attend to this gentleman! Le' me go! Le' me go. D' you hear?'

He tore himself free, and was gone while he spoke, leaving Clement to climb the stairs. On the landing he encountered another clerk, whom he supposed to be 'Cocky Sands,' and he attacked him. 'Mr Bourdillon? Is he here?' he asked.

But Mr Sands eluded him, shouted over his shoulder for 'Tom!' and clattered down the stairs. 'Can't wait!' he flung behind him. 'Find someone!'

However, Clement lost nothing by this, for the next moment one of the partners appeared at a door. Clement knew him, and 'Is Mr Bourdillon here?' he cried for the third time, and he seized the broker by the button-hole. He, at any rate, should not escape him.

'Mr Bourdillon?' The broker stared, unable on the instant to recall his thoughts, and from the way in which he wiped his bald and steaming head with a yellow bandanna, it was plain that he had just got something of moment off his mind. 'Pheugh! What times!' he ejaculated, fanning himself and breathing hard. 'What a morning! You've heard, I suppose? Everitt's are gone. Gone within the hour, d—n them! Oh, Bourdillon? It was Bourdillon you asked for? To be sure, it's Mr Ovington, isn't it? I thought so; I never forget a face, but he didn't tell me that you were here. By Jove!' He raised his hands – he was a portly gentleman, wearing a satin under-vest and pins and chains innumerable, all at this moment a little awry. 'By Jove, what a find you have there! Slap, bang, and up to the mark, and no mistake! Hard and sharp as nails! I take off my hat to him! There's not a firm,' mopping his heated face anew, 'within half a mile of us that wouldn't be glad to have him! I'll take my Davy there are not ten men in country practice could have pushed the deal through, and squeezed eleven thousand in cash out of Snell & Higgins on such a day as this! He's a marvel, Mr Ovington! You can tell your father I said so, and I don't care who says the contrary.'

'But is he here?' Clement cried, dancing with impatience. 'Is he here, man?'

'Gone to the India House this' – he looked at his watch – 'this half-hour, to complete. He had to drop seven per cent, for cash on the nail – that, of course! But he got six thousand odd in Bank paper, and five thou. in gold, and I'm damned if any one else would have got that today, though the stuff he had was as good as the ready in ordinary times. My partner's gone with him to Leadenhall Street to complete – glad to oblige you, for God knows how many clients we shall have left after this – and they've a hackney coach waiting in Bishopsgate and an officer to see them to it. You may catch him at the India House, or he may be gone. He's not one to let the grass grow under his feet. In that case—'

'Send a clerk with me to show me the Office!' Clement cried. 'It's urgent, man, urgent! And I don't know my way inside the House. I must catch him.'

'Well, with so much money – here, Nicky!' The broker stepped aside to make room for a client who came up the stairs three at a time. 'Nicky, go with this gentleman! Show him the way to the India House. Transfer Office – Letter G! Sharp's the word. Don't lose time. – Coming! Coming!' to someone in the office. 'My compliments to your father. He's one of the lucky ones, for I suppose this will see you through. It's Boulogne or this' – he made as if he held a pistol to his head – 'for more than I care to think of!'

But Clement had not waited to hear the last words. He was half-way down the stairs with his hand on the boy's collar. They plunged into Cornhill, but the lad, a London-bred urchin, did not condescend to the street for more than twenty yards or so. Then he dived into a court on the same side of the way, crossed it, threaded a private passage through some offices, and came out in Bishopsgate Street. Stemming the crowd as best they could they crossed this, and by another alley and more offices the lad convoyed his charge into Leadenhall Street. A last rush saw them landed, panting and with their coats wellnigh torn from their backs, on the pavement on the south side of the street, in front of the pillared entrance, and beneath the colossal Britannia that, far above their heads and flanked by figures of Europe and Asia, presided over the fortunes of the greatest trading company that the world has ever seen. Through the doors of that building – now, alas, no more – had passed all the creators of an oriental empire, statesmen, soldiers, merchant princes, Clive, Lawrence, Warren Hastings, Cornwallis. Yet today, the mention of it calls up as often the humble figure of a black-coated, white-cravated clerk with spindle legs and a big head, who worked within its walls and whom Clement, had he called a few months earlier, might have met coming from his desk.

Here Clement, had he been without a guide, must have wasted precious minutes. But the place had no mysteries for the boy, even on this day of confusion and alarm. Skilled in every twist and turning, he knew no doubt. 'This way,' he snapped, hurrying down a long passage which faced the entrance, and appeared to penetrate into the bowels of the building.

Then, 'No! Not that way, stupid! What are you doing?'

But Clement's eyes, as he followed, had caught sight of a party of three, who, issuing from a corridor on the right at a considerable distance before them, had as quickly disappeared down another corridor on the left. The light was not good, but Clement had recognised one of them, and 'There he is!' he cried. 'He has gone down there! Where does that lead to?'

'Lime Street entrance!' the lad replied curtly, and galloped after the party, Clement at his heels. 'Hurry!' he threw over his shoulder, 'or they'll be out, and, by gum, you'll lose him! Once out and we're done, sir!'

They reached the turning the others had taken and ran down it. The distance was but short, but it was long enough to enable Clement to collect his wits, and to wonder, while he prepared himself for the encounter, how Arthur would bear himself at the moment of discovery. Fortunately, the party pursued had paused for an instant in the east vestibule before committing themselves to the street, and that instant was fatal to them. 'Bourdillon!' Clement cried, raising his voice. 'Hi! Bourdillon!'

Arthur turned as if he had been struck, saw him and stared, his mouth agape. 'The devil!' he ejaculated.

But to Clement's surprise his face betrayed neither the guilt nor the fear which he had expected to see, but only amazement that the other should be there – and some annoyance. 'You?' he said. 'What the devil are you doing here? What joke is this? Did your father think that I could not be trusted to see things through? Or that you were likely to do better?'

'I want a word with you,' said Clement. He was in no mood to mince matters.

'But why are you here?' with rising anger. 'Why have you come after me? What's up?'

'I'll tell you, if you'll step aside.'

'You can tell me on the coach, then, for I have no time to lose now. I mean to catch the three o'clock coach, and—'

'No!' Clement said firmly. 'I must speak to you here.'

But on that the broker interposed, his watch in his hand. 'Anyway, I can't stop,' he said. 'Who is this gentleman?'

'Mr Ovington, junior,' Arthur said, with something of a sneer. 'I don't know what he has come up for, but—'

'But, at any rate, he'll see you safe to the coach,' the other rejoined. 'And I must be off. I give you joy of it, Mr Bourdillon. Fine work! Fine work, by Jove! And I shall tell Mr Ovington so when I see him. You're a marvel! My compliments to your father, young gentleman,' addressing Clement. 'Glad to have met you, but I can't stay now. Fifty things to do, and no time to do 'em in. The world's upside down today. Good morning! Good morning!' With a wave of the hand, his watch in the other, he turned on his heel and strode back towards the main entrance.

The two looked at one another and the third, who made up the party, a burly man in a red waistcoat and a curly-brimmed Regency hat, surveyed them both. 'Well, I'm hanged,' Arthur exclaimed, reverting sourly to his first surprise. 'Is everybody mad? Must you all come to town? I should have thought that you'd had enough to do at the bank without this! But as you must—' then to the officer, who was carrying a small leather valise, the duplicate of one which Arthur held in his hand – 'wait a minute, will you? And keep an eye on us. We shall not be a minute. Now,' drawing Clement into a corner of the lodge, five or six paces away, where, though a stream of people continually brushed by them, they could talk with some degree of privacy. 'What is it, man? What is it? What has brought you up? And how the deuce have you come to be here – by this time?'

'I posted.'

'Posted? From Aldersbury? In heaven's name, why? Why, man?'

Clement pointed to the bag. 'To take that over,' he said.

'This? Take this over?' Arthur turned a deep red. 'What – what the devil do you mean, man?'

'You ought to know.'

'I?'

'Yes, you,' Clement retorted, his temper rising. 'It's stolen property, if you will have it.' And he braced himself for the fray.

'Stolen property?'

'Just that. And my father has commissioned me to take charge of it, and to restore it to its owner. Now you know.'

For one moment the handsome face, looking into his, lost some of its colour. But the next, Arthur recovered himself, the blood flowed back to his cheeks, he laughed aloud, laughed in defiance. 'Why – you – you fool!' he replied, in bitter contempt, 'I don't know what you are talking about. Your father – your father has sent you?'

'It's no good, Bourdillon,' Clement answered. 'It's all known. I've seen the Squire. He missed the certificates yesterday afternoon – almost as soon as you were gone. He sent for you, I went over, and he knows all.'

He thought that that would finish the matter. To his astonishment Arthur only laughed afresh. 'Knows all, does he?' he replied. 'Well, what of it. And he found out through you, did he? Then a pretty fool you were to put your oar in! To go to him, or see him, or talk to him! Why, man,' with bravado, though Clement fancied that his eyes wavered and that the brag began to ring false, 'what have I done? Borrowed his money for a month, that's all! Taken a loan of it for a month or two – and for what? Why, to save your father and you and the whole lot of us. Ay, and half Aldersbury from ruin! I did it and I'd do it again! And he knows it, does he? Through your d—d interfering folly, who could not keep your mouth shut, eh! Well, if he does, what then? What can he do, simpleton?'

'That's to be seen.'

'Nothing! Nothing, I tell you! He signed the transfer, signed it with his own hand, and he can't deny it. The rest is just his word against mine.'

'No, it's Miss Griffin's, too,' Clement said, marvelling at the other's attitude and his audacity – if audacity it could he called.

But Arthur, though he had been far from expecting a speedy discovery, had long ago made up his mind as to the risk he ran. And naturally he had considered the line he would take in the event of detection. He was not unprepared, therefore, even for Clement's rejoinder, and, 'Miss Griffin?' he retorted, contemptuously, 'Do you think that she will give evidence against me? Or he – against a Griffin? Why, you booby, instead of talking and wasting time here, you ought to be down on your knees thanking me – you and your father! Thanking me, by heaven, for saving you and your bank, and taking all the risk myself! It would have been long before you'd have done it, my lad, I'll answer for that!'

'I hope so,' Clement replied with emphasis. 'And you may understand at once that we don't like your way, and are not going to be saved your way. We are not going to have any part or share in robbing your uncle – see! If we are going to be ruined, we are going to be ruined with clean hands! No, it's no good looking at me like that, Bourdillon. I may be a fool in the bank, and you may call me what names you like. But I am your match here, and I am going to take possession of that money.'

'Do you think, then,' furiously, 'that I am going to run away with it?'

'I don't know,' Clement rejoined. 'I am not going to give you the chance. I am going to take it over and return it to the owner; it will not go near our bank. I have my father's authority for acting as I am acting, and I am going to carry out his directions.'

'And he's going to fail? To rob hundreds instead of borrowing from one money that you know will be returned – returned with interest in a month? You fool! You fool!' with savage scorn. 'That's your virtue, is it? That's your honesty that you brag so much about? Your clean hands? You'll rob Aldersbury right and left, bring half the town to beggary, strip the widow and the orphan, and put on a smug face! "All honest and above board, my lord!" when you might save all at no risk by borrowing this money for a month. Why, you make me sick! Sick!' Arthur repeated, with an indignation that went far to prove that this really was his opinion, and that he did honestly see the thing in that light. 'But you are not going to do it. You shall not do it,' he continued, defiantly. 'I'll see you – somewhere else first! You'll not touch a penny of this money until I choose, and that will not be until I have seen your father. If I can't persuade you I think I can persuade him!'

'You'll not have the chance!' Clement retorted. He was very angry by now, for some of the shafts which the other had loosed had found their mark. 'You'll hand it over to me, and now!'

'Not a penny!'

'Then you'll take the consequences,' was Clement's reply. 'For as heaven sees me, I shall give you in charge, and you will go to Bow Street. The officer is here. I shall tell him the facts, and you know best what the result will be. You can choose, Bourdillon, but that is my last word.'

Arthur stared. 'You are mad!' he cried. 'Mad!' But he was taken aback at last. His voice shook, and the colour had left his cheeks.

'No, I am not mad. But we will not be your accomplices. That is all. That is the bed-rock of it,' Clement continued. 'I give you two minutes to make up your mind.' He took out his watch.

Rage and alarm do not better a man's looks, and Arthur's handsome face was ugly enough now, had Clement looked at it. Two passions wrestled within him: rage at the thought that one whom he had often out-manœuvred and always despised should dare to threaten and thwart him; and fear – fear of the gulf that he saw gaping suddenly at his feet. For he could not close his eyes, bold and self-confident as he was, to the danger. He saw that if Clement said the word and made the thing public, his position would be perilous; and if his uncle proved obdurate, it might be desperate.

His lips framed words of defiance, and he longed to utter them; but he did not utter them. Had they been alone, it had been another matter! But they were not alone; the Bow Street man, idly inquisitive, was watching him, and a stream of people, immersed each in his own perplexities and unconscious of the tragedy at his elbow, was continually brushing by them.

To do him justice, Arthur had hitherto seen the thing only by his own lights. He had looked on it as a case of all for fortune and the rest well lost, and he had even pictured himself in the guise of a hero, who took the risks and shared the benefits. If the act were ill, at least, he considered, he did it in a good cause; and where, after all, was the harm in assuming a loan of something which would never be missed, which would be certainly repaid, and which, in his hands, would save a hundred homes from ruin? The argument had sounded convincing at the time.

Then, for the risk, what was it, when examined? It was most unlikely that the Squire would discover the trick, and if he did he could not, hard and austere as he was, prosecute his own flesh and blood. Nay, Arthur doubted if he could prosecute, since he had signed the transfer with his own hand – it was no forgery. At the worst then, and if discovery came, it would mean the loss of the Squire's favour and banishment from the house. Both of these things he had experienced before, and in his blindness he did not despair of reinstating himself a second time. He had a way with him, he had come to think that few could resist him. He was far, very far, from understanding how the Squire would view the act.

But now the mists of self-deception were for the moment blown aside, and he saw the gulf on the edge of which he stood, and into which a word might precipitate him. If the pig-headed fool before him did what he said he would, and preferred a charge, the India House might take it up; and, pitiless where its interests were in question, it might prove as inexorable as the Bank had proved in the case of Fauntleroy only the year before. In that event, what might not be the end? His uncle had signed the transfer, and at the time that had seemed enough; it had seemed to secure him from the worst. But now – now when so much hung upon it, he doubted. He had not inquired, he had not dared to inquire how the law stood, but he knew that the law's uncertainties were proverbial and its ambages beyond telling.

And the India House, like the Bank of England, was a terrible foe. Once launched on the slope, let the cell door once close on him, he might slip with fatal ease from stage to stage, until the noose hung dark and fearful before him, and all the influence, all the help he could command, might then prove powerless to save him! It was a terrible machine – the law! The cell, the court, the gallows, with what swiftness, what inevitableness, what certainty, did they not succeed one another – dark, dismal stages on the downward progress! How swiftly, how smoothly, how helplessly had that other banker traversed them! How irresistibly had they borne him to his doom!

He shuddered. The officer of the law, who a few minutes before had been his servant, fee-bound, obsequious, took on another shape, and grew stern and menacing. The man was even now observing him, and possibly had already his suspicions. Arthur's colour ebbed at the thought and his face betrayed him. The peril might be real or unreal – it might be only his imagination that he had to fight. But he could not face it. He moistened his dry lips, he forced himself to speak. He surrendered – sullenly, with averted eyes.

'Have it your own way,' he said. 'Take it.' And with a last attempt at bravado, 'I shall appeal to your father!'

'That is as you will,' Clement said. He was not comfortable, and sensible of the other's humiliation, his only wish was to bring the scene to an end as quickly as possible. He took up the bag and signed to the officer that they were ready.

'It's some hundreds short. You know that?' Arthur muttered.

'I can't help it.'

'He'll be the loser.'

'Well – it must be so.' Yet Clement hesitated, a little taken aback. He did not like the thought, and he paused to consider whether it might not be his duty to return to the brokers' and undo the bargain. But it would be necessary to repeat all the formalities at a cost of time that he could not measure, and it was improbable that he would be able to recoup the whole of the loss. Rightly or wrongly, he decided to go on, and he turned to the officer. 'I take on the business now,' he said, sharply. 'Where is the hackney-coach? In Bishopsgate? Then lead the way, will you?' And, the bag in his hand, he moved towards the crowded street.

But with his foot on the threshold, something spoke in him, and he looked back. Arthur was standing where he had left him, gloom in his face; and Clement melted. He could not leave him, he could not bear to leave him thus. What might he not do, what might he not have it in his mind to do? Pity awoke in him, he put himself in the other's place, and though there was nothing less to his taste at that moment than a companionship equally painful and embarrassing, he went back to him. 'Look here,' he said, 'come with me. Come down with me and face it out, man, and get it over. It's the only thing to do, and every hour you remain away will tell against you. As it is, what is broken can be mended – if you're there.'

Arthur did not thank him. Instead, 'What?' he cried. 'Come? Come with you? And be dragged at your chariot wheels, you oaf! Never!'

'Don't be a fool,' Clement remonstrated, pity moving him more strongly now that he had once acted on it. He laid his hand on the other's arm. 'We'll work together and make the best of it. I will, I swear, Bourdillon, and I'll answer for my father. But if I leave you here and go home, things will be said and there'll be trouble.'

'Trouble the devil!' Arthur retorted, and shook off his hand. 'You have ruined the bank,' he continued, bitterly, but with less violence, 'and ruined your father and ruined me. I hope you are content. You have been thorough, if it's any satisfaction to you. And some day I shall know why you've done it. For your honesty and your clean hands, they don't weigh a curse with me. You're playing your own game, and if I come to know what it is, I'll spoil it yet, d—n you!'

'I don't mind how much you curse me, if you will come,' Clement answered, patiently. 'It's the only thing to be done, and when you think it over in cold blood, you'll see that. Come, man, and put a bold face on it. It is the brave game and the only game. Face it out now.'

Arthur looked away, his handsome face sullen. He was striving with his passions, battling with the maddening sense of defeat. He saw, as plainly as Clement, that the latter's advice was good, but to take it and to go with him, to bear for many hours the sense of his presence and the consciousness of his scorn – his gorge rose at the thought. Yet, what other course was open to him? What was he going to do? He had little money with him, and he saw but two alternatives: to blow out his brains, or to go, hat in hand, and seek employment at the brokers' where he was known. He had no real thought of the former alternative – life ran strong in him and he was sanguine; and the latter meant the overthrow of all his plans, and a severance, final and complete, from Ovington's. His lot thenceforth would be that of a man who had 'crossed the fight,' done something dubious, put himself outside the pale.

Whereas if he went with Clement, humiliation would indeed be his. But he would still be himself, and with his qualities he might live it down, and in the end lose nothing.

So at last, 'Go on,' he said, sulkily. 'Have it your own way. At any rate, I may spoil your game!' He shut his eyes to Clement's generosity. If he gave a thought to it at all, he fancied that he had some purpose to serve, some axe of his own to grind.

They went out into the babel of the street, and, deafened by the cries of the hawkers, elbowed by panic-stricken men who fancied that if they were somewhere else they might save their hoards, shouldered by stout countrymen, adrift in the confusion like hulks in a strange sea, they made their way into Bishopsgate Street. Here they found the hackney-coach awaiting them, and drove by London Wall to the Bull and Mouth. A Birmingham coach was due to start at three, and after a gloomy wrangle they booked places by it, and, while the officer guarded the money, they sat down in the Coffee Room to a rare sirloin and a foaming tankard. They ate and drank in unfriendly silence, two empty chairs intervening; and more than once Arthur repented of his decision. But already the force of circumstances was driving them together, for the thoughts of each had travelled forward to Aldersbury – and to Ovington's. What was happening there? What might not already have happened there? Hurried feet ran by on the pavement. Ominous words blew in at the windows. Scared men rushed in with pallid, sweating faces, ate standing, and went out again. Other men sat listless, staring at the table before them, eating nothing – or here and there, apart in corners, whispered curses over their meat.

Chapter Thirty-Six

The news of the failures which convulsed the City on that Black Monday did not reach Aldersbury until late on the Tuesday – the tidings came in with the mails. But hours before that, and even before the opening of the bank, things in the town had come to a climax. The women, always more practical than the men and less squeamish, had taken fright and been talking. In many a back parlour in Maerdol, and the Foregate, and on the Cop, wives had spoken their minds. They wouldn't be scared out of asking for their own, by any banker that ever lived, they said. Not they! 'Would you, Mrs Gittins?' quoth one.

'Not I, ma'am, if I had it to ask for, as your goodman has. I'd not sleep another night before I had it tight and right.'

'No more he shall! What, rob his children for fear of a stuffy old man's black looks? But I'll see him into the bank myself, and see that he brings it out, too! I'll answer for that!'

'And you're in the right, ma'am, seeing it's yours. Money's not that easy got we're to be robbed of it. Now those notes with C.O. on them they're money anyways, I suppose? There's nothing can alter them, I'm thinking. I've two of them at home, that my lad—'

'Oh, Mrs Gittins!' And superior information raised its hands in horror. 'You understand nothing at all. Don't you know they're the worst of all? If those shutters – go – up at that bank,' dramatically, 'they'll not be worth the paper they're printed on! You take my advice and go this very minute and buy something at Purslow's or Bowdler's, and get them changed. And you'll thank me for that word, Mrs Gittins, as long as you live.'

Upset was not the word for Mrs Gittins, who had thought herself outside the fray. 'Well, they be thieves and liars!' she gasped. 'And Dean's too, ma'am? You don't mean to say—'

'I wouldn't answer even for them,' darkly. 'If you ask me, I'd let someone else have 'em, Mrs Gittins. Thank the Lord, I've none of them on my mind!'

And on that Mrs Gittins waddled away, and two minutes later stood in Purslow's shop, inwardly, 'all of a twitter,' but outwardly looking as if butter would not melt in her mouth. But, alas! Purslow's was out of change that day; and so, strange to say, was Bowdler's. Most unlucky – great scarcity of silver – Government's fault – should they book it? But Mrs Gittins, although she was all of a twitter, as she explained afterwards, was not so innocent as that, and got away without making her purchase.

Still, that was the way talk went, up and down Bride Hill and in Shocklatch, at front door and back door alike. And the men were not ill-content to be bidden. Some had passed a sleepless night, and had already made up their minds not to pass another. Others had had a nudge or a jog of the elbow from a knowing friend, and had been made as wise by a raised eyebrow as by an hour's sermon. Worse still, some had got hold of a story first set afloat at the Gullet – the Gullet was the ancient low-browed tavern in the passage by the Market Place, where punch flowed of a night, and the tradesmen of the town and some of their betters were in the habit of supping, as their fathers and grandfathers had supped before them. Arthur's departure, quickly followed by Clement's – after dark and in a post-chaise, mark you! – had not passed without comment; and a wiseacre had been found to explain it. At first he had confined himself to nods and winks, but being cornered and at the same time uplifted by liquor – for though the curious could taste saloop at the Gullet, Heathcote's ale was more to the taste of the habitués, when they did not run to punch – he had whispered a word, which had speedily passed round the circle and had not been slow to go beyond.

'Gone! Of course they're gone!' was the knowing one's verdict. 'And you'll see the old man will be gone, too, before morning, and the strong-box with him! Open? No, they'll not open? Never again, ten o'clock or no ten o'clock. Well, if you must have it, I got it from Wolley not an hour back. And he ought to know. Wasn't he hand in glove with them? Director of the – oh, the Railroad Shares? Waste paper! Never were worth more, my lad. If you put your money into that, it's on its way to London by this time!'

'And Boulogne tomorrow,' said another, going one better, as he knocked the ashes out of his pipe. 'I'm seventy-five down by them, and that's the worst and the best for me! Those that are in deeper, I'm sorry for them, but they've only themselves to thank! It's been plain this month past what was going to happen.'

One or two were tempted to ask him why he hadn't drawn out his seventy-five pounds, if he had been so sure. But they refrained, having a wambling, a sort of sick feeling in the pit of their stomachs. He was a rude, overbearing fellow, and there was no knowing what he might not bring out by way of retort.

The upshot of this and of a hundred other reports which ran about the town like wild-fire, was that a full twenty minutes before the bank opened on the Tuesday, its doors were the butt of a hundred eyes. Many, assembled by twos and threes, in the High Street and on the Market Place, awaited the hour; while others took up their stand in the dingy old Butter Cross a little above the bank, where day in and day out old crones sat knitting and the poultry women's baskets stood on market days. Few thought any longer of concealment; the time for that was past, the feeling of anxiety was too deep and too widespread. Men came together openly, spoke of their fears and cursed the banker, or nervously fingered their pass-books, and compared the packets of notes that they had with them.

Some watched the historic clock, but more watched, and more eagerly, the bank. The door, the opening of which, if it were ever opened, meant so much to so many, must have shrunk, seasoned wood as it was, under the intensity of the gaze fixed upon it, while the windows of the bank-house – ugh! the pretender, to set himself up after that fashion, while all the time he was robbing the poor! – were exposed to a fire as constant. Not a curtain moved or a blind was lowered, but the action was marked and analysed, deductions drawn from it, and arguments based upon it. That was Ovington's bedroom! No, that. And there was his girl at the lower window – but he would not have taken her with him in any case.

As a fact, had they been on the watch a little earlier, they would have been spared one anxiety. For about nine o'clock Ovington had disclosed his presence. He had left the house, crossed with a grave face to the Market Place, and rung the bell at Dean's. He had entered after a brief parley with an amazed manservant, had been admitted to see one of the partners, and at a cost to his pride, which only he could measure, the banker had stooped to ask for help. Between concerns doing business in the same town, relations must exist and transactions must pass even when they are in competition; and Dean's and Ovington's had been no exception to the rule. But the elder bank had never forgotten that they had once enjoyed a monopoly. They had neither abandoned their claims nor made any secret of their hostility, and Ovington knew that it was to the last degree unlikely that they would support him, even if they had the power to do so.

But he had convinced himself that it was his duty to make the attempt, however hopeless it might seem, and however painful to himself – and few things in his life had been more painful. To play the suppliant, he who had raised his head so high, and by virtue of an undoubted touch of genius had carried it so loftily, this was bad enough. But to play the suppliant to the very persons on whom he had trespassed, and whom he had defied, to open his distresses to those to whom he had pretended to teach a newer and sounder practice, to acknowledge in act, if not in word, that they had been right and he wrong, this indeed was enough to wring the proud man's heart, and bring the perspiration to his brow.

Yet he performed the task with the dignity, of which, as he had risen in the world, he had learned the trick, and which even at this moment did not desert him. 'I am going to be frank with you, Mr Dean,' he said when the door had closed on the servant and the two stood eye to eye. 'There is going, I fear, to be a run on me today, and unfortunately I have been disappointed in a sum of twelve thousand pounds, which I expected to receive. I do not need the whole, two-thirds of the sum will meet all the demands which are likely to be made upon me, and to cover that sum I can lodge undeniable security, bills with good names – I have a list here and you can examine it. I suggest, Mr Dean, that in your own interests as well as in mine you help me. For if I am compelled to close – and I cannot deny that I may have to close, though I trust for a short time only – it is certain that a very serious run will be made upon you.'

Mr Dean's eyes remained cold and unresponsive. 'We are prepared to meet it,' he answered frostily. 'We are not afraid.' He was a tall man, thin and dry, without a spark of imagination, or enterprise. A man whose view was limited to his ledger, and who if he had not inherited a business, would never have created one.

'You are aware that Poles' and Williams' have failed?'

'Yes. I believe that our information is up to date.'

'And that Garrard's at Hereford closed yesterday?'

'I am sorry to hear it.'

'The times are very serious, Mr Dean. Very serious.'

'We have foreseen that,' the other replied. They were both standing. 'The truth is, we are paying for a period of reckless trading, encouraged in my humble opinion, Mr Ovington' – he could not refrain from the stab – 'by those who should have restrained it.'

Ovington let that pass. He had too much at stake to retort. 'Possibly,' he said. 'Possibly. But we have now to deal with the present – as it exists. It is on public rather than on private grounds that I appeal to you, Mr Dean. A disaster threatens the community. I appeal to you to help me to avert it. As I have said, securities shall be placed in your hands, more than sufficient to cover the risk. Approved securities to your satisfaction.'

But the other shook his head. He was enjoying his triumph – a triumph beyond his hopes. 'What you suggest,' he said, a faint note of sarcasm in his tone, 'comes to this, Mr Ovington – that we pool resources? That is how I understand you?'

'Practically.'

'Well, I am afraid that in justice to our customers I must reply that we cannot do that. We must think of them first, and of ourselves next.'

Ovington took up his hat. The other's tone was coldly decisive. Still he made a last effort. 'Here is the list,' he said. 'Perhaps if you and your brother went over it at your leisure?'

But Dean waved the list away. 'It would be useless,' he said. 'Quite useless. We could not entertain the idea.' He was already anticipating the enjoyment with which he would tell his brother the news.

With a heavy heart, Ovington replaced the list in his breast pocket. 'Very good,' he said. His face was grave. 'I did not expect – to be frank – any other answer, Mr Dean. But I thought that it was my duty to see you. I regret your decision. Good-morning.'

'Good-morning,' the other banker replied, and he rang for his manservant.

'They're gone,' he reflected complacently, as the door closed behind his visitor. 'Smashed, begad!' and with the thought he rid himself of a sense of inferiority which had more than once troubled him in his rival's presence. He sat down to eat his breakfast with a good appetite. The day would be a trying one, but Dean's, at any rate, was safe. Dean's, thank God, had never put its hand out farther than it could draw it back. How pleased his brother would be!

That was the worst, immeasurably the worst, of Ovington's experiences, but it was not the only painful interview that was in store for him before the bank opened that morning. Twice, men, applying, stealthy and importunate, at the back door, forced their way in to him. They were not of those who had claims on the bank and feared to be losers by it. They were in debt to it, but desperate and pushed for money they saw in the bank's necessity their opportunity. They – one of the two was Purslow – required only small sums, and both had conceived the idea that, as the bank was about to fail, it would be all one to Ovington whether he obliged them or not. It would be but a hundred or so the less for the creditors, and as the bank had sold their pledged stocks they thought that it owed them something. They had still influence, their desperate straits were not yet known; if he obliged them they would do this and that and the other – nebulous things – for him.

Ovington, of course, could do nothing for them, but to harden his heart against their appeals was not a good preparation for the work before him, and when he entered the bank five minutes before ten, he had to brace himself in order to show an unmoved front to the clerks.

He need not have troubled himself. Rodd knew all, and the two lads, on their way to the bank that morning, had been badgered out of such powers of observation as they possessed. They had been followed, cornered, snatched in this direction and that, rudely questioned, even threatened. Were they going to open? Where was the gaffer? Was he gone? They had been wellnigh bothered out of their lives, and more than once had been roughly handled. It seemed as if all Aldersbury was against them – and they did not like it. But Ovington had the knack of attaching men to him, the lads were loyal, and they had returned only hard words to those who waylaid them. Pay? They could pay all the dirty money in Aldersbury! Mr Ovington? Well, they'd see. They'd see where he was, and be licking his boots in a week's time. And they'd better take their hands off them! The stouter even threatened fisticuffs. A little more and he'd give his questioners a lick over the chops. Come now, give over, or he'd show them a trick of Dutch Sam's they wouldn't like.

The two arrived at the bank, panting and indignant, their coats half off their backs; and Rodd, whose impeccable respectability no one had ventured to assail, had to say a few sharp words before they settled down and the counter assumed the calm and orderly aspect that, in his eyes, the occasion required. He was himself simmering with indignation, but he let no sign of it appear. He had made all his arrangements beforehand, seen every book in its place, and the cash where it could be handled – and a decent quantity, sufficient to impose on the vulgar – laid in sight. After a few words had been exchanged between him and Ovington, the latter retired to the desk behind the curtain, and the other three took their places. Nothing remained but to watch – the seniors with trepidation, the juniors with a not unpleasant excitement – the minute hand of the clock. It wanted three minutes of ten.

And already, though from their places behind the counter the clerks could not see it, the watching groups before the bank had grown into a crowd. It lined the opposite pavement, it hung a fringe two-deep on the steps of the Butter Cross, it extended into the Market Place, it stretched itself half-way down the hill. And it made itself heard. The voices of those who passed along the pavement, the scraps of talk half caught, the sudden exclamation, blended in a murmur not loud but continuous, and fraught with something of menace. Once, on the fringe of the gathering, there was an outburst of booing, but it ceased as suddenly as it had risen, suppressed by the more sober element. And once a hand tried the doors, a voice surprisingly loud, cried, 'They're fast enough!' and footsteps retreated across the pavement. The driver of a cart descending the hill called to 'Make way! Make way!' and that, too, reached those within almost as plainly as if it had been said in the room. Something, too, happened on it, for a shout of laughter followed.

It wanted two – it wanted one minute of ten. Rodd gave the order to open.

The younger clerk stepped forward and drew the bolts. He turned the key, and opened one leaf of the door. The other was thrust open from without. The clerk slid under the counter to his place. They came in.

They came in, three abreast, elbowing and pushing one another in their efforts to be first. In a moment they were at the counter, darting suspicious glances at the clerks and angry looks at one another, and with them entered an atmosphere of noise and contention, of trampling feet and peevish exclamations. The bank, so still a moment before, was filled with clamour. There were tradesmen among them, a little uncertain of themselves and thankful that Ovington was not visible, and one or two bluff red-faced farmers who cared for nobody, and slapped their books down on the counter; and there were also a few, of the better sort, who looked straight before them and endeavoured to see as little as possible – with a sprinkling of small fry, clerks and lodging-house keepers and a coal-hawker, each with his dirty note gripped tight in his fist. The foremost rapped on the counter and cried 'Here, Mister, I'm first!' 'No, I!' 'Here, you, please attend to me!' They pressed their claims rudely, while those in the rear uttered impatient remonstrances, holding their books or their notes over the heads of others in the attempt to gain attention. In a moment the bank was full – full to the doors, full of people, full of noise.

Rodd's cold eye travelled over them, measured them, weighed them. He was filled with an immense contempt for them, for their folly, their greed, their selfishness. He raised his hand for silence. 'This is not a cock-fight,' he said in a tone as withering as his eye. 'This is a bank. When you gentlemen have settled who comes first, I will attend to you.' And then, as the noise only broke out afresh and more loudly, 'Well, suppose I begin at the left hand,' he said. He passed to that end of the counter. 'Now, Mr Buffery, what can I do for you. Got your book?'

But Mr Buffery had not got his book, as Rodd had noticed. On that the cashier slowly drew from a shelf below the counter a large ledger, and, turning the leaves, began a methodical search for the account.

But this was too much for the patience of the man last on the right, who saw six before him, and had left no one to take care of his shop. 'But, see here,' he cried imperiously. 'Mr Rodd, I'm in a hurry! If that young man at the desk could attend to me I shouldn't take long.'

Rodd, keeping his place in the book with his finger, looked at him. 'Do you want to pay in, Mr Bevan?' he asked gravely.

'No. I want forty-two, seven, ten. Here's my cheque.'

'You want cash?'

'That's it.'

'Well, I'm the cashier in this bank. No one else pays cash. That's the rule of the bank. Now, Mr Buffery,' leisurely turning back to the page in the ledger, and running his finger down it. 'Thirty-five, two, six. That's right, is it?'

'That's right, sir.' Buffery knuckled his forehead gratefully.

'You've brought a cheque?'

But Buffery had not brought a cheque. Rodd shrugged his shoulders, called the senior clerk forward, and entrusted the customer, who was no

great scholar, to his care. Then he closed the ledger, returned it carefully
to the shelf, and turned methodically to the next in the line. 'Now, Mr
Medlicott, what do you want? Are you paying, or drawing?'

Mr Medlicott grinned, and sheepishly handed in a cheque. 'I'll draw
that,' he mumbled, perspiring freely, while from the crowd behind him,
shuffling their feet and breathing loudly, there rose a laugh. Rodd brought
out the ledger again, and verified the amount. 'Right,' he said presently,
and paid over the sum in Dean's notes and gold.

The man fingered the notes and hesitated. Rodd, about to pass to
the next customer, paused. 'Well, ain't they right?' he said. 'Dean's notes.
Anything the matter with them?'

The man took them without ado, and Rodd paid the next and the
next in the same currency, knowing that it would be remarked. 'I'll give
them a jog while I can,' he thought. 'They deserve it.' And, sure enough,
every note of that bank that he paid out was presented across the counter at
Dean's within the hour. It gave Mr Dean something to think about.

No one, in truth, could have done the work better than Rodd. He
was so cool, so precise, so certain of himself. Nothing put him out. He
plodded through his usual routine at his usual leisurely pace. He recked
nothing of the impatient shuffling crowd on the other side of the counter,
nothing of the greedy eyes that grudged every motion of his hand. They
might not have existed for him. He looked through them. A plodder, he
had no nerves. He was the right man in the right place.

At noon, taking with him a slip of paper, he went to report to
Ovington, who had retired to the parlour. They had paid out seventeen
hundred pounds in the two hours. At this rate they could go on for a long
time. There was only one large account in the room – should he call it up
and pay it? It might have a good effect.

Ovington agreed, and Rodd returned to the counter. His eye sought
out Mr Meredith. 'I don't know what you're doing here,' he said austerely.
'But I suppose your time is worth something. If you'll pass up your cheque
I'll let you go.'

The small fry clamoured, but Rodd looked through them. 'Eight
hundred and ten,' said Meredith with a sigh of relief, passing his cheque
over the heads of those before him. He was not ashamed of his balance,
but for the moment he was ashamed of himself. He began to suspect that
he had let himself be carried away with a lot of silly small chaps – yet his

fingers itched to hold the money.

Rodd confirmed the account, fluttered a packet of notes, counted them thrice and slowly, and tossed them to Mr Meredith. 'I make them right,' he said, 'but you'd better count them.' Then, to one or two who were muttering something about illegal preference, 'Bless your innocent hearts,' he said, 'you'll all be paid!' And he took the next in order as if nothing had happened.

It had its effect, and so had a thing that half an hour later broke the dreary monotony of paying out. A man at the back who had just pressed in – for the crowd, reinforced by new arrivals, was very nearly as large as at the hour of opening – raised his voice, complaining bitterly that he could not stay there all day, and that he wanted to pay in some money and go about his business.

There was a stir of surprise. A dozen turned to look at him.

'Good lord!' someone exclaimed.

Only Rodd was unmoved. 'Get a pay slip,' he said to the senior clerk, who had been pretty well employed filling in cheques for the illiterate and examining notes. 'Now, gentlemen, fair play. Let him pass through. Oh, it's Mr Walker, is it? How much, Mr Walker?'

'Two seven six, ten,' said Mr Walker, laying a heavy canvas bag on the counter. Rodd untied the neck of the bag and upset the contents, notes and gold, before him. He counted the money with professional deftness, whilst the clerk filled in the slip. 'How's your brother?' he asked.

'Pretty tidy.'

'And how are things in Wolverhampton?'

'So, so! But not so bad as they were.'

'Thank you. You're the only sensible man I've seen today, and we shall not forget it. Now, gentlemen, next please.'

Mr Walker was closely inspected as he pushed his way out, and one or two were tempted to say a word of warning to him, but thought better of it, and held their peace. About two in the afternoon a Mr Hope of Bretton again broke the chain of withdrawals. He paid in two hundred. Him a man did pluck by the sleeve, muttering, 'Have a care, man! Have a care what you're doing!' But Mr Hope, a bluff tradesman-looking person, only answered, 'Thank ye, but I am up to snuff. If you ask me I think you're a silly set of fools.'

News of him and of what he had said, and indeed of much more than he had said, ran quickly through the crowd that wondered and waited all day before the bank; that snapped up every rumour, and devoured the wildest inventions. The bank would close at one! It would close at three – the speaker had it on the best authority! It would close when so and so had been paid! Ovington, the rascal, had fled. He was in the bank, white as a sheet. He had attempted suicide. There was a warrant out for him. The crowd moved hither and thither, like the colours in a kaleidoscope. On its outer edges there was horse-play. Children chased one another up and down the Butter Cross steps, fell over the old women who knitted, were cuffed by the men, driven out by the Beadle – only to return again.

But under the trivialities there was tense excitement. Now and again a man who had been slow to take the alarm forced his way, pale and agitated, through the crowd, to vanish within the doors; or a countryman, whom the news had only just reached in his boosey-close or his rickyard – as they call a stackyard in Aldshire – rode up the hill, hot with haste and cursing those who blocked his road, flung his reins to the nearest bystander, and plunged into the bank as into water. And on the fringe, hiding themselves in doorways, or in the dark mouths of alleys, were men who stood biting their nails, heedless or unconscious of what passed about them; or who came staggering up from the Gullet with stammering tongues and eyes bloodshot with drink – men who a year before had been well-to-do, sober citizens, fathers of families.

All one to them now whether Ovington's stood or fell! They had lost their all, and to show for it and for all that they had ever been worth had but a few pieces of printed paper, certificates, or what not, which they took out and read in corners, as if something of hope might still, at the thousandth time of reading, be derived from them, or which they brandished aloft in the tavern with boasts of what they would have gained if trickery had not robbed them. So, though the crowd had its humours and was swept at times by gusts of laughter, the spectre of ruin stood, gaunt and bleak, in the background, and many a heart quailed before grim visions of bailiffs and forced sales and the workhouse – the workhouse, that in Aldersbury, where they were nothing if not genteel, they called the House of Industry.

And Ovington, as he sat over his books, or peered from time to time from a window, knew this, and felt it. He would not have been human if he had not thought with longing of that twelve thousand, the use of which had so nearly been his; ay, and with passing regret – for after all was not the greatest good for the greatest number sound morality? – of the self-denying ordinance which had robbed him of it. But harassed and heavy-hearted as he was, he remained master of himself, and his bearing was calm and dignified, when at a quarter to four, he showed himself, for the first time that day, in the bank.

It was still half-full, and the approach of closing time and the certainty that they could not all be paid that day, along with the fear that the doors would not open on the morrow, mightily inflamed those who were not in the front rank. They clamoured to be paid, brandishing their books or their notes. Some tried prayers, addressing Rodd by name, pleading their poverty or their services. Others reproached him for his slowness, and swore that it was purposeful. And they would not be still, they pushed and elbowed one another, rose on tiptoe and shuffled their feet, quarrelled among themselves.

Their voices filled the bank, passed beyond it, were heard in the street. Rodd worked on bravely, but the perspiration stood on his brow, while the clerks, flurried and nervous, looked now at the clock and now at the malcontents whose violence and restlessness seemed to treble their numbers.

Then it was that Ovington came in, and on the instant the noise died down, and there was silence. He advanced without speaking to within a few feet of the counter. He was cold, composed, upright, dignified. And still he did not speak. He surveyed his customers, his spectacles in his hand. His eyes took in each. At length, 'Gentlemen,' he said quietly, 'there is no need for this excitement. You will all be paid. We are short-handed today, but I had no reason to suppose that those who know me as well as most of you do know me – and there are some here who have known me all my life – would distrust me. However, as we are shorthanded, the bank will remain open today until half-past four. Mr Rodd, you will see, if you please, that the requirements of those now in the room are met. I need not add that the bank will open at the usual time tomorrow. Good-day, gentlemen.'

They raised a feeble cheer in their relief, and in the act of turning away, he paused. 'Mr Ricketts,' he said, singling out one, 'you are here about those bills? They are important. If you will bring them through to me – yes, if you please?'

The man whom he had addressed, a banker's clerk, followed him thankfully into the parlour. His uneasiness had been great, for, though he had not joined in his neighbours' threats, his employers' claim exceeded those of all the rest put together.

'We daren't wait, Mr Ovington,' he said apologetically. 'Our people want it. I take it, it is all right, sir?'

'Quite,' Ovington said. 'You have them here? What is the total?'

'Eighteen hundred and twenty-eight, six, eight, sir.'

Ovington examined the bills with a steady hand and wrote the amount on a slip of paper. He rang the bell, and the younger clerk came in. 'Bring me that,' he said 'as quickly as you can.' Then to his visitor, 'My compliments to Mr Allwood. Will you tell him that his assistance has been of material use to me, and that I shall not forget it? I was sorry to hear of Gibbons' failure.'

'Yes, sir. Very unfortunate. Very unfortunate, indeed!'

'He is no loser by them, I hope?'

'Well, he is, sir, I am sorry to say.'

'Ah, I am sorry.' And when the lad had brought in the money, and the account was settled, 'Are you returning tonight?'

'No, sir. My instructions were to travel by daylight.'

'Then you have an opportunity of stating outside, that you have been paid? I am anxious, of course, to stop this foolish run.'

The man said he would not fail to do so, and Ovington thanked him and saw him out by the private door. Then, taking with him certain books and the slips of paper that Rodd had sent in to him hour by hour, he went into the dining-room. Things were no worse than he had expected, but they were no better. Or, yes, they were, a few hundreds better.

Betty was there, awaiting him with an anxious face. She had had no slips to inform her from hour to hour how things went, and she had been too wise to intrude on her father. But many times she had looked from the windows on the scene before the bank, on the shifting crowd, the hasty arrivals, the groups that clung unwearied to the steps of the Butter Cross; and though poverty – she was young – had few terrors for her, she comprehended only too well what her father was suffering – ay, and, though it was a minor evil, what a blister to his pride was this gathering of his neighbours to witness his fall!

So, though she could have put on an appearance of cheerfulness, she felt that it would not accord with his mood, and instead, 'Well, Father,' she said, with loving anxiety, 'is it bad or good?' And, as he sank wearily into his chair, she passed her arm about his shoulders.

'Well,' he replied, with the sigh of a tired man, 'it is pretty much as we expected. I don't know, child, that it is better or worse. But Rodd will be here presently and he will tell us. He must be worn out, poor chap. He has borne the brunt of the day, and he has borne it famously. Famously! I offered to take his place at the dinner-hour but he would not have it. He has not left the counter for five minutes at a time, and he has shown splendid nerve.'

'Then you have not missed the others much?'

'No. We did not wish to pay out too quickly. Well – let us have some tea. Rodd will be glad of it. He has not tasted food since ten o'clock.'

'Did you go in, Father?'

'For a minute,' smiling, 'to scold them.'

'Oh, they are horrid!'

'No, they are just frightened. Frightened, child! We should do the same in their place.'

'No,' Betty said stoutly. 'I shouldn't! And I could never like anyone who did! Never!'

'Did what?'

'Took money from you when you wanted it so much! I think they're mean! Mean! And I shall never think anything else!' Betty's eyes sparkled, she was red with indignation. But the heat passed, and now she was paler than usual, she looked sad. Perhaps she had forgotten how things were, and now remembered; or perhaps – at any rate the glow faded and she was again the Betty of late days – a tired and depressed Betty.

She had seen to it that the fire was clear and the lamps burned brightly; had she not visited the room a dozen times to see to it? And now the curtains had been drawn, the tea-tray had come in, the kettle sang on the hob, the silver and china, reflecting the lights, twinkled a pleasant welcome to the tired man. Or they would have, if he could have believed that the comfort about him was permanent. But how long – the doubt tortured him – would it be his? How long could he ensure it for others? The waiting, anxious crowd, the scared faces, the clamorous customers, these were the things he saw, the things that blotted out the room and darkened the future. These were the only realities, the abiding, the menacing facts of life. He let his chin fall on his hand, and gazed moodily into the fire. A Napoleon of finance? Ay, but a Napoleon, crushed in the making, whose Waterloo had met him at Arcola!

He straightened himself when Rodd's step was heard in the passage, and he rose to take the last slip from the cashier's hand.

'Sit down, man, sit down,' he said. 'Betty, give Rodd a cup of tea. He must need it. Well?' putting on his glasses to consult the slip.

'We've paid out thirteen thousand two hundred and ten, sir.'

'Through one pair of hands! Well done! A fine feat, Rodd, and I shall not forget it. Umph!' thoughtfully, 'that is just about what we expected. Neither much better nor much worse. What we did not expect – but sit down and drink your tea, man. Betty!'

'Yes, Father.'

'Pass the toast to him. He deserves all we can do for him. What we did not expect,' reverting to the slip with a wrinkled brow, 'were the payments in. Four hundred and seventy odd! I don't understand that. No other sign of returning credit, Rodd? Was it someone we've obliged? Very unlikely, for long memories are rare at such times as these. Who was it?'

Rodd was busy with his toast. Betty had passed it to him with a polite smile. 'There were two, sir, I think,' he said. He spoke as if he were not quite certain.

The banker looked up in surprise. 'Think!' he said. 'Why, you must know.'

'Well, there were two, sir, I am sure. But paying out all day—'

'You'd remember who paid in, I should think. When there were but two. You must remember who they were.'

'One was from Wolverhampton, I know,' Rodd replied, 'Mr Watkins – or Walker.'

'Walker or Watkins? Of Wolverhampton? I don't remember any customer of that name. And the other? Who was he?'

'From somewhere Bretton way. I could look him up.'

The banker eyed Rodd closely. Had the day's work been too much for him? 'You could look him up?' he rejoined. 'Why, man, of course you could. Four hundred and seventy! A bank has failed before now for lack of less. All good notes, I suppose? No Gibbons' or Garrards', eh?' an idea striking him. 'But you'd see to that. If someone had the idea of washing his hands that way – and the two banks already closed!'

But Rodd shook his head. 'No, sir. It was in gold and Bank of England notes. I saw to that.'

'Then I don't understand it,' the banker decided. He sat pondering – the thing had taken hold of his mind. Was it a trick? Did they mean to draw out the amount next morning? But no, they would not risk the money, and he would stand no worse if they drew it. An enemy could not have done it, then. A friend? But such friends were rare and the sum was no trifle. The amount was more than he had received upon his plate, the proceeds of which had already gone into the cash-drawer. He pondered.

Meanwhile, 'Another cup of tea?' Betty said politely. And as Rodd, avoiding her eyes, handed her his cup, 'It's so nice to hear of strangers helping us,' she continued with treacherous sweetness. 'One feels so grateful to them.'

Rodd muttered something, his mouth full of toast.

'It's so fine of them to trust us, when they don't know how things are – as we do, of course. I think it is splendid of them,' Betty continued. 'Father, you must bring them to me, some day, when all these troubles are over – that I may thank them.'

But her father had risen to his feet. He was standing on the hearthrug, a queer look on his face. 'I think that they are here now,' he said. 'Rodd, why did you do it?'

The cashier started. 'I, sir? I don't think I—'

'Oh, you understand, man!' The banker was much moved. 'You understand very well. Walker of Wolverhampton? You've a brother at Wolverhampton, I remember, though I don't think I've ever seen him. This is your three hundred, and all you could add to it. My G–d, man—' Ovington was certainly moved, for he seldom swore, 'but if we go you'll lose it! You must draw it out before the bank opens tomorrow.'

'No,' said Rodd, who had turned red. 'I shall do nothing of the sort, sir. It's as safe there as anywhere. I'm not afraid.'

'But I don't understand,' Betty said, looking from one to the other. It couldn't be true. It could not be that she had made such a – a dreadful mistake!

'There's no Mr Walker,' her father explained, 'and no gentleman from Bretton. They are both Rodd. It's his money.'

'Do you mean—' in a very small voice. 'I thought that Mr Rodd took his money out!'

'Only to put it in again when he thought that it might help us more. But we can't have it. He mustn't lose his money, all I expect that he—'

'It came out of the bank,' Rodd said. 'And there's where it belongs, and I'm not going,' stubbornly, 'to take it out. I've been here ten years – very comfortable, sir. And if the bank closed where'd I be? It's my interest that it shouldn't close.'

The banker turned to the fire and put one foot on the fender as if to warm it. 'Well, let it stay,' he said, but his voice was unsteady. 'If we have to close you'll have done a silly thing – that's all; but if we don't, you'll not have been such a fool!'

'Oh, we shall not close,' Rodd boasted, and he gulped down his tea, his ears red.

There was an embarrassing silence. Ovington turned. 'Well, Betty,' he said, attempting a lighter tone. 'I thought that you were going to thank – Mr Walker of Wolverhampton?'

But Betty, murmuring something about an order for the servants, had already hurried from the room.

Chapter Thirty-Seven

That the Squire suffered was certain; whether he suffered more deeply in pocket or in pride, whether he felt more poignantly the loss of his hoarded thousands or the dishonour that Arthur had done to his name, even Josina could not say. His ruling passions through life had been pride of race and the desire to hoard, and it is certain that sorely wounded in both points he suffered as acutely as age with its indurated feelings can suffer. But after the first outburst, after the irrepressible cry of anguish which the discovery of his nephew's treachery had wrung from him, he buried himself in silence. He sat morose and unheeding, his hands clasping his stick, his sightless eyes staring at the fire. He gave no sign, and sought no sympathy. He was impenetrable. Even Josina could not guess what were his thoughts.

Nor did she try to learn. The misfortune was too great, the injury on one side beyond remedy, and the girl had the sense to see this. She hung over him, striving to anticipate his wishes and by mute signs of affection to give him what comfort she might. But she was too wise to trouble him with words or to attempt to administer directly to a mind which to her was a mystery, darkened by the veil of years that separated them.

She was sure of one thing, however, that he would not wish anything to be said in the house; and she said nothing. But she soon found that she must set a guard also on her looks. On the Tuesday Mrs Bourdillon 'looked in,' as it was her habit to look in three or four times a week. She had usually some errand to put forward, and her pretext on this occasion was the Squire's Christmas list. Near as he was, he thought much of old customs, and he would not for anything have omitted to brew a cask of October for his servants' Christmas drinking, or to issue the doles of beef to the men and of blankets to the women which had gone forth from the Great House since the reign of Queen Anne. Mrs Bourdillon was never unwilling to gain a little reflected credit, or to pay in that way for an hour's job-work, so that there were few years in which she did not contrive to graft a name or two on the list.

That was apparently her business this afternoon. But Josina, whose faculties were quickened by the pity which she felt for the unconscious mother, soon perceived that this was not her only or, indeed, her real motive. The visitor was not herself. She was nervous, the current of her small talk did not run with its usual freedom, she let her eyes wander, she broke off and began again. By and by as the strain increased she let her anxiety appear, and at last, 'I wish you would tell me,' she said, 'what is the matter with Arthur. He is not open with me,' raising her eyes with a piteous look to Josina's face. 'And – and he's something on his mind, I'm sure. I noticed it on Sunday, and I am sure you know. Is there' – and Josina saw with compassion that her mittened hands were trembling – 'is there anything – wrong?'

The girl had her answer ready, for she had already decided what she would say. 'I am afraid that they are anxious about the bank,' she said. 'There is what they call a "run" upon it.'

The explanation was serious enough, but, strange to say, Mrs Bourdillon looked relieved. 'Oh! And I suppose that they all have to be there?'

'Yes, I suppose so.'

'And that's all?'

'I am afraid that that is enough.'

'But – but you don't mean that there may be a – a failure?'

'I hope not. Indeed, I hope not. But people are so silly! They think that they can all have their money out at once. And of course,' Josina continued, speaking from a height of late-acquired knowledge, 'a bank lends its money out and cannot get it in again in a minute. But I've no doubt that it will be all right. Mr Ovington is very clever.'

Mrs Bourdillon sighed. 'That's bad,' she said. And she seemed to think it over. 'You know that all our money is in the bank now, Josina! I don't know what we should do if it were lost! I don't know what we should do!' But, all the same, Josina was clear that this was not the fear that her visitor had had in her mind when she entered the room. 'Nor why Arthur was so set upon putting it in,' the good lady continued. 'For goodness knows,' bridling, 'we were never in trade. Mr Bourdillon's grandfather – but that was in the West Indies and quite different. I never heard any one say it wasn't. So where Arthur got it from I am sure I don't know. And, oh dear, your father was so angry about it, he will never forgive us if it is lost.'

'I don't think that you need be afraid,' Josina said, as lightly as she could. 'It's not lost yet, you know. And of course we must not say a word to anyone. If people thought that we were afraid—'

'We? But I can't see' – Mrs Bourdillon spoke with sudden sharpness – 'what you have to do with it?'

Josina blushed. 'Of course we are all interested,' she said.

Mrs Bourdillon saw the blush. 'You haven't – you and Arthur haven't – made it up?' she ventured.

Josina shook her head.

'But why not? Now – now that he's in trouble, Josina?'

'I couldn't! I couldn't, indeed.'

The mother's face fell, and she sighed. She stared for awhile at the faded carpet. When she looked up again, the old anxiety peeped from her eyes. 'And you don't think that – that there's anything else?' she asked, as she prepared to rise.

'I am afraid that that is enough – to make them all anxious!'

But later, when the other was gone, Josina wondered. What had aroused the mother's misgivings? What had brought that look of alarm to her eyes? Arthur's sudden departure might have vexed her, but it could hardly have done more, unless he had dropped some hint, or she had other grounds for suspicion? But that was impossible, Josina decided. And she dismissed the thought.

She went slowly upstairs. After all she had troubles enough of her own. She had her father to think of – and Clement. They were her world, hemispheres which, though her whole happiness depended upon it, she could hardly hope to bring together, divided as they were by an ocean of prejudice. How her father now regarded Clement, whether his hatred of the name were in the slightest degree softened, whether under the blow which had stunned him, he thought of her lover at all, or remembered that it was he, and not Arthur, who had saved his life, she had no notion.

Alas! it would be but natural if the name of Ovington were more hateful to him than ever. He would attribute – she felt that he did attribute Arthur's fall to them. He had said that it was the poison of trade, their trade, their cursed trade, which had entered his veins, and, contaminating the honest Griffin blood, had destroyed him. It was they who had ruined him!

And then, as if the stain were not enough, it was from them again that it could not be hid. They knew of it, they must know of it. There must be interviews about it, dealings about it, dealings with them. They might feign horror of it, they who in the Squire's eyes were the real cause of it; they might hold up their hands at the fact and pity him! Pity him! If anything, anything, she was sure, could add to her father's mortification, it was that the Ovingtons were involved in the matter.

With every stair, the girl's heart sank lower. Once more in her father's room, she watched him. But she was careful not to let her solicitude appear, and though she was assiduous for his comfort and conduced to it by keeping Miss Peacock and the servants at a distance, she said almost as little to him as he to her. From time to time he sighed, but it was only when she reminded him that it was his hour for bed that he let a glimpse of his feelings appear.

'Ay,' he muttered, 'I'm better there! Better there, girl!' And with one hand on his stick and the other on his chair he raised himself up by his arms as old men do. 'I can hide my head there.'

She lent him her shoulder across the room and strove by the dumb show of her love to give him what comfort she might. But tears choked her and she thought with anguish that he was conquered. The unbreakable old man was broken. Shame and not the loss of his money had broken him.

It would not have surprised her had he kept his bed next day. But either there was still some spring of youth in him, or old age had hardened him, for he rose as usual, though the effort was apparent. He ate his breakfast in gloomy silence, and about an hour before noon he declared it his will to go out. Josina doubted if he was fit for it, but whatever the Squire willed his womenfolk accepted, and she offered to go with him. He would not have her, he would have Calamy – perhaps because Calamy knew nothing. 'Take me to the stable,' he said. And Josina thought 'He is going to see the old mare – to bid her farewell.'

It certainly was to his old favourite that he went, and he stood for some minutes in her box, feeling her ears and passing his hand between her forelegs to learn if she were properly cleaned; while the grey smelled delicately about his head, and nuzzled with her lips in his pockets.

'Ay,' said Calamy after a while, 'she were a trig thing in her time, but it's past. And what are the legs of a horse when it's a race wi' ruin?'

'What's that?' The Squire let his stick fall to the ground. 'What do you mean?' he asked, and straightened himself, resting his hand on the mare's withers.

'They be all trotting and cantering,' Calamy continued with zest, as he picked up the stick, 'trotting and cantering into town since morning, them as arn't galloping. They be covering all the roads wi' the splatter and sound of them. But I'm thinking they'll lose the race.'

'What do you mean?' the Squire growled. Something of his old asperity had come back to him.

'Mean, master? Why, that Ovington's got the shutters up, or as good. Their notes is no better than last year's leaves, I'm told. And all the country riding and spurring in on the chance of getting change for 'em before it's too late! Such-like fools I never see – as if the townsfolk will have left anything for them! Watkins o' the Griffin, he's three fi-pun notes of theirs, and he was away before it was light, and Blick the pig-killer and the overseer with him, in his tax-cart. And parson he's gone on his nag – trust parson for ever thinking o' the moth and rust except o' Sunday! They've tithe money of his. And the old maid as lives genteel in the villa at the far end o' the street, she've hired farmer Harris' cart – white as a sheet she was, I'm told! Wouldn't even stay to have the mud wiped off, and she so particular! And there's three more of 'em started to walk it. I'm told the road is black with them – weavers from the Valleys and their missuses, every sort of 'em with a note in his fist! There was two of them came here, wanted to see Mr Arthur – thought he could do something for 'em.'

'D—n Mr Arthur!' said the Squire. But inwardly he was thinking, 'There goes the last chance of my money! A drowning man don't think whether the branch he can reach is clean or dirty! But there never was a chance. That young chap came to bamboozle me and gain time, and that's their play.' Aloud, 'Give me my stick,' he said. 'Who told you – this rubbish?'

'Why, it's known at the Cross! The rooks be cawing it. Ovington is over to Bullon or some-such foreign place, these two days! And Dean he won't be long after him! They're talking of him, too. Ay, Parson should ha' thought of the poor instead of laying up where thieves break through and steal. But we're all things of a day!'

'Take me to the house,' said the Squire.

'Shadows as pass! Birds i' the smoke!' continued the irrepressible Calamy, smacking his lips with enjoyment. 'Leaves and the wind blows!'

Mr Arthur – but there, your honour knows best where the shoe pinches. Squire Acherley's gone through on his bay, and Parson Hoggins with him, and 'Where's that d—d young banker?' he asks. Thinks I, if the Squire heard you, you'd get a flip o' the tongue you wouldn't like! But he's a random-tandem talker as ever was! And' – halting abruptly – 'by gum, I expect here's another for Mr Arthur! There's someone drove up the drive now, and gone to the front door.'

'Take me in! Take me in!' said the Squire peevishly, his heart very bitter within him. For this was worse than anything that he had foreseen. His twelve thousand pounds was gone, but even that loss – monstrous, incredible, heart-breaking loss as it was – was not the worst. Ruin was abroad, stalking the countryside, driving rich and poor, the widow and the orphan to one bourne, and his name – his name through his nephew – would be linked with it, and dragged through the mire by it, no man so poor that he might not have a fling at it. He had held his head high, he had refused to stoop to such things, he had condemned others of his class, Woosenham and Acherley, and their like, because they had lowered themselves to the traffic of the market-place. But now – now, wherever men met and bragged of their losses and cursed their deluders, the talk would be of his nephew! His nephew! They might even say that he had had a share in it himself, and canvass and discuss him, and hint that he was not above robbing his neighbours – but only above owning to the robbery!

This was worse, far worse than the worst that he had foreseen when the lad had insisted on going his own way. Worse, far worse! Even his sense of Arthur's dishonour, even his remembrance of the vile, wicked, reckless act which the young man had committed, faded beside the prospect before him; beside the certainty that wherever, in shop or tavern, men cursed the name of Ovington, or spoke of those who had ruined the countryside, his name would come up and his share in the matter be debated.

Ay, he would be mixed up in it! He could not but be mixed up in it! His nephew! His nephew! He hung so heavily on Calamy's arm, that the servant for once held his tongue in alarm. They went into the house – the house that until now dishonour had never touched, though hard times had often straitened it, and more than once in the generations poverty had menaced it.

Chapter Thirty-Eight

But before they crossed the threshold they were intercepted. Miss Peacock, her plumage ruffled, and that which the Squire was wont to call her 'clack' working at high pressure, met them at the door. 'Bless me, sir, here's a visitor,' she proclaimed, 'at this hour! And won't take any denial, but will see you, whether or no. Though I told Jane to tell him—'

'Who is it?'

'Goodness knows, but it's not my fault, sir! I told Jane – but Jane's that feather-headed, like all of them, she never listens, and let him in, and he's in the dining-parlour. All she could say, the silly wench, was, it was something about the bank – great goggle-eyes as she is! And of course there's no one in the way when they're wanted. Calamy with you, and Josina trapesing out, feeding her turkeys. And Jane says the man's got a portmanteau with him as if he's come to stay. Goodness knows, there's no bed aired, and I'm sure I should have been told if—'

'Peace, woman!' said the Squire. 'Did he ask to see me, or—' with an effort, 'my nephew?'

'Oh, you, sir! Leastwise that's what Jane said, but she's no more head than a goose! To let him in when she knows that you're hardly out of your bed, and can't see every Jack Harry that comes!'

'I'll see him,' the Squire said heavily. He bade Calamy take him in.

'But you'll take your egg-flip, Mr Griffin? Before you—'

'Don't clack, woman, don't clack!' cried the Squire, and made a blow at her with his stick, but with no intention of reaching her. 'Begone! Begone!'

'But, dear sir, the doctor! You know he said—'

'D—n you, I'll not take it! D'you hear? I'll not take it! Get out!' And he went on through the house, the tap of his stick on the stone flags going before him and announcing his coming. Half-way along the passage he paused. 'Did she say,' he asked, lowering his voice, 'that he came from the bank?'

'Ay, ay,' Calamy said. 'And like enough. Ill news has many feet. Rides apace and needs no spurs. But if your honour will let me see him, I'll sort him! I'll sort him, I'll warrant! One'd think,' grumbling, 'they'd more sense than to come here about their dirty business as if we were the bank!' The man was surprised that his master took the matter with any patience, for, to him, with all the prejudices of the class he served, it seemed the height of impertinence to come to Garth about such business. 'Let me see him, your honour, and ask what he wants,' he urged.

But the Squire ruled otherwise. 'No,' he said wearily, 'I'll see him.' And he went in.

The front door stood open. 'There's a po-chay, right enough,' Calamy informed him. 'And luggage. Seems to ha' come some way, too.'

'Umph! Take me in. And tell me who it is. Then go.'

The butler opened the door, and guided the old man into the room. A glance informed him who the visitor was, but he continued to give all his attention to his master, in this way subtly conveying to the stranger that he was of so little importance as to be invisible. Nor until the Squire had reached the table and set his hand on it did Calamy open his mouth. Then, 'It's Mr Ovington,' he announced.

'Mr Ovington?'

'Ay, the young gentleman.'

'Ah!' The old man stood a moment, his hand on the table. Then, 'Put me in my chair,' he said. 'And go. Shut the door.'

And when the man had done so, 'Well!' heavily, 'what have you come to say? But you'd best sit. Sit down! So you didn't go to London? Thought better of it, eh, young man? Ay, I know! Talked to your father and saw things differently? And now you've come to give me another dose of fine words to keep me quiet till the shutters go up? And if the worst comes to the worst, your father's told you, I suppose, that I can't prosecute – family name, eh? That's what you've come for, I suppose?'

'No, sir,' Clement answered soberly. 'I've not come for that. And my father—'

The Squire struck his stick on the floor. 'I don't want to hear from him!' he cried with violence. 'I want no message from him, d'you hear? I'm not come down to that! And as for your excuses, young gentleman—'

'I am not come with any excuses,' Clement answered, restraining himself with difficulty – but after all the old man had had provocation enough to justify many hard words, and he was blind besides. As he sat there, glaring sightlessly before him, his hands on his stick, he was a pathetic figure in his anger and helplessness. 'I've been to town, as I said I would.'

The Squire was silent for some seconds. 'And come back?' he exclaimed.

'Well, yes, sir,' with a smile. 'I'm here.'

'Umph? How did you do it?'

'I posted up and came down as far as Birmingham by the Bull and Mouth coach. I posted on this morning.'

'Well, you've been devilish quick!' The Squire admitted it reluctantly. He hardly knew whether to believe the tale or not. 'You didn't wait long there, that's certain. And did as little, I suppose. Bank's going, I hear?'

'I hope not.'

'Pooh!' the Squire said impatiently. 'You may speak out! Speak out, man! There is no one here.'

'There's some danger, I'm afraid,' Clement admitted.

'Danger! I should think there was! More than danger, as I hear!' The Squire drummed for a moment with his fingers on the table. He was thinking not of the bank, or even of his loss, but of his nephew and the scandal that would not pass by him. But he would not refer to Arthur, and after a pause, 'Well,' with an angry snort, 'if that's all you've come to tell me, you might ha' spared yourself – and me. I cannot say that your company's very welcome, so if you please, we'll dispense with compliments. If that's all—'

'But that's not all, sir,' Clement interposed. 'I wish I could have brought back the securities, or even the whole of the money.'

The Squire laughed. 'No doubt,' he said.

'But I was too late to ensure that. The stock had already been transferred.'

'So he was quick, too!'

'And selling for cash in the middle of such a crisis he had to accept a loss of seven per cent on the current price. But he suggests that if you reinvest immediately, a half, at least, of this may be recovered, and the eventual loss need not be more than three or four hundred. I ought perhaps to have stayed in town to effect this, but I had to think of my father, who was alone at the bank. However, I did what I could, sir, and—'

Clement paused; the Squire had uttered an exclamation which he did not catch. The old man turned a little in his chair so as to face the speaker. 'Eh?' he said. 'Do you mean that you've got the money, any of the money – here?'

'I've eleven thousand and a bit over,' Clement explained. 'Five thousand in gold and the rest—'

'What?'

'Sir?'

'Do you mean' – the Squire spoke haltingly, after a pause; he did not seem to be able to find the right words. 'Do you mean that you've brought back the money?'

'Not all. What I've told you, sir. There's six thousand and odd in notes. The gold is in two bags in the chaise.'

'Here?'

'At the door, sir. I'll bring it in.'

'Ay,' said the Squire passively. 'Bring it in.' Clement went out and returned, carrying in two small leather bags. He set them down at the Squire's feet. 'There's the gold, sir,' he said. 'I've not counted it, but I've no doubt that it is right. It weighs a little short of a hundred pounds.'

The old man felt the bags, then, standing up, he lifted them in turn a few inches from the floor. 'What does a thousand pounds weigh?' he asked.

'Between eighteen and nineteen pounds, sir.'

'And the notes?'

'I have them here.' Clement drew a thick packet from the pocket of his inner vest and put it into the Squire's hands. 'They're Bank of England paper. They were short even at the bank, and wanted Bourdillon to take it in one-pound notes, but he stood out and got these in the end.'

The Squire handled the packet, felt its thickness, weighed it lovingly in his hand. So much money, so much money in so small a space! Six thousand and odd pounds! It seemed as if he could not let it go, but in the end he placed it in the breast pocket of his high-collared old coat, the shabby blue coat with the large gilt buttons that was his common wear at home.

The money secured, he sat, looking before him, while Clement, a little mortified, waited for the word of acknowledgment that did not come. At last,

'Did you call at your father's?' the old man asked – irrelevantly, it seemed.

Clement coloured. He had not expected the question. 'Well, I did, sir,' he admitted. 'Bourdillon—'

'He was with you?'

'As far as the town. He was anxious that the money should be seen to arrive. He thought that it might check the run, and I agreed that it might do some good, and that we might make that advantage of it. So I took it through the bank.'

'Pretty full, I expect, eh? Pretty full?'

'Well,' ruefully, 'it was, sir.'

'A strong run, eh?'

'I'm afraid so. It looked like it. It was full to the doors. That's why,' glancing at his watch as he stood by the window, the table between him and the Squire, 'I must get back to my father. We took it through the bank and out by the garden, and put it in the chaise again in Roushill.'

'Umph! He came back to town with you?'

'Bourdillon, sir? Yes – as far as the East Bridge. He left me there.'

'Where is he?'

Clement hesitated. 'I hope that he's gone to the bank, sir,' he said.

He did not add, as he might have, that, after Arthur and he had left the coach at Birmingham and posted on, there had been a passionate scene between them. No doubt Arthur had never given up hope, but from the first had determined to make another fight for it; and there was no police officer at their elbows now. He had appealed to Clement by all that he loved to take the money to the bank, and there to deal with it as his father should decide.

Finding Clement firm and his appeals useless, he had given way to passion, he had stormed and threatened and even shed tears; and at last, seizing the pistol case that lay at their feet, he had sworn that he would shoot himself before the other's eyes if he did not give way. In his rage he had seemed to be capable of anything, and there had been a struggle for the pistol, blows had been exchanged, and worse might have come of it if the noise of the fracas had not reached the post-boy's ears. He had pulled up, turned in his saddle, and asked what the devil they would be at; he would have no murder in his master's carriage.

That had shamed them. Arthur had given way, had flung himself back, white and sullen, in his corner, and they had continued the journey on such terms as may be imagined. But even so, Arthur had proved his singular power of adaptation. The environs of the town in sight, he had suggested that at least they should take the money through the bank. Clement, anxious to make peace, had consented to that, and on the East Bridge Arthur had called on the post-boy to stop, had jumped out, and, turning his back on his companion, had made off without a word.

Clement said nothing of this to the Squire, though the scene had been painful, and though he felt that something was due to him, were it but a word of thanks, or an expression of acknowledgment. It had not been his fault or his father's, that the money had been taken; it was through him that the greater part of it had been recovered, and now reposed safe in the Squire's pocket and in the bags at his feet.

At the least, it seemed to him, the old man might remember that his father was alone and needing him – was facing trouble, and, it might be, ruin. He took up his hat. 'Well, sir, that's all,' he said curtly. 'I must go now.'

'Wait!' said the Squire. 'And ring the bell, if you please.'

Clement stepped to the fireside and pulled the faded drab cord, which once had been blue, that hung near it. The bell in the passage had hardly tinkled before Calamy entered. 'Bid your mistress come here,' said the old man. 'Where is she? Fetch her?'

The blood mounted to Clement's face, and his pulses began to throb, his ideas to tumble over one another. The old man, who sat before him, his hands on his stick, stubbornly confronting the darkness, the old man, whom he had thought insensible, took on another hue, became instead inscrutable, puzzling, perplexing. Why had he sent for his daughter? What was in his mind? What was he going to say? What had he – but even while Clement wondered, his thoughts in a whirl, strange hopes jostling one another in his brain, the door opened, and Josina came in.

She came in with a timid step, but as soon as her eyes met Clement's, the colour rose vividly to her cheeks, then left her pale. Her lip trembled. But her look, fleeting as it was and immediately diverted to her father – how he blessed her for that look! For it bade him take confidence, it bade him have no fear, it bade him trust her. Silently and incredibly, it took him under her protection, it pledged her faith to him.

And how it changed all for him! How it quelled, in a moment, the disappointment and anger he was feeling, ay, and even the vague hopes which the Squire's action in summoning her had roused in him! How it gave calmness and assurance where his aspirations had been at best to the extravagant and the impossible.

But, whatever his feelings, to whatever lover's heaven that look raised him, he was speedily brought to earth again. The old man had proved himself thankless; now, as if he were determined to show himself in the worst light, he proceeded to prove himself suspicious.

'Come here, girl,' he said, 'and count these notes.' Fumbling, he took the parcel from his pocket and handed it to her. 'Ha' you got them? Then count them! D'you hear, wench? Count them! And have a care to make no mistake! Lay 'em in piles o' ten. They are hundreds, are they? Hundreds, eh?'

She untied the parcel, and brought all her faculties to bear on the task, though her fingers trembled, and the colour, rising and ebbing in her cheeks, betrayed her consciousness that her lover's eyes were upon her. 'Yes, sir, they are hundred-pound notes,' she said.

'All?'

'Yes, all, I think, sir.'

'Bank of England?' He poked at her skirts with his stick. 'Bank of England, eh? Are you sure?'

'Yes, sir, so far as I can see.'

'Ay, ay. Well, count 'em! And mind what you are doing, girl!'

Clement did not know whether to smile or to be angry, but a moment later he felt no bent towards either. For with a certain dignity, 'I ha' been deceived once,' the Squire continued. 'I ha' signed once and paid for it. I'm in the dark. But I don't act i' the dark again. If I can't trust my own flesh and blood, I'll not trust strangers. No, no! I don't know as there's any one I can trust.'

'I quite understand, sir,' Clement said – though it was the last thing he had had in his mind to say a moment earlier.

'I don't mind whether you understand or not,' the Squire retorted. 'Ha' you done, girl?' after an interval of silence.

'Not quite, sir. I have five heaps of ten.'

'Well, well, get on. We are keeping the young man.'

He spoke as he would have spoken of any young man in a shop, and Clement winced, and Josina knew that he winced and she reddened. But she went on with her work. 'There are sixty-one,' she said. 'That makes—'

'Six thousand one hundred pounds. Ay, it's right so far. Right so far. And the gold' – he paused and seemed to be at a nonplus – 'I'm afraid 'twould take too long to count it. Well, let it be. Get some paper and write a receipt as I tell you.'

'There is no need, sir,' Clement ventured.

'There's every need, young man. I'm doing business. Ha' you got the pen, girl? Then write as I tell you. "I, George Griffin of Garth, in the County of Aldshire, acknowledge that I have this 16th day of December 1825 received from Messrs. Ovington, of Aldersbury, six thousand one hundred pound in Bank of England notes, and " – ha' you got that? Ha' you got that? – "two bags stated by them to contain five thousand pounds in gold." Ha' you got that down? Then show me the place, and—'

But as she put the pen in his hand he let it drop. He sat back in his chair. 'Ay, he showed me the place before,' he muttered, his chin on his breast. 'It was he gave me the pen, then, girl. And how be I to know? How be I to know?'

It came home to them – to them both. In his voice, his act, his attitude was the pathos of blindness, its helplessness, its dependence, its reliance on others – on the eyes, the hand, the honesty of others. The girl leant over him. 'Father,' she said, tears in her voice, 'I wouldn't deceive you! You know I wouldn't. I would never deceive you.'

'Ha' you never deceived me? Wi' that young man?' sternly.

'But—'

'Ay, you have! You have deceived me – with him.'

She could not defend herself, and, suppressing her sobs, 'I will call Calamy,' she said. 'He can read. He shall count the notes.'

But he put out his hand and grasped her skirts. 'No,' he said. 'What'll I be the better? Give me the pen. If you deceive me in this, wench – what matter if the notes be short or not, or what comes of it?'

'I would cut off my hand first!' she cried. 'And Clement—'

'Eh?' He sat up sharply.

She was frightened, and she did not continue. 'This is the place, sir,' she said meekly.

'Here?'

'Yes, sir, where you are now.'

He wrote his name. 'Dry it,' he said. 'And ring the bell. And there, give it to him. He wants to be off. Odds are the shutters 'll be up afore he gets there. Calamy!' to the man who had appeared at the door, 'see this gentleman off, and be quick about it. He's no time to lose. And, hark you, come back to me when he's gone. No, girl,' sternly, 'you stay here. I want you.'

Chapter Thirty-Nine

In ordinary times, news is slow to make its way to the ears of the great. Protected from the vulgar by his deer park, looking out from the stillness of his tall-windowed library on his plantations and his ornamental water, Sir Charles Woosenham was removed by six miles of fine champaign country from the common fret and fume of Aldersbury. He no longer maintained, as his forefathers had maintained, a house in the town, and in all likelihood he would not have heard the talk about the bank, or caught the alarm in time, if one of his neighbours had not made it his business to arouse him.

Acherley, baffled in his attempt at blackmail, and thirsting for revenge, had bethought him of the Chairman of the Valleys Railroad. He had been quick to see that he could use him, and perhaps he had even fancied that it was his duty to use him. At any rate, one fine morning, some days before this eventful Wednesday, he had mounted his old hunter, Nimrod, and had cantered across country by gaps and gates from Acherley to Woosenham Park. He had entered by a hunting wicket, and leaping the ha-ha, he had presented himself to Sir Charles ten minutes after the latter had left the breakfast table, and withdrawn himself after his fashion of a morning, into a dignified seclusion.

Alas, two minutes of Acherley's conversation proved enough to destroy the baronet's complacency for the day. Acherley blurted out his news, neither sparing oaths nor mincing matters. 'Ovington's going!' he declared. 'He's bust-up – smashed, man!' And striking the table with a violence that made his host wince, 'He's bust-up, I tell you,' he repeated, 'and I think you ought to know it! There's ten thousand of the Company's money in his hands, and if there's nothing done, it will be lost to a penny!'

Sir Charles stared, stared aghast. 'You don't say so?' he exclaimed. 'I can't believe it!'

'Well, it's true! True, man, true, as you'll soon find out!'

'But this is terrible! Terrible!'

Acherley shrugged his shoulders. 'It'll be terrible for him,' he sneered.

'But – but what can we do?' the other asked, recovering from his surprise. 'If it is as bad as you say—'

'Bad? And do, man? Why, get the money out! Get it out before it is too late – if it isn't too late already. You must draw it out, Woosenham! At once! This morning! Without the delay of a minute!'

'I!' Sir Charles could not conceal the unhappiness which the proposal caused him. No proposal, indeed, could have been less to his taste. He would have to make up his mind, he would have to act, he would have to set himself against others, he would have to engage in a vulgar struggle. A long vista of misery and discomfort opened before him. 'I? Oh, but—' and with the ingenuity of a weak man he snatched at the first formal difficulty that occurred to him – 'but I can't draw it out! It needs another signature besides mine.'

'The Secretary's? Bourdillon's? Of course it does! But you must get his signature. D—n it, man, you must get it. If I were you I should go into town this minute. I wouldn't lose an hour!'

Sir Charles winced afresh at the idea of taking action so strong. He had not only a great distaste for any violent step, but he had also the feelings of a gentleman. To take on himself such a responsibility as was now suggested was bad; but to confront Ovington, who had gained no slight influence over him, and to tell the banker to his face that he distrusted his stability – good heavens, was it possible that such horrors could be asked of him? Flustered and dismayed, he went back to his original standpoint. 'But – but there may be nothing in this,' he objected weakly. 'Possibly nothing at all. Mere gossip, my dear sir,' with dignity. 'In that case we might be putting ourselves in the wrong – very much in the wrong.'

Acherley did not take the trouble to hide his contempt. 'Nothing in it?' he replied, and he tossed off a second glass of the famous Woosenham cherry-brandy which the butler, unbidden, had placed beside him. 'Nothing in it, man? You'll find there's the devil in it unless you act! Enough in it to ease us of ten thousand pounds! If the bank fails, and I'll go bail it will, not a penny of that money will you see again! And I tell you fair, the shareholders will look to you, Woosenham, to make it good. I'm not responsible. I've no authority to sign, and the others are just tools of that

man Ovington, and afraid to call their souls their own! You're Chairman
– you're Chairman, and, by G–d, they'll look to you if the money is left in
the bank and lost!'

Sir Charles quailed. This was worse and worse! Worse and worse! He
dropped the air of carelessness which he had affected to assume, and no
more flustered man than he looked out on the world that day over a white
lawn stock or wore a dark blue coat with gilt buttons, and drab kerseymeres
with Hessians. But, again, true to his instincts, he grasped at a matter of
form, hoping desperately that it might save him from the precipice towards
which his friend was so vigorously pushing him. 'But – my good man,'
he argued, 'I can't draw out the money – the whole of the capital of the
concern, so far as it is subscribed – on my own responsibility! Of course I
can't!' wiping the perspiration from his brow. 'Of course I can't!' peevishly.
'I must have the authority of the Board first. We must call a meeting of the
Board. That's the proper procedure.'

Acherley rose to his feet, openly contemptuous. 'Oh, hang your
meeting!' he said. 'And give a seven days' notice, eh? If you are going
to stand on those P's and Q's I've said my say. The money's lost already!
However, that's not my business, and I've warned you. I've warned you.
You'll not forget that, Woosenham? You'll exonerate me, at any rate.'

'But I can't – God bless my soul, Acherley,' the poor man remonstrated,
'I can't act like that in a moment!' And Sir Charles stared aghast at his too
violent associate, who had brought into the calm of his life so rude a blast
of the outer air. 'I can't override all the formalities! I can't, indeed, even if
it is as serious as you say it is – and I can hardly believe that, with such a
man as Ovington at the helm!'

'You'll soon see how serious it is!' the other retorted. And satisfied
that he had laid the train, he shrugged his shoulders, tossed off a third
glass of the famous cherry-brandy, and took himself off without much
ceremony.

He left a flustered, nervous, unhappy man behind him. 'Good G–d!'
the baronet muttered, as he rose and paced his library, all the peace and
pleasantness of his life shattered. 'What's to be done? And why – why in
the world did I ever put my hand to this matter!' One by one, and plainly,
all the difficulties of the position rose before him, the awkwardness and
the risk. He must open the thing to Bourdillon – in itself a delicate matter
– and obtain his signature. If he got that, he doubted if he had even then

power to draw the whole amount in this way, and doubted, too, whether Ovington would surrender it, no meeting of the Board having been held? And if he obtained the money, what was he to do with it? Pay it into Dean's? But if things were as bad as Acherley said, was even Dean's safe? For, of a certainty, if he removed the money to Dean's and it were lost, he would be responsible for every penny – every penny of it! There was no doubt about that.

Yet if he left it at Ovington's and it were lost, what then? It was not his custom to drink of a morning, but his perturbation was so great that he took a glass of the cherry-brandy. He really needed it.

He could not tell what to do. In every direction he saw some doubt or some difficulty arise to harass him. He was no man of business. In all matters connected with the Company he had leant on Ovington, and deprived of his stay, he wavered, turning like a weathercock in the wind, making no progress.

For two days, though terribly uneasy in his mind, he halted between two opinions. He did nothing. Then tidings began to come to his ears, low murmurs of the storm which was raging afar off; and he wrote to Bourdillon asking him to come out and see him – he thought that he could broach the matter more easily on his own ground. But two days elapsed, during which he received no answer, and in the meantime the warnings that reached him grew louder and more disquieting. His valet let drop a discreet word while shaving him. A neighbour hoped that he had nothing in Ovington's – things were in a bad way, he heard. His butler asked leave to go to town to cash a note. Gradually he was wrought up to such a pitch of uneasiness that he could not sleep for thinking of the ten thousand pounds, and the things that would be said of him, and the figure that he would cut if, after Acherley's warning, the money were lost. When Wednesday morning came, he made up his mind to take advice, and he could think of no one on whose wisdom he could depend more surely than on the old Squire's at Garth; though, to be sure, to apply to him was, considering his attitude towards the Railroad, to eat humble pie.

Still, he made up his mind to that course, and at eleven he took my lady's landau and postilions, and started on his sixteen-mile drive to Garth. He avoided the town, though it lay only a little out of his way, but he saw enough of the unusual concourse on the road to add to his alarm. Once, nervous and fidgety, he was on the point of giving the order to turn the horses' heads for Aldersbury – he would go direct to the bank and see Ovington! But before he spoke he changed his mind again, and half-past twelve saw him wheeling off the main road and cantering, with some pomp and much cracking of whips, up the rough ascent that led to Garth.

He was so far in luck that he found the Squire not only at home, but standing before the door, a gaunt, stooping figure, leaning on his stick, with Calamy at his elbow. 'Who is it?' the old man asked, as he caught the sound of galloping hoofs and the roll of the wheels. He turned his sightless eyes in the direction of the approaching carriage.

'I think it's Sir Charles, sir,' Calamy answered. 'It's his jackets.'

'Ay! Well, I won't go in, unless need be. Go you to the stables and bid 'em wait.'

Sir Charles alighted, and bidding the postilions draw off, greeted his host. 'I want your advice, Squire,' he said, putting his arm through the old man's, and, after a few ceremonial words, he drew him a few paces from the door. It was a clear, mild day, and the sun was shining pleasantly. 'I'm in a position of difficulty, Griffin,' he said. 'You'll tell me, I know, that I've only myself to thank for it, and perhaps that is so. But that does not mend matters. The position, you see, is this.' And with many apologies and some shamefacedness he explained the situation.

The Squire listened with gloomy looks, and, beyond grunting from time to time in a manner far from cheering, he did not interrupt his visitor. 'Of course I ought not to have touched the matter,' the baronet confessed, when he had finished his story. 'I know what you think about that, Griffin.'

'Of course you ought not!' The Squire struck his stick on the gravel. 'I warned you, man, and you wouldn't take the warning. You wouldn't listen to me. Why, damme, Woosenham, if *we* do these things, if we once begin to go on 'Change' and sell and buy, where'll you draw the line? Where'll you draw the line? How are you going to shut out the tinkers and tailors and Brummagem and Manchester men when you make yourselves no better than them! How? By Jove, you may as well give 'em all votes at once, and in ten years' time we shall have bagmen on the Bench and Jews in the House! Aldshire – we've kept up the fence pretty well in Aldshire, and kept our hands pretty clean, too, and it's been my pride and my father's to belong to this County. We're pure blood here. We've kept ourselves to ourselves, begad! But once begin this kind of thing—'

'I know, Griffin, I know,' Woosenham admitted meekly. 'You were right and I was wrong, Squire. But the thing is done, and what am I to do now? If I stand by and this money is lost—'

'Ay, ay! You'll have dropped us all into a pretty scalding pot, then!'

'Just so, just so.' The baronet had pleaded guilty, but he was growing restive under the other's scolding, and he plucked up spirit. 'Granted. But, after all, your nephew's in the concern, Griffin. He's in it, too, you know, and—'

He stopped, shocked by the effect of his words. For the old man had withdrawn his arm and had stepped back, trembling in all his limbs. 'Not with my good will!' he cried, and he struck his stick with violence on the ground. 'Never, never!' he repeated, passionately. 'But you are right,' bitterly, 'you are right, Woosenham. The taint is in the air, the taint of the City and the 'Change, and we cannot escape it even here – even here in this house! In the concern? Ay, he is! And I tell you I wish to heaven that he had been in his grave first!'

The other, a kindly man, was seriously concerned. 'Oh, come, Squire,' he said; and he took the old man affectionately by the arm. 'It's no such matter as all that. You make too much of it. He's young, and the younger generation look at these things differently. After all, there's more to be said for him than for me.'

The Squire groaned.

'And, anyway, my old friend,' Woosenham continued gently, 'advise me. Time presses.' He looked at his watch. 'What shall I do? What had I better do? I know I am safe in your hands.'

The Squire sighed, but the other's confidence was soothing, and with the sigh he put off his own trouble. He reflected, his face turned to the ground at his feet. 'Do you think him honest?' he asked, after a pause.

'Who? Ovington?'

'Ay,' gloomily. 'Ovington? The banker there.'

'Well, I do think he is. Yes, I do think so. I've no reason to think otherwise.'

'He's a director, ain't he?'

'Of the Railroad? Yes.'

'Responsible as you are?'

'Yes, I suppose he is!'

'A kind of trustee, then, ain't he – for the shareholders.'

Sir Charles had not seen it in that light before. He looked at his adviser with growing respect. 'Well, I take it he is – now you mention it, Griffin,' he said.

'Then' – this, it was plain, was the verdict, and the other listened with all his ears – 'if he is honest, he'll not have mixed the money with his own. He'll not have put it to an ordinary account, but to a Trust account – so that it will remain the property of the Company, and not be liable to calls on him. That's what he should have done, anyway. Whether he has done it or not is another matter. He's pressed, hard pressed, I hear, and I don't know that we can expect the last spit of honesty from such as him. It's not what I've been brought up to expect. But,' with a return of his former bitterness, 'we may be changing places with 'em even in that! God knows! And I do know something that gives me to believe that he may behave as he should.'

'You do?' Sir Charles exclaimed, his spirits rising. 'You do think so?'

'Well, I do,' reluctantly. 'I'll speak as I know. But if I were you I should go to him now and tell him, as one man to another, that that's what you expect; and if he hangs back, tell him plain that if that money's not put aside he'll have to answer to the law for it. Whether that will frighten him or not,' the Squire concluded, 'I'm not lawyer enough to say. But you'll learn his mind.'

'I'll go in at once,' Sir Charles replied, thankfully.

'I'm going into town myself. If you'll take me in – you've four horses – it will save time, and my people shall fetch me out in an hour or so.'

Sir Charles assented with gratitude, thankful for his support; and Calamy was summoned. Two minutes later they got away from the door in a splutter of flying gravel and dead beech leaves. They clattered down the stony avenue, over the bridge, and into the high road.

Probably of all those – and they were many – who travelled that day with their faces set towards the bank, they were the last to start. If Tuesday had been the town's day, this was certainly the country's day. For one thing, there was a market; for another, the news of something amiss, of something that threatened the little hoard of each – the slowly-garnered deposit or the hardly-won note – had journeyed by this time far and wide. It had reached alike the remote flannel-mill lapped in the folds of the border-hills, and the secluded hamlet buried amid orchards, and traceable on the landscape only by the grey tower of its church. On foot and on horse-back, riding and tying, in gigs and ass-carts, in market vans and carriers' carts; the countryside came in – all who had anything to lose, and many who had nothing at stake, but were moved by a vague alarm. Even before daybreak the roads had begun to echo the sound of their marching. They came by the East Bridge, labouring up the steep, winding Cop; by the West Bridge and under the gabled fronts of Maerdol; along the river bank, before the house of the old sea-dog whose name was a household word, and whose portrait hung behind the mayor's chair, and so up the Foregate – from every quarter they came. Before ten the streets were teeming with country-folk, whose fears were not allayed by the news that all through the previous day the townsfolk had been drawing their money. Sullen tradesmen, victims of the general depression, eyed the march from their shop doors, and some, fearing trouble, put up half their shutters. More took a malicious amusement in telling the rustics that they were too late, and that the bank would not open.

The alarm was heightened by a chance word which had fallen from Frederick Welsh. The lawyer's last thought had been to do harm, for his interest in common with all substantial men lay the other way. But that morning, before he had dressed, or so much as shaved, his office and even his dining-room had been invaded. Scared clients had overwhelmed him with questions – some that he could answer and more that he could not. He could tell them the law as to their securities, whether they were lodged for safety, or pawned for loans, or mortgaged on general account. But he could not tell them whether Ovington was solvent, or whether the bank would open, or whether Dean's was affected; and it was for answers to these questions that they clamoured. In the end, badgered out of all patience, he had delivered a curt lecture on banking.

'Look here, gentlemen,' he had said, imposing silence from his hearthrug and pressing his points with wagging forefinger, 'do you know what happens when you pay a thousand pounds into a bank? No, you don't? Well, I'll tell you. They put a hundred pounds into the till, and they lend out four thousand pounds on the strength of the other nine hundred. If they lend more than that, or lend that without security, they go beyond legitimate banking. Now you know as much as I do. A banker's money is out on bills payable in two months or four, it's out on the security of shares and farms and shop-stock, it's lent on securities that cannot be realised in five minutes. But it's all there, mark me, somewhere, in something, gentlemen, and I tell you candidly that it's my opinion that if you would all go home and wait for your money till you need it, you'd all get it in full, twenty shillings in the pound.'

He meant no harm, but unfortunately the men who heard the lecture paid no heed to the latter part, but went out, impressed with the former, and spread it broad-cast. On which some cried, 'That's banking, is it! Shameful, I call it!' while others said, 'Well, I call it robbery! The old tea-pot for me after this!' A few were for moving off at once and breaking Ovington's windows, and going on to Dean's and serving them the same. But they were restrained, things had not quite come to that; and it was an orderly if excited throng that once more waited on Bride Hill and in the Market Place for the opening of the doors.

Not all who gathered there had anything to lose. Many were mere onlookers. But here and there were to be seen compressed lips, pale faces, anxious eyes. Here and there women gripped books in feverish fingers or squeezed handkerchiefs into tight balls; and now and again a man broke into bad words and muttered what he would do if they robbed him. There were country shopkeepers who had lodged the money to meet the traveller's account, and trembled for its safety. There were girls who saw their hard-earned portions at stake, and parsons whose hearts ached as they thought of the invalid wife or the boy's school-bill; and there were at least a score who knew that if the blow fell the bailiff, never far from the threshold, would be in the house. Before the eyes of not a few rose the spectres of the poorhouse and a pauper funeral.

Standing in groups or dotted amid the crowd were bigger men – wool-brokers and cattle-dealers – men loud in bar-parlours and great among their fellows, whose rubicund faces showed flabby and mottled, and whose fleshy lips moved in endless calculations. How was this bill to be met, and who would renew that one? Too often the end of their calculations spelled ruin – if the bank failed. Ruin – and many were they who depended on these big men: wage-earners, clerks, creditors, poor relations! One man walking up and down under the arcade of the Market House was the centre for many eyes. He was an auctioneer from a neighbouring town, a man of wide dealings, who, it was whispered, had lodged with Ovington's the proceeds of his last great sale – a sum running into thousands and due every penny to the vendor.

His case and other hard cases were whispered by one to another, and, bruited about, they roused the passions even of those who were not involved. Yet when the bank at length opened on the stroke of ten an odd thing happened. A sigh, swelling to a murmur, rose from the dense crowd, but no one moved. The expected came as the unexpected, there was a moment of suspense, of waiting. No one advanced. Then someone raised a shout and there was a rush for the entrance; men struggled and women were thrust aside, smaller men were borne in on the arms of their fellows. A wail rose from the unsuccessful, but no man heeded it, or waited for his neighbour, or looked aside to see who it was who strove and thrust and struggled at his elbow. They pushed in tumultuously, their country boots drumming on the boards. Their entrance was like the inrush of an invading army.

The clerks, the cashier, Ovington himself, stood at the counter waiting motionless to receive them, confronting them with what courage they might. But the strain of the preceding day had told. The clerks could not conceal their misgivings, and even Rodd failed to bear himself with the chilling air which had yesterday abashed the modest. He shot vindictive glances across the counter, his will was still good to wither, but the crowd was today made up of rougher material, was more brusque and less subservient. They cared nothing for him, and he looked, in spite of his efforts, weary and dispirited. There was no longer any pretence that things were normal or that the bank was not face to face with a crisis. The gloves were off. They were no longer banker and customers. They were enemies.

It was Ovington himself who this morning stood forward, and in a few cold words informed his friends that they would all be paid, requesting them at the same time to be good enough to keep order and await their turns, otherwise it would be impossible to proceed with the business. He added a single sentence, in which he expressed his regret that those who had known him so long should doubt, as he could only suppose that they did doubt, his ability to meet his engagements.

It was well done, with calmness and dignity, but as he ceased to speak – his appearance had for the moment imposed silence – a disturbance broke out near the door. A man thrust himself in. Ovington, already in the act of turning, recognised the newcomer, and a keen observer might have noted that his face, grave before, turned a shade paler. But he met the blow. 'Is that Mr Yapp?' he asked.

It was the auctioneer from Iron Ferry. 'Ay, Mr Ovington, it is,' he said, the perspiration on his face, 'and you know my position.'

Ovington nodded. Yapp was one of five depositors – big men – whose claims had been, for the last twenty-four hours, a nightmare to him. But he let nothing be seen, and 'Kindly let Mr Yapp pass,' he said; 'I will deal with him myself.' Then, as one or two murmured and protested, 'Gentlemen,' he said sternly, 'you must let me conduct my business in my own way, or I close my doors. Let Mr Yapp pass, if you please.'

They let him through then, some grumbling, others patting him on the back – 'Good luck to you, Jimmy!' cried one well-wisher. The counter was raised and resettling his clothes about him, the auctioneer followed Mr Ovington into the parlour. The banker closed the door upon them.

'How much is it, Mr Yapp?' he asked.

The man's hand shook as he drew out the receipt. 'Two thousand, seven hundred and forty,' he said. 'I hope to God it's all right, sir?' His voice shook. 'It's not my money, and to lose it would three parts ruin me.'

'You need not fear,' the banker assured him. 'The money is here.' But for a moment he did not continue. He stood, his eyes on the man's face, lost in thought. Then, 'The money is here, and you can have it, Yapp,' he said. 'But I am going to be plain with you. You will do me the greatest possible favour if you will leave it for a few days. The bank is solvent – I give you my honour it is. No one will lose a penny by it in the end. But if this and other large sums are drawn today I may have to close for a time, and the injury to me will be very great. If you wish to make a friend who may be able to return the favour tenfold—'

But Yapp shook his head. 'I daren't do it!' he declared, the sweat springing out anew on his face. 'It isn't my money and I can't leave it! I daren't do it, sir!'

Ovington saw that it was of no use to plead further, and he changed his tone. 'Very good,' he said, and he forced himself to speak equably. 'I quite understand. You shall have the money.' Sitting down at the table he wrote the amount on a slip, and struck the bell that stood beside his desk. The younger clerk came in. He handed him the slip.

Yapp did not waver, but he remembered that good turns had been done to him in that room, and he was troubled. 'If it was my money,' he said awkwardly, 'or if there was anything else I could do, Mr Ovington?'

'You can,' Ovington replied. He had got himself in hand, and he spoke cheerfully.

'Well—'

'You can hold your tongue, Yapp,' smiling.

'It's done, sir. I won't have a tongue except to say that the money's paid. You may depend upon me.'

'Thank you. I shall not forget it.' The clerk brought in the money, and stayed until the sum was counted and checked and the receipt given. 'That's right, Mr Yapp,' the banker said, and sat back in his chair. 'Show Mr Yapp out, Williams.'

Yapp followed the clerk. His appearance in the bank was greeted by half a dozen voices. 'Ha' you got it?' they cried.

He was a man of his word, and he slapped his pocket briskly. 'Every penny!' he said, and something like a cheer went up. 'I'd not have worried, but it wasn't my money.'

Ovington's appeal to him had been a forlorn hope, and much, now it had failed, did the banker regret it. But he had calculated that that twenty-seven hundred pounds might just make the difference, and he had been tempted. Left to himself he sat, turning it over, and wondering if the auctioneer would be silent; and his face, now that the mask was off, was haggard and careworn. He had slept little the night before, and things were working out as he had feared that they would.

Presently he heard a disturbance in the bank. Something had occurred to break the orderly course of paying out. He rose and went out, a frown on his face. He was prepared for trouble, but he found to his relief that the interruption was caused by nothing worse than his son's return.

Having given his word to Arthur to carry the money through the bank, Clement had sunk whatever scruples he felt, and had made up his mind to do it handsomely. He had driven up to the door with a flourish, had taken the gold from the chaise under the public eye, and now, with all the parade he could, he was bringing it into the bank. His brisk entrance and cheery presence, and the careless words he flung on this side and that as he pushed through the crowd, seemed in a trice to clear the air and lift the depression. Not even Arthur could have carried the thing through more easily or more flamboyantly. And that was saying much.

'Make way! Make way, if you please, gentlemen!' he cried, his face ruddy with the sharp, wintry air. 'Let me in, please! Now, if you want to be paid, you must let the money come through! Plenty of money! Plenty for all of you, gentlemen, and more where this comes from! But you must let me get by! Hallo, Rawlins, is that you? You're good at dead weights. Here, lift it! What do you make of it?' And he thrust the bag he carried into a stout farmer's hands.

'Well, it be pretty near fifty pund, I'd say,' Rawlins replied. 'Though, by gum, it don't look within a third of it, Mr Clement.'

Clement laughed. 'Well done!' he said. 'You're just about right. And you can say after this, Rawlins, that you've lifted fifty pound weight of gold! Now, make way, gentlemen, make way, if you please. There's more to come in! Plenty more!'

He bustled through with the bag, greeted his father gaily, and placed his burden on the floor beside him. Then he went back for the other bag. He made a second countryman weigh this, grinned at his face of astonishment, then taking up the two bags he went through with his father to the parlour.

His arrival did good. The clerks perked up, smiled at one another, went to and fro more briskly. Rodd braced himself and, though he knew the truth, began to put on airs, bandied words with a client, and called contemptuously for order. And the customers looked sheepish. Gold! Gold coming in like that in bags as if 'twere common stuff. It made them think twice. A few, balancing in their minds a small possible loss against the banker's certain favour, hesitated and hung back. Two or three even went out without cashing their notes and shrugged their shoulders in the street, declaring that the whole thing was nonsense. They had been bamboozled. They had been hoaxed. The bank was sound enough.

But behind the parlour door things wore a different aspect.

Chapter Forty

The banker looked at the money lying at his feet. Clement looked at his father. He noted the elder man's despondent attitude, he read the lines which anxiety had deepened on his brow, and his assumed gaiety fell from him. He longed to say something that might comfort the other, but *mauvaise honte* and the reserve of years were too much for him, and instead he rapidly and succinctly told his tale, running over what had happened in London and on the road. He accounted for what he had brought, and explained why he had brought it and at whose request. Then, as the banker, lost in troubled thought, his eyes on the money, did not speak, 'It goes badly then, sir, does it?' he said. 'I see that the place is full.'

Ovington's eyes were still on the bags, and though he forced himself to speak, his tone was dull and mechanical. 'Yes,' he said. 'We paid out fifteen thousand and odd yesterday. About six thousand in odd sums today. I have just settled with Yapp – two thousand seven hundred. Mills and Blakeway have drawn at the counter – three thousand and fifty between them. A packet of notes from Birmingham, eleven hundred. Jenkins sent his cheque for twelve hundred by his son, but he omitted to fill in the date.'

'And you didn't pay it?'

'No, I didn't pay it. Why should I? But he will be in himself by the two o'clock coach. The only other account – large account outstanding – is Owen's for eighteen hundred. Probably he will come in by the same coach. In the meantime' – he took a slip of paper from the table – 'we have notes for rather more than two thousand still out; half of these may not, for one reason or another, be presented. And payable on demand we still owe something like two or three thousand.'

'You may be called upon for another six thousand, then, sir?'

'Six at best, seven thousand or a little more at worst. And we had in the till to meet it, a quarter of an hour ago, about three thousand. We should not have had as much if Rodd had not paid in four hundred and fifty.'

'Rodd?' Clement's eyes sparkled. 'God bless him! He's a Trojan, and I shan't forget it! Bravo, Rodd!'

The banker nodded, but in a perfunctory way. 'That's the position,' he said. 'If Owen and Jenkins hold off – but there's no hope of that – we may go on till four o'clock. But if either comes in we must close. Close,' bitterly, 'for the lack of three thousand or four thousand pounds!'

Clement sighed. Young as he was he was beginning to feel the effect of his exertions, of his double journey, and his two sleepless nights. At last, 'No one will lose, sir?' he said.

'No, no one, ultimately and directly, by us. And if we were an old bank, if we were Dean's even' – there was venom in the tone in which he uttered his rival's name '– we might resume in a week or a fortnight. We might reopen and go on. But,' shrugging his shoulders, 'we are not Dean's, and no one would trust us after this. It would be useless to resume. And, of course, the sacrifices that we have made have been very costly. We have had to re-discount bills at fifteen per cent, and sell a long line of securities at a loss, and what is left on our hands may be worth money some day, but it is worthless at present.'

'Wolley's Mill?'

'Ay, and other things. Other things.'

Clement looked at the floor, and again the longing to say something or do something that might comfort his father pressed upon him. To himself the catastrophe, save so far as it separated him from Josina, was a small thing. He had had no experience of poverty, he was young, and to begin the world at the bottom had no terrors for him. But with his father it was different, and he knew that it was different. His father had built up from nothing the edifice that now cracked and crumbled about them. He had planned it, he had seen it rise and grow, he had rejoiced in it and been proud of it. On it he had spent the force and the energy of the best twenty years of his life, and he had not now, he had no longer, the vigour or the strength to set about rebuilding.

It was a tragedy, and Clement saw that it was a tragedy. And all for the lack – pity rose strong within him – all for the lack of – four thousand pounds. To him, conversant with the bank's transactions, it seemed a small sum. It was a small sum.

'Ay, four thousand!' his father repeated. His eyes returned mechanically to the money at his feet, returned and fixed themselves upon it. 'Though in a month we may be able to raise twice as much again! And here – here' – touching it with his foot – 'is the money! All, and more than all that we need, Clement.'

Then at last Clement perceived the direction of his father's gaze, and he took the alarm. He put aside his reserve, he laid his hand gently on the elder man's shoulder, and by the pressure of his silent caress he strove to recall him to himself, he strove to prove to him that whatever happened, whatever befell, they were one – father and son, united inseparably by fortune. But aloud, 'No!' he said firmly. 'Not that, sir! I have given my word. And besides—'

'He would be no loser.'

'No, we should be the losers.'

'But – but it was not we, it was Bourdillon, lad!'

'Ay, it was Bourdillon. And we are not Bourdillons! Not yet! Nor ever, sir!'

Ovington turned away. His hand shook, the papers that he affected to put together on his desk rustled in his grasp. He knew – knew well that his son was right. But how great was the temptation! There lay the money at his feet, and he was sure that he could not be called to account for it. There lay the money that would gain the necessary time, that would meet all claims, that would save the bank!

True, it was not his, but how great was the temptation. It was so great that what might have happened had Clement not been there, had he stood there alone and unfettered, it is impossible to say – though the man was honest. For it was easy, nothing was more easy, than to argue that the bank would be saved and no man, not even the Squire, would lose. It was so great a temptation, and the lower course appeared so plausible that four men out of five, men of average honesty and good faith, might have fallen.

Fortunately the habit of business integrity came to the rescue, and reinforced and supported the son's argument – and the battle was won. 'You are right,' the banker said huskily, his face still averted, his hands trembling among the papers. 'But take it away! For God's sake, boy, take it away! Take it out of my sight, or I do not know what I may do!'

'You'll do the right thing, sir, never fear!' the son answered confidently.

And with an effort he lifted the two heavy bags and moved towards the door. But on the threshold and as the door closed behind him, 'Thank God!' he whispered to himself, 'Thank God!' And to Betty, who met him in the hall and flung her arms about his neck – the girl was in tears, for the shadow of anxiety hung over the whole house, and even the panic-stricken maids were listening on the stairs or peering from the windows – 'Take care of him, Betty,' he said, his eyes shining. 'Take care of him, girl. I shall be back by one o'clock. If I could stay with him now I would, but I cannot. I cannot! And don't fret. It will come right yet!'

'Oh, poor father!' she cried. 'Is there no hope, Clement?'

'Very little. But worse things have happened. And we may be proud of him, Betty. We've good cause to be proud of him. I say it that know! Cheer up!'

She watched him go with his heavy burden and his blunt common-sense down the garden walk; and when he had disappeared behind the pear-tree espaliers she went back to listen outside the parlour door. She had been her father's pet. He had treated her with an indulgence and a familiarity rare in those days of parental strictness, and she understood him well, better than others, better even than Clement. She knew what failure would mean to him. It was not the loss of wealth which would wound him most sorely, though he would feel that; but the loss of the position which success had gained for him in the little world in which he lived, and lived somewhat aloof. He had been thought, and he had thought himself, cleverer than his neighbours. He had borne himself as one belonging to, and destined for, a wider sphere. He had met the pride of the better-born and the older-established with a greater pride; and believing in his star, he had allowed his contempt for others and his superiority to be a little too clearly seen.

For all this he would now pay, and his pride would suffer. Betty, lingering in the darker part of the hall, where the servants could not spy on her, listened and longed to go in to him and comfort him. But all the rules forbade this, she might not distract him at such a time. Yet, had she known how deep was his depression as he sat sunk in his chair, had she known how the past mocked him, and the long chain of his successes rose and derided him, how the mirage of long-cherished hopes melted and left all cold before him – had she guessed the full bitterness of his spirit, she had broken through every rule and gone in to him.

The self-made man! Proudly, disdainfully he had flung the taunt back in men's faces. Could they make, could they have made themselves, as he had? And now the self-ruined man! He sat thinking of it, and the minutes went by. Twice one of the clerks came in and silently placed a slip beside him and went softly out. He looked at the slip, but without taking in its meaning. What did it matter whether a few more or a few less pounds had been drawn out, whether the drain had waxed or waned in the last quarter of an hour? The end was certain, and it would come when the two men arrived on the Chester coach. Then he would have to bestir himself. Then he would have to resume the lead and play the man, give back hardness for hardness, and scorn for scorn, and so bear himself in defeat that no man should pity him. And he knew that he could do it. He knew that when the time came his voice would be firm and his face would be granite, and that he would pronounce his own sentence and declare the bank closed with a high head. He knew that even in defeat he could so clothe himself with power that no man should browbeat him.

But in the meantime he paid his debt to weakness, and sat brooding on the past, rather than preparing for the future; and time passed, the relentless hand moved round the clock. Twice the clerk came in with his doom-bearing slips, and presently Rodd appeared. But the cashier had nothing to say that the banker did not know. Ovington took the paper and looked at the figures and at the total, but all he said was, 'Let me know when Owen and Jenkins come.'

'Very good, sir.' Rodd lingered a moment as if he would gladly have added something, would have ventured, perhaps, some word of sympathy. But his courage failed him and he went out.

Nor when Clement, half an hour afterwards, returned from his mission to Garth did he give any sign. Clement laid his hand on his shoulder and said a cheery word, but, getting no answer, or as good as none, he went through to his desk. A moment later his voice could be heard rallying a too conscious customer, greeting another with contemptuous good humour, bringing into the close, heated atmosphere of the bank, where men breathed heavily, snapped at one another, and shuffled their feet, a gust of freer brisker air.

Another half-hour passed. A clerk brought in a slip. The banker looked at it. No more than seven hundred pounds remained in the till. 'Very good,' he said. 'Let me know when Mr Owen and Mr Jenkins come.'

And as the door closed behind the lad he fell back into his old posture of depression. There was nothing to be done.

But five minutes later Clement looked in, his face concerned. 'Sir Charles Woosenham is here,' he said in a low voice. 'He is asking for you.'

The banker roused himself. The call was not unexpected nor quite unwelcome. 'Show him in,' he said, and he took up a pen and drew a sheet of paper towards him that he might appear to be employing himself.

Sir Charles came in, tall, stooping a little, his curly-brimmed hat in his hand; the dignified bearing with which he was wont to fence himself against the roughness of the outer world a little less noticeable than usual. He was a gentleman, and he did not like his errand.

Ovington rose. 'Good morning, Sir Charles,' he said, 'you wanted to see me? I am unfortunately busy this morning, but I can give you ten minutes. What is it, may I ask?' He pushed a chair toward his visitor.

But Woosenham would not sit down. If the man was down he hated to – but, there, he had come to do it. 'I am sure it is all right, Mr Ovington,' he said awkwardly, 'but I am concerned about the – about the Railway money, in fact. The sum is large, and – and—' stammering a little – 'but I think you will understand my position?'

The banker smiled. 'You wish to know if it's safe?' he said.

'Well, yes – precisely,' with relief. 'You'll forgive me, I am sure. But people are talking.'

'They are doing more,' Ovington answered austerely – he no longer smiled. 'They are doing their best to ruin me, Sir Charles, and to plunge themselves into loss. But I need not go into that. You are anxious about the Railroad money? Very good.' He rang the bell and the clerk came in. 'Go to the strong-room,' the banker said, taking some keys from the table, 'with Mr Clement, and bring me the box with the Railway Trust.'

'I am sorry,' Sir Charles said, when they were alone, 'to trouble you at this time, but—'

Ovington stopped him. 'You are perfectly in order,' he said. 'Indeed, I am glad you have come. The box will be here in a minute.'

Clement brought it in, and Ovington took another key and unlocked it. 'It is all here,' he explained, 'except the small sum already expended in preliminary costs – the sum passed, as you will remember, at the last meeting of the Board. Here it is.' He took a paper which lay on the top of the contents of the box. 'Except four hundred and ten pounds, ten shillings.

The rest is invested in Treasury Bills until required. The bills are here, and Clement will check them with you, Sir Charles, while I finish this letter. We have, of course, treated this as a Trust Fund, and I think that the better course will be for you to affix your seal to the box when you have verified the contents.'

He turned to his letter, though it may be doubted whether he knew what he was writing, while Sir Charles and Clement went through the box, verified the securities, and finally sealed the box. That done, Woosenham would have offered fresh apologies, but the banker waved them aside and bowed him out, directing Clement to see him to the door.

That done, left alone once more, he sat thinking. The incident had roused him and he felt the better for it. He had been able to assert himself, and he had confirmed in goodwill a man who might yet be of use to him. But he was not left alone very long. Sir Charles had not been gone five minutes before Rodd thrust a pale face in at the door, and in an agitated whisper informed him that Owen and Jenkins were coming down the High Street. A scout whom the cashier had sent out had seen them and run ahead with the news. 'They'll be here in two minutes, sir,' Rodd added in a tone which betrayed his dismay. 'What am I to do? Will you see them, sir?'

'Certainly,' Ovington answered. 'Show them in as soon as they arrive.'

He spoke firmly, and made a brave show in Rodd's eyes. But he knew that up to this moment he had retained a grain of hope, a feeling, vague and baseless, that something might yet happen, something might yet occur at the last moment to save the bank. Well, it had not, and he must steel himself to face the worst. The crisis had come and he must meet it like a man. He rose from his chair and stood waiting, a little paler than usual, but composed and master of himself.

He heard the disturbance that the arrival of the two men caused in the bank. Someone spoke in a harsh and peremptory tone, and something like an altercation followed. Raised voices reached him, and Rodd's answer, civil and propitiatory, came, imperfectly, to his ear. The peremptory voice rose anew, louder than before, and the banker's face grew hard as he listened. Did they think to browbeat him? Did they think to bully him? If so, he would soon – but they were coming. He caught the sound of the counter as Rodd raised it for the visitors to pass, and the advance of feet, slowly moving across the floor. He fixed his eyes on the door, all the manhood in him called up to meet the occasion.

The door was thrown open, widely open, but for a moment the banker could not see who stood in the shadow of the doorway. Two men, certainly, and Rodd at their elbow, hovering behind them; and they must be Owen and Jenkins, though Rodd, to be sure, should have had the sense to send in one at a time. Then it broke upon the banker that they were not Owen and Jenkins. They were bigger men, differently dressed, of another class; and he stared. For the taller of the two, advancing slowly on the other's arm, and feeling his way with his stick, was Squire Griffin, and his companion was no other than Sir Charles, mysteriously come back again.

Prepared for that which he had foreseen, Ovington was unprepared for this, and the old man, still feeling on his unguarded side with his stick, was the first to speak. 'Give me a chair,' he grunted. 'Is he here, Woosenham?'

'Yes,' Woosenham said, 'Mr Ovington is here.'

'Then let me sit down.' And as Sir Charles let him down with care into the chair which the astonished banker hastened to push forward, 'Umph!' he muttered, as he settled himself and uncovered his head. 'Tell my man' – this to Rodd – 'to bring in that stuff when I send for it. Do you hear? You there? Tell him to bring it in when I bid him.' Then he turned himself to the banker, who all this time had not found a word to say, and indeed had not a notion what was coming. He could only suppose that the Squire had somehow revived Woosenham's fears, in which case he should certainly, Squire or no Squire, hear some home truths. 'You're surprised to see me?' the old man said.

'Well, I am, Mr Griffin. Yes.'

'Ay,' drily. 'Well, I am surprised myself, if it comes to that. I didn't think to be ever in this room again. But here I am, none the less. And come on business.'

The banker's eyes grew hard. 'If it is about the Railroad moneys,' he said, 'and Sir Charles is not satisfied—'

'It's none of his business. Naught to do with the Railroad,' the Squire answered. Then sharply, 'Where's my nephew? Is he here?'

'No, he is not at the bank today.'

'No? Well, he never should ha' been! And so I told him and told you. But you would both have your own way, and you know what's come of it.

Hallo!' breaking off suddenly, and turning his head, for his hearing was still good. 'What's that? Ain't we alone?'

'One moment,' Ovington said. Rodd had tapped at the door and put in his head.

The cashier looked at the banker, over the visitors' heads. 'Mr Owen and Mr Jenkins are here,' he said in a low tone. 'They wish to see you. I said you were engaged, sir, but—' his face made the rest of the sentence clear.

Ovington reddened, but retained his presence of mind. 'They can see me in ten minutes,' he said, coldly. 'Tell them so.'

But Rodd only came a little farther into the room. 'I am afraid,' he said, dropping his voice, 'they won't wait, sir. They are—'

'Wait?' The word came from the Squire. He shot it out so suddenly that the cashier started. 'Wait? Why, hang their infernal impudence,' wrathfully, 'do they think their business must come before everybody's? Jenkins? Is that little Jenkins – Tom Jenkins of the Hollies?'

'Yes, sir.'

'Then d—n his impudence!' the old man burst forth again in a voice that must have wellnigh reached the street. 'Little Tom Jenkins, whose grandfather was my foot-boy, coming and interrupting my business! God bless my soul and body, the world is turned upside-down nowadays. Fine times we live in! Little – but, hark you, sirrah, d'you go and tell him to go to the devil! And shut the door, man! Shut the door!'

'Tell them I will see them in ten minutes,' said the banker.

But the old man was still unappeased. 'That's what we're coming to, is it?' he fumed. 'Confound their impudence,' wiping his brow, 'and they've put me out, too! I dunno where I was. Is the door closed? Oh, 'bout my nephew! I didn't wish it, I've said that, and I've said it often, but he's in. He's in with you, banker, and he's lugged me in! For, loth as I am to see him in it, I'm still lother that any one o' my name or my blood should be pointed at as the man that's lost the countryside their money! Trade's bad, out of its place. But trade that fails at other folks' cost and ruins a sight of people who, true or false, will say they've been swindled—'

'Stop!' the banker could bear it no longer, and he stepped forward, his face pale. 'No one has swindled here! No one has been robbed of his money. No one – if it will relieve your feelings to know it, Mr Griffin – will lose by the bank in the end. I shall pay all demands within a few months at most.'

'Can you pay 'em all today?' asked the Squire, at his driest.

'It may be that I cannot. But every man to whom the bank owes a penny will receive twenty shillings in the pound and interest, within a few weeks – or months.'

'And who will be the loser, then, if the bank closes? Who'll lose, man?'

'The bank. No one else.'

'But you can't pay 'em today, banker?'

'That may be.'

'How much will clear you? To pay 'em all down on the nail,' truculently, 'and tell 'em all to go and be hanged? Eh? How much do you need for that?'

Ovington opened his mouth, but for a moment, overpowered by the emotions that set his temples throbbing, he could not speak. He stared at the gaunt, stooping figure in the chair – the stooping figure in the shabby old riding-coat with the huge plated buttons that had weathered a dozen winters – and though hope sprang up in him, he doubted. The man might be playing with him. Or, he might not mean what he seemed to mean. There might be some mistake. At last, 'Five thousand pounds would pull us through,' he said in a voice that sounded strange to himself, 'as it turns out.'

'You'd better take ten,' the Squire answered. 'There,' fumbling in his inner pocket and extracting with effort a thick packet, 'count five out of that. And there's five in gold that my man will bring in. D'you give me a note for ten thousand at six months – five per cent.'

'Mr Griffin—'

'There, no words!' testily. 'It ain't for you I'm doing it, man. Understand that! It ain't for you. It's for my name and my nephew, little as he deserves it! Count it out, count it out, and give me back the balance, and let's be done with it.'

Ovington hesitated, his heart full, his hands trembling. He was not himself. He looked at Woosenham. 'Perhaps, Sir Charles,' he said unsteadily, 'will be good enough to check the amount with me!'

'Pshaw, man, if I didn't think you honest I shouldn't be here, whether or no. No such fool! I satisfied myself of that, you may be sure, before I came in. Count it, yourself. And there! Bid 'em bring in the gold.'

The banker rang the bell and gave the order. He counted the notes, and by the time he had finished, the bags had been brought in. 'You'll ha' to take that uncounted,' the Squire said, as he heard them set down on the floor, 'as I took it myself.'

'My son will have seen to that,' Ovington replied. He was a little more like himself now. He sat down and wrote out the note, though his hand shook.

'Ay,' the Squire agreed, 'I'm thinking he will have.' And turning his head towards Woosenham, 'He's a rum chap, that,' he continued, with a chuckle and speaking as if the banker were not present. 'He gave me a talking-to – me! D'you know that he got to London in sixteen hours, in the night-time?'

'Did he, by Jove! Our friend at Halston could hardly have beaten that.'

'And nothing staged either! Railroads!' scornfully. 'D'you think there's any need o' railroads when a man can do that? Or that any railroad that's ever made will beat that? Sixteen hours, by George, a hundred and fifty-one miles in the night-time!'

Sir Charles, who had been an astonished spectator of the scene, gave a qualified assent, and by that time Ovington was ready with his note. The Squire pouched it with care, but cut short his thanks. 'I've told you why I do it,' he said gruffly. 'And now I'm tired and I'll be getting home. Give me your arm, Woosenham. But as we pass I've a word to say to that little joker in the bank.'

He had his word, and a strange scene it was. The two great men stood within the counter, the old man bending his hawk-like face and sightless eyes on the quailing group beyond it, while the clerks looked on, half in awe and half in amusement. 'Fools!' said the Squire in his harshest tone. 'Fools, all of ye! Cutting your own throats and tearing the bottom out of your own money-bags! That's what ye be doing! And you, Tom Jenkins, and you, Owen, that should know better, first among 'em! You haven't the sense to see a yard before you, but elbow one another into the ditch like a pair of blind horses! You deserve to be ruined, every man of you, and it's no fault o' yourn that you're not! Business men? You call yourselves business men, and run on a bank as if all the money was kept in a box under the counter ready to pay you! Go home! Go home!' poking at them with his stick. 'And thank God the banker has more sense than you, and a sight more money than your tuppenny ha'penny accounts run to! Damme, if I were master here, if one single one o' you should cross my door again! But there, take me out, Woosenham; take me out! Pack o' fools! Pack o' dumb fools, they are!'

The two marched out with that, but the Squire's words ran up and down the town like wild-fire. What he had said and how he had said it, and the figure little Tom Jenkins of the Hollies had cut, was known as far as the Castle Foregate before the old man had well set his foot on the step of his carriage. The crowd standing about Sir Charles' four bays in the Market Place and respectfully gazing on the postilion's yellow jackets had it within two minutes. Within four it was known at the Gullet that the old Squire was supporting the bank, and had given Welsh Owen such a talking-to as never was. Within ten, the news was being bandied up and down the long yard at the Lion, where they stabled a hundred horses, and was known even to the charwomen who, on their knees, were scrubbing the floors of the Assembly Rooms that looked down on the yard. Dean's, at which a persistent and provoking run had been prosecuted since morning, got it among the first; and Mr Dean, testy and snappish enough before, became for the rest of the day a terror and a thunder-cloud to the junior clerks. Nay, the news soon passed beyond Aldersbury, for the three o'clock up-coach swept it away and dropped it with various parcels and hampers at every stage between the Falcon at Heygate and Wolverhampton. Not a turn-pike man but heard it and spread it, and at the Cock at Wellington they gave it to the down-coach, which carried it back to Aldersbury.

Owen, it was known, had drawn his money. But Jenkins had thought better of it. He had gone out of the bank with his cheque in his hand, and had torn it up *coram publico* in the roadway; and from that moment the run, its force already exhausted, had ceased.

Half an hour later he would have been held a fool who looked twice at an Ovington note, or distrusted a bank into which, rumour had it, gold had been carried by the sackful. Had not the Bank of England sent down a special messenger bearing unstinted credit? And had not the old Squire of Garth, the closest, stingiest, shrewdest man in the county, paid in thirty, forty, fifty thousand pounds and declared that he would sell every acre before the bank should fail? Before night a dozen men were considering ruefully the thing that they had done or pondering how they might, with the least loss of dignity, undo it. Before morning twice as many wives had told their husbands what they thought of them, and reminded them that they had always said how it would be – only they were never listened to!

At the Gullet in the Shut off the Market Place, where the tap never ceased running that evening, and half of the trade of the town pressed in to eat liver and bacon, there was no longer any talk of Boulogne. All the talk ran the other way. The drawers of the day were the butts of the evening, and were bantered and teased unmercifully. Their friends would not be in their shoes for a trifle – not they! They had cooked their goose with a vengeance – no more golden eggs for them! And very noticeable was it that whenever the banker's name came up, voices dropped and heads came together. His luck, his power, his resources were discussed with awe and in whispers. There were not a few thoughtful faces at the board, and here and there were appetites that failed, though the suppers served in the dingy low-ceiled room at the Gullet, dark even at noon-day, were famous for their savouriness.

Very different was the scene inside the bank. At the counter, indeed, discipline failed the moment the door fell to behind the last customer. The clerks sprang to their feet, cheered, danced a dance of triumph, struck a hundred attitudes of scorn and defiance. They cracked silly jokes, and flung paper darts at the public side; they repaid by every kind of monkey trick the alarms and exertions from which they had suffered during three days. They roared, 'Oh, dear, what can the matter be!' in tones of derision that reached the street. They challenged the public to come on – to come on and be hanged! They ceased to make a noise only when breath failed them.

But in the parlour, whither Clement, followed after a moment's hesitation by Rodd, had hastened to join and to congratulate his father, there was nothing of this. The danger had been too pressing, the margin of safety too narrow to admit of loud rejoicing. The three met like shipwrecked mariners drawn more closely together by the ordeal through which they had passed, like men still shaken by the buffeting of the waves. They were quiet, as men amazed to find themselves alive. The banker, in particular, sat sunk in his chair, overcome as much by the scene through which he had passed as by a relief too deep for words. For he knew that it was by no art of his own, and through no resources of his own that he survived, and his usual self-confidence, and with it his aplomb, had deserted him. In a room vibrating with emotion they gazed at one another in thankful silence, and it was only after a long interval that the older man let his thoughts appear. Then 'Thank God!' he said unsteadily, 'and you, Clement! God bless you! If we owe this to any one we owe it to you, my boy! If you had not been beside me, God knows what I might not have done!'

'Pooh, pooh, sir,' Clement said; yet he did but disguise deep feeling under a mask of lightness. 'You don't do yourself justice. And for the matter of that, if we have to thank any one it is Rodd, here.' He clapped the cashier on the shoulder with an intimacy that brought a spark to Rodd's eyes. 'He's not only stuck to it like a man, but if he had not paid in his four hundred and fifty—'

'No, no, sir, we weren't drawn down to that – not quite.'

'We were mighty near it, my lad. And easily might have been.'

'Yes,' said the banker; 'we shall not forget it, Rodd. But, after all,' with a faint smile, 'it's Bourdillon we have to thank.' And he explained the motives which, on the surface at least, had moved the Squire to intervene. 'If I had not taken Bourdillon in when I did—'

'Just so,' Clement assented drily. 'And if Bourdillon had not—'

'Umph! Yes. But – where is he? Do you know?'

'I don't. He may be at his rooms, or he may have ridden out to his mother's. I'll look round presently, and if he is not in town I'll go out and tell him the news.'

'You didn't quarrel?'

Clement shrugged his shoulders. 'Not more than we can make up,' he said lightly, 'if it is to his interest.'

The banker moved uneasily in his chair. 'What is to be done about him?' he asked.

'I think, sir, that that's for the Squire. Let us leave it to him. It's his business. And now – come! Has any one told Betty?'

The banker rose, conscience-stricken. 'No, poor girl, and she must be anxious. I quite forgot,' he said.

'Unless Rodd has,' Clement replied, with a queer look at his father. For Rodd had vanished while they were talking of Arthur, whom it was noteworthy that neither of them now called by his Christian name.

'We'll go and tell her,' said Ovington, reverting to his everyday tone. And he turned briskly to the door which led into the house. He opened it, and was crossing the hall, followed by Clement, who was anxious to relieve his sister's mind, when both came to a sudden stand. The banker uttered an exclamation of astonishment – and so did Betty. For Rodd, he melted with extraordinary rapidity through a convenient door, while Clement, the only one of the four who was not taken completely by surprise, laughed softly.

'Betty!' her father cried sternly. 'What is the meaning of this?'

'Well, I thought – you would know,' said Betty, blushing furiously. 'I think it's pretty plain.' Then, throwing her arms round her father's neck, 'Oh, Father, I'm so glad, I'm so glad, I'm so glad!'

'But that's an odd way of showing it, my dear.'

'Oh, he quite understands. In fact' – still hiding her face – 'we've come to an understanding, Father. And we want you' – half laughing and half crying – 'to witness it.'

'I'm afraid I did witness it,' gravely.

'But you're not going to be angry? Not today? Not today, Father.' And in a small voice, 'He stood by you. You know how he stood by you. And you said you'd never forget it.'

'But I didn't say that I should give him my daughter.'

'No, Father, she gave herself.'

'Well, there!' He freed himself from her. 'That's enough now, girl. We'll talk about it another time. But I'm not pleased, Betty.'

'No?' said Betty, gaily, but dabbing her eyes at the same time. 'He said that. He said that you would not be pleased. He was dreadfully afraid of you. And I said you wouldn't be pleased, too. But—'

'Eh?'

'I said you'd come to it, Father, by and by. In good time.'

'Well, I'm—' But what the banker was, was lost in the peal of laughter that Clement could no longer restrain.

Chapter Forty-One

Arthur, after he had dropped from the post-chaise that morning, did not at once move away. He stood on the crown of the East Bridge, looking down the river, and the turmoil of his feelings was such as for a time to render thought of the future impossible, and even to hold despair at bay. The certainty that his plan would have succeeded if it had not been thwarted by the very persons who would have profited by it, and the knowledge that but for their scruples all that he had at stake in the bank would have been saved – this certainty and this knowledge, with the fact that while they left him to bear the obloquy they had denied him the prize, so maddened him that for a full minute he stood, grasping the stone balustrade of the bridge, and whispering curses at the current that flowed smoothly below.

The sunshine and the fair scene did but mock him. The green meadows, and the winding river, and the crescent of stately buildings, spire-crowned, that, curving with the stream, looked down upon it from the site of the ancient walls, did but deride his misery. For, how many a time had he stood on that spot and looked on that scene in days when he had been happy and care-free, his future as sunny as the landscape before him! And now – oh, the cowards! The cowards, who had not had the courage even to pick up the fruit which his daring had shaken from the bough.

Ay, his daring and his enterprise! For what else was it? What had he done, after all, at which they need make mouths? It had been but a loan he had taken, the use for a few weeks of money which was useless where it lay, and of which not a penny would be lost! And again he cursed the weakness of those who had rendered futile all that he, the bolder spirit, had done, who had consigned themselves and him to failure and beggary. He had bought their safety at his own cost, and they had declined to be saved. He shook with rage, with impotent rage, as he thought of it.

Presently, a man, passing over the bridge, looked curiously at him, paused and went on again, and the incident recalled him to himself. He remembered that he was in a place where all knew him, where his movements and his looks would be observed, where every second person who saw him would wonder why he was not at the bank. He must be going. He composed his face and walked on.

But whither? The question smote him with a strange and chilly sense of loneliness. Whither? To the bank certainly, if he had courage, where the battle was even now joined. He might fling himself into the fray, play his part as if nothing had happened, smile with the best, ignore what he had done and, if challenged, face it down. And there had been a time when he could have done this. There had been a time, when Clement had first alighted on him in town, when he had decided with himself to play that rôle, and had believed that he could carry it off with a smiling face. And now, now, as then, he maintained that he had done nothing that the end did not justify, since the means could harm no one.

But at that time he had believed that he could count on the complicity of others, he had believed that they would at least accept the thing that he had done and throw in their lot with his, and the failure of that belief, brag as he might, affected him. It had sapped his faith in his own standards. The view Clement had taken had slowly but surely eclipsed his view, until now, when he must face the bank with a smile, he could not muster up the smile. He began to see that he had committed not a crime, but a blunder. He had been found out!

He walked more and more slowly, and when he came, some eighty yards from the bridge and at the foot of the Cop, to a lane on his left which led by an obscure short-cut to his rooms, he turned into it. He did not tell himself that he was not going to the bank. He told himself that he must change his clothes, and wash, and eat something before he could face people. That was all.

He reached his lodgings, beneath the shadow of an old tower that looked over the meadows to the river, without encountering any one. He even stole upstairs, unseen by his landlady, and found the fire alight in his sitting-room, and some part of a meal laid ready on the table. He washed his hands and ate and drank, but instinctively, as he did so, he hushed his movements and trod softly. When he had finished his meal he stood for a moment, his eyes on the door, hesitating. Should he or should he not go to the bank? He knew that he ought to go. But the wear and tear of three days of labour and excitement, during which he had hardly slept as many hours, had lowered his vitality and sapped his will, and the effort required was now too much for him. With a sigh of relief he threw up the sponge, he owned himself beaten. He sank into a chair and, moody and inert, he sat gazing at the fire. He was very weary, and presently his eyes closed, and he slept.

Two hours later his landlady discovered him, and the cry which she uttered in her astonishment awoke him. 'Mercy on us!' she exclaimed. 'You here, sir! And I never heard a sound, and no notion you were come! But I was expecting you, Mr Bourdillon. 'He won't be long,' I says to myself, 'now that that plaguy bank's gone and closed – worse luck to it!'

'Closed, has it?' he said, dully.

'Ay, to be sure, this hour past.' Which of course was not true, but many things that were not true were being said in Aldersbury that day. 'And nothing else to be expected, I am told, though there's nobody blames you, sir. You can't put old heads on young shoulders, asking your pardon, sir, as I said to Mrs Brown no more than an hour ago. It was her Johnny told me – he came that way from school and stopped to look. Such a sight of people on Bride Hill, he said, as he never saw in his life, 'cept on Show Day, and the shutters going up just as he came away.'

He did not doubt the story – he knew that there was no other end to be expected. 'I am only just from London,' he said, feeling that some explanation of his ignorance was necessary. 'I had no sleep last night, Mrs Bowles, and I sat down for a moment, and I suppose I fell asleep in my chair.'

'Indeed, and no wonder. From London, to be sure! Can I bring you anything up, sir?'

'No, thank you, Mrs Bowles. I shall have to go out presently, and until I go out, don't let me be disturbed. I'm not at home if any one calls. You understand?'

'I understand, sir.' And on the stairs, as she descended, a pile of plates and dishes in her arms, 'Poor young gentleman,' she murmured, 'it's done him no good. And some in my place would be thinking of their bill. But his people will see me paid. That's where the gentry come in – they're never the losers, whoever fails.'

For a few minutes after she had retired he dawdled about the room, staring through the window without seeing anything, revolving the news, and telling himself, but no longer with passion, that the game was played out. And gradually the idea of flight grew upon him, and the longing to be in some place where he could hide his head, where he might let himself go and pity himself unwatched. Had his pockets been full he would have returned to London and lost himself in its crowds, and presently, he thought – for he still believed in himself – he would have shown the world what he could do.

But he had spent his loose cash on the journey, he was almost without money, and instinct as well as necessity turned his thoughts towards his mother. The notion once accepted grew upon him, and he longed to be at the Cottage. He felt that there he might be quiet, that there no one would watch him, and stealthily – on fire to be gone now that he had made up his mind – he sought for his hat and coat and let himself out of the house.

There was no one in sight, and descending from the Town Wall by some steps, he crossed the meadows to the river. He passed the water by a ferry, and skirting the foot of the rising ground on the other side, he presently struck into the Garthmyle road a little beyond the West Bridge.

He trudged along the road, his hat drawn down to his eyes, his shoulders humped, his gaze fixed doggedly on the road before him. He marched as men march who have had the worst of the battle, yet whom it would be unwise to pursue too closely. At first he walked rapidly, taking where he could a by-path, or a short-cut, and though the hills, rising from the plain before him, were fair to see on this fine winter day, as the sun began to decline and redden their slopes, he had no eye for them or for the few whom he met, the roadman, or the carter, who, plodding beside a load of turnips or manure, looked up and saluted him.

But when he had left the town two or three miles behind he breathed more freely. He lessened his pace. Presently he heard on the road behind him the clip-clop of a trotting horse, and not wishing to be recognised, he slipped into the mouth of a lane, and by and by he saw Clement Ovington ride by. He flung a vicious curse after him and, returning to the road, he went on more slowly, chewing the sour cud of reflection, until he came to the low sedgy tract where the Squire had met with his misadventure, and where in earlier days the old man had many a time heard the bittern's note.

He was in no hurry now, for he did not mean to reach the Cottage until Clement had left it, and he stood leaning against the old thorn tree, viewing the place and thinking bitterly of the then and the now. And presently a spark of hope was kindled in him. Surely all was not lost – even now! The Squire was angry – angry for the moment, and with reason. But could he maintain his anger against one who had saved his life at the risk of his own? Could he refuse to pardon one, but for whom he would be already lying in his grave? With a quick uplifting of the spirit Arthur conceived that the Squire could not. No man could be so thankless, so unmindful of a benefit, so ungrateful.

Strange, that he had not thought of that before! Strange, that under the pressure of difficulties he had let that claim slip from his mind. It had restored him to his uncle's favour once. Why should it not restore him a second time? Properly handled – and he thought that he could trust himself to handle it properly – it should avail him. Let him once get speech of his uncle, and surely he could depend on his own dexterity for the rest.

Hope awoke in him, and confidence. He squared his shoulders, he threw back his head, he strode on, he became once more the jaunty, gallant, handsome young fellow, whom women's eyes were wont to follow as he passed through the streets. But, steady, not so fast. There was still room for management. He had no mind to meet Clement, whom he hated for his interference, and he went a little out of the way, until he had seen him pass by on his return journey. Then he went on. But it was now late, and the murmur of the river came up from shadowy depths, the squat tower of the church was beginning to blend with the dark sky, lights shone from cottage doors, when he passed over the bridge. He hastened on through the dusk, opened the garden-gate and saw his mother standing in the lighted doorway. She had missed Clement, but had gathered from the servant who had seen him that Arthur might be expected at any moment, and she had come to the door with a shawl about her head, that she might be on the look-out for him.

Poor Mrs Bourdillon! She had passed a miserable day. She had her own, her private grounds for anxiety on Arthur's account, and that anxiety had been strengthened by her last talk with Josina. She was sure that something was wrong with him, and this had so weighed on her spirits and engrossed her thoughts, that the danger that menaced the bank and her little fortune had not at first disturbed her. But as the tale of village gossip grew, and the rumours of disaster became more insistent, she had been forced to listen, and her fears once aroused, she had not been slow to awake to her position. Gradually Arthur's absence and her misgivings on his account had taken the second place. The prospect of ruin, of losing her all and becoming dependent on the Squire's niggard bounty, had closed her mind to other terrors.

So at noon on this day, unable to bear her thoughts alone, she had walked across the fields and seen Josina. But Josina had not been able to reassure her. The girl had said as little as might be about Arthur, and on the subject of the bank was herself so despondent that she had no comfort for another. The Squire had gone to town – for the first time since he had been laid up – in company with Sir Charles, and Josina fancied that it might be upon the bank business. But she hardly dared to hope that good could come of it, and Mrs Bourdillon, who flattered herself that she knew the Squire, had no hope. She had returned from Garth more wretched than she had gone, and had she been a much wiser woman than she was, she would have found it hard to meet her son with tact.

When she heard his footsteps on the road, 'Is it you?' she cried. And as he came forward into the light, 'Oh, Arthur!' she wailed, 'what have you brought us to? What have you done? And the times and times I've warned you! Didn't I tell you that those Ovingtons—'

'Well, come in now, Mother,' he said. He stooped and kissed her on the forehead. He was very patient with her – let it be said to his credit.

'But, oh dear, dear!' She had lost control of herself and could not stay her complaints if she would. 'You would have your way! And you see what has come of it! You would do it! And now – what am I to say to your uncle?'

'You can leave him to me,' Arthur replied doggedly. 'And for goodness' sake, Mother, come in and shut the door. You don't want to talk to the village, I suppose? Come in.'

He shepherded her into the parlour and closed the door on them. He was cold, and he went to the fire and stooped over it, warming his hands at the blaze.

'But the bank?'

'Oh, the bank's gone,' he said.

She began to cry. 'Then, I don't know what's to become of us!' she sobbed. 'It's everything we have to live upon! And you know it wasn't I signed the order to – to your uncle! I never did – it was you – wrote my name. And now – it has ruined us! Ruined us!'

His face grew darker. 'If you wish to ruin us,' he said, 'at any rate if you wish to ruin me, you'll talk like that! As it is, you'll not lose your money, or only a part of it. The bank can pay everyone, and there'll be something over. A good deal, I fancy,' putting the best face on it. 'You'll get back the greater part of it.' Then, changing the subject abruptly, 'What did Clement Ovington want?'

'I don't – know,' she sobbed. But already his influence was mastering her; already she was a little comforted. 'He asked for you. I didn't see him – I could not bear it. I suppose he came to – to tell me about the bank.'

'Well,' ungraciously, 'he might have spared himself the trouble.' And under his breath he added a curse. 'Now let me have some tea, Mother. I'm tired, dog-tired. I had no sleep last night. And I want to see Pugh before he goes. He must take a note for me – to Garth.'

'I'm afraid the Squire—'

'Oh, hang the Squire! It's not to him,' impatiently. 'It's to Josina, if you must know.'

She perked up a little at that – she had always some hope of Josina; and the return to everyday life, the clatter of the tray as it was brought in, the act of giving him his tea and seeing that he had what he liked, the mere bustling about him, did more to restore her. The lighted room, the blazing fire, the cheerful board – in face of these things it was hard to believe in ruin, or to fancy that life would not be always as it had been. She began again to have faith in him.

And he, whose natural bent it was to be sanguine, whose spirits had already rebounded from the worst, shared the feeling which he imparted. That she knew the worst was something; that, at any rate, was over, and confidently he began to build his house again. 'You won't lose,' he said, casting back the locks from his forehead with the gesture peculiar to him. 'Or not more than a few hundreds at worst, Mother. That will be all right. I'll see to that. And my uncle – you may leave him to me. He's been vexed with me before, and I've brought him round. Oh, I know him. I've no doubt that I can manage him.'

'But Josina?' timidly. 'D'you know, she was terribly low, Arthur, about something yesterday. She wouldn't tell me, but there was something. She didn't seem to want to talk about you.'

He winced, and for a moment his face fell. But he recovered himself, and, 'Oh, I'll soon put that right,' be answered confidently. 'I shall see her in the morning. She's a good soul, is Josina. I can count on her. Don't you fret, Mother. You'll see it will all come right – with a little management.'

'Well, I know you're very clever, Arthur. But Jos—'

'Jos is afraid of him, that's all,' And laughing, 'Oh, I've an arrow in my quiver, yet, Mother. We shall see. But I must see Jos in the morning. Is Pugh there? I'll write to her now and ask her to meet me at the stile at ten o'clock. Nothing like striking while the iron is hot.'

On the morrow he did not feel quite so confident. The sunshine and open weather of the day before had given place to rain and fog, and when, after crossing the plank-bridge at the foot of the garden, he took the field path which led to Garth, mist hid the more distant hills, and even the limestone ridge which rose to their knees. The vale had ceased to be a vale, and he walked in a plain, sad and circumscribed, bounded by ghostly hedges, which in their turn melted into grey space. That the day should affect his spirits was natural, and that his position should appear less hopeful was natural, too, and he told himself so, and strove to rally his courage. He strode along, swinging his stick and swaggering, though there was no one to see him. And from time to time he whistled to prove that he was free from care.

After all, the fact that it rained did not alter matters. Wet or dry he had saved the Squire's life, and a man's life was his first and last and greatest possession, and not least valued when near its end. He who saved it had a claim, and much – much must be forgiven him. Then, too, he reminded himself that the old man was no longer the hard, immovable block that he had been. The loss of sight had weakened him; he had broken a good deal in the last few months. He could be cajoled, persuaded, made to see things, and surely, with Josina's help, it would not be impossible to put such a colour on the – the loan of the securities as might make it appear a trifle. Courage! A little courage and all would be well yet.

He was still hopeful when he saw Josina's figure, muffled in a cloak and poke-bonnet, grow out of the mist before him. The girl was waiting for him on the farther side of the half-way stile, which had been their trysting place from childhood; and what slight doubt he had felt as to her willingness to help him died away. He whistled a little louder, and swung his stick more carelessly, and he spoke before he came up to her.

'Hallo, Jos!' he cried cheerfully. 'You're before me. But I knew that I could count on you, if I could count on any one. I only came from London last night, and' – his stick over his shoulder, and his head thrown back – 'I knew the best thing I could do was to see you and get your help. Why' – in spite of himself his voice fell a tone – 'what's the matter?'

'Oh, Arthur!' she said. That was all, but the two words completed what her look had begun. His eyes dropped. 'How could you? How could you do it?'

'Why – why, surely you're not going to turn against me?' he exclaimed.

'And he was blind! Blind, and he trusted you. He trusted you, Arthur.'

'The devil!' roughly – for how could he meet this save by bluster? 'If we're going to talk like that – but you don't understand, Jos. It was business, and you don't understand, I tell you. Business, Jos.'

'He does.'

Two words only, but they rang a knell in his ears. They gripped him in the moment of his swagger, left him bare before her, a culprit, dumb.

'He has felt it terribly! Terribly,' she continued. 'He was blind, and you deceived him. Whom can he trust now, Arthur?'

He strove to rally his confidence. He could not meet her gaze, but he tapped a rail of the stile with his stick. 'Oh, but that's nonsense!' he said. 'Nonsense! But, of course, if you are against me, if you are not going to help me—'

'How can I help you? He will not hear your name.'

'I can tell you how – quite easily, if you will let me explain?'

She shook her head.

'But you can. If you are willing, that is. Of course, if you are not—'

'What can I do? He knows all.'

'You can remind him of what I did for him,' he answered eagerly. 'I saved his life. He would not be alive now but for me. You can tell him that. Remind him of that, Jos. Tell him that some time after dinner, when he is in a good humour. He owes his life to me, and that's not a small thing – is it? Even he must see that he owes me something. What's a paltry thousand or two thousand? And I only borrowed them; he won't lose a penny by it – not a penny!' earnestly. 'What's that in return for a man's life? He must know—'

'He does know!' she cried, and the honest indignation in her eyes, the indignation that she could no longer restrain, scorched him. For this was too much, this was more than even she, gentle as she was, could bear. 'He does know all – all, Arthur!' she repeated severely. 'That it was not you – not you, but Clement, Mr Ovington, who saved him! And fought for him – that night! Oh, Arthur, for shame! For shame! I did not think so meanly of you as this! I did not think that you would rob another—'

'What do you mean?' He tried to bluster afresh, but the stick shook in his hand. 'Confound it, what do you mean?'

'What I say,' she answered firmly. 'And it is no use to deny it, for my father knows it. He knows all. He has seen Clement—'

'Clement, eh?' bitterly. 'Oh, it's Clement now, is it?' He was white with rage and chagrin, furious at the failure of his last hope. 'It's that way, is it? You have gone over to that prig, have you? And he's told you this?'

'Yes.'

'And you believe him?'

'I do.'

'You believe him against me?'

'Yes,' she said, 'for it is the truth, Arthur. I know that he would not tell me anything else.'

'And I? Do you mean to say that I would?'

She was silent.

It was check and mate, the loss of his last piece, the close of the game – and he knew it. With all in his favour he had made one false move, then another and a graver one, and this was the end.

He could not face it out. There was no more to be said, nothing more to be done, only shame and humiliation if he stayed. He flung a word of passionate incoherent abuse at her, and before she could reply he turned his back on her and strode away. Sorrowfully Jos watched him as he hurried along the path, cutting at the hedge with his stick, cursing his luck, cursing the trickery of others, cursing at last, perhaps, his own folly. She watched him until the ghostly hedges and the misty distances veiled him from sight.

Ten minutes later he burst in upon his mother at the Cottage and demanded twenty pounds. 'Give it me, and let me go!' he cried, 'Do you hear? I must have it! If you don't give it me, I shall cut my throat!'

Scared by his manner, his haggard eyes, his look of misery, the poor woman did not even protest. She went upstairs and fetched the sum he asked for. He took it, kissed her with lips still damp with rain, and bidding her send his clothes as he should direct – he would write to her – he hurried out.

Chapter Forty-Two

'I wun't do it! I wun't do it!' the Squire muttered stubbornly. 'Mud and blood 'll never mix. Shape the chip as you will, 'tis part of the block! Girls' whimsies are women's aches, and they that's older must judge for them. She'd only repent of it when 'twas too late, and I've paid my debt and there's an end of it.'

From the hour of that scene at Ovington's he had begun to recover. From that moment he began to wear a stiff upper lip and to give his orders in hard, sharp tones, as he had been wont to give them in days when he could see; as if, in truth, his irruption into the life of the town and his action at the bank had re-established him in his own eyes. Those about him were quick to see the change – he had taken, said they, a new lease of life. 'Maybe, 'tis just a flicker,' Calamy observed cautiously; but even he had to admit that the flame burned higher for a time, and privately he advised the new man who filled Thomas' place 'to hop it when the master spoke,' or he'd hop it to some purpose.

The result was that there was a general quickening up in the old house. The master's hand was felt, and things moved to a livelier time. To some extent pride had to do with this, for the rumour of the Squire's doings in Aldersbury had flown far and wide and made him the talk of the county. He had saved the bank. He had averted ruin from hundreds. He had saved the countryside. He had paid in thirty, forty, fifty thousand pounds. Naturally his people were proud of him.

And doubtless the bold part he had played had given the old man a fillip; others had stood by, while he, blind as he was, had asserted himself, and acted, and rescued his neighbours from a great misfortune. But the stiffness he showed was not due to this only. It was assumed to protect himself. 'I wun't do it! I wun't do it! It's not i' reason,' he told himself over and over again; and in his own mind he fought a perpetual battle. On the one side contended the opinions of a lifetime and the prejudices of a caste, the beliefs in which he had been brought up, and a pride of birth that had come down from an earlier day; on the other, the girl's tremulous gratitude, her silence, the touch of her hand on his sleeve, the sound of her voice, the unceasing appeal of her presence.

Ay, and there were times when he was so hard put to it that he groaned aloud. No man was more of a law to himself, but at these times he fell back on the views of others. What would Woosenham say of it? How he would hold up his hands! And Chirbury – whose peerage he respected, since it was as old as his own family, if he thought little of the man? And Uvedale and Cludde? Ay, and Acherley, who, rotten fellow as he was, was still Acherley of Acherley? They had held the fort so stoutly in Aldshire, they had repelled the moneyed upstarts so proudly, they had turned so cold a shoulder on Manchester and Birmingham! They had found in their Peninsular hero, and in that little country churchyard where the maker of an empire lay resting after life's fever, so complete a justification for their own claims to leadership and to power! And no one had been more steadfast, more dogged, more hide-bound in their pride and exclusiveness than he.

Now, if he gave way, what would they say? What laughter would there not be from one end of the county to the other, what sneers, what talk of an old man's folly and an old man's weakness! For it was not even as if the man's father had been a Peel or the like, a Baring or a Smith! A small country banker, a man just risen from the mud – not even a stranger from a distance, or a merchant prince from God knows where! Oh, it was impossible. Impossible! Garth, that had been in the hands of gentlefolk, of Armigeri from Harry the Eighth, to pass into the hands, into the blood of – no, it was impossible! All the world of Aldshire would jeer at it, or be scandalised by it.

'I wun't do it!' said the Squire for the hundredth time. It was more particularly at the thought of Acherley that he squirmed. He despised Acherley, and to be despised by Acherley – that was too much!

'Of course,' said a small voice within him, 'he would take the name of Griffin, and in time—'

'Mud's mud,' replied the Squire silently. 'You can't change it.'

'But he's honest,' quoth the small voice.

'So's Calamy!'

'He saved—'

'And I ha' paid him! Damme, I ha' paid him! Ha' done!' And then, 'It's that blow on the head has moithered me!'

Things went on in this way for a month, the Squire renewing his vigour and beginning to tramp his fields again, or with the new man at his bridle-hand to ride the old grey from point to point, learning what the men were doing, inquiring after gaps, and following the manure to the clover-ley, where the oats and barley would presently go in. Snow lay on the upper hills, grizzling the brown sheets of bracken, and dappling the green velvet of the sloping ling; the valley below was frost-bound. But the Squire had a fire within him, a fire of warring elements, that kept his blood running. He was very sharp with the men and scolded old Fewtrell. As for Thomas' successor, the lad learned to go warily and kept his tongue between his teeth.

The girl had never complained; it seemed as if that which he had done for her had silenced her, as if, she, too, had taken it for payment. But one day she was not at table, and Miss Peacock cut up his meat. She did not do it to his mind – no hand but Jos' could do it to his mind – and he was querulous and dissatisfied.

'I'm sure it's small enough, sir,' Miss Peacock answered, feebly defending herself. 'You said you liked it small, Mr Griffin.'

'I never said I liked mince-meat! Where is the girl? What ails her?'

'It's nothing, sir. She's been looking a little peaky the last week or two. That's all. And today—'

'Why didn't you tell me?'

'It's only a headache, sir. She'll be well enough when the spring comes. Josina was always nesh – like her mother.'

The Squire huddled his spoon and fork together, and pushed his plate away, muttering something about d—d sausage meat. Her mother? How old had her mother been when she – he could not remember, but certainly a mere child beside him. Twenty-five or so, he thought. And she was nesh, was she? He sat, shaving his chin with unsteady fingers, eating nothing; and when Calamy, hovering over his plate, hinted that he had not finished, he blew the butler out of the room with a blast of language that made Miss Peacock, hardened as she was, hold up her hands. And though Jos was at breakfast next morning, and answered his grumpy questions as if nothing were amiss, a little seed of fear had been sown in the Squire's mind that grew as fast as Jonah's gourd, and before noon threatened to shut out the sun.

A silk purse could not be made out of a sow's ear. But a good leather purse, that might pass in time – the lad was stout and honest. And his father, mud, certainly, and mud of the pretentious kind that the Squire hated: mud that affected by the aid of gilding to pass for fine clay. But honest? Well, in his own way, perhaps: it remained to be seen. And times were changing, changing for the worse; but he could not deny that they were changing. So gradually, slowly, unwelcome at the best, there grew up in the old man's mind the idea of surrender. If the money were paid back, say in three months, say in six months – well, he would think of it. He would begin to think of it. He would begin to think of it as a thing possible some day, at some very distant date – if there were more peakiness. The girl did not whine, did not torment him, did not complain; and he thought the more of her for that. But if she ailed, then, failing her, there was no one to come after him at Garth, no one of his blood to follow him – except that Bourdillon whelp, and by G–d he should not have an acre or a rood of it, or a pound of it. Never! Never!

Failing her? The Squire felt the air turn cold, and he hung, shivering, over the fire. What if, while he sought to preserve the purity of the old blood, the old traditions, he cut the thread, and the name of Griffin passed out of remembrance, as in his long life he had known so many, many old names pass away – pass into limbo?

Ay, into limbo. He saw his own funeral procession crawl – a long black snake – down the winding drive, here half-hidden by the sunken banks, there creeping forth again into the light. He saw the bleak sunshine fall on the pall that draped the farm-wagon, and heard the slow heavy note of the Garthmyle bell, and the scuffling of innumerable feet that alone broke the solemn silence. If she were not there at window or door to see it go, or in the old curtained pew to await its coming – if the church vault closed on him, the last of his race and blood!

He sat long, thinking of this.

And one day, nearly two months after his visit to the bank – in the meantime he had been twice into town at the Bench – he was riding on the land with Fewtrell at his stirrup, when the bailiff told him that there was a stranger in the field.

'Which field?' he asked.

'Where they ha' just lifted the turnips,' the man said.

'Oh!' said the Squire. 'Who is it? What's he doing there?'

'Well, I'm thinking,' said Fewtrell, 'as it's the young gent I've seen here more 'n once. Same as asked me one day why we didn't drill 'em in wider.'

'The devil, he did!' the Squire exclaimed, kicking up the old mare, who was leaning over sleepily.

'Called 'em Radicals,' said Fewtrell, grinning. 'Them there Radical Swedes,' says he. Dunno what he meant. 'If you plant Radicals, best plant 'em Radical fashion,' says he.'

'Devil he did!' repeated the Squire. 'Said that, did he?'

'Ay, to be sure. He used to come across with a gun field-way from Acherley; oh, as much as once a week I'd see him. And he'd know every crop as we put in, a'most same as I did. Very spry he was about it, I'll say that.'

'Is it the banker's son?' asked the Squire on a sudden suspicion.

'Well, I think he be,' Fewtrell answered, shading his eyes. 'He be going up to the house now.'

'Well, you can take me in,' to the groom. 'I'll go by the gap.'

The groom demurred timidly; the grey might leap at the gap. But the Squire was obstinate, and the old mare, who knew he was blind as well as any man upon the place, and knew, too, when she could indulge in a frolic and when not, bore him out delicately, stepping over the thorn-stubs as if she walked on eggs.

He was at the door in the act of dismounting when Clement appeared. 'D'you want me?' the old man asked bluntly.

'If you please, sir,' Clement answered. He had walked all the way from Aldersbury, having much to think of, and one question which lay heavy on his mind. That was – how would it be with him when he walked back?

'Then come in.' And feeling for the door-post with his hand, the Squire entered the house and turned with the certainty of long practice into the dining-room. He walked to the table as firmly as if he could see, and touching it with one hand he drew up with the other his chair. He sat down. 'You'd best sit,' he said grudgingly. 'I can't see, but you can. Find a chair.'

'My father has sent me with the money,' Clement explained. 'I have a cheque here and the necessary papers. He would have come himself, sir, to renew his thanks for aid as timely as it was generous and – and necessary. But' – Clement boggled a little over the considered phrase, he was nervous and his voice betrayed it – 'he thought – I was to say—'

'It's all there?'

'Yes, sir, principal and interest.'

'Have you drawn a receipt?'

'Yes, sir, I've brought one with me. But if you would prefer that it should be paid to Mr Welsh – my father thought that that might be so?'

'Umph! All there, is it?'

'Yes, sir.'

The old man did not speak for awhile. He seemed to be at a loss, and Clement, who had other and more serious business on his mind, and had his own reasons for feeling ill at ease, waited anxiously. He was desperately afraid of making a false step.

Suddenly, 'Who was your grandfather?' the Squire asked.

Clement started and coloured. 'He had the same name as my father,' he said. 'He was a clothier in Aldersbury.'

'Ay, I mind him. I mind him now. And his father, young man?'

'His name was Clement,' and foreseeing the next question, 'he was a yeoman at Easthope.'

'And his father?'

Clement reddened painfully. He saw only too well to what these questions were tending. 'I don't know, sir,' he said.

'And you set up – you set up,' said the Squire, leaning forward and speaking very slowly, 'to marry my heiress?'

'No, sir, your daughter!' Clement said, his face burning. 'If she'd not a penny—'

'Pho! Don't tell me!' the old man growled, and to Clement's surprise – whose ears were tingling – he relapsed into silence again. It was a silence very ominous. It seemed to Clement that no silence had ever been so oppressive, that no clock had ever ticked so loudly as the tall clock that stood between the windows behind him. 'You know,' said the old man at last, 'you're a d—d impudent fellow. You've no birth, you're nobody, and I don't know that you've much money. You've gone behind my back and you've stole my girl. You've stole her! My father 'd ha' shot you, and good reason, before he'd ha' let it come to this. But it's part my fault,' with a sigh. 'She've seen naught of the world and don't know the difference between silk and homespun or what's fitting for her. You're nobody, and you've naught to offer – I'm plain, young gentleman, and it's better – but I believe you're a man, and I believe you're honest.'

'And I love her!' Clement said softly, his eyes shining.

'Ay,' drily, 'and maybe it would be better for her if her father didn't! But there it is. There it is. That's all that's to be said for you.' He sat silent, looking straight before him with his sightless eyes, his hands on the knob of his stick. 'And I dunno as I make much of that – 'tis easy for a man to love a maid – but the misfortune is that she thinks she loves you. Well, I'm burying things as have been much to me all my life, things I never thought to lose or part from while I lived. I'm burying them deep, and God knows I may regret it sorely. But you may go to her. She's somewhere about the place. But' – arresting Clement's exclamation as he rose to his feet – 'you'll ha' to wait. You'll ha' to wait till I say the word, and maybe 'tis all moonshine, and she'll see it is. Maybe 'tis all a girl's whimsy, and when she knows more of you she'll find it out.'

'God bless you, sir!' Clement cried. 'I'll wait. I'm not afraid. I've no fear of that. And if I can make myself worthy of her—'

'You'll never do that,' said the old man sternly, as he bent lower over his stick. He heard the door close and he knew that Clement had gone – gone on wings, gone on feet lighter than thistle-down, gone, young and strong, his pulses leaping, to his love.

The Squire was too old for tears, but his lip trembled. It was not alone the sacrifice that he had made that moved him – the sacrifice of his pride, his prejudices, his traditions. It was not only the immolation of his own will, his own hopes and plans – his cherished plans for her. But he was giving her up. He was resigning that of which he had only just learned the worth, that on which in his blindness he depended every hour, that which made up all of youth and brightness and cheerfulness that was left to him between this and the end. He had sent the man to her, and they would think no more of him. And in doing this he had belied every belief in which he had been brought up and the faith which he had inherited from an earlier day – and maybe he had been a fool.

But by and by it appeared that they had not forgotten him, or one, at any rate, had not. He had not been alone five minutes before the door opened behind him, and closed again, and he felt Josina's arms round his neck, her head on his breast. 'Oh, Father, I know, I know,' she cried. 'I know what you have done for me! And I shall never forget it – never! And he is good. Oh, Father, indeed, indeed, he is good!'

'There, there,' he said, stroking her head. 'Go back to him. But, mind you,' hurriedly, 'I don't promise anything yet. In a year, maybe, I'll talk about it.'

THE END

Appendix

The essay below gives an account of Stanley Weyman's life and explains how he came to be such a successful novelist. Since it contains no 'spoilers', you can if you wish read it before *Ovington's Bank* itself. Jim Lawley, August 2018

Stanley Weyman (1855-1928) – the first syllable of 'Weyman' is pronounced as 'why', not 'way' – was one of the most illustrious British writers of the last decade of the nineteenth and the early decades of the twentieth centuries. At that time he was as well-known and highly regarded as HG Wells, Oscar Wilde, Rudyard Kipling and Robert Louis Stevenson. Stevenson in fact sent Weyman letters of admiration, Oscar Wilde petitioned the Home Office from Reading Gaol to make Weyman's novels available to convicts, and Hugh Walpole described him as 'one of the finest masters of the narrative gift the English novel has known'. Graham Greene was later to refer to Weyman's novels as 'key books in my life'. Yet by the late twentieth century Weyman's novels were all out of print.

A number of reviewers have suggested that *Ovington's Bank* (1922), published when Weyman was at the height of his powers, is the finest of these twenty-four novels. Serialised on BBC television in the 1960s as *Heiress of Garth*, it is a great shame that this magnificent story, worthy of Trollope, has lain so long forgotten. Although published in the same year as TS Eliot's *The Waste Land* and James Joyce's *Ulysses*, there is nothing modernist about *Ovington's Bank*: it belongs to a different literary tradition – the tradition of the Victorian novel.

* * *

Stanley John Weyman was born on Tuesday, 7 August 1855 in Ludlow in the county of Shropshire in England. He was the second surviving child of Thomas Weyman (1819-1873), and Mary Maria (née Bluck, 1827-1901).

Stanley had an older brother, Henry (1850-1941), a sister Maria who was born and died in 1852, a younger brother, Arthur (1860-1935), and a younger sister, Louisa (1863-1930). In due course, Stanley was to dedicate his novel *Shrewsbury* (1898) to his brother Henry, *Count Hannibal* (1901) to his sister Louisa, and give the name Arthur to the hero of *Chippinge* (1906).

Stanley's father, Thomas, was a prosperous solicitor, one of the most prominent and respected men in the small county town of Ludlow (population of about 5,000 in 1850). The family lived near the centre of town at 54, Broad Street. While externally unchanged, in 2017 this fine Georgian building houses a driving school, the Conservative party's local office, and a hair-dressing salon, but in the nineteenth and early twentieth centuries, it was known to all Ludlow as the imposing town house of the Weyman family. Described in Stanley's novel *The New Rector* (1891) as a 'substantial respectable residence of brick, not detached nor withdrawn from the roadway' it remains a fine example of a Georgian town house with a large walled garden behind, eloquent of the family's prosperity and social status. The journalist Robert Harborough Sherard described it in 1895 as 'the typical house of the prosperous citizen of an English provincial town. It is built of red brick, and, from the colour of the oak panellings, doors, and rafters – which may be admired in the various rooms inside – must have been standing for over a century'. The Weymans were at the top of the social hierarchy in Ludlow – big fish in a small pond; in his early years Stanley doubtless grew accustomed to his position of status as a 'young master' regarded with respect and even deference.

Ludlow is an ancient market town in which the original mediaeval street layout survives to this day. Turning left out of his front door, a couple of minutes' walk brought Stanley to the imposing Norman castle dating from 1086. Interviewed in 1895, Stanley explained why he never made use of Ludlow Castle in any of his historical novels: 'No doubt, it teems with romance; but all is so familiar to me. This was my earliest playground. My first recollections are of Ludlow Castle, and of all the stories of which it was the scene. And over-familiarity, perhaps, you know … So I look abroad, and explore periods less familiar to me, which, for this very reason, have for me all the charm of the unforeseen.'

Meanwhile, turning right out of the front door, Stanley had only to go a couple of hundred yards down the hill and across the bridge over the

River Teme to find himself in beautiful countryside: Whitcliffe Common, Bringewood Chase, Mortimer's Forest and other delights were all only minutes away. It seems likely that as a boy Stanley explored and learned to love these places which are especially rich in wildlife. The rare Ghost Orchid, for example, was found in 1876 in Evens Wood near Ludlow by Stanley's neighbour and near contemporary Fanny Louisa Lloyd (1857-1933). Stanley's own brother, Arthur, another keen naturalist, found the rare moss, *Cinclidotus riparius*, new to Britain in 1890 in the River Teme just down the hill from the family home. Indeed, Clement in *Ovington's Bank* who could not observe 'a rare flower without wondering why it grew in that position' may, at least in part, be a portrait of Stanley's younger brother. References to nature and wildlife abound in Stanley's novels, sometimes offering an ironic counterpoint to human activity. In *Count Hannibal* (1901), for example, the ruthless eponymous hero sets out in hot pursuit of his enemy: 'His feet as he strode along the river-bank trampled the flowers, and slew the pale water forget-me-not which grew among the grasses'. This sentence is quintessential Weyman: who else would remember the forget-me-nots at such a moment?

Count Hannibal is set in sixteenth century France and indeed almost all of Weyman's novels are historical novels. His interest in history started at an early age: 'The very first book that I can remember as a child was *Little Arthur's History of England*. I was very pleased with it, and read it in preference to my toy-books,' he told Sherard in 1895. When he was seven he was sent to a boarding school, at Tenbury, about ten miles from Ludlow. 'I remember that I read a great deal, but I do not remember any of the books which I read, nor anything about them, except that there was something very striking about beavers in the book of which I was most fond.' He stayed at Tenbury two years, being forced to leave it 'one night, sick of scarlet fever, wrapped in a blanket'. Next he went to a dame's school at Shrewsbury, and it was there that he discovered *Jane Eyre*: 'One of the governesses lent it to me, and I was so enthralled that I read and re-read it, taking it up to bed with me.' Then, 'at the age of eleven I returned to Ludlow, and was placed at the Grammar School here. Our head-master's hobby was English history, and in his study he used to drill us in a most effective manner. We were made to stand in line – he facing us, cane in hand – and each boy had an English king named to him, and was required to reel off all the dates of importance in his reign. If he made a mistake, down came the cane. It was effective, in my case at least, for even today I am strong on the dates in English history. I remember him with gratitude, for I believe that it was he who laid the foundation of my – well – of this taste for history. He gave me the framework, and what one wants at the outset is the skeleton, which one can afterwards clothe at leisure.

'At the same time,' Weyman told Sherard in 1895, 'that is to say whilst the head-master at Ludlow Grammar School was thus effectively grounding me in the rudiments of English history, I was bribed by my father to read Macaulay's history, at the rate of sixpence a volume. I hardly needed the stimulus of the bribe, however, for I delighted in Macaulay. He has the wonderful gift of making history all living, and I found his books much more entertaining than a novel … and used to take them to my bed with me. Together with Macaulay, I read *Ivanhoe*. I was fond of Scott at the time, and am so still, though there are some of his books – as for instance, *Count Robert of Paris* – which I cannot and never could read. On the other hand, I can re-read *Quentin Durward* with the most complete satisfaction.

'I left Ludlow Grammar School at the age of fifteen and went to Shrewsbury School, where, as I was fifteen, I was placed in the Senior House. But I was such a little chap that the big boys in the Senior House resented my presence. They were very indignant that so small a boy should be put amongst them, and they bullied me frightfully. I led rather a lonely life there, and used to spend most of my time in the House Library. *Hypatia* and *Adam Bede* were my favourite books, and impressed me very much at the time. However, later, I won some respect from my fellows by a good performance in a school steeplechase. They saw that though I was a very little chap I had some pluck, and they treated me much better afterwards.'

His time at Shrewsbury must have been difficult in other ways too; in 1873 his father died from injuries sustained in a fox-hunting accident. The bullying he was meanwhile enduring at Shrewsbury School and the fact that he was later able to earn the bullies' respect seems to have made a profound impression on him. While in his home town of Ludlow, he was recognizable to all as a Weyman and was treated with due respect, at Shrewsbury School, one of the famous schools of England, he clearly enjoyed no such privileges; doubtless many of the boys were from wealthier and more aristocratic backgrounds and may have looked down on him not only because of his small stature but because he came 'only' from a professional family. At school and later, as we shall see, on the legal circuit and travelling in France, the Weyman name counted for nothing; only by his actions could he prove himself and earn respect. In his novels again and again we see the bullied and downtrodden eventually proving their worth and either winning the respect of their tormentors or getting the better of them; in Weyman's fictional world rights are wronged, scores settled and vengeance wreaked.

'I was a bad classical scholar,' he told Sherard, 'and had no taste for mathematics. No history was taught at Shrewsbury. Though I did not distinguish myself, I attained a respectable position in the school, and passed out with an exhibition at Christ Church, Oxford. I was rather sorry to have to go to the 'House' [Christ Church College]. It was hardly the place for a man who had only a moderate allowance. I enjoyed my 'Varsity life very much. My principal amusement was running with the college pack of beagles. I grew amazingly at Oxford, perhaps because I was better fed. I went up in 1874, and took my degree in 1877 – a second in history. I studied history mainly under Professor Kitchin ... Together with my degree I took away from Oxford a great number of debts. At the age of twenty-two, I went as classical master and teacher of history to King's School, at Chester, and had a very good time there, and was able to save money. The head-master was an old Shrewsbury man, a very good fellow and one of my best friends... and on his account I regretted leaving the School. I did this in 1878, and entered as a student at the Inner Temple, where I read law with a man called Bosanquet, who, curiously enough, was of an old Huguenot family. My best friends... were made in Bosanquet's chambers. I was called to the Bar in 1881, and joined the Oxford Circuit, which we always think the most gentlemanly Circuit. My practice at the Bar was uneventful, and not very remunerative. Some days I would make 15 Pounds, on other days nothing at all. My average income as a barrister was 200 Pounds a year; and if in my best year I earned 300 Pounds, there was a year in which I earned only 20 Pounds. I remember that after I had been a few years at the Bar I was challenged by the Income-tax Commissioners to show cause why, and so on – and went to Westminster and produced my fee-book, from which it became patent that, at that time, my entire earnings from my profession did not exceed 130 Pounds. Thereupon the Commissioners said: 'Good morning, Mr Weyman; we hope you will have better luck in the future.' My very first brief of all, was for the defendant in a case about a tailor's bill, in the Westminster County Court. The plaintiff was Charles Dickens, the son of the novelist. I lost the case. And I have often thought since that if they had had a better man they would have won their case.

'I was, perhaps, too nervous, too sensitive, to succeed at the Bar. I remember being once so bullyragged by the Judge that I had to go outside, and was so sick that in order to recover myself I had to take a pint of champagne. But I liked the work, and the Circuit took me to pleasant places, full of historic souvenirs – yes, souvenirs of English history – Reading, Oxford, Monmouth, Gloucester, Worcester, Hereford, Shrewsbury, and Stafford.

'When [in 1891] I left the Bar and came back to Ludlow to live with my people, I considered myself – then a man of thirty-five – a complete failure. At the Bar I saw men of perhaps less capacity outstripping me. I could not speak – I do not think that writers ever do speak well in public – and I had little presence – men of better presence trampled me under foot.'

This out-manoeuvring of the worthy by the worldly is a recurrent theme in Weyman's novels and features significantly in *Ovington's Bank*.

Weyman was faring little better in his attempts to make a living by writing: 'Nor had my other endeavour,' he told Sherard 'namely as a writer, been more successful. For at the time that I was at the Bar, I tried – God knows how hard – to eke out my altogether insufficient income with my pen. How I wrote! I had begun by contributing fancy sketches to the St. James's Gazette, at that time under the editorship of Greenwood. Greenwood rather liked my work, and one day asked me to report for his paper. He sent me down to Windsor to describe the marriage of Prince Leopold, and I went, and was excellently placed, and saw it all, but my report was considered altogether unsatisfactory. It was not printed nor was I paid for it, and that was the end of my journalistic experiences. So then I tried short stories for the magazines, and failed at that; until one day there came into my hands Anstey's tale, The Black Poodle, about which everybody was talking. I said to myself: 'Let me see why everybody is talking about this story,' and I took it home and read and re-read it, till I came to the conclusion that its captivation lay in the fact of the extreme carefulness of its workmanship. I pulled it to pieces, sentence by sentence, and saw that each sentence had been polished and elaborated till no further elaboration was possible. So I determined that I also would elaborate and polish, and these things I did in a story which I wrote and called, King Pippin and Sweet Clive. I sent it to the Cornhill. James Payn read it, and so greatly approved of it that he asked me up to the office, and encouraged me to continue writing. 'But' he said, 'why do you not write a novel? You can never make an income out of writing short stories.' I answered, 'Sir, I have no idea of plot construction such as is necessary for the production of a novel.' And then the kind man gave me a full hour of his time in a paternal discourse on the carpentry of fiction. He encouraged me to try, and I did try, and again I failed. I wrote a novel of modern life, and it was lamentably bad. I think that it was called *The New Rector*, a title which I have since used again. And as to that first novel, I am putting it to its best use, and am writing on the back of the pages of the manuscript. But of my writings at that time, why should I speak of them. I never made more than 50 Pounds a year during all those years, and was a failure in this profession as I was at the Bar. So the day came when I sickened of unsuccess, and turned my steps back to the house where I was born, and where there was a home and a refuge for me … [But] I did not put my pen altogether away. History had always fascinated me, and amongst the first things which I wrote here, was a study on Oliver Cromwell's Kinsfolk, which appeared in the Historical Review.

'It was, however, by a mere accident that I was put on the road which has led me, well, to – to – well, to being respectfully greeted by the clerks at that bank over the way, who formerly, – enfin. I was up in London, and was sitting in the smoking-room of my club in St. James's Street, the New University Club, thinking rather despondently of my past, and even more despondently of my future, when I happened to notice, on the little table which stood by the chair on which I was sitting, a copy of Professor Baird's History of the Huguenots. I took it up, and rather mournfully turned over its leaves. Those were Rider Haggard's imperial days, the days when fiction, to be popular and marketable, had to rumble with thunder, and drip with blood. And the book in my hand set me thinking that one might successfully write of carnage and the stir of arms in a period which was elegant and refined. I thought of the Huguenots and St. Bartholomew's Eve; and, later, as I was washing my hands, I thought out the plot of *The House of the Wolf*. At the same time, I had not forgotten what I had learned as to the absolute necessity of taking pains, and over that story I spent infinite labour. I polished and re-wrote, and touched and re-touched, and I could, with difficulty, in the end allow myself to let it go forth, wondering whether all had been well said, no word or deed forgot. It was accepted, and from the serial use of it and the book-rights I derived, in all, the sum of 200 Pounds.

'*The House of the Wolf* was written for, and accepted by, Comyns Carr, of the English Illustrated Magazine, who was pleased with it, and asked me to write him another story for the same magazine. So I set to work and produced The Story of Francis Cludde. In the meanwhile, however, the editor of the English Illustrated Magazine had been changed, and the young man who had taken Comyns Carr's place said about my Story of Francis Cludde, 'Oh, hang it! I won't have this story. I don't like it.' It was a great blow, as at that time I had no footing. *The House of the Wolf* was no great success then, though from certain letters which I received, I knew that a certain number of people liked it. So I had to take my Story of Francis Cludde into the market, and eventually succeeded in selling it for serial publication in The Leisure Hour. The editor, Mr Stephens, said to me in making our arrangement: 'If it takes, we will give you a little more money.' Some time later, he sent me a cheque for 60 guineas more than I had bargained for. It was afterwards published in book form by Cassell's, and this year [1895] had a 'boom' in America, so that altogether out of that contemptuously-rejected Story of Francis Cludde I have made from 700 to 800 Pounds.'

In his article about Weyman, published in 1895, Sherard concluded: 'It is very evident to anyone who speaks to Stanley Weyman, that here is a man who has suffered bitterly and long – maybe too long – for, though he is at all times winning, sympathetic, genial, and of a hospitality of which there is record only in the courtly days of which he writes, his face bears the imprint of disappointment, and, even when speaking of unrivalled successes achieved, the quiet voice has none of that enthusiasm of the man who has striven and conquered. There is an evident grudge against the past in one who, in the irony of fate, has torn his triumph from the very vitals of the past.'

'My real success,' Weyman told Sherard, 'began with *A Gentleman of France*,' of which, I may say, that I bestowed upon it, in almost feverish anxiety, all the care of which I was capable. I gave it a whole year of unremitting labour. I have told you what were my materials. I might add that the volumes of the London Library, a most excellent collection, greatly assisted me in matters of detail. Thus, for my information on cut and thrust – my technicalities of fencing – I am much indebted to Castle's excellent *Schools and Masters of Fence from the Middle Ages to the Eighteenth Century*. But, in fact, I am not diffuse in matters of detail or of stage properties. For instance, I invent the costumes in which my characters parade. I think that Scott was the last writer who was conscientious as to his documentation on these points.'

From 1890 until 1908 Weyman published an average of one novel a year. These books proved immensely successful and he soon became very wealthy.

* * *

So what turned Weyman from a failure at the Bar and in the embryonic stages of his literary career into a man capable of success? It may have been an adventure that Weyman had in December 1885 when on a walking holiday with his brother Arthur in the Pyrenees which galvanised his writing career. Certainly, the dramatic events seared into his consciousness and similar scenes feature in one form or another in many of his novels. The story is best told in Weyman's own words:

LE NOMMÉ W

In the department of the Basses Pyrénées in December, 1885, I temporarily lost my name. I became known as Le Nommé W. Thieves and murderers in that country are commonly designated in this way, and obtain consideration in plenty. Extenuating circumstances arise on their behalf, self-generated in a night like the mushrooms. But the crime of which my brother and I were accused was one that admitted of no palliation, the mere suspicion of which placed us at once beyond the pale of native sympathy; converted a *procureur*, who may at other times have been a gentleman, into a rough *bureaucrat*, and conjured up about us a Cadmean crop of revolvers and fetters. We were German spies.

About the middle of that December we were at Pau. The early part of the winter in the district had been exceptionally mild. We had spent three weeks in exploring the better known passes and valleys of the Hautes Pyrénées, and now proposed to make our way to Biarritz by a roundabout road through the forest of Iraty, a wild and interesting part of the French Basque country. Accordingly, we sent our heavy baggage by rail to Biarritz, and started ourselves after lunch on the 14th by train to Oloron, our equipment consisting of a knapsack and light pack, a railway rug, two light overcoats, and two walking sticks. The weather was fine and bright, though cold, and we were in high spirits, anticipating a delightful excursion.

At Oloron station we sought out the *diligence* for Tardets. We intended to sleep that evening at this place on the outskirts of the forest, with a view to making an early start on foot next morning. The *diligence* discovered, we put our slight baggage inside, and asked for two places. Then, learning that the vehicle would not leave the town for half-an-hour, we told the driver to pick us up by the way, and started blithely – unwitting lambs as we were – to stir our blood by a brisk walk along the road. This – if a cabinet minister well acquainted with French manners is to be believed – this was the cause of all our woe! To pay for a ride and then to walk is a thing so foreign to the thrifty French nature, that it might form the basis for an accusation of the most abominable crimes. We paid to ride: we walked. From that moment the eye of the French law saw in us German spies.

Once clear of Oloron, we strode along merrily, noting the softer character of the landscape, and admiring the rolling hills and woods, until the *diligence* overtook us some two miles or so beyond the town.

We stepped in, so far as I could afterwards remember, without hesitation, and greeted our fellow-travellers cheerily. They were two – a farmer or peasant-proprietor, and a bluff, ruddy, well-set-up man of middle height, wearing a cocked hat and uniform of dark blue faced with white, of the kind worn by the *gendarmes*. He sported epaulettes, however, and a profusion of silver lace, with a decoration and medal, and a handsome sword; so that I did not set him down either as an ordinary *gendarme* (a conclusion to which my brother had come) or as that which he was in fact, a brigadier of that force. I did not know what he was, but on lighting a cigarette offered him one. He preferred a cigar, and declined. His companion, however, accepted my offer, and we fell into a desultory conversation. To what place were we going? What was our nationality? What cigarettes were they? Had we come from Pau? What was our purpose in visiting that part of the country? All these questions our smart friend asked, and I, who had never been 'wanted,' answered without any suspicion that I was being interrogated with a purpose. We were English, I said, travelling for pleasure, and going to Tardets: we had come from Pau: our cigarettes were of Egyptian manufacture.

After this, wearied by the rattling of the omnibus and the strain which the use of a foreign tongue imperfectly known imposed, I was glad to fall into silence. I examined – these details are important – my letter-case to see if I had any gold-beater's skin. And, my brother calling my attention to the sun-set sky behind us, we speculated on the chance of the highest peak in sight being the Pic du Midi d'Ossau, on whose shoulder, six thousand feet above the sea, we had been some weeks before.

About five o'clock the *diligence* stopped in the street of a small village. Near at hand, and apparently awaiting it, stood a *gendarme*. The brigadier, stepping out nimbly, exchanged, as I noticed, a word with him, and passed across the road. The *gendarme* came to the door. 'Look here!' exclaimed my brother, 'he has left this!' And taking up a smart leather satchel, which the brigadier had left in his place, he handed it to the *gendarme*, telling him that 'the monsieur' had left it.

'Thank you,' said the man civilly. 'Are you going to Tardets?'

'Certainly!' we answered.

'Then you descend here. This is Tardets.'

We were astonished. We had not looked to be at Tardets before half-past six. But we had no suspicions, and thanking him cordially, we alighted. The *gendarme* pointed out the inn, a very poor place, and we entered it with him: we were about to ask for a bedroom, when he intervened, opening the door of a room down stairs, and inviting us by a gesture to enter. We did so, and saw immediately that we had fallen into a trap. Before us, looking very stern and uncompromising, stood the brigadier: behind us we heard the door slammed to with unnecessary emphasis.

'This is not Tardets, but Aramits,' the Brigadier said harshly. 'I wish to ask you some questions. If you answer them satisfactorily, you shall proceed on your journey, gentlemen.' Then he began by asking, as he sat down at the table before us, what was my name. I told him, and that I had a passport, which I produced, not doubting that this would end the matter. Nothing of the kind! It was in English, and our inquisitor knew nothing of that language. Despite his decorations and epaulettes, he could not write with facility, could not spell at all, and I suspect could read but little. He pounced upon the word Majesty, and persisted for some time that that was my name. Then the passport, although countersigned for Spain and Italy, bore no French *visé*. Rejecting it, therefore, he proceeded to put to me, in a tone which grew more loud and imperious each minute, a series of questions. He asked my name, nationality, and profession: where I had entered France: how long I had been in the country: how long I proposed to stay in it: what was my object in travelling: where did I intend to sleep that night – the next – and the next? Then came my brother's turn, our inquisitor's tone growing more bim-bam-bom-like each minute. He disregarded our protestations that he spoke too quickly, and that we did not understand all he said; and, telling us that we had spoken French excellently in the *diligence*, paid us the only compliment which passed at the interview.

'Now, attend to me!' he cried presently, passing from examination-in-chief to cross-examination. 'Why did you, when you were about to enter the vehicle, show hesitation at the sight of me – of me – the Brigadier?' I laughed outright. The idea that I should shrink at sight of even a superintendent of police seemed to me, being an Englishman and not an official-ridden Frenchman, funny in the extreme. 'I did not,' I said.

'Why did you tell me in the *diligence* that you were Belgians? Answer me that!' And he thumped the table.

'It is not true. I did not tell you so.'

'Very well!' in a menacing accent. 'Why did you tell me that you were friends, not brothers?'

'I did not tell you so.'

'What! You said you were Belgians. That is so?'

'No! No! No!'

'Where is the map which you consulted in the *diligence*?'

'I had no map in the *diligence*.'

'You took something from your pocket, and examined it. Produce it!'

I handed to him a tiny packet containing gold-beater's skin. He looked at it curiously, almost fearfully. He consulted the *gendarme* upon it. He held it up to the light. Finally he put it carefully aside.

'And now the map! Be quick! The map I say!' he roared.

'The only map we have is an authorised French map, that of the *État -major*. But it is in the knapsack. We did not have it in the *diligence*. The knapsack was in the care of the driver.'

'You had a pencil. You made a map of the country as you came?'

'I had no pencil. I made no map. I do not draw.'

'You made signs.'

At this I shrugged my shoulders, and exchanged a glance of wonder with my brother – making signs again, you see!

'You looked behind you at the country,' he persisted doggedly. I told him what I have already set down regarding the sunset and the Pic du Midi.

'Why did you not speak to one another in French? Attend! Tell me that,' with another thump upon the table.

'It is not our language. We speak it badly, and with difficulty.'

'Chut! You understand it perfectly! You said you were travelling for your pleasure.'

'Yes, that is so.'

'But you said also that you were travelling for your health.'

'Yes, that is so, too. Partly for pleasure and partly for health.'

'Are you wealthy?'

'No, I wish I were!' And so he continued in an endless round of the same questions. I have set some of them down at length, because they convey an idea of the French system of examining the accused; and offer an example of the false assumptions, the deliberate traps, and the bullying tone by which the prosecution seek to extract either the truth, or something that may weigh against the prisoner.

At the end of three quarters of an hour of this the brigadier announced himself to be dissatisfied. He must make an arrest.

I protested loudly. I warned him that we were British subjects. I produced two *lettres d'indication* addressed to a number of foreign bankers, and written in French. I showed him that the name engraved upon my compass, knife-haft, and other things corresponded with that in the passport.

I solemnly warned him – well, that we should not perish unavenged: and I probably referred to *Son Excellence l'Ambassadeur de sa Majesté Britannique*, honestly believing at the time in the efficacy of this conjuration.

But he was not afraid of a name! He smiled a Napoleonic smile, and conducted us at once to the police-station. Here, in a little office, he wrote down his version of what we had said of ourselves, mingling with it, without distinguishing marks of any kind, his own evidence and his opinion of us generally. It may be imagined that the result was a very wonderful document: particularly as I took pity upon his incapacity, spelled some of the French words for him, and occasionally even wrote a sentence, or struck the pen through one which contained too gross a perversion of our statements. This done he took from us our money (for which he gave us a receipt) and our papers, watches, compasses, and walking-sticks; our knapsacks and pack also. But he did not search us, so that we retained our matches and cigarettes. With great difficulty I obtained leave to send a telegram to the vice-consul at Pau.

By this time it was about a quarter-past six and quite dark. I anticipated that we should be lodged in the *gendarmes'* quarters, and was peering about in no apprehensive mood, when the brigadier bade us follow him. Guarded by two *gendarmes* we marched down stairs to a yard at the back of the house. Facing us stood a small detached outhouse with two doors. It would have been in England a pig-sty, or a hen-house, or at best a neglected dog-kennel; but in France, and here, it was the lock-up of Aramits! The two doors were thrown open, the two *gendarmes* bowed, and, immensely astonished, but too proud to complain or make a useless resistance, we stepped in, and the doors were locked behind us. We were in prison: the prison surely of some wild uncivilised country!

Our cells were about eight feet long by four wide and eight high: rough and mean beyond description. The walls and floor were of stones and trodden earth respectively, as we discovered when daylight came. At present we were in the dark: no fires, no lights! Windows proper, there were none, though an oblong aperture over the door admitted light in the day, and air (cold or warm as luck might have it) at all times. A board covered by a frowsy, dark-coloured blanket, and a pitcher in one case, a bucket in the other, formed the whole and only furniture in each cell. The sole alleviation of our discomfort lay in the fact that the partition between us was of rough planks, so that we could talk to one another – an arrangement, I fancy, not entirely matter of accident.

A quarter of an hour later our doors were opened, and I was taken to my brother's cell. One *gendarme* held a smoky, guttering candle: three others stood partly within, and partly without the doorway, around which a dozen women and children clustered, peeping at us. Our dinner, some greasy soup, with bits of bread and cabbage floating in it, was produced: we had only one basin, but, thank heaven, a spoon apiece: a lump of bread, and a bottle of thin sour wine completed the meal.

Anxious not to seem cast down, we fell upon the horrid mess with apparent appetite, at intervals drinking toasts and bantering the police; and laughing very loudly at our own jokes. *'Vive la Republique!'* to which a glance round our cell gave point, was well received; so was *'Le Beau Sexe',* but it was reserved for our third toast, *'Madame la femme de M. le Brigadier!'* to bring down the house, the vicious emphasis which we threw into our enemy's name sending his subordinates into a frenzy of delight. The more they laughed – and the most taciturn face wore a grin – the more fluent grew our French, and the wilder our folly; and when we wound up by begging them to bring our hot water at eight and to see that our beds were well aired and our boots well varnished – when this was done, and we were back in our cells, we had at least the satisfaction of feeling that our entertainment had been as successful as unique; and that M. le Brigadier's importance had not gained much at our hands.

By the way, – 'Can we not,' my brother had asked, 'sleep at the inn, if we pay for our room, and for a room for a guard?'

'No, it is out of the question,' was the decisive answer – twice given.

At a quarter to seven our doors were locked, and were not again opened until eight o'clock next morning. For thirteen hours no one came near us. They were thirteen hours of intense cold and misery, as may be understood when I say that the thermometer fell in that neighbourhood on that night several degrees below freezing point. My brother had fortunately been carrying our travelling rug, and it had not been taken from him; yet he felt the cold severely.

I had merely my walking suit and a thin dust-coat. The frowsy blanket I at first put from me, shuddering at the least contact with it, and picturing the French tramp who had last used it. But necessity knows no daintiness: before morning I was hugging the blanket about me, and wishing that it were five times as thick. The night air poured in through the unglazed window, and through a dozen chinks and apertures besides. I did not get even ten minutes' sleep: by five o'clock my feet were numbed, my teeth chattering, and my shoulders shaking. For very fear lest the cold should kill me then and there, I rose, and for three hours tramped up and down the cell unceasingly – two steps and a half each way: it was dreary work!

Soon after eight the brigadier came in his shirt-sleeves, and let us out. For some time we had been loudly clamouring, and I think that he was alarmed on finding how cold the night had been; for he took us both to his room, and placed chairs for us before the wood-fire which was burning in the great open fireplace. His wife and child were still in bed in the room. He offered us a glass of Armagnac, and telling us he should take us early in the day to the *procureur* at Oloron, went down stairs. I have no doubt he did this last with a purpose. For almost immediately his wife, ignoring our presence, got up, and, after partly dressing herself, brought the child to the fire. She was a young woman, but thin and careworn. If it were not that wives in France have the upper hand, one would have said that Monsieur Bim-bam-bom began his bullying at home. She sat on the one side of the fire, dressing the child: we sat respectfully on the other.

'You say you are English. Is it not so?' she begins, pausing with an uplifted sock in her hand, and fixing us suddenly with her keen eyes. We cheerfully acquiesce. 'You do not speak German?'

'Not a word.'

'Belgian?'

'Most certainly not.'

'But you have no papers,' she continues, shaking her head. 'Papers? Oh dear yes! Abundance of papers! Papers signed by the Marquis of Salisbury, Chevalier de la Jarrètiere, & c & c !' we cry.

'No, you have no papers! Dear, dear me!'

'No papers!' we reply warmly. 'And if it be so? Do we look like brigands, madam: thieves, madam?'

'No, gentlemen!' And madam's polite breeding interferes with her duties as assistant police-examiner. She cries, '*Mon Dieu, non!*' many times, and we are comforted.

At nine o'clock the brigadier brought in a telegram. It was addressed to me, but he had opened it. The sender, the vice-consul at Pau, announced that he had telegraphed to the mayor of Aramits respecting us. This second telegram was presently brought. It certified that we were harmless tourists, known to the vice-consul. Upon this the brigadier was so kind as to say that we should soon be permitted to go. I thought he meant that he would release us without taking us before the *procureur*, and I replied sharply, 'Our release is not the question now. We have a complaint to make.'

'Of what?' he asked.

'Of the treatment we have received. It was your turn yesterday; it is ours to-day.'

'What?' he roared. 'I have gone out of my way to treat you well, and you threaten me? Take care! If you had not said that you were Belgians, this would not have happened!'

'We did not say so!' we both cried.

'You did!' he shouted.

'We did not!' I retorted as loudly.

'No! No! No! It is false!' And we stood glaring into one another's eyes. I thought he was going to strike me. Over his shoulder I had a glimpse of his wife's frightened face, and the smiling *gendarmes* in the doorway. Then he flung away with a torrent of oaths, leaving us to enjoy some bread and coffee, which we had been allowed to order at the inn, and found delicious. We thought that now our troubles were over and our enemy's beginning; but we reckoned without our host. Back presently came the brigadier, and sternly bade us follow him. He conducted us back to the cells, and locked us up – this time together. I fear we looked a little foolish.

So from half-past nine until about twelve we kicked our heels in my cell. It was in vain that we asked for water, that we might wash, and for our knapsack, that we might brush our hair, and so forth. The *gendarmes* visited us from time to time, but it was for other things than these – in part to see if even yet we would vary our story, and partly, I think, to gather our intentions. I made mine plain. I was sorry, I said, for the brigadier's wife and child; for himself – well, it was a pity that so promising a career should end thus miserably. And I drew a moral from the story. 'Too much zeal!' I concluded sadly, 'too much zeal!' My words, no doubt, were carried straight to the person concerned, and I think – yes, still I think – that under the bluff, stern exterior he showed us to the end, there was a heart quivering like a jelly.

At noon they let us out to eat a substantial luncheon in the sunny yard. Of course we paid for our chicken and claret, in spite of which it was wonderful how cheerful we grew as the warmth stole through us.

The *gendarmes*, moreover, were civil and kindly. In the midst of our meal a visitor came upon the scene in the shape of the *curé* of the parish – a young man, thin and ascetic looking, but with a pleasant smile. I suppose he had come to see us in the ordinary course of his duties, for, after saluting us, he said, 'My sons, this is sad! I trust that it will be a warning to you for the future.' Now that was not at all the light in which we were looking at the matter, and I told him so very quickly. His perplexity, as we detailed our story and showed the cells in which we had spent the night ('at the Hôtel de la Poste one night!' commented a gendarme sympathetically, 'here the next!') was most amusing. But when we went on to explain our intentions in regard to the brigadier, he took us up. 'Revenge, my sons, is an empty thing,' he said gravely.

'But the cells were cold, my father; very cold last night,' I replied.

'It is true. Yet let it pass. You will go far away and forget it. You think much of it now, but viewed from afar it will seem a small thing.'

'Perhaps. At present I say with St. Paul, *Civis Romanus sum*, and I will not go out privily.'

He pricked up his ears. 'You know Latin!' he exclaimed.

I told him that I had been at Oxford; and was amused to find that this gave him a graver opinion of the wrongs we had suffered than all my complaints. He made another pilgrimage to the cells: he shrugged his shoulders inimitably; and then, perching himself upon a wall, talked to us for some time. He had a knowledge of English politics most surprising in a man stationed in that obscure village, and was altogether a charming specimen of a charming class.

At two we were ordered to make ready to start. The brigadier ostentatiously loaded his revolver and charged us to make no attempt at escape. He also directed us to carry our baggage. We declined; he blustered. In the end, the *gendarme* who accompanied him agreed to carry the knapsack, and we took up the lesser articles. I noticed that every person, gentle or simple, whom we met on the road, saluted the brigadier, while he ignored many of their greetings. He was a little king in his district; justice of the peace as well as superintendent of police; and to me at that moment a standing argument in his arrogance for our resident county magistrates. In France such men are wanting, or have no power. There is no one to check official arbitrariness, or to come between the executive and the people.

At a bridge half-way between Aramits and Oloron, the brigadier of the latter place met us and took charge of us, giving our old enemies, from whom we here parted, a written receipt for us. In one respect we had cause to regret the change: our new master bade us carry the luggage: we demurred. Thereupon he produced a long chain with handcuffs at each end.

'You can make your choice,' he said, 'either take up the baggage and carry it, or repeat your refusal. In the latter case we shall handcuff you, chain you together, and force you to carry it.'

This he said without a trace of passion; and being quite sure that he would keep his word, my brother took up the knapsack and I the rug and coats. After the night we had spent we were in anything but good condition; and it was not without difficulty that, thus burdened, we walked the remaining distance, over four miles, to Oloron. At the time we were treated in this way, the police, it will be remembered, had the vice-consul's telegram in their possession, and knew that we were English tourists. On our arrival at Oloron we were taken to the house of the *procureur*. He was not at home, and we proceeded to his public office. I believe that our arrest had been noised abroad, for the streets were full of people, who stood and watched our little procession go by. No one was uncivil to us, though we heard the words '*Espions Allemands,*' freely exchanged; yet the ordeal of passing, burdened as we were, and in custody, under the eyes of hundreds of Frenchmen, was not to our English taste.

The *procureur* received us in a moderately large room, in the middle of which we were told to stand, while he sat at an ordinary writing-table. The police arranged themselves behind us, and round the room sat a number of men whom I judged to be respectable inhabitants of the town. I at once asked to be furnished with an interpreter, saying that I had had only too much experience of the danger of answering questions in a language imperfectly known. Unfortunately I had well conned the sentences in which I expressed this, and my glibness defeated my object. The *procureur*, a tall, dark, harsh-voiced man, politely assured me that I spoke French sufficiently well, and, save for the aid which one of the gentlemen present who spoke a little English gave us, we fought our own battle. Here, at any rate, I thought, we shall get justice!

And at first all went well. I need not give the magistrate's questions, which were not many. There was abundant evidence of our nationality and identity, and with little loss of time he gave his decision: We were free, we might go.

Upon this I stated that I wished to lay a formal complaint against the brigadier of Aramits. I submitted (1) That we had about us sufficient papers of identity, and that therefore the arrest was illegal from the first. (2) That if the arrest and detention were in themselves legal, they were attended by circumstances of illegal and unnecessary severity.

What passed upon this I give in detail, because it may make the position clear to other travellers in France, and solve in some degree a vexed question. 'Very well,' was the *procureur*'s answer, 'I understand. Then firstly where are your papers, if you please?'

'I had a British Foreign-Office passport which identified me.'

'It bore no French *visé*, and was without weight here on that account.'

'Do I understand then,' I asked slowly, 'that it is absolutely necessary for every Englishman travelling in France to have a passport countersigned by the French authorities?'

'It is absolutely necessary,' was his answer.

'And yet,' I cried, 'there are hundreds of Englishmen at Pau, and you know that there are not ten such passports among them all! But I leave that. There is my banker's *lettre d'indication*.'

'It is a foreign recommendation on the same footing as your passport.'

'Not at all! The bankers who sign it are French as well as English bankers.'

That clearly puzzled him, and he spoke a while with his clerk: finally, 'It is printed, not written,' he said.

I laughed aloud. As a fact, my name, the essential part of the document, was written, but I missed that point. I abandoned under protest my first head of complaint, and passed on to the treatment we had received.

To this his sole answer was that it was unlucky for us that we had been arrested at Aramits and not at Oloron, where there was a comfortable prison. It was our misfortune, not the *gendarmes'* fault: they had only done their duty. As for an apology, he would not assist us to any form of one. 'If,' he concluded harshly, his patience worn thin by my importunity, 'you think you have cause for complaint, go to your ambassador!'

'We will!' we cried with one voice, and gave up the fight for that time. Our money – less the cost of telegram, luncheon and breakfast – and papers were returned to us. Our volunteer interpreter kindly told us that there was a train just starting for Pau; and another gentleman, undertaking to show us the way to the station, we left *M. le Procureur* with less ceremony than haste. Once in the train, I lay back in my corner of the carriage fairly exhausted, and morally depressed beyond belief by the continuous bullying to which we had been subjected.

Our first impulse was to keep the whole matter to ourselves; but friendly greetings and a good dinner at our hotel put us in heart again. We sent a brief epitome of the story to the newspapers, and raised our bitter cry before the ambassador. In the issue, both from Lord Lyons and Sir John Walsham, who at the time was his representative, we received most courteous treatment. But, unfortunately, we have never got farther than that, although Mr Addison, Q.C., Member of Parliament for Ashton-under-Lyne, asked a question in the House on the matter, and the Government expressed themselves dissatisfied with the French minister's explanations. True, we have been informed that the chief officer of *gendarmes* in the district has privately called upon the vice-consul at Pau to express his regret; and that the brigadier at Aramits has been punished by some days' detention – not, I fear, in his own cells. But no public apology has been made at Oloron, in the newspapers, or elsewhere: no public reprimand has been administered. Nay, the very document from which I learn this, states that the indiscretion of the police was palliated by the suspects' conduct; and goes on to narrate a pure fiction, to the effect that on the day of our arrest we retired under surveillance into a wood with certain instruments, and did very dreadful things indeed!

* * *

This adventure, which Weyman later described as the only great adventure in his otherwise quiet life, is worthy of the pages of one of his novels: '… we stood glaring into one another's eyes. I thought he was going to strike me. Over his shoulder I had a glimpse of his wife's frightened face, and the smiling *gendarmes* in the doorway.'

But in this case it is of course fact, not fiction. The adventure clearly made a profound impression on Weyman; over the years reworkings of incidents and snatches of dialogue from this episode appear and reappear in his novels. We have seen for example how (echoing the French diplomat Talleyrand) Weyman taunted the Brigadier: "'Too much zeal,' I concluded sadly, 'too much zeal!'"

A few years later in *The House of the Wolf* (1890), the hero, finding himself surrounded by his enemies, warns their leader that he is exceeding his authority: 'Beware of too much zeal, Captain Pallavicini! It is a dangerous thing!' While in *The Story of Francis Cludde* (1891), the eponymous hero, threatened with arrest, says, 'You will do so at your peril … I am travelling in the Queen's name and on her service.' The bullying bailiff backs down and later sends an intermediary to convey his apologies; laconically, Cludde replies, 'Tell him from me that he is zealous – perhaps overzealous.'

More generally, victories over bullies, with might but not right on their side, feature again and again in Weyman's novels. His adventure in Aramits taught him a good deal about the risks of such encounters ('He conducted us back to the cells, and locked us up … I fear we looked a little foolish'), but he clearly looked back with some pride at the part he had played: '… we had at least the satisfaction of feeling that our entertainment had been as successful as unique; and that M. le Brigadier's importance had not gained much at our hands.' However, perhaps the most interesting aspect of his account is the way in which Weyman himself, to some extent, actually creates the adventure. At a number of points it is his spirited defiance, his verve and wit, and his refusal to submit which enrage the Brigadier and, by goading the official to further abuse of his power, drive the story forward. In this sense Weyman's conduct, while from a practical point of view surely unwise, made a gripping story happen. It may indeed have been by standing up to the bullying Brigadier that Weyman discovered how he could quickly – indeed on the spur of the moment – produce a compelling tale from a clash of personalities in tense circumstances. While for the rest of his life Stanley was only to imagine such scenes in the quiet of his study, on this first occasion he created an adventure 'live' in real time. The episode not only galvanised Weyman by showing how quickly such stirring adventures can be produced, but also perhaps provided him with a source of strong emotion which he could recollect in tranquillity and which would help him start and carry on the composition of new stories. In the 1890s a string of successful novels set in France in which, against all odds, heroes win satisfying victories over powerful oppressors gave sublimated expression to his frustration at not receiving the public apology he felt to be his due for the arrest at Aramits. Composed at the rate of a thousand words a day, these swashbuckling romances became international best-sellers: a remarkable demonstration of the maxim that novel-writing is the art of turning misfortune into money.

Much later in Weyman's literary career, the hero of *The Great House* (1919), Peter Basset (who seems to be Weyman's self-portrait), is drifting through the years without making much of a mark, worsted at every turn by others with more presence and less substance, when he has an adventure in which he has to stick up for himself and which changes the course of his life: 'He was one of those to whom a spice of danger is a fillip, whom a little peril shakes out of themselves.' In Stanley's case the fillip was of course his arrest at Aramits.

* * *

Weyman resigned from the bar in 1891 to devote himself to full-time writing and by 1895 was wealthy enough to marry Charlotte, the daughter of the Rev. Richard Panting, formerly headmaster of Shrewsbury School. They went to live in the Vale of Clwyd (Denbighshire) perhaps in part on health grounds (it seems that at some point around 1890 suffering from phthisis Stanley had spent eight or nine months at a sanatorium on the Continent). Weyman is quoted as saying he was going to 'grow books and cows, the former for profit and the latter for pleasure'. While his brothers, Henry and Arthur, worked in the law firm that their father had established, Stanley longed for the life of his grandfathers as a yeomen farmer. There are good reasons for thinking that his brother Arthur was of a similar disposition and laboured in the family law firm from necessity rather than vocation, escaping to the country whenever he could. There are obvious parallels with Clement in *Ovington's Bank*.

The Weymans were happily married for 33 years. Their home, Llanrhydd Hall, a country mansion about two miles from Ruthin, was built around 1620. Although now very well-off, the Weymans rented and never bought the house although they paid for many additions. Weyman soon became a leading figure in Denbighshire affairs and public matters; he was governor of several schools, gave speeches and prizes, and supported local charities including hospitals, the RSPCA, and the Ruthin War Memorial Fund. In 1900 in his capacity as Chairman of the Ruthin Christmas Show he advised farmers to pay more attention to 'the production of butter, poultry, eggs and fruit' since these 'smaller branches' of agriculture might turn out to be more profitable than others. He was a mainstay of the local Conservative party, a County Councillor, a churchwarden at St. Meugan's, reading the lesson every Sunday for many years, and a Commissioner of the Inland Revenue. As a magistrate and Chairman of the Ruthin Bench for fifteen years he delivered stern lectures and lenient sentences. On one occasion, two penniless youths were bound over under the First Offenders Act for stealing 'a sovereign and other small coins' and, the local newspaper tells us, 'as they had no money to pay their train fare, Mr Weyman at once contributed the necessary amount.' *The Denbighshire Free Press* (6 August 1904) informs us that: 'At the invitation of Mr and Mrs Stanley Weyman, of Llanrhydd Hall, all the inmates of the workhouse… were entertained to a sumptuous tea served on the lawn in front of the Hall, on Friday afternoon last. Mr and Mrs Weyman, and other ladies and gentlemen, tended to the wants of the visitors who spent a most enjoyable afternoon and feelingly expressed their gratitude for the kindness and generosity extended to them.' Local golfers competed each year for 'The Stanley Weyman Cup'. Nor was his fame merely local; both a fishing trawler and a minesweeper were named 'The Stanley Weyman'.

Weyman continued to travel extensively sometimes in the company of his great friend and fellow novelist H. Seton Merriman. In 1914 he visited Ulster to study the Irish question and subsequently wrote to *The Times* with advice for Prime Minister Asquith. This was one of a number of letters he wrote to *The Times* over the years on matters as diverse as the recruitment of soldiers for the First World War, book clubs and newspaper reviews.

In 1908 Weyman announced his retirement as a novelist: 'I think I have told all the tales I have to tell. I have had a long run and would far sooner quit the stage now, while I am still playing to a full house, than go on and risk tiring the audience and having to bring the curtain down at last on half-empty benches.' The 1911 census shows him, now a 'retired novelist', living at Llanrhydd Hall with his wife and six servants (cook, parlour maid, maid, housemaid, kitchen maid and chauffeur/coachman). In that year in a General Preface to his collected works, he wrote: '... by and by, with youth and energy behind him, [the novelist] will discover that he has done his best. He may possess greater skill – experience is a powerful helper – but the freshness of fancy is past, the well of imagination sinks low, the pen flags. Then if he be wise, and necessity do not drive, he will own that the world belongs to the young ... and he will withdraw from that rivalry with himself which can now have but one ending.

'It was reasoning such as this which led me to lay down the pen when I had told the full tale of twenty volumes. It still holds good: the passage of four years does but add cogency to it. And though I do not propose, now or at any time, to frame a self-denying ordinance of which the chances of life or the changes of humour might lead me to repent, I see no ground to suppose that I shall return to the desk.'

Indeed in a letter to Kipling, after completion of *The Red Cockade* (1895), Weyman had written that he felt he was beginning to repeat himself. A novelist's 'constant effort' Weyman had written in the General Preface 'is to produce something higher and better, more imaginative or more realistic than his earlier work... To produce something better will be his morning and evening ambition.' After 1895 he largely abandoned the practice of setting his novels in France, focussing increasingly on England in the eighteeth and early nineteenth centuries. *Chippinge* (1906) for example is set at the time of the Great Reform Bill of 1832. Sir John Marriot described this novel as 'a striking illustration of the invaluable help that fiction can give to history.' But Weyman was not satisfield: *Chippinge* 'was not that step in advance which I had hoped it might prove to be.'

Weyman knew that he wanted to set a novel in the early nineteenth century but he had to wait over a decade before he felt ready to try again. In *The Great House* (1919) he returns more successfully to describe 'the opening movement in that transfer of power from the few to the many, of which we are witnessing the completion in our day ... to depict the attitude of mind towards it of different classes – the despair of those who looked back, the hopes of those who looked forward, the ardour of the young, the doubts of the old …' But it is in *Ovington's Bank* (1922), set in 1825 when the country is just recovering from the economic slump following the Napoleonic wars, that Weyman explores most successfully the themes of old money versus new, the clash between the ancient landowning class (represented by Squire Griffin) and the new commercial interests (represented by Ovington and the Squire's nephew, Arthur). Ovington wishes to bring the railway to town, the Squire fighting for the old ways and the old values, is virulently opposed. A rich cast of characters with their own ambitions and aspirations are caught up in the struggle, allowing Weyman to explore important themes of integrity and moral courage and to throw much light on the eternal question of what living a good life entails, while, as always, telling an enthralling story.

The back cover of the Pan edition of *Ovington's Bank* (1972) describes the novel as Weyman's last book, but in fact it was followed by three more excellent novels: *The Traveller in a Fur Coat* (1924), a thriller set in Germany in 1809, and then *Queen's Folly* (1925) and the posthumous *The Lively Peggy* (1928), both exciting romances set in early nineteenth century England.

Stanley Weyman died after a short illness on 11 April 1928. He left an estate valued at just under £100,000 (several million pounds in today's money) with generous bequests to his family, friends and servants as well as to the Pension Fund of the Society of Authors, to the Welsh Church and to the parish Church of St. Meugan's just opposite the gates of his house. The man whose thrilling stories helped countless thousands of readers through life's journey now lies in the churchyard of his beloved St. Meugan's. May he rest in peace.

Jim Lawley

Bibliography

Wildlife in the Marches (2015) by Mark Lawley published by Marches Publications. This book contains previously unpublished genealogical information about the Weyman family.

Stanley Weyman (1895) by Robert Harborough Sherard in *The Idler*, Volume VII February 1895 to July 1895. An interview with Weyman.

Le Nommé W. (1886) by Stanley Weyman in *MacMillan's Magazine*, Vol LV, pp199-206. Weyman's account of his arrest in France.

Acknowledgements

I thank my friend Simon Butt for his help in researching the events at Aramits.

We have been unable to trace the copyright holder of the painting of Garth by C.L. Cary and would appreciate any information which would enable us to do so.

Also by Merlin Unwin Books

The Yellow Earl Douglas Sutherland £20

Maneaters of Kumaon Jim Corbett £14.99

The Byerley Turk Jeremy James £9.99

The Temptation and Downfall of the Vicar of Stanton Lacy Peter Klein £12

The Stalking Party D.P. Hart-Davis £14.99

Death of a High Flyer D.P. Hart-Davis £14.99

Ascension: The Story of a South Atlantic Island Duff Hart-Davis £16.99

How the Other Half Lived Derek Beattie £14.99

The Nearest Earthly Place to Paradise – the literary landscape of Shropshire £20

A Shropshire Lad A.E. Housman £20